Murray Hoffman

Ecclesiastical law in the State of New York

Murray Hoffman

Ecclesiastical law in the State of New York

ISBN/EAN: 9783742843371

Manufactured in Europe, USA, Canada, Australia, Japa

Cover: Foto ©Andreas Hilbeck / pixelio.de

Manufactured and distributed by brebook publishing software
(www.brebook.com)

Murray Hoffman

Ecclesiastical law in the State of New York

ECCLESIASTICAL LAW

IN THE

STATE OF NEW YORK.

BY

MURRAY HOFFMAN.

Entered according to Act of Congress, in the year 1868, by
MURRAY HOFFMAN,
in the Clerk's Office of the District Court for the Southern District of New York.

PREFACE.

QUESTIONS connected with the incorporation of Religious Societies under the statutes of the State of New York, have come very frequently, of late years, before our courts of justice. These questions are often influenced by the ecclesiastical system of the church or body, in connection with which they arise. An attempt is made in the following pages to set forth, in a convenient form, the statute law, the decisions of courts of justice, and such ecclesiastical regulations as are useful in explaining the positive law and its mode of execution. An historical notice is introduced of all those churches which had a place of any importance in the Colony, before the Revolution.

The following table shows the distribution of the subjects.

TABLE OF CONTENTS.

CHAPTER XI.

CHAPTER XII.

CHAPTER XIII.

CHAPTER XIV.

CHAPTER XV.

CHAPTER XVI.

CHAPTER XVII.

CHAPTER XVIII.

CHAPTER XIX.

CHAPTER XX.

CHAPTER XXI.

CHAPTER XXII.

CHAPTER XXIII.

ECCLESIASTICAL LAW

IN THE

STATE OF NEW YORK.

CHAPTER I.

CHURCH OF ENGLAND IN THE COLONY.

THE legal and actual position of the Church of England in the Colony of New York is of importance upon some questions even at this day. It is of much interest to all Churchmen. The Protestant Episcopal Church will be very imperfectly understood if we do not comprehend the state of the Church of England in the Colony.

From the time that Master Wolfall, in Hudson's Bay, after a godly sermon, administered the Holy Communion after the order of the Church of England,[1] and from the time when the first services were held according to the Book of Common Prayer, on the bank of James River,[2] efforts were made to make the Church of England the established Church of many of the colonies, and to compel a general contribution for its support. At the same time the system of toleration, as it prevailed in England, was allowed.

In Hoffman's "Law of the Church" (p. 19, *et seq.*), are authorities, showing that in South Carolina, Virginia, and Maryland, the establishment was complete. Conformity was enjoined, and the support of the ministry enforced. All this was the act of the legislative assemblies, the then representatives of the people, and undoubtedly representing

---

[1] Hakluyt, vol. iii. p. 166 (1578).　　　　[2] A. D. 1607.

1

their actual opinion in those colonies. The English Toleration Acts were recognized or reënacted.

An impartial examination of the annals of the period will support the assertion, that the system of an established Church was enforced with far more moderation and justice, in what may be termed the Church of England Colonies, than in any other.

We may now advert to the enactments bearing upon this subject.

By the laws of the Duke of York of 1664, " no minister was to be allowed to officiate, unless he should produce testimonials to the Governor, that he had received ordination, either from some Protestant bishop or minister within some part of His Majesty's dominions, or the dominions of some foreign prince, of the Reformed Religion."

" Upon this the Governor shall induct the minister into the parish, that shall make presentation of him as duly elected by the major part of the inhabitants, householders." [1]

By an order of the Court of Assizes in 1672, it was directed, that although divers persons may be of different judgments, yet all shall contribute to the minister established and allowed of. The laws were to be duly observed as to parochial churches. And in 1675, a similar order was made to levy a rate upon all the towns which had not already a sufficient maintenance for a minister.

By another of the Duke's laws of 1664, it was ordered, that for the orderly management of all parochial affairs, eight of the most able men of each parish should be chosen by the major part of the householders, to be overseers, out of which number, the constable and such eight overseers shall yearly make choice of two to be church-wardens; and in case of the death of any of the said overseers and church-wardens, or his or their departure out of the parish, the said constable and overseers shall make choice of another to supply his room.

These church-wardens were to make presentment at the

<hr />

[1] *Church,* 4. *Coll. Hist. Society,* vol. i. p. 332.

sessions of misdemeanors which had come to their knowledge, as swearing, Sabbath-breaking, etc.

" The minister of every parish was to preach every Sunday, to pray for the King, etc. He was publicly to administer the Sacrament of the Lord's Supper once every.year at least in his parish church, not denying it to persons that for want of health shall require it at their houses. He was not to refuse the Sacrament of Baptism to the children of Christian parents, when they shall be tendered."

" No person shall be molested, fined, or imprisoned for differing in judgment in matters of religion, who professes Christianity."

This is a remarkable body of laws to have proceeded from a governor of the Duke of York, afterwards James the Second, and by his authority. It may perhaps be regarded as springing from the same motives which afterwards led him to form that strange union with the Dissenters in England—his animosity to the Anglican Church, and his intention to plant the Roman Catholic Church upon her ruins. (Macaulay's History, vol. ii. p. 195 etc.).

The following are important documents upon the present subject.

One article of the instructions to Governor Dongan of 1686 is: " You are to take especial care that God Almighty be devoutly served throughout the government, the Book of Common Prayer as it is now established read every Sunday and Holy Day, and the blessed Sacraments administered according to the rites of the Church of England."

" You shall be careful that the churches already built, be well and orderly kept, and more be built in the Colony. And that besides a competent maintenance be assigned to the minister of each church, a convenient house be built at the common charge for each minister; and a competent proportion of land be assigned for a glebe."

" And you are to take care that the parishes be so limited and settled, as you shall find most convenient for accomplishing this good work." (Art. 32.)

" Our will and pleasure is, that no minister be preferred

by you to any ecclesiastical benefice in our Province, without a certificate from the Archbishop of Canterbury, of his being conformable to the doctrine and discipline of the Church of England, and of a good life and conversation." (Art. 33.)

And by Article 35, — " to the end that the ecclesiastical jurisdiction of the Archbishop of Canterbury may take place in our Province as far as conveniently may be, you are to give all countenance and encouragement in the exercise of the same, except only the collating of benefices, granting licenses for marriages, and probate for wills, which we have reserved to you, our Governor for the time being."

" You are to permit liberty of conscience to all persons except Papists, so that they be content with a quiet enjoyment of the same."[1]

The instructious to Governor Sloughter of 1689 were the same, except that the Bishop of London was substituted for the Archbishop of Canterbury. Those to the Governor, the Earl of Bellemont, of 1697, and to Governor Hunter of 1709, are also nearly identical. In the latter is this clause : " We authorize you to collate any person or persons to any churches, chapels, or other ecclesiastical benefices within our said Province and territories aforesaid as often as any of them shall happen to be void."

The term " Collation," used in these documents, has in general the same meaning in the English law as " Institution," except that it is the term exclusively used when the benefice is in the Bishop. Then there is no presentation, but immediate institution.

The clerk by institution or collation, hath the care of souls committed to him. In virtue of collation as well as of institution, the clerk can enter into the glebe, and take the tithes; though for want of induction, he cannot yet grant or sue for them. (Burns, vol. i. pp. 104, 170.) In the letter of the Society for the Propagation of the Gospel, to Queen Anne, of the 20th of August, 1712, it is stated, "that out of her pious concern that all her subjects in all

___
[1] *Colonial Documents*, vol. iii. p. 872.

parts of her dominion should be instructed in the principles of our most holy religion, she had been pleased to give instructions to the governors of the plantations in America, and particularly to the governors of New York and New Jersey, that the Book of Common Prayer, as by law established, shall be read each Sunday and Holy Day, and the Sacraments administered, according to the rites of the Church of England."

The letter of the Bishop of London, Dr. Sherlock, on the subject of the Church in the colonies, addressed to the King in Council, of February 1759, is full of valuable information and facts.[1]

" In 1696 the King directed, that the President, Council, and Ministers should provide that the live word and service of God should be preached, planted, and used, according to the rites and doctrines of the Church of England."

He gives many details respecting the Southern and West India Colonies not pertinent to our present inquiry, and adds : " The Church of England being established in America, the Independents and other Dissenters who went to settle in New England, could only have a toleration, and in fact they had no more, as appears by their several charters, and more particularly by the Rhode Island charter granted in the 14th year of Charles II."

" Thus stands the right of the Church of England in America. And in fact at least one half of the plantations are of the established Church, and have built churches and ministers' houses, and have, by laws of their respective Assemblies, confirmed by the Crown, provided maintenance for the Church of England clergy."

But upon this subject certain acts of the Colonial Assembly are of great importance.

An act was passed in September 1693, for settling a ministry and raising a maintenance for them in the city of New York, and counties of Richmond, ^{Act of 1693.} Westchester, and Queens. It provided that there should be called, inducted, and established, a good and sufficient Protestant minister to officiate and have the cure of souls, as follows: "In the City of New York, one ; in the County of Richmond, one ; in the County of Westchester, two ; one to have the care of Westchester, Eastchester, Yonkers, and the Manor of Pelham, the other to have the care of Rye, Mamaroneck, and Bedford ; in Queens County, two ; one to have the charge of Jamaica and the adjacent towns and farms, the other to have the care of Hempstead, and the next adjacent towns and farms."   (§ 1.)

By the second section, there was to be assessed, levied, and paid, in every such city and county, for the maintenance of each of such respective ministers the sum specified, namely, £100 in New York, £60 in Richmond, etc., £120 in Queens, etc.

The third section directed a warrant to be issued by the justices, to summon the freeholders of those places to choose annually ten vestrymen and two church-wardens ; and this body was vested with the power of making the assessment and collection before prescribed.

The fifth section is as follows : —

" That all and every the respective ministers, that shall be settled in the respective city, counties, and precincts aforesaid, shall be called to officiate in their respective precincts, by the respective vestrymen and church-wardens aforesaid."

This statute received the King's assent in Council the 11th May, 1697.

It may be noticed that by the fourth section of the Act of 27th June, 1704 (the act relating to Trinity Church), the £100 to be raised in the city of New York, was absolutely appropriated to the Rector of Trinity Church for the time being, after the death of the Rev. Mr. Vesey, the then Rector.

An act was passed on the fourth of August 1705 (confirmed by the Queen on the eleventh of April 1706), explaining and enforcing the Statute of 1693.

By the second section, the payments of the sums specified were to be made to the ministers then inducted and established at the places named, and hereafter to be presented and inducted to the said places, namely, Richmond, Kings and Queens Counties. New York is not mentioned, no doubt because of the Act of 1704.

And by section 4, "the vestrymen and church-wardens were to present the ministers, which ministers shall be instituted and inducted to the said churches respectively."

We may here follow ont this series of statutes.

An Act of July 17th, 1721 (S. & L. p. 146), prescribed an oath to be taken by the vestrymen to assess the freeholders impartially. An Act of June 22d 1731 (S. & L. p. 216), adopted all the English statutes relating to the affirmations of Quakers. An Act of the 2d of September 1744 (S. & L. 349), was merely to alter the time of holding elections in Richmond County, for the choice of the wardens and vestrymen appointed by the Act of 1693. And the Act of the 29th November, 1745, changed the number of vestrymen in the city of New York. Fourteen were to be chosen, two for each Ward.

The vestrymen and wardens constitnted by the Act of 1693, was an anomalous body chosen by the freeholders, not the body known by that title in the English, or in our general Ecclesiastical Law.

In the Session of 1695 the Colonial Assembly resolved, that the wardens and vestrymen had power to call a dissenting minister under the Act of 1693.

In April of that year, the Assembly being summoned to the Council Chamber, Governor Fletcher rebuked them for assuming that they alone could explain an act which they alone had not made. He had also, in September 1693, admonished them, that they did not constitute the sole legislative power; that the judges were to interpret the law.

There was a proceeding in 1699 very important upon this question. A bill had passed the Assembly for settling a ministry of Dissenters. The Earl of Bellemout writes, that it being contrary to his instructions, he would not give his assent to the bill, but had rejected it.[1]

---

[1] *Colonial Documents*, vol. iv. p. 586.

The action of the Council upon this bill was as follows : —
" At a Council held at the Fort the 10th of May, 1699, William Smith, Chief Justice, and Chairman of the Committee, reported that as to the bill for the support of ministers, schoolmasters, etc., the Governor had communicated to the Committee his instructions respecting the settlement of religion in the Province, and they were of opinion, that by such instructions, His Excellency ought not to pass the bill." An application to the King for a modification and relief was earnestly recommended.[1]

This chief justice was the father of William Smith the historian, a writer whose unfairness where the Church is concerned is marked. His statement of the transactions at Jamaica, hereafter adverted to, is proof of this charge. His denunciations of Lord Cornbury's proceedings are violent, perhaps no more than they deserve; while of the course of Hunter, of Morris, of their moderation and justice, and of the ultimate success at law of the Dissenters by the decision of a Churchman, he has not one word. Doctor Johnson's strong animadversions upon his history are well merited.[2]

This leads me to the detail of the transactions at Jamaica, by which the meaning of the statutes was tested and determined.

In 1702 the first vestrymen and wardens were chosen at that place by the freeholders, under the Act of 1693. In the same year Mr. Hubbard, a dissenting minister, was called. Whether he was inducted by the Governor or not, does not appear.[3]

In 1704 Mr. Urquhart, of the Church of England, was inducted by Lord Cornbury, and put into possession of the church and glebe by his warrant alone. After his death, his widow put a dissenting minister, who had married her daughter, into possession. This was about 1710, as nearly as I can ascertain it.

---

[1] *Journals of the Council,* vol. i. p. 138.

[2] Letter to Archbishhop Secker, March 20, 1759, *Colonial Documents,* vol. vii p. 870.   [3] *Ibid.,* vol. v. 321, 328.

In 1712 Governor Hunter granted an instrument of induction unto the church at Jamaica, a dissenting clergyman being in possession. Proceedings were then had of which we have a full and reliable account, and which are very creditable to that governor.

The Rev. Mr. Henderson, a missionary of the Church, represents the case thus:[1] "That the two Colonial statutes made it plain that the ministry of the Church of England was intended to be maintained, and that the Dissenters had taken forcible possession of the church at Jamaica through the counivance of Governor Hunter in turning out well-affected Justices."

An answer to this statement appeared, in which it was alleged, that Hunter had illegally favored the Rev. Mr. Poyer in granting a letter of induction to him, although not legally presented.

Mr. Poyer sued the church-wardens of Queens County before the Justices of Session, for refusing to pay him a quarter's salary. They defended on the grounds — 1. That they had no money. 2. That there was no order of the Justices to pay the amount. 3. Because they thought him not qualified under the act to demand the salary, or any part of it. The court gave judgment for the defendants.[2]

In a letter of Governor Hunter to John Chamberlain, of February 1711–12, he says: " Mr. Poyer having the Society's Mission, and the Lord Bishop of London's recommendation to the church, I, upon the first application, granted him induction.

" The Dissenters being in possession of the manse house, by the contrivance of the widow of Mr. Urquhart, whose daughter had married a dissenting minister there, I consulted the Chief Justice, Mompesson, how far I might proceed in putting Mr. Poyer in possession, who gave his opinion in writing, *that it could not be done otherwise than in course of law, without a high crime and misdemeanor.*"

He proceeds to detail the action of the Justices of Queens County, and that he had urged Mr. Poyer to try the question

---

[1] *Colonial Documents,* vol. v. p. 311.   [2] *Ibid.,* p. 334.

at law, offering to aid him in bearing the expense. That "he had urged Mr. Poyer to commence a suit; all other measures, except those that were legal, being a real detriment to the interests of the church."

There is also a letter from Colonel Morris upon the subject, which deserves notice.

He states that Governor Fletcher, and James Graham, Speaker of the Assembly, sought to benefit the church, the Assembly being inclined to maintain a ministry. Graham, who had the drawing of the bill, prescribed a method of induction, and so managed it, that it would not do well for the Dissenters, and but lamely for the church, though it would do with the help of the Governor, and that it was not all wished, but it was the most that could be got at the time, the Assembly being for the most part Dissenters, who would have defeated the act, had they seen through the artifice."

Colonel Morris also states the interview between Judge Coe and the Governor in relation to Poyer's course, and the action brought by him; the representations that the Dissenters had the great majority in the Assembly, and that the act was meant to be for the Dissenters; that he had urged that the Council and Governor made part of the Legislature, and their intention was probably exactly the reverse. As to the Governor, this was a certainty. The act must be construed by its language, and that plainly appears to be in favor of the Church of England.

He adverts to the loose wording of the act, and that the claim of the Dissenters that it was for their benefit as well as for our own, might be supported without much wresting. He sensibly observes, "that if by force the salary is taken from them and paid to the ministers of the Church, it may be the means of subsisting these ministers, but they will not make many converts among a people who think themselves injured. Whereas, let this matter be once regularly determined, they will live in peace, and the Church will in all probability flourish, and I believe would at this day have been in a better position had there been no act in her favor."

In 1733 Governor Cosby removed Chief Justice Morris from his place as chief justice, and among others assigned the following reason : " That some years since, the Dissenters in the parish of Jamaica brought an ejectment against the minister of the Church of England for the church he preached in and was possessed of. When the trial came on, the defendant demurred to the plaintiffs' evidence. The chief justice desired them to waive the demurrer, telling them that if the jury found for the plaintiffs he would grant a new trial. The defendant's counsel, fearing the worst, did consent, and the jury found for the plaintiffs. The defendant's counsel moved for a new trial, and urged his promise. He denied it at first, but when they offered to make oath of it, he said a rash promise ought not to be kept, and never would grant it; whereby they lost their church, and the Dissenters have since had it."

From this period before 1733, perhaps as early as 1712, the Dissenters have had uninterrupted possession of the property and glebe.[1]

In Thompson's " History of Long Island," it is stated that the chief justice answered this accusation against him in a printed letter. I have not met with this production, but very little should be required to exonerate a judge from an accusation so extremely improbable, as well as disgraceful.

In considering the question on these facts in a legal view, two points arise : the effect of the royal instructions upon the statute, and the true construction of the statute.

Those instructions before and after the act, commanded the induction of ministers of the Church of England only, but undoubtedly they were overruled by an act of Assembly with the royal assent. The assent of the Governor was the same as that of the King in Council, but a statute could be annulled by the King. Unless and until so annulled, it was of perfect force and legality.[2] In the present instance the assent had been actually given in Council.

---

[1] *Col. Doc.*, vol. viii. Letter of Rev. Wm. L. Johnson to the writer.

[2] Hoffman's *Estate, etc., of the Corporation*, vol. i. p. 29 ; 22 N. Y. Rep. p. 44.

Chief Justice Morris was a strong asserter of the invalidity of royal instructions when opposed by a colonial statute.[1]

The meaning of the Statute of 1693, we have observed, was much contested. Its language was ambiguous.

But while the right of presentation was vested in that particular body of wardens and vestrymen created by the act, there was no provision requiring the Governor to induct. The instructions were not inconsistent with the statute. The English law was observed. The presentation was exclusively in one body, induction in another. And Lord Cornbury may not have been wrong in denying the right of the dissenting minister, however unjustifiable in dispossessing him by force. Governor Fletcher in 1693, insisted that collation was vested in him, and that the act had not robbed him of it.

But after the Statute of 1705, it seems to me, the Governor was bound to induct the minister presented by the body of wardens and vestrymen. The language of the fourth section of the act of that year is very strong.

With the exception, then, of the unwarrantable conduct of Lord Cornbury, whom the historian and the novelist combine to denounce,[2] the course of those in power and of the Bench was signally moderate, just, and legal. Reference was made to the courts to expound the law. That was pronounced, and submission followed.

The statutes referred to were offensive to every class of Dissenters, except those who had the predominance of freeholders in the particular counties.[3] The Presbyterians controlled at Jamaica, and finally obtained the glebe.

Hence efforts were made in 1706, and afterwards, to repeal or modify these laws. A bill was introduced to exempt the Protestants of the Counties of New York, Westchester, Queens and Richmond, from any taxation for the support of ministers of churches to which they did not belong. It was rejected.[4]

---

[1] *Colonial Documents*, vol. v. p. 19.
[2] Smith's History. Thompson's *Long Island.* The *Water Witch*, p. 22.
[3] Letter of Colonel Morris, before cited.
[4] *Journals of Council*, vol. ii. p. 1706.

So in 1769 attempts were made by the Assembly to have
an act passed for allowing churches of reformed Protestants to the northward of the Counties of Dutchess and
Ulster, to take and hold real estate to the value of one hundred pounds per annum, given to them for the support of
the gospel and the uses of schools. The Council refused
its assent.[1]

It has been before noticed that the Bishop of London
(Sherlock) considered the Statutes of Uniformity and Toleration to prevail in the colony. But while this is true as to
several of the southern colonies by virtue of legislation
of their own, it does not appear to be accurate as to New
York. Counselor West gave an opinion in 1724, that such
acts did not extend to New York. The Bishop of Hereford
had taken the same view; and Bishop Gibson also.[2] There
is in Smith's "History of New York," p. 221, an able examination of the subject, in which the Statute of 5th Anne,
made upon the union with Scotland, is fully considered.
The weight of authority and argument appears to be against
the proposition.

[1] *Journals of Council*, vol. ii.   Sts. 1698, 1706, 1742.
[2] Hoffman's *Law of the Church*, p. 18.

CHAPTER II.

CHARTERS TO CHURCHES OF THE CHURCH OF ENGLAND.

§ 1. *Particular Charters.* There was no general act or authority in colonial days, under which churches could organize and acquire corporate powers. Special charters were granted by royal governors, as the needs of the Church appeared to demand them in particular places.

The earliest of these was that to Trinity Church in the city of New York in 1697. There was one to St. Andrew's, Richmond County, in 1713; to St. George's, Hempstead, in 1735; to Grace Church, Jamaica, and to St. George's, Flushing, on the 17th June, 1761; to St. James', Newtown, on the 9th of September, 1761; to St. Peter's, Albany, on the 2d of December, 1762; to the Parish Church of Rye (Grace Church), the 19th of December, 1764; to Trinity Church of New Rochelle, the 2d of June, 1762; to St. Peter's, Westchester, the 2d of December, 1762; to St. Peter's, in the Manor of Courtlandt, near Peekskill, the 18th of August, 1770; to the Church in Poughkeepsie, the 9th of March, 1773.

§ 2. In a note[1] I have made a summary of the charter and laws as to Trinity Church, New York. It is needless, I think, to state these, or the questions upon them, in detail. It may be hoped that the matters agitated are finally settled. I have but to repeat here that it would have been far better had Trinity Church rested upon the charter, and the act changing her name. Her position and claims were as absolute and extensive under these, as under the Act of 1814; and I do not doubt that we should have had them now assured by judicial determination in her favor, had she rested upon them. The Act of 1814, in my judgment, did not strengthen her, and led to aggression, and that before the legislature, where defeat would have seriously injured her.

[1] Note L

That Act of 1814 has been ably defended.[1] It may be sustained fully and mainly upon the ground, that it was a declaratory act of what the charter prescribed or allowed.

§ 3. *Protected by Constitution.* These church charters were preserved in force by the 36th section of the Constitution of 1777, providing that nothing in such Constitution contained should be construed to affect any grant of land within this State, made by the authority of the said king, or his predecessors, or to annul any charters to bodies politic by him or them or any of them made prior to that date, (14th of October, 1775).

So the 14th section of the Act of April, 1784, chapter 18, renewed in the 12th section of the General Act of April 5th, 1813, recognizes the legality of religious corporations, created under the great seal of the Colony.

§ 4. *Alteration of Name.* In many instances, particular acts of the State legislature have been obtained altering the style and name from " in communion with the Church of England as by law established," to " in communion with (or of) the Protestant Episcopal Church in the State of New York."

Thus by an Act of the 3d of March, 1789 (chapter 51), the style of St. Peter's in Albany was so changed. By an Act of the 12th of March, 1793 (3 Greenl. 88), a similar change was authorized as to Grace Church, Jamaica, St. George's Church, Flushing, and St. James', Newtown. By an Act of 5th April, 1792 (chapter 46), the same was done as to the church in Poughkeepsie.

As to several such charters no such act has been passed. The Church of St. George's, Hempstead, of St. Andrew's, Richmond, and Trinity Church, New Rochelle, are I believe in this position. Some views upon this point are hereafter submitted.

The provisions of these charters are in many particulars substantially the same. There are differences, and some of importance, which will be noticed.

§ 5. *St. George's, Hempstead.* I take the charter of St.

_____

[1] Among others by Judge Redfield of Vermont. Boston, 1858.

George's Church, Hempstead, as an example, and will endeavor to point out the important variations in other charters.

(1.) *Preamble.* The petition of Robert Jenner, Rector, and Robert Cornell, and others named, inhabitants of the Parish of Hempstead, in Queens County, to Governor Cosby, was recited, stating that they had lately built a new church in the said parish, and had dedicated it to the service of God, according to the rites and ceremonies of the Church of England, as by law established, by the name of St. George's Church, which church they hold, together with a parsonage house and glebe lands in said parish. That for want of being incorporated, they were not capable of receiving such donations as pious persons might be disposed to give unto them, or of purchasing lands and tenements for the use of such church, or carrying on its affairs, as otherwise they might do.

They prayed that for accomplishing these purposes, they and other of the communicants of the said church might be created a body politic and corporate.

(2.) *Corporation created.* It was then ordained, constituted, and declared, etc., that the said Robert Jenner, John Cornell, etc., etc., and the rest of the communicants of the said church in the Parish of Hempstead aforesaid, be, and they and their successors, *communicants of the said church,* shall be from time to time, and at all times forever hereafter, a body politic and corporate, in deed, fact, and name, by the name of

(3.) *Title. The Rector and Inhabitants of the Parish of Hempstead in Queens County, on Long Island, in Communion of the Church of England, as by law established.* And them and their successors, communicants of the said church by the name of the rector and inhabitants, etc., etc., (*as above*), one body politic and corporate, we do erect, make, constitute and declare.

The usual clause as to perpetual succession, and as to suing and being sued, is inserted.

(4.) *To take and hold Lands.* "They and their successors,

by the same name, be, and shall forever hereafter be capable and able in the law to take, accept of, acquire and purchase, have, hold, and enjoy in fee forever, or for life or lives, or for years, or in any other manner, messuages, lands, tenements, and hereditaments; and the same to lease or demise for one or more years, or to grant, alien, bargain, sell and dispose of for life or lives, or forever under certain yearly rents; and also to accept of, take, possess and purchase any goods, chattels or personal estate, and the same to hire, let, sell or dispose of, at their will and pleasure; and all this as fully as any other corporation or body politic within that part of our kingdom called England, or this our Province of New York, may lawfully do. *Provided*, that such real estate shall not at any one time exceed the yearly rent of two hundred pounds over and above the church and grounds, and the parsonage and glebe land."

The grant of a common seal, and to alter, break, and change the same is made.

(5.) *Rector, Wardens, Vestrymen.* "For the better ordering the affairs of such corporation, there shall be one rector or parochial minister of the Church of England as by law established, duly qualified for the cure of souls, two church-wardens, and a number of vestrymen from time to time elected as hereafter expressed."

(6.) *Power in whom vested.* "Which vestrymen, or the major part of them, and the two church-wardens, or one of them, *together with the rector* for the time being, shall apply themselves to take care for the best disposing, governing, and ordering the general business and affairs of and concerning said church, and of or concerning all such lands, tenements, and real and personal estate as shall or may be acquired as aforesaid."

(7.) *Tenure of first Wardens, etc.* The Rev. Robert Jenner, the then rector, was then named and constituted rector during his natural life; John Cornell and Micah Smith wardens; William Cornell, etc., to the number of ten vestrymen, to continue in their offices during their natural lives respectively, or until others were duly chosen in their stead."

(8.) *Call of Vestry and Transaction of Business.* " We ordain and direct, that the rector of the church for the time being, or in his absence by sickness, one church-warden by consent of the rector, may from time to time assemble and call together the said church-wardens or one of them, and vestrymen for the time being, or the greater number of them, to consult, advise, and do the business and affairs of the said church, and to hold vestries for that purpose."

(9.) *In case of Vacancy, etc.* " In case of a vacancy of a rector, or that the rector for the time being should absent himself from his said parish, then, and in either of such cases, during such vacancy or absence, the church-wardens for the time being, or one of them, may call and hold such vestries as the rector might do."

Provisions, applicable to the death or removal of the original ten named vestrymen are made, which need not be noticed.

(10.) *Annual Elections.* After the death, removal, or refusal to act, of the vestrymen and wardens named in the charter, it was provided : " Then and from thenceforth the choice as well of the vestrymen as of the church-wardens of the said church, shall be annual ; and that yearly, once in the year forever hereafter, that is to say, on Thursday in Whitsun-week in every year, at the said church, the communicants of the said church for the time being, or the major part of them present, shall elect, choose, and appoint two of the communicants of the said church to be church-wardens and six other communicants of the said church to be vestrymen, for the ensuing year.

(11.) *Tenure of Office.* " Which church-wardens and vestrymen so chosen, and hereafter to be chosen, shall enter immediately upon their respective offices, from the respective times they shall be so chosen, until other fit persons be respectively elected in their respective places.

Powers. " They shall have full power and lawful authority to execute and perform their respective offices in as full and ample manner, as any church-wardens or vestrymen in that part of Great Britain called England, or this Province, have or lawfully may do."

(12.) *Vacancy, etc.* In case of the death, resignation, or removal, or refusal to serve, of a warden or vestryman, it was made lawful for the communicants of the church for the time being, or the major part of them, to proceed in manner aforesaid, and make a new election of one or more of their communicants in the room or place of such officer, etc.

(13.) *Call of Rectors.* "The patronage, advowson, donation, or presentation of and to the said church and parish, after decease or removal of the said Robert Jenner the then rector, or next avoidance thereof, shall appertain and belong to, and is hereby vested in the church-wardens and vestrymen of Saint George's in the Parish of Hempstead aforesaid for the time being and their successors forever, or the major part of them, whereof one church-warden is always to be one."

(14.) *Assessment, £60.* The rector or minister for the time being was to have and receive the sum of sixty pounds yearly; to be levied, assessed, collected, and paid by the inhabitants of the precinct or parish of Hempstead in Queens County aforesaid, towards the maintenance provided by the act, for settling a ministry, etc., and the act for the better explaining thereof.

(15.) *Clerk, Sexton, etc.* The rector, at a vestry or meeting, by and with the advice and consent of the major part of the members then present, may nominate and appoint a clerk, sexton, or bell-ringer, to and for the said church. Also, a clerk and messenger, and such other under-officers as they shall stand in need of, to remain in their respective offices so long as the rector, church-wardens, and vestrymen for the time being, or the major part of them, shall see fit.

(16.) *By-laws.* The rector, church-wardens, or one of them, and the vestrymen, or the major part of them in vestry, shall have power from time to time, to make rules and ordinances for the good discipline and weal of the members of the said church and corporation, as they, or the major part of them shall see fit, but not repugnant to the laws of England or of the Province. Such rules, etc, to be entered in a book, or books, to be kept for that purpose.

(17.) *Confirmation of Title.* It proceeded to grant, ratify and confirm unto the said " Rector and inhabitants of the Parish of Hempstead, in communion of the Church of England, as by law established, and their successors," the church and ground on which it stood, and which doth belong to the same, containing about half an acre of land; and the parsonage-house and lot commonly known as the parsonage-house lot, in the town of Hempstead aforesaid, now in possession of the said Robert Jenner and his successors forever, rectors of the said church — to have and to hold the premises unto the said rector, etc. *(as above,)* to their only proper use and behoof forever. To be holden in fee and common socage of our Manor of East Greenwich in the County of Kent, paying annually on the feast of the Annunciation, at the city of New York, the annual rent of one shilling, current money of the Province.

I have marked the various clauses of this charter by numbers, and proceed to some observations upon them.

(1.) It is shown in the preamble of the charter of St. George's Church, Hempstead, that the church had already a rector. Thus the ecclesiastical organization was so far complete. The same is found in the charter of Grace Church, Jamaica. In the charter of St. George's, Flushing, it is recited, that the three churches of Jamaica, Newtown, and Flushing, had but one pastor to officiate among them, and the inconvenience arising from this is stated. The petition is by inhabitants of the particular places respectively.

(2.) *Members.* A very marked feature of this charter is, that the clause which constitutes the corporation is — Robert Jenner, etc., — and the rest of the *communicants* of the said church in the parish of Hempstead aforesaid, and their successors, *communicants* of the said church shall be, etc.,

— by the name, etc. In no other charter that I have seen is this phrase to be found. In general, the language is merely "in communion of the Church of England as by law established." This subject is considered hereafter under subdivision 10, " Elections."

(3.) *Title.* The title given in these charters varies considerably. That to the church in Hempstead we have seen is, " The Rector and Inhabitants of the said Parish of Hempstead, in Queens County, on Long Island, in communion of the Church of England as by law established." That of Grace Church, Jamaica, " The Rector and Inhabitants of the Parish and Township of Jamaica, in Queens County, in communion with the Church of England," etc. That of St. George's, Flushing, is — " The Inhabitants of the Township of Flushing, in Queens County, in communion of the Church of England as by law established." That of St. Peter's, Westchester, " The Rector and Inhabitants of the borough town of Westchester, in communion, etc. ; " of St. Andrew's, Richmond, " The Minister, Church-Wardens, and Vestrymen of St. Andrew's Church, in the County of Richmond ; " of Rye, " The Rector and Inhabitants of the Parish of Rye," etc.; of New Rochelle, " The Minister and Members of Trinity Church, New Rochelle, in the County of Westchester, in communion of," etc. ; of Poughkeepsie, " The Rector and Inhabitants of Poughkeepsie, Dutchess County, in communion," etc.

(4.) *Power to hold Lands.* The clause authorizing the acquisition and holding of real estate and personal property is almost the same in all the charters, with the exception of the limit of annual value, which varies.

As to this limitation it is well settled, that it furnishes the rule of value only at the time of the acquisition. If by the course of time and contingencies, the property has increased to any extent, the charter and grant will not be affected.

If they could take by Devise. There is one important question under these charters, Whether the churches so incorporated before the Revolution, could take real estate by devise ?

There was no Colonial act authorizing devises, nor any act of the State until that of the 3d of March, 1787 (1 Greenleaf, 386). It is the received opinion that the Statute of Henry VIII., or Statute of Wills, was in force here. The whole question is examined *post*, chapter 16, § 4, and an attempt made to prove that the Statute of Elizabeth prevailed, and by force of that statute devises were valid, until the Act of March 3d, 1787, our own Statute of Wills.

(5–6.) The provisions of this charter contained in subdivisions 5 and 6 are of great importance. It will be seen, that a call of a vestry meeting, and the transaction of the business of the church in it, depends upon the rector, or if absent by reason of sickness, then one warden, *with the rector's assent*, may call a meeting, and perform the business of the church.

And again, in case of a vacancy, or, if the rector absent himself from his parish, the acts of the warden and a majority of the vestrymen are valid.

It is obvious, that the absence from the parish must be a wilful abandonment of his duty there, or an absence so protracted and unexplained, as to warrant such conclusion.

With this qualification, the great principle of the English law of rectorial authority is fully observed.

" The minister is not in consideration of law a mere individual of a vestry. On the contrary, he is always described as the first and as an integral part of the parish. He is denominated *Præses Ecclesiasticus, Rector Parochiæ*." The parish in vestry is described as " The Minister, Church-wardens and Parishioners in vestry assembled." With us it would be *vestrymen* instead of *parishioners*. His right to preside is undoubted. (Wilson *v.* Mackmath, 3 Phill. 67.)

In The Queen *v.* Doyly, (4 Perry and Davidson, 58,) it was held that " the president of the vestry (the rector if present) has authority to regulate the proceedings ; to decide what they shall be, so as to insure the voters of the parish a reasonable time to vote ; to adjourn the poll if he see fit, and to do all necessary acts, being amenable to a court of justice."

But under our law fixing a day for an election, there can be no adjournment to any other day. It may be from one hour to another on the same day.

This rule is even more absolutely recognized in the charter of St. Peter's, Westchester: "We do ordain that the said rector, and one of the church-wardens for the time being, together with a majority of the vestrymen of the said church, being met in vestry, shall have power and authority, by a majority of their voices, to do, etc., and to direct, order and manage the business of such corporation."

The provision in the charter of the church at Rye is similar.

In such cases the rector's presence is essential. He has the right to preside, an equal vote, and there are sometimes cases (as hereafter shown), though rare, of a casting vote, in the sense of a double vote.

But there are two charters, perhaps more, which present a marked exception to the English law.

The charter of Trinity Church, New Rochelle, after providing that there should be one minister of the Church of England, two church-wardens, and six vestrymen, declares: "Which minister and church-wardens, *or any two of them*, together with the vestrymen, or the major part of them for the time being, shall have, and are hereby vested with, full power and authority to dispose, order and govern the business and affairs of and concerning such church, and concerning all such lands, tenements or hereditaments, real or personal estate, as shall or may be purchased or acquired for the use thereof as aforesaid."

And so by another section: "We ordain and direct, that the minister and church-wardens of the said church for the time being, *or any two of them*, together with the said vestrymen, or the major part of them, shall be, and by these presents are, authorized and empowered, to consult, advise and consider, and by a majority of voices to do, direct and transact the interests, business and affairs of the said church, and to hold vestries for that purpose."

So in the case of the charter of St. George's, Flushing. "The minister and church-wardens of the said church for the time being, *or any two of them*, shall and may from time to time, call and assemble the said minister, church-wardens, and vestrymen, or the greater number of them, the said vestrymen; which said minister and church-wardens, *or any two of them*, together with the said vestrymen, or the major part of them, are anthorized and empowered to consult, advise and consider, and by a majority of voices, to do, manage and transact, and carry on, the business and affairs of the said church, and to hold vestries for that purpose."

The charter of St. James' Church, Newtown, 9th September 1761, is alike in this respect.

Thns the minister and church-wardens are put together colleetively.   Any two of these — therefore two wardens — with a majority of the vestrymen, arc competent to hold vestries, and transact business.

In the casc of a contested election in the church of New Rochelle (1864), the present writer's opinion was given that such was necessarily the meaning of the charter of that ehurch.   The royal charters underwent the supervision of the Attorney-General.   The lawyers of that day did not use language on such matters loosely and unadvisedly.   The deviation from the usnal phraseology and the general English rulc, must have been intended.   I was informed that some of the chief founders of the Episcopal Church at New Rochelle were French Protestants, and this clause of the charter was an offering to their principles, for the purpose of securing them to the Church, at the surrender of a true Church rule.

(10.) *Elections and Qualifications.*   The charter of St. George's, Hempstead, I have before noticed as peculiar upon the qualification of voters at the annual elections.   They are to be " communicants of the said church for the time being."   No other qualification is prescribed.

If we turn to the 21st Canon of the English Church of 1603, in force when this charter was granted, we may conclude, that receiving the communion three times in the year preceding, is sufficient.   I am not prepared to say that once wonld not suffice.

It is clear that the voter must be a communicant of that identical church, within its walls, at its separate altar. A communicant of a particular church, is a member of such church. Communing in it two or three times a year, and communing elsewhere as frequently, does not make him a member, and he cannot be a voter. But this is subject to the qualification, that communing elsewhere when temporarily absent, would not invalidate his right.

It seems to me no question of difficulty can arise as to the qualifications of voters in this church except in the frequent case of a communing in the church for a large portion of the year, and elsewhere for an equal, or nearly equal portion. The solution of this question will depend upon the same rules as the decision of the question of inhabitancy, as hereafter fully stated. The substantial inquiry is, which is the real domicile or home. His church communnion will follow his civil abode.

The position is strengthened by the language used in constituting the corporate body, "Communicants of the said church *in the parish* of Hempstead aforesaid."

After careful examination, and some doubt, I think that inhabitancy within the parish is also necessary for the qualification of a voter. The doubt arises from the fact that in the clause as to the electors at the annual election, no term is used, except, "communicants of the said church for the time being," and by the English law there could be a parishioner without residence, as by holding a freehold estate within the parish limits. On the other side the corporators are the rector and inhabitants of the parish of Hempstead, and clear language must be used to extend the right to vote beyond the corporators. Parishioners may be a larger term than corporators.

If this is so, then an inhabitant of the parish of Hempstead is, I presume, the same as an inhabitant of the town of Hempstead; and as to the meaning of this phrase, see *post*, this subdivision. Of course ownership of, or hiring a pew or seat, without being a communicant, will not suffice.

But in general the charters are similar in this particular to that of St. Andrew's, Richmond.   "It shall be lawful for the inhabitants of the said island in communion of the Church of England as by law established, to meet and choose two church-wardens, etc.   That of the church at Flushing, and at Newtown, are alike, that is, the inhabitants of such towns respectively, in communion, etc.

It may be here noticed that an act was passed the 13th day of March, 1843, by which the charter of Grace Church, Jamaica, was amended as follows : "In addition to the persons now qualified to vote at the elections, and eligible to the offices hereafter mentioned, it shall be lawful for all other male persons, of full age, of the congregation of Grace Church, in the village and town of Jamaica, in communion with the Protestant Episcopal Church of this State, who shall have belonged to such church or congregation, for the last twelve months preceding such election, and who shall have been baptized in the Episcopal Church, or shall have been received therein, either by the rite of confirmation, or by receiving the Holy Communion, or by purchasing or hiring a pew or seat in said church, or by some joint act of the parties and the rector, whereby they have attached themselves to the Protestant Episcopal Church, at any election for wardens and vestrymen of said church, to vote for and be eligible as such wardens and vestrymen."

We have then two material questions to consider under these colonial charters, as to voters.   What is the interpretation of inhabitant of the town or township, and what is the sense of being "in communion with the Church of England," where the name has not been changed ; and of, "in communion with the Protestant Episcopal Church, in the State of New York," where it has been.

Inhabitant.   Inhabitancy is a term of large and not easily defined meaning.   It cannot be said to be strictly synonymous with domicile.   It may be in one place when the domicile either of birth or adoption has been in another and has not been lost.   It may at least be said, that a fixed residence, a personal dwelling in a place, is an essential element. This would not be incousistent with temporary absences for business or pleasure; but the return to the abode, and the *animus morandi* in the place, euter into and form an essential part of the meauing.[1]

The *Incola* of the Latin is the *Parochias* of the Greek; and Caius defines *Incolam* to be the place where one establishes his abode (*domicilium*). Domat includes in the term personal residence, the atteudance upon religions services on festival days, the beàring a part in the public charges, and a sharing public privileges. ("Civil Law," vol. ii. p. 485. IV.)

"A mere lodger," says Lord Hardwicke, "cannot be said to be an inhabitant." (Cases Temp. Hard. 308.)

Iu The Attorney-Geueral *v.* Parker (3 Atk. 376), the language of a deed was, "The Parishioucrs and Inhabitauts of Clerkenwell." "Parishioners," said Lord Hardwicke, "takes in not only inhabitauts of the parish, but occupiers of lands that pay rates and duties, though not residents. Inhabitants is a still larger word, and takes in housekeepers, as for instance, those who have gained a settlement, and so become inhabitauts. Usage may be resorted to, to construe ancient grants. Contemporaneous exposition is the best way to go by." The custom was proven of admittiug all householders to vote.

In The Attorney-General *v.* Davy (2 Atkyn's 212), the case was this. By a charter of Edward VI. twelve persons were incorporated to elect a chaplain of the church at Kirton, and three of them were euipowered to choose a chaplain for the church of Sanford within the parish of Kirton, with the cousent and approbation of the major part of the inhabitants of Sanford. As reported in Atkyn's, the only point decided was, that two of the three persons could do the corporate act. But in The Attorney-General *v.* Parker, (*ante,*) his lordship states, that under this charter he had

---

[1] Bouvier's *Law Dict. in verbo*, Frost *v.* Wisble, 19 Wendell, 11; Bartlett *v.* The City of New York, 5 Sandf. Supr. Ct. Reps. 44; Matter of Wragby, 8 Wendell, 184; Isham *v.* Gibbons, 1 Bradford, 69.

held that *inhabitants* ought to be restrained to persons paying scot and lot.   Lord Eldon has spoken of the uncertainty of this phrase, and its different meanings (10 Vescy's Rep. 339).   If we look into the law dictionaries, we find, that at least this is clear, that it comprises a contribution in value to some parish, town, or borough objects.

In Rex *v.* Allard (4 Barn. & Cress. 772), it is said, that the term varies in its import, according to the subject to which it is applied.   A non-resident occupier of lands is not an inhabitant.

The case of The King *v.* Davie (6 Adol. & Ellis, 374), is important.   A charter of Edward VI. granted that the inhabitants of the ville of S. within the parish of C. should have a chapel for such inhabitants, with a chaplain to be paid out of the profits of the vicarage of C., and that they should elect chapel wardens.   That certain governors, appointed in the mode prescribed, with the assent of a majority of the inhabitants of the said ville, should nominate and appoint the chaplains.   Upon a nomination and notice to the inhabitants to meet, for the purpose of assenting or dissenting, the resident payers of church and poor rates were allowed to vote.   Some persons not rated tendered votes. Proof was given of the course in two previous elections in 1771 and 1814, and evidence of aged persons, as to the usage being to admit only those who paid rates.   It was held, that from the text of the charter and usage, the term inhabitants might be construed to be limited to the particular class.

In some charters a power to vote or assess for church repairs, etc., was conferred.[1]   And some of these authorities would indicate the sense in which the term may have been used, to be resident rate-payers.

But this right may be treated as surrendered or superseded.   Indeed it was doubtful if a charter alone could confer this power, which is a power in substance of taxation.

We are led back to other definitions.   It may be safely stated that a mere lodger or sojourner for a time, without

---

[1] Trinity Church, Reformed Dutch Church, and a few others.

the indication of the *animus morandi*, the intent to make it a home, is not enough.   A permanent abode and subjection to public taxes and duties is enough.   There may be cases of difficulty between these two points.   It will be remembered that if votes are illegally admitted or rejected, it will only invalidate the election, when a different result would have been reached.

In Ennes *v.* Smith, 14 Howard's U. S. Rep. 400, it is said, "There must be actual residence within the place, with the intention that it is to be permanent."

Towns.   The charters quite generally require the party to be an inhabitant of a particular designated town or township.

These towns or townships in many cases, particularly on Long Island, were constituted by Dutch patents, and are unchanged in some cases to this day.   Bolton's "History of Long Island" and Broadhead's "History of New York" afford information on this point. The boundaries of the towns are settled by acts of the legislature.   They are defined in the laws of 1801, and the Revised Statutes (vol. iii.) contain them fully.

It may be observed that the limits would be the same as the limits at the date of the charters respectively, whether subsequently changed or not.

In Communion, etc.   What is the sense of being in communion of or with the Church of England ?

First, it is to be examined as to charters where the title has not been changed, but remains as it was in the charter.

The communion of the Church of England, in the mere ecclesiastical sense — the union or identity of faith, worship, orders, and observances, is not touched or varied by anything in our Revolution, our Constitution, or our Laws.   The exceptions are few, and are as follows, or of the same nature.

Whatever is inconsistent with the Constitution of 1777, or the laws of 1784 connected with a supremacy of such Church, or the power of the Bishop of London within the limits of the State, is abrogated.   But if exclusively confined to mere spiritual ecclesiastical matters, a church might be incorporated to-morrow, under our law, by the name of St. James, in the city of New York, in communion of the Church of England.

But again, the Protestant Episcopal Church is the successor of the Church of England. It is very important to understand this proposition.

When any such chartered church has allied itself with the Protestant Episcopal Church of the United States, by uniting in the Diocesan Convention, it accedes to the explicit declaration of that Church, "that it has not intended to depart from the Church of England in any essential point of doctrine, discipline, or worship, or further than local circumstances require." So the avowal and admission of each such church, and of each member of the same, is clearly, that the Protestant Episcopal Church is in communion of the Church of England; is the successor of such church, varied in some matters. A court of justice would act upon such an admission and recognition.

Some authorities may be usefully noticed bearing upon this point.

In Mason v. Mulcater (6 Wheaton, 454), it was decided, —

1. That by the law in Virginia prior to the Revolution, each parish was authorized to elect a vestry, twelve persons, to manage the parochial affairs; and however numerous might be the churches in the parish, the same vestry had charge of them all. There were two churches within the parish of Fairfax : the Church of Alexandria and the Falls Church ; but they were under one rector and one vestry. In 1819, a vestry was chosen by persons professing to belong to the Falls Church, and to that portion of the parish of Fairfax not included within the District of Columbia.

2. Before the Revolution, the Episcopal Church was the established church in Virginia, and all the parishioners were liable to be rated for parish taxes, and were entitled to vote in the choice of the vestry. But the Church establishment fell with the Revolution, and the compulsory power of taxation ceased; and as no person could be compelled to worship in the Episcopal Church, or pay taxes for its sup-

port, the parishioners of the Episcopal Church, in the ecclesiastical sense of the term, afterwards consisted only of the Episcopal contributors and members.

3. The Statute of 1786, chap. 12, saved the management of their property and regulation of their discipline, according to the rules of their own sect, to all religious societies. By the Canons of the Episcopal Church, subsequently passed, the right to elect vestries is confined to the freeholders and housekeepers who are members of the Protestant Episcopal Church within the parish, and regularly contribute towards the support of the minister, and to the common exigencies of the Church within the parish.

4. That the Episcopal Chnrch at Alexandria then known as Christ Church, was the regular vestry in succession of the parish of Fairfax; and in connection with the minister, had the care and management of the temporalities. A sale of church-lands, with the assent of the minister, under a judgment of the conrt, conveyed a good title.

In The Town of Pawlett *v.* Clark (9 Cranch 292), Justice Story says: "The Chnrch of England, so familiar in our laws and judicial treatises, is nothing more than a compendious expression for the religious establishment of the realm, considered in the aggregate. In this seuse it is said to have peculiar rights aud privileges, not as a corporation, but as an ecclesiastical institution." So it is nsed iu Magna Charta, chapter 1, where it is declared, *Ecclesia Anglicana libera sit,* and *habeat omnia jura integra et libertates suis illæsas.*

Aud it was held, that where there was a grant of land, in part for the use of the Church of England, an Episcopal church erected by the Crown before the Revolution, or by the State since, would have been entitled to take. Bnt there being none such, the land was at the disposal of the State, and a grant to a town was valid.

Considering that the phrase "in communion of the Church of Eugland," where the title of a chnrch is unchanged, is the same for the matters now treated of, as "iu communiou of the Protestant Episcopal Chnrch," the question is, What is the sense and extent of the term?

Of course the actual reception of the Sacrament is such communion. This means reception in the parish church of the place of which the persons are inhabitants, or its chapels. By Canons 21 and 22 of 1603 the Holy Communion was to be administered in every parish church and chapel, so that each parishioner might communicate thrice in every year; and every lay person was bound to receive the communion thrice in each year. Canon 27 strictly prescribes the reception in the communicant's own parish church.

But I apprehend this is not the exclusive sense. Something short of this, will place a person in communion.

The Prayer-Book uses the phrase "in communion of the Catholic Church." Stillingfleet calls communion "a union in the common worship of a church." And Calvin, after speaking of a church retaining the Word of God and use of sacraments, says: "It is a dangerous temptation to think of separating from such a church, the communion whereof is never to be rejected, so long as it continues the true use of the Word and Sacraments." (Inst. Lib. 4, cap. 10.)

There are several articles of the Church of England, declaring that for certain offenses, the guilty party shall be excommunicated *ipso facto.* For example, — "Whoever shall affirm that the form of God's worship established by law, and contained in the Book of Common Prayer, is a corrupt or unlawful worship, or containeth anything contrary to the scripture, shall be so excommunicated." Article 4.

Now to hold and affirm the converse of what justifies excommunication, would establish communion. An expressed adhesion to the doctrines and order of the Prayer-Book would so far be sufficient.

Excommunication, we are to remember, was not merely exclusion from the Holy Communion, which was the lesser kind, but also absolute expulsion from the Church, *a liminibus sacræ matris ecclesiæ,* which was the greater. (Bishop Tomline, Spelman's Glossary *in verbo.*)

Conformity, as defined in the English law, may be communion, in the sense of that law. Conformity to our own worship, order, constitution, and canons, proven by open avowal or acts of plain adhesion, may be enough in our Church.

Again, in the ministration of baptism in our own and in the English Book of Common Prayer, thanks are given that the baptized child is *incorporated* into the Holy Church; and in the case of adults, that he is grafted into the body of Christ's Church." Clearly both the child and the adult are thus in communion of the Church, and without partaking of the Holy Eucharist. Confirmation is communion in the sense we are discussing; but where confirmation has been given upon one baptized according to the order of the Church, it adds nothing to the qualification.

While the theological meaning may thus be satisfied, something more is, I apprehend, included. The union or communion must be evinced by an outward act. Attendance upon the public worship was such an act. This was enjoined to be at the parish church or chapel by the Statute of 5 and 6 Edward VI., by that of 1 Elizabeth, cap. 2, and by the 9th Canon of 1603. The Act of 31 George III. continued the former acts in force, except as to persons who came within the Toleration Acts of 1 William and Mary.

Attendance at a customary chapel within the parish was a compliance with these requisitions.

Another question arises for consideration. Lay baptism, as it is termed, cannot of itself be the entering into communion with the Church. It is not being baptized *therein*. But the communion may be formed, notwithstanding this, though not by it.

The communion, I presume, may lawfully be administered to those who have received a lay baptism. There is also authority to prove that confirmation may be administered upon such baptism.

By a clause of the 15th Canon of 1798 of the duty of ministers to keep a register, and which clause remained in force until 1832, it was provided, " And no minister shall place on the said list the names of any persons except those who, on due inquiry, he shall find to have been baptized in this Church, or who, *having been otherwise baptized,* shall have been received into this Church, either by the holy rite of confirmation, or by receiving the holy communion, or by some other joint act of the parties and of a minister of this Church, whereby such persons shall have attached themselves to the same." (See Wheatley's Book of Common Prayer, p. 394.)

Chapels of Ease. There is a power attached to a parochial church of importance. It is the right to establish chapels of ease, as they are termed in the English law. Such chapels arose from the increase of the worshipers beyond what the parish church could support, or for the convenience of parishioners residing at a great distance from it. The theory of such chapels was subordination to the mother church, shown by the duty of resorting to it for baptism, the communion, marriages, and burials. They were also bound to account to the rector for all oblations, fruits, and tithes, and by attending the parish church on certain holy days. The curate was generally appointed by the rector, who could officiate himself whenever he chose. The support of the curate and chapel fell upon the mother church. Modifications of these rules arose by license or prescription.[1] For example in Line *v.* Harris (1 Lee's Rep. 146), the general rule that the nomination to the curacy belonged to the incumbent was recognized, and an exception was established by custom and license. (Burns' Ecc. Law, ed. 1842, vol. i. p. 296.)

The chapels of St. George and St. Paul, erected in the city of New York, and the chapel at Factoryville in Richmond County, were chapels of this character. No doubt there were others. They were under the rector of the parish church, who employed ministers as assistants or not, according to circumstances. They had no independent minister; but the right to baptize and administer the communion was attached to them. They were supported partly by the

[1] Gibson's *Codex,* p. 292.

parent church, partly by contributions of the worshipers in them. Chapels of this nature did not cease to be chapels of ease by acquiring the right of administering the sacraments.

The consent of the ordinary, the patron, and the incumbent was necessary for their erection. The vestry under the charters answer to the patron. Patronage and advowson was expressly conferred upon them. The incumbent was the rector. The Governor had the power of induction, and this involved the lesser authority, and made him the ordinary for such purposes.

But the worshipers in these chapels were as much members of the parish church as the worshipers there. In the case of a contested election in St. Andrew's Church, Richmond County (1857), the writer's opinion was given that the attendants upon a chapel erected by that church, not separately organized or incorporated, were, under the charter, as fully entitled to vote as the worshipers at the parish church.

Parochial Chapels. But there was also known to the English ecclesiastical law, what were termed parochial churches or chapels. They possessed the privileges of baptism and sepulture, a separate minister, and generally a separate endowment, often from the parish church. The assent of the ordinary, the patron, and incumbent was here also required. They could be established by prescription, where nothing was shown to repel the presumption of a deed.

I refer to the cases of The Attorney-General *v.* Mowerton, 2 Vesey sen. 26; Morysey *v.* Hillcoat, 2 Hagg. Ecc. Rep. 30; Dent *v.* Rob, 1 Young & Coll. 1.

The case of Bateman *v.* Cox (7 Bro. Parl. Cases, 59, Dublin Ed.), deserves particular notice. The peculiar or ancient parish of the Church of Dorchester, being very extensive, with many villages or hamlets within it, remote from the mother church, occasioned the erection of many chapels within its peculiar rectory, and subsequent to the division of the dioceses into parochial cures and the establishment of tithes in the kingdom, some of these chapels were independent chapels, endowed with a revenue in perpetuity for maintenance of a priest to perform divine service, and for the better accommodation of the inhabitants. They were allowed the privileges of sacraments and burials, and other parochial rights; and presentation being made of some of them by their founder or endower, became from that time presentative, and institution was practiced and allowed. Others, through the presentation of their patrons or common reputation, had acquired the character of parish churches, and the hamlets of distinct parishes. The one in question had, besides, the characteristics of a parish church, in having baptisms and sepulture.

There was no proof of any subordination to Fort Balden as a mother church, no right to seats there, no contributing to its repairs, no resorting thither on stated days, no oblations paid over, no oath of obedience to the rector or vicar, as required by ancient canons.[1]

"The *Capella Parochialis*, as it is called by Hobart, has belonging to it all sorts of parochial rights, as clerks, wardens, etc.; all rights of performing divine service, baptism, sepulture, etc.; which is very strong evidence itself that this is not barely a chapel of ease to the parish to which it belongs, but stands on its own foundation." (Lord Hardwicke in Attorney-General *v.* Mowerton, 2 Vesey sen. 426.)

The assent of the ordinary, the incumbent, and patron was necessary for the establishment of such churches. The patron was the vestry, the incumbent of course the rector, and the ordinary for these purposes was the Governor. The admission of ministers and establishment of churches was vested in him.

At present, the consent of the bishop would be necessary for the ecclesiastical organization of a separate church of this nature, as well as of the vestry and rector. They may become incorporated of course under the general act.

These separated churches or chapels, as they possessed entire independence of the mother church, and were freed

---

[1] See this oath, 1 Burns' *Ecc. Law*, 808; Constitution of Archbishop Winchester.

from all duty to it and from its supervision, so they lost all claim to its privileges, franchises, or emoluments, and all voice in its government. This is shown by the cases before cited, and by The Attorney-General *v.* St. Cross Hospital (38 Law & Eq. Rep. 500). It would necessarily result from separation and independence, without any authority.

These churches then were parochial churches, because they were within the parish limits, yet entirely disconnected and independent. So fully does this system continue, that by an Act of 1 and 2 Victoria (chapter 107), a parish may be divided into separate parishes, or into district parishes, or chapelries. The boundaries were to be fixed and enrolled in chancery, and in the registry of the diocese.

Guided by these principles, we are able to meet most of the questions which may arise as to churches separately organized and incorporated within the limit of a parish created by Royal Charter.

And no point can be more clear than this, that the right to vote at elections of wardens and vestrymen, and every right of participation in the management of the affairs of the Mother Church, is lost and voluntarily surrendered. To belong at the same time to two independent organized incorporated churches, is an impossibility. We have before noticed some rules applicable to cases of doubt. If the person's attendance is about equal in the city and in the country, the rule which indicates his domicile would determine his place for voting. Voting at one place clearly would debar voting at another.

In the case of St. Andrew's Church, Richmond, where the charter as before noticed made the whole island the parish, several separate churches had been organized and incorporated. In 1864 the opinion of the present writer was given, that persons were not entitled to a vote at the parish church of St. Andrew's, who regularly belonged to such independent churches.

Notice. In several charters there is a clause directing notice to be given in a particular manner of the annual election. This must be carefully attended to. Where there is no such provision, au election would not be invalid without it, the members being bound to know the day established by the charter. A good custom, however, prevails of giving a notice on the Sunday previous.

Time of Polling. The period for which the poll should be kept open is to be regulated by the convenieuce aud number of votes to be taken. Custom here has a great influence. The rule has been stated in several cases that reasonable time must be allowed for the taking all the votes proffered. It would be illegal to close the election while voters are ready aud desirous of voting. If there is a custom to conclude the poll at a certain time, that being a reasonable time, the voters must tender their votes within it. See Burns, vol. i. p. 15.

Where the directors, in ordering an election, limited the time of keeping the polls open to one hour, it was held, that the inspectors could still extend the time in their discretion to accommodate voters. (Matter of the Mohawk R. R. Co., 19 Wendell, 133. See Rex *v.* Mayor of Carmæthen, Maule & Selwyn, 697.)

Class from which to be Chosen. In almost every one of these charters there is a designation of the class from which the choice is to be made. Iu the case of the Hempstead charter it is "the communicants of the said church." In the charter of St. George's, Flushing, and others, it is "of their members, etc." The persons capable of holding the office must be of such specified class, and none others are eligible.

(11.) *Tenure.* I believe that invariably the tenure of office is for the ensuing year, or until others be chosen in their stead. See this subject examined, *post*, chapter 4, § 18.

Quorum and Majority. Under these charters the common-law rule prevails. All being convened, by notice, or from presumed knowledge of the appointed day, when fixed by charter or by-law, they who attend form a quorum, and a majority of that quorum decide the questions. But in general the presence of one warden is essential.

(12.) *Vacancy.* Where a vacancy occurs, by death, etc., the communicants in the church at Hempstead, and those entitled to vote in other cases, are to supply it. Where the charter does not specify the mode of holding such election, it can be fixed by a by-law of the members, and, as I think, by the vestry.

(13.) The patronage, advowson, presentation, is in effect the call and settlement of a rector, as now known in our law, and is vested in all the charters in the wardens and vestrymen. The important questions of the effect of a call with or without institution, as to property or income, duration of the connection, and other points, are examined *post*, chapter 4, § 24, and chapter 20. It is sufficient to say here, that so far as the general legislation of the Church affects these questions, the ministers of chartered churches are in the same position as those attached to churches organized under the General Incorporation Act.

(14.) The assessment of £60, sanctioned by the Act of 1693, was abolished in 1784. See *post*, chapter 3, § 2.

(15.) The power of appointing subordinate officers is common to all the charters. See *post*, chapter 16, § 7.

(16.) The authority to make rules and ordinances is also found in all these charters. See, as to this power, *post*, chapter 16, § 6.

CHAPTER III.

§ 1. *Constitution of* 1777.   The 35th Article of the Constitution of 1777, after recognizing as the law of the State
such parts of the common law of England, and of the
statute law of England and Great Britain, and of the acts
of the legislature of the Colony of New York, as together
formed the law of such Colony, on the 19th of April, 1775,
ordained, " That all such parts of the common law, and
all such of the said statutes and acts aforesaid or parts
thereof as may be construed to establish or maintain any
particular denomination of Christians or their ministers,
or concern the allegiance heretofore yielded to, and the
supremacy, sovereignty, government, or exercise by, the
King of Great Britain, and his predecessors over the Colony of New York, and its inhabitants, or are repugnant to
this Constitution, be, and they are hereby, abrogated and
repealed."

So in the 30th Article it was ordained, that the free exercise and enjoyment of religious profession and worship,
without discrimination or preference, shall forever hereafter
be allowed within this State to all mankind.

By the 31st Article, it was declared, " Whereas the ministers of the gospel are by their profession dedicated to the
service of God, and the cure of souls, and ought not to be
diverted from the great duties of their function: Therefore, no minister of the gospel, or priest of any denomination whatsoever, shall be eligible to or capable of holding
any civil or military office within this State."

The 36th Article had this clause: that " Nothing in the

Constitution contained should be construed to affect any grants of lands within the State, made by the authority of the King or his predecessors, or to annul any charters to bodies politic, by him or them, or any of them, made prior to the 14th of October 1775."

§ 2. *Act of April* 6, 1784.   On the 6th of April, 1784 (Laws, chapter 18), an act was passed to enable all the religious denominations in the State to appoint trustees, who shonld be a body corporate for the purpose of taking care of the temporalities of their respective congregations, aud for other pnrposes therein mentioued."

The preamble is as follows: "Whereas by the 38th article of the Constitution of the State of New York, it is ordained that the free exercise and enjoyment of religious profession and worship without discrimination or preference should forever thereafter be allowed within the State to all mankind.   And whereas many of the churches, congregations, and religious societies in this State (while it was a colony) have been put to great difficulties to support the public worship of God, by reason of the illiberal aud partial distribution of charters of incorporatiou to religious societies, whereby many charitable and well-disposed persons have been prevented from contributing to the support of religion for want of proper persons authorized by law to take charge of their pious donations, and many estates purchased and given to the support of religious societies, now rest in private hands, to the great insecurity of the societies for whose benefit they were purchased or given.   And whereas it is the duty of all free and virtuous governments to enconrage virtue and religion, and to enable every religious denomination for the decent aud honorable support of divine worship agreeable to the dictates of conscience and sound jndgment, therefore," etc.

This act formed the model of all subsequent legislation, and has been superseded by such. It is only useful to notice a few of its provisions.

The distinction between the qualifications of voters at the first and at subsequent elections was made.   For the first election, every male person, who had statedly worshiped with the congregation, and been considered as belonging to it, was entitled to vote. But for subsequent elections, he must have been a stated attendant on divine worship in said church or congregation for one year before such election, and must have contributed to the support of the church according to the usages and customs thereof.

A register of such attendants was directed to be kept.

By the 9th section, " Nothing in the act contained was to be construed to alter or change the religious constitutions or governments of either of the said churches, congregations, or societies, so far as respects or in any wise concerns the doctrine, discipline, or worship thereof."

And by the 14th section, " The religious corporations created by letters patent under the great seal of the Colony of New York, were recognized in allowing them to hold lands of the yearly value of twelve hundred pounds, although restricted by their charter to a less sum."

§ 3. *Act of 17th April* 1784. Most of the sections of the Act of the 17th of April 1784 (chapter 23), relate to Trinity Church only. But by the 6th section, to remove all doubts as to the continuance and effect of the acts specified, it was expressly enacted, that the Act of the 27th September 1693, that of the 27th June 1704, of the 4th of August 1705, of the 27th July 1721, of the 21st September 1744, certain parts of an Act of the 29th November 1745, which do grant certain emoluments and privileges to the Episcopal Church, or that mode of religious worship commonly called the Church of England, in the city and county of New York, and in the counties of Richmond, Queens, and Westchester, and do establish and maintain the ministers of that denomination within the said counties, and do also declare or imply a preëminence or distinction of the said Episcopal Church or Church of England over all other churches and other religious denominations, be absolutely abrogated and repealed.

§ 4. *Act of 20th April* 1784. Again by an Act of the 20th of April 1784 (chapter 38), it was recited : —

"Whereas by virtue of sundry acts hereinafter enumerated, passed by the legislature of the late Colony of New York, the inhabitants of the city and county of New York, county of Richmond, Westchester, and Queens counties, without distinction, have for many years been compelled to pay taxes for the support of the Episcopal Church in the said counties, contrary to the principles of justice and sound policy. And whereas by color of such laws, it has been pretended that the Episcopal churches were established in such counties, and claims in consequence thereof, to have been set up, and prosecutions commenced injurious to the rights and privileges of other religious denominations. And whereas, although the spirit of the said laws is repugnant to the Constitution of this State, it appears incumbent on the legislature, in order to remove every ground of uneasiness, that the said law should be repealed," etc.

Then the statute proceeded to repeal in terms the Acts of 1693, of 1705, of 1721, of 1745, of 1755, of 1756, of the 20th January 1770, of the 31st January 1775, and the Act against Jesuits and Popish priests of July 31, 1700.

§ 5. *Constitution of 1822.* The fourteenth section of the 7th Article of the Constitution of 1822 was the same as the 36th Article of that of 1777, cited (*ante*, § 1). The 18th Article of the Constitution of 1846 is similar.

"Thus it is manifest that all the royal charters incorporating churches, and all the franchises and powers they confer are recognized and in full validity at this hour, excepting such provisions in them as may declare or involve the exercise within the State of any authority by a foreign prince or potentate, or imply any supremacy in a particular church.

"Grants of land to them, whether by private individuals or by the Crown, for the purposes of their creation, and without conditions or reservations, are beyond recall or control. Incorporations of churches in communion of that of England in the colonies, were regarded the same as collegiate and academical incorporations, as being of a private and independent character, the same, precisely, as to their private character, as would be the incorporation of a Presbyterian or Lutheran congregation." (Judge Redfield.)

CHAPTER IV.

THE PROTESTANT EPISCOPAL CHURCH.

§ 1. *Act of April* 1784.   The Act of April 6th, 1784, before referred to, was general in its provisions, prescribing the same regulations for the incorporation of churches of every denomination.   It was found unsuitable to the system of the Episcopal Church, and on the 17th of March, 1795 (Laws, chapter 25), an act was obtained, entitled "An Act for the Relief of the Protestant Episcopal Church in the State of New York."

Act of 1795.   The preamble is as follows : "Whereas the Protestant Episcopal Church in this State, by the petition of the standing committee of its convention, hath represented that the act entitled, 'An Act to enable,' etc., passed 6th of April, 1784, directs a mode of incorporation which exposes it to a variety of difficulties, leaving the corporations not incorporated by charter to the alternative of foregoing the benefit of incorporation, or submitting to an entire alteration and subversion of the usual and peculiar government of the respective congregations of said Church. For remedy thereof," etc.

The provisions enacted were so nearly the same as those now in force under the Act of 1813, that I shall only notice a few variations of some significance, and illustrative of the present law.

The clause as to the constitution of a vestry is the same, but there is added : "Which vestry shall be, to all intents and purposes, a body corporate, and enjoy and exercise all the power, rights, and privileges granted to trustees by the 4th and 6th sections of the act entitled, 'An Act, etc.'" (the Act of April 6th, 1784.)

The present act makes the trustees and their successors the body corporate.

Again, section 4 declared the qualification of voters thus: " That the persons qualified to vote at all such elections shall be such male adult persons as shall have belonged to such church or congregation for the last twelve months at least, preceding such election. *Provided always*, that they shall have been baptized in the Episcopal Church, or shall have been received into the said church, either by the rite of confirmation, or by receiving the Holy Communion, or by purchasing or hiring a pew or seat in such church, or by some other joint act of the parties and of the rector, whereby they shall have attached themselves to the Protestant Episcopal Church."

The first section of the General Act of the 27th of March 1801 (Laws, chap. 79), is a transcript of this Act of 1795, with a few variations, and is copied verbatim, in the first section of the existing Act of 1813.

§ 2. *First Election, etc.* " It shall be lawful for the male persons of full age belonging to any church, congregation, or religious society, in which divine service shall be celebrated according to the rites of the Protestant Episcopal Church in this State, and not already incorporated, to meet for the purpose of incorporating themselves, and of electing church-wardens and vestrymen, and to proceed to make such election and to effect such incorporation, in like manner as by the first section of the act hereby amended, is authorized to be done by persons possessing the qualifications therein specified."[1]

Every other qualification prescribed in the Act of 1813, amended by this Act of 1819, is dispensed with for the first election. Twelve months' union with the church or congregation was required by the Act of 1813. No time is now prescribed. But as notice of the meeting must be given for two preceding Sundays, the belonging to the church during that period may be requisite.

---

[1] Act of March 5th, 1819, § 1, to amend the act entitled, " An Act to provide for the Incorporation of Religious Societies." Laws of 1819, chap. 88.

The qualifications are merely being a male of full age, and belonging to a congregation, in which worship is celebrated according to the rites of the Church. The use of the services according to the Book of Common Prayer would satisfy this last provision.

What is the meaning of the phrase "belonging to any church?" etc. The phrase is not "belonging to the Protestant Episcopal Church," nor, "in communion with the Protestant Episcopal Church;" it is, "belonging to a church or congregation, in which divine services are held, according to the rites of such Church."

The statute itself makes a discrimination. It renders valid an incorporation by persons not possessing all the qualifications specified in the Act of 1813. And then it declares, that no person not possessing those qualifications (enumerated in the Act of 1813), shall be permitted to vote at any subsequent election. (Sect. 1, Act of 1819.)

It seems an inevitable consequence, that the Statute of 1819 meant to dispense, at this first election, not merely with the prior connection of twelve months, but with the other qualifications specified, such as baptism, confirmation, or reception of the Holy Communion, or purchasing or hiring a pew or seat. A usual attendance seems enough.

This is strengthened by reference to the Act of 1813 itself. The phrase, "who shall have belonged to such church or congregation," is used distinctively from the phrase of "being in communion with the Protestant Episcopal Church," and the other enumerated qualifications.

In the discussions upon the proposed changes in the Act of Incorporation in the Convention of New York, it was stated, that the change in 1819 was made as matter of policy, to spread the Church in new regions. If the persons had evinced a disposition and preference for this Church, even for a short period, it was expedient to bring them together and increase, by uniting, their attachment and energy. They would soon be led to a more decided and consistent faith.

The standing committee of the Western Diocese strongly

urged the expediency of the amendment of 1819 continuing. Bishop Delancy was willing that it should remain. The latter, after an experience at Albany, most earnestly and publicly deprecated any attempt to obtain an alteration in the law as it stood. Its inconveniences or defects had far better be submitted to, than to encounter the risk of most radical and injurious provisions which would be urged.

Organization. There may have been, previous to these steps for an incorporation, a complete ecclesiastical organization, a congregation or church, rector, wardens, and vestrymen. A clause of the first section of the Act of 1813 presupposes this, directing that the rector, if any, or in his absence, or if there be none, one of the church-wardens or vestrymen, shall be called to the chair.

But such organization is not made necessary by the statute. Any other person may be called to preside. While the ecclesiastical organization may exist, it is not indispensable that it should exist. In the case of St. Mark's Church, it did exist for some time before the incorporation.

This fact and distinction will be found of importance in many cases that arise. In Hoffman's " Law of the Church," p. 276, the report of a committee of the Diocese of Wisconsin is stated, accurately distinguishing the cases. " The organization of a parish is strictly and solely an ecclesiastical procedure, constituting the parish a component part of the Protestant Episcopal Church, and as such duly entitling it to ecclesiastical rights and privileges. The ecclesiastical organization gives no civil or corporate powers to the parish."

While the ecclesiastical organization confers no corporate powers, yet, in many cases, the civil incorporation will control a canonical or diocesan regulation. Thus all regulations of the mode of a vestry's acting, its succession, rules as to property of the Church, will be exclusively governed by the statutes applicable to the body incorporated. In our State, and in the other States, as far as I am aware, the legislature has never gone beyond its proper limit; has never attempted to act as to matters of doctrine, discipline, or religious practice.

There is, I apprehend, an inaccuracy in the precedent, in the Journal of the Convention of New York, in stating that there cannot be a rector until there is a corporation.

§ 3. *Object of the Meeting.* The object of the meeting is to incorporate themselves under the Act of 1813 as amended in 1819. They are by a majority of voices "to elect two church-wardens and eight vestrymen, and to determine on what day of the week called Easter-week, the said offices of church-wardens and vestrymen shall annually thereafter cease, and their successors in office be chosen. Also, to fix the name or title by which such church or congregation shall be known in law."[1]

§ 4. *Notice.* Of this first election, "notice shall be given in the time of *morning* service on two Sundays previous thereto, by the rector, or if there be none, by any other person belonging to such church or congregation."[2]

Here again, the organization of a church with a rector is supposed as possibly existing.

This notice, if given by a layman, may be given from a pew or on a step of the chancel. The election would be legal if given by such anywhere, but Church regulations forbid that it should be given from within the chancel, from the desk, or pulpit. The writer, at least, upon examination, gave an opinion to that effect.

It is to be given "in the time of morning service." It is legal to give it at any period during such service. Custom regulates it as to be done next after the reading of the gospel. It must not be given during evening service. It ought not to be given by a clergyman officiating who is not the rector. Most probably an incorporation, otherwise unobjectionable, would not be held invalid on this account, but it is easy and secure to follow the letter of the statute.

§ 5. *Presiding Officer.* At this meeting for this incorporation and first election, "the rector, or if there be none,

[1] Sect. 1 of Laws of 1813.   [2] *Ibid.*

or he be necessarily absent, then one of the church-wardens or vestrymen, or any other person called to the chair, shall preside at such first election." [1]

If there is a rector, and he be present, he must preside. If absent, (the necessity will be presumed,) and there are wardens and vestrymen, then a warden or a vestryman must preside; if both wardens are absent, then one of the vestrymen. All this presumes an ecclesiastical organization. But if there is no such organization, then any other person called to the chair shall preside.

In stating that if there is a warden present he presides in preference to a vestryman, I state the custom rather than the strict law. The statute has not pointed out any order of presiding, except as to the rector. If insisted upon, I apprehend that the persons assembled may choose a presiding officer, though of course, only out of wardens or vestrymen. If not one of either class is present, then another person may be chosen.

It is quite a common case, when there is no rector, for the clergyman who has officiated during the service to preside at the election. The committee of the Convention on the Incorporation of Churches in 1864, recognize this in the case of the Rev. Mr. Dyer, he being stated as assisting in the organization and presiding, although they held the certificate defective in not adding that he had been called to the chair. Still the tenor of the provisions rather indicates that the person so called and presiding should be one of the congregation, — one belonging to it.

The number to be chosen are eight vestrymen and two wardens, neither more nor less. The election may be by ballot, or by open nomination, and *viva voce* voting. This point the meeting will first decide. Two persons of those present should be called by the chair to assist in counting the ballots, or to join in declaring the result upon an election by nomination. They are to join in the certificate. It is advisable to appoint a secretary, and that minutes be kept, to be copied into a regular book, and attested by the

---

[1] Sect. 1 of Laws of 1813.

presiding officer and secretary. The notice and days of giving it should be stated with the course of proceedings, and names of the persons chosen. It is expedient to enter all this in the book intended as the Vestry Minute Book.

§ 6. *Certificate.* "The person who presides, together with two other persons, shall make a certificate, under their hands and seals, of the church-wardens and vestrymen so selected; of the day in Easter-week so fixed on for the annual election of their successors; and of the name or title by which such church or congregation shall be known in law."[1]

For the form of this certificate, see Appendix No. 2.

All which the statute requires to be stated in the certificate is the names of the wardens and vestrymen, the day in Easter-week fixed for the annual elections, and the name by which the church shall be known in law.

In the case of All Saints Church *v.* Lovett (1 Hall's Superior Ct. Reps. 195), it appeared as a fact, that there was a rector, and that another person presided at the election. The Court held, that as the statute did not require that the certificate should state that the rector presided, or some one else in the cases prescribed, it would assume that the rector was absent to sustain the incorporation.

The Methodist Union Church *v.* Richet (23 Barbour's Reps. 437), arose under the third section of the Act of 1813, applicable to other churches or congregations; but the provisions as to notice, the holding the elections, and the certificate, are so similar as to make the decision pertinent.

The Court say, that although it is manifestly proper to show in the certificate that all the requirements of the statute have been followed, the omission of particulars not necessary to be stated, does not affect the validity of the certificate. A compliance with the statute, beyond what is required to be set forth, may be presumed.

In the case of the Church of the Redemption in 1864, the certificate stated that the Rev. Robert I. Dickson pre-

[1] Sect. 1 of Laws of 1813.

sided, but did not state that he was the rector, or had been called, etc. In point of fact he was the rector.

The Committee of the Convention on the Incorporation of Churches, reported against admission upon this and another ground, namely, the want of a stamp under the United States Laws. This last point is afterwards more fully noticed. The author's opinion being asked, he stated, that under the above authority the omission was not fatal, although the irregularity should be discouraged. It could not be doubted that the fact would be presumed, or would be open to proof.

But if we look narrowly into this point, we may probably conclude that it is best that the certificate should be rigidly confined to what the law exacts, and go no further. It is merely the record of what took place at the meeting. Sometimes the certifiers might not be able conscientiously to state the previous action. Simplicity is attained. The certificate is clearly presumptive evidence of the incorporation. All the prerequisites are open to proof, whether stated or not.

§ 7. *Signing, etc.* The certificate is to be signed and sealed by the presiding officer and by two other of the persons present."[1]

Care should be taken that these persons have been at the meeting for the whole time it lasted.

§ 8. *Acknowledgment or Proof.* 1. "Such certificate shall be duly acknowledged or proved by one or more of the subscribing witnesses, before the Chancellor, or one of the Judges of the Supreme Court, or one of the Judges of the Court of Common Pleas of the county where such church or place of worship of such congregation shall be situated." (Sect. 1 of Act of April 5, 1813.)

2. " Certificates of incorporation authorized by the ' Act to provide for the Incorporation of Religious Societies,' passed April 5, 1813, which shall be hereafter made or executed, may be acknowledged or proved before any officer authorized to take acknowledgments or proofs of conveyances of

---

[1] Sect. 1 of Laws of 1813.

real estate, and in the same manner, and of the like effect; and upon being so acknowledged or proved, shall be entitled to be recorded as in the said act provided." (Sect. 1 of Act of April 16, 1844, chap. 158.)

Judges of the Supreme Court, Judges of the County Courts, (at least out of the county of New York,) Commissioners of Deeds and Notaries Public, in their particular counties, are authorized to take the acknowledgment of deeds.

3. "All such certificates which have been heretofore acknowledged or proven, before any officer authorized to take acknowledgments or proofs of conveyances of real estate, shall and are hereby declared to be of the same force and validity as if the same had been acknowledged or proven before any one of the officers named in the first section of the act hereby amended; but nothing herein contained shall be construed to impair or affect the rights of any person or persons, in any case where any legal proceedings shall be instituted for enforcing such rights before the passage of this act." (Sect. 2 of Act of April 16, 1844, chap. 158.)

In The First Baptist Society *v.* Rapelye (16 Wendell, 605, 1837), the acknowledgment of the certificate was before a Commissioner of Deeds, and it was held, that there was no valid incorporation on that account. Then the law of 1844 above cited was passed.

A certificate may be executed, and will be received in evidence, in a suit testing the validity of an election, although not executed until several months after the election. (The People *v.* Peck, 11 Wendell, 604.)

In the case of the Church of the Redemption, a meeting was held for the purpose of incorporating on the 12th of April, 1864. A certificate was executed, duly proven and recorded in the Register's office of the city of New York, on the 22d of April, 1864. The certificate was defective, and the record unavailing from the want of a stamp, under the law of the United States. (See *post.*) An election took place in April, 1865, on the day fixed upon, and some

changes were made. An application for admission to the
Convention in September, 1865, was reported against, because of this want of a stamp, and that there was no incorporation. On Saturday, the 31st of March, 1866, a new
certificate was executed by the same three persons who
signed the former one, was duly acknowledged and stamped,
and was recorded on Monday, the 2d day of April, 1866, in
the Register's office. On Sunday, the 1st of April, 1866,
notice was given that the annual election would be held on
the Tuesday ensuing. Such election was held and certain
changes in the vestrymen made.

The new certificate was a precise transcript of the former
of the same date, excepting it stated the presiding officer
to be the rector. The subscribing witnesses were different.

The author submitted the following results in an opinion.
(The effect of the want of a stamp was first discussed. See
post.)

That assuming the first record to be totally void, and no
corporation constituted, the renewed certificate was a valid
instrument properly executed, and the corporation was created when it was recorded. That the old certificate could
have been used, and stamped and recorded anew, with the
same effect. There was however no objection to the issuing
of the new one. The statute had nowhere prescribed a
time for such an instrument to be acknowledged, or even
for its execution. A defective certificate could be supplied
subsequently by a new one. That had the new and regular
certificate been filed in the proper office within a year from
the organization, every thing would have been valid; and
that the better opinion appeared to be that if nothing had
been done requiring corporate powers, nor any thing acquired as a corporation, the old vestry held their places, and
the proceedings would be valid. The provision of the
statute formed rules by which the members had agreed to
be controlled. That as the statute did not require any
notice to be given of a subsequent election, nor any rule
existed requiring notice, that given in the case on the preceding Sunday was sufficient.

4. *Stamp.* As before observed, the application of the Church of the Redemption for admission into Convention, was reported against on the ground of the want of a stamp upon the certificate. The Committee quote the 152d section of the Act of Congress of June 30, 1864, providing that it should not be lawful to record any instrument required by law to be stamped, unless a stamp of the proper amount be affixed. And the record of any such instrument upon which the stamp or stamps shall not have been affixed, shall be utterly void, and shall not be used in evidence.

The author, in the opinion before referred to, observed, that as the certificate was executed April 12th, and recorded April 22d, 1864, an act of the ensuing June could scarcely invalidate an instrument then on record, if it was before valid. The question would seem therefore to be governed by the law in force at the previous dates.

By the Act of July 1st, 1862, stamp duties are imposed on the instruments enumerated in Schedule B annexed to it. Among such instruments was "a certificate of any other description than those specified." A duty of ten cents was imposed, afterwards reduced to five.

The Commissioner of the Revenue held, that "a stamp was requisite upon every certificate which has or may have a legal force in law or equity." Section 95 imposed a penalty for signing or issuing any instrument without the proper stamp; and declared, "that such instrument as aforesaid should be invalid and of no effect."

Various provisions were quoted, relaxing the law under particular circumstances.

The 163d section of the Act of June 30th, 1866, was cited, and is as follows: " No deed or instrument so required by law to be stamped, and heretofore signed or issued without being duly stamped, nor any copy thereof, shall be recorded, or be admitted to be used as evidence in any court, until a legal stamp shall be affixed; and a party interested is authorized to affix such stamp in the presence of the Register, Recorder, etc. *Provided*, that no instrument, etc., issued prior to this act without being stamped, shall for that cause, if the stamps required be affixed, be deemed invalid and of no effect."

The certificate in the case was invalid and of no effect, not under the 152d section of the law of June, 1864, but under the original Act of 1862 (§ 94–95), as amended to five cents. But under the clauses cited, the old certificate (at least prior to July 13th, 1866,) could have been stamped, and have been then duly recorded anew, or the old rendered legal. From that time certainly, the corporation would be constituted.

And it might be that such stamping would render every thing operative and valid from the beginning, so that if stamps were now affixed, the corporation would be deemed in existence from April 22, 1864, and every corporate act established. (Brown *v.* Savage, 5 Jurist, 1070; Rogers *v.* James, 7 Taunton, 747.)

The Act of the 13th of July, 1866, § 9, was, however, the act in force, and was the same as section 152 of the Act of June 30th, 1864. There might perhaps be a question whether the clauses referred to are not repealed. But without considering this point, as the new certificate was duly stamped and recorded in April, 1866, before this act, the strong ground was, that the corporation commenced April 2d, 1866. It was stated that there was nothing, connected with property or otherwise, which would make the fact that there was no legal incorporation from 1864 until this period, of importance.

As above noticed, the law of 1866, now in force, forbids the recording of any instrument on which stamps are required, without such stamps are affixed; otherwise, the record is wholly void, and cannot be given in evidence,

§ 9. *Record of Certificate.* (1.) The certificate thus executed, and acknowledged or proven, shall be recorded by the Clerk of such county (the county where the church or place of worship of such congregation shall be situated), in a book, to be by him provided for that purpose. (§ 1 of Act of April 5th, 1813.)

(2.) "All that part of the former duty of the Clerk of

the city and county of New York, which appertains and relates to the registering of mortgages, and to the recording of deeds, conveyances, and other writings, which by law are directed, or hereafter may be directed, to be registered or recorded, shall continue to be held, exercised and enjoyed, by a person to be appointed as is hereafter mentioned, and be called the Register in and for the city and county of New York ; and he shall have and enjoy all the rights and powers, and perform all the duties which were formerly performed by the Clerk of the city and county of New York, in relation to the recording and registering of deeds, conveyances, mortgages, and other writings." (§ 99 of Act of April 9, 1813, as amended by subsequent acts.)

(3.) The Clerk of the city and county of New York shall forever hereafter be relieved, restrained, and precluded from doing or performing any duties or services, or any act, matter, or thing whatsoever, as Clerk of the city and county of New York, so far as the same relates to the registering of mortgages, and recording of deeds, conveyances, and other writings, which by law are, or hereafter may be, directed and required to be recorded or registered. (Ibid. § 160.)

These provisions are found in the act to reduce the laws relating to the city of New York into one act. (2 R. L., 1813, p. 412.)

The first act was that of March 13, 1812. (6 Webster, 163.)

(4.) " Whereas several religious societies whose places of worship are in the city of New York, seeking to incorporate themselves under the provisions of an act entitled, ' An Act to provide for the Incorporation of Religious Societies,' passed April 5th, 1813, have, through mistake, caused the certificate provided for by the first section of this act to be recorded in the office of the Clerk of the city and county of New York : Now, therefore, be it enacted, that the recording of every such certificate in the said office of the Clerk of the city and county of New York, prior to the passage of this act, be regarded and construed, and such recording is hereby declared to be, of the same validity, force, and effect, as would have been the recording of such certificate in the office of the Register of the city and county of New York; and every act, deed, matter, and thing, done or performed by every such religious society since the recording of its certificate in the office of said Clerk, is hereby ratified and confirmed, and declared to be valid in all respects, as if said certificate had been recorded in the office of said Register; but this act shall not affect any suit or proceeding already commenced arising out of such original mistake." (§ 1 of Act of April 29, 1863, chap. 287.)

In the case of the Church of the Atonement, before mentioned, the certificate of an election in November 1865, had been filed in the County Clerk's office. An opinion was given that this was not the proper office, but the Register's only.

Among other points the Revised Statutes were referred to (1 R. S. 762, § 38), defining a conveyance "an instrument by which the title to any real property may be affected in law or equity." And also the provisions by which for recording conveyances, the Register of the city of New York, was, by section 43, made in effect the County Clerk. A doubt was expressed whether a certificate by which no title was directly affected, but through the recording of which a body might acquire title, and in a particular mode transfer it, was within the clause. However, the Act of April 29, 1863 (*ante*), was a clear legislative declaration, that the Register's office was the proper place, and not the Clerk's office.

The filing in the wrong office was equivalent to an omission to file and record at all. And hence no corporation had been constituted. The language was, " that the trustees and their successors shall *thereupon* be a corporate body," etc. The recording was a prerequisite as absolutely necessary to be followed as any other prescription of the statute.

§ 10. *Certificate Evidence.* By the Act of 1813 (chap. 271, § 9), this certificate, duly proved or acknowledged, with the certificate of the proper officer endorsed thereon, may be received in evidence, on the trial of any action, in the same manner as if such instrument were a conveyance of real estate.

And by the Revised Statutes (1 R. S. 377, § 76), copies of all papers duly filed in the office of the County Clerk, and transcripts from the book of records kept therein, certified by such Clerk, with the seal of his office affixed, shall be evidence in all courts, in like manner as if the originals were produced. The transcript of all records certified by the said Register may be read in evidence in any court of this State, without further proof of such deed, conveyance, or other writing, so recorded, in the said office. (§ 161 of Act of April 9, 1813, " To reduce," etc.).

§ 11. *Vestry are Trustees.* " The church-wardens and vestrymen so created, and their successors in office, of themselves; but if there be a rector, they, together with the rector, shall form a vestry and be the trustees of such church or congregation."   (§ 1, Act of 1813.)

In the first place, the wardens and vestrymen, if there is no rector, constitute a vestry; but if there is a rector, then they, together with him, form it; and it cannot be formed without him. In the same manner, they, or they with the rector, are constituted trustees.

The Church phraseology is thus preserved. A vestry is constituted resembling the select vestries of the English law, and representing the mass of the parishioners. The assembling of these with the rector, forms a vestry generally, as known to that law.

So by the second section of the Vestry Act of Maryland, the rector of the parish, with all the eight vestrymen chosen at the election, shall be deemed and considered the vestry of the parish for the ensuing year, and the rector of the parish shall always be one of the vestry.

The Act of 1785 of Virginia, and the ordinance of the Convention after the repeal of that act, contain similar provisions. The statute of Wisconsin is to the same effect.

§ 12. *Corporate Body.* Such trustees and their successors shall thereupon, by virtue of this act, be a body corporate, by the name or title expressed in such certificate. (Ibid.)

This language is precisely the same as that used in the third section of the act, under which it has been held, that trustees do not form the corporation, so as to enable them to sue in their own names. (See *post*, chap. 16, § 3.)

§ 13. *Subsequent Elections.* "The persons *qualified as aforesaid*, shall in every year thereafter (*after the first election*), on the day in Easter-week, so to be fixed for that purpose, elect such church-wardens and vestrymen." (§ 1 of Act of 1813.)

" No person *not possessing those qualifications*, shall be permitted to vote at any subsequent election of church-wardens and vestrymen." (§ 1 of Act of March 5, 1819, chap. 38.)

The qualifications thus prescribed are those stated in the first section of the Act of 1813, and which, until the Act of 1819, were all required for the first, as well as subsequent elections. They are, —

(1.) Being a male person of full age.

(2.) Being of a church or congregation in communion with the Protestant Episcopal Church in this State.

(3.) Having belonged to such church or congregation for the last twelve months preceding such election.

We pause here to notice that these qualifications are separate, and each essential. The qualifications subsequently stated are adjuncts to these, though distinctive in themselves. Great errors are fallen into by not understanding or neglecting this point.

The essential and indispensable prerequisites of a voter are, — 1. That he is a male adult. 2. That he shall be of a church which is in communion with the Protestant Episcopal Church in this State. 3. That he has belonged to the particular church where he proposes to vote, for twelve months preceding the election.

Then follow other qualifications, each of which is adjunctive to, or explanatory of, the preceding qualifications.

(4.) *And* who shall have been baptized in the Episcopal Church.

Or, shall have been received therein either by the rite of confirmation, or by receiving the Holy Communion ; or, by purchasing or hiring a pew or seat in said church ; or, by some joint act of the parties and of the rector, whereby they shall have attached themselves to the Protestant Episcopal Church.

Apparently there is a class of what may be termed ecclesiastical, and another of secular qualifications.

It has been claimed that one who hires a pew or seat, although an avowed Dissenter or Romanist, and who had frequented the church sufficiently during the year, might vote.

But this view is clearly erroneous. The church or congregation to which he shall have belonged for a year, is to be one in communion with the Protestant Episcopal Church. He is to be of that Church. Hence he is to be of such communion. Reception into the Convention is a plain proof of this communion of the Church. But it is not the only test. Avowal of the doctrine and discipline, worshiping according to its formularies, is also such. The individual member must have the same belief and give the same indications and proofs of it as the body.

Again, being *baptized in the Episcopal Church* (meaning, according to its prescribed forms and order, excluding in this instance, I apprehend, lay baptism,) is a definite proof of this communion.

Then the other qualifications specified contemplate a *reception into the Church* of persons not in it by virtue of baptism. They are designated as having been *received* by confirmation or through the holy communion. These evidences are not local but general. The next is local: or, by purchasing or hiring a pew or seat in said church. But the true version of this is, the hiring or purchasing a seat in the particular church by one in communion with the Church, — the general spiritual body, — but in a very loose sense.

Thus a person may have been baptized with lay baptism, or never baptized, nor confirmed, nor taken the communion, yet if he professes to unite himself with the Episcopal Church, and evinces it by worshiping in a church of that faith for a year previous, then the holding or hiring a pew or seat in it, is a reception into it, for the purpose of voting.

Many years ago this subject was submitted to the late Chief Justice Jones, and the author. The opinion was very clear, that thus far the provisions were plain and consistent.

No one could vote who was not of the communion; in other words, a professed Episcopalian, and had belonged to the particular church for a year previous; and the meaning of this phrase was, the statedly worshiping at the church, or whenever he attended public worship, with the exception of necessary absences; or at least, that there was not a greater or equal degree of attendance on public worship elsewhere, during the year.

But the remaining clause has always been a subject of difficulty. A person may be qualified to vote " by a joint act of himself and the rector, whereby he attaches himself to the Protestant Episcopal Church."

This again is subordinate to the yearly attendance.

It would of course shock every one to state the proposition, that a rector could make a person a member of the Church, the body of Christ, in any way but through the ordinances of the Church. That is not the sense which can be admitted.

I have known of a case in which a rector received a money contribution for his own support, or for the general use of the church, a few weeks before the election, and admitted the party to vote. Besides the decisive objection of the want of attendance for the year previous, this was a flagrant misconstruction of the provision. That payment was not attaching himself to the church.

It is clear that the clause means something positive and permanent, by which the person declares an adherence to the Protestant Episcopal Church, its doctrine, discipline, and worship. Cases may be imagined in which one seeking to come within it, is not yet prepared for its ordinances of admission. In such a case, for the purposes of voting, the statute permits an act of avowed adhesion, made to and with the assent of the rector, to avail. Manifestly, a mere pecuniary contribution is not within its scope. The joint act should always be put in writing.

This clause of the statute receives illustration from a portion of Canon XV. of 1798, "of the duty of ministers to keep a register." This remained part of the law of the Church until 1832. "And no minister shall place on the said list the names of any persons except those who, on due inquiry, he shall find to have been baptized in this Church, or who, having been otherwise baptized, shall have been received into this Church, either by the holy rite of confirmation, or by receiving the holy communion, or by some other joint act of the parties and of a minister of this Church, whereby such persons shall have attached themselves to the same."

This was omitted in the revision of 1832.

We see from this provision, that it was considered that lay baptism was sufficient for confirmation. Wheatley says, that in the early Church, confirmation preceded the eucharist, except there was extraordinary cause to the contrary, such as in the case of clinic baptism, of the absence of a bishop, or the like; in which cases the eucharist is allowed before confirmation. (Book of Common Prayer, p. 394.) See the Rubric to the communion office.

The statute is almost word for word with the canon in force when it was passed. We may presume members of the Church drew it. It seems quite clear, that the joint act must be one indicating an adhesion to the Church, its doctrines, and order.

In The People *ex rel. v.* Lacoste (Supreme Court, 1865), the Judge, upon a trial as to a contested election, charged the jury, that the clause meant something of a spiritual or ecclesiastical character.

The sense of the phrase, " who shall have belonged to such church for the last twelve months," may be gathered from the following cases : —

In The People *v.* Tuttle (31 N. Y. Rep. 550), it was held, that the words " stated attendant on divine worship in the said congregation, at least one year before the election," was held to mean, attendance regularly, at regular fixed times, not occasional. The attendance must be personal. It cannot be supplied by another. The regular attendance of a wife or other member of the family will not suffice. And no amount of contribution can be accepted in lieu of this personal presence statedly.

In the case of The People *v.* Phillips (1 Denio, 388), arising under the third section of the Act of 1813, a decision was made pertinent to the case now considered. The qualifications of voters at the first election are these: " Every male person of full age, who has statedly worshiped with such church, congregation, or society, and has formerly been considered as belonging thereto." But at subsequent elections, no member shall be permitted to vote until " he shall have been a stated attendant on divine worship in the said church, congregation, or society, at least one year before such election, and shall have contributed to the support of such church, according to the usages and customs thereof." (Ibid. § 7.)

The Court say: "These qualifications could neither be abridged nor extended by any act of the trustees or of the corporators. Every corporation has power to make by-laws, but they must be consistent with its charter or they will be invalid. As far as any by-law required qualifications for the right of voting, not recognized by the statute, they were wholly unauthorized. A by-law making a formal act of admission by the trustees, and payment of a particular sum of money therefor, was not warranted." See Angell & Ames on Corp. 267, 273, etc.

The highly important case of Petty *v.* Tooker (21 N. Y. Rep. 267), is hereafter examined at length. It is attempted to be shown that it does not apply to Episcopal churches incorporated under the first section. It adjudged that corporations formed under the third section were not denominational, and individuals did not lose their right to vote by abandoning the doctrine and ecclesiastical organization of the Church.

There are some disqualifications under the general law of the State which I proceed to notice.

Infants. The rules of the common law, it is to be noticed, applicable to civil corporations established by statute or charter, apply to incorporations of an ecclesiastical character. (Robertson *v.* Bullions, 11 N. Y. Rep. 243.)

The rule requiring voters to be adults is taken from the common law. In the case of Trinity Church, New Rochelle, under a charter of 1762, where the phrase was merely " the members in communion with the Church of England," etc., the opinion was given that the votes of minors were illegally admitted.

" The members of corporations may be natural persons, that is, in municipal corporations, males of years of majority." (Grant on Corporations, p. 5.)   " In general, infants cannot be corporators." (p. 6.)   " An infant cannot be an attorney, bailiff, factor, or receiver," (McPherson on Infancy, p. 448); " nor steward of a manor, or of the court of a bishop, because he has not sufficient knowledge or experience to use the office ; nor can he appoint a deputy," (Hobart, 525) ; " nor can he be a member of the House of Commons." (McPherson, 448; 2 Inst. 47.)

The statement in some books (Bingham, for example), that a minor may be the mayor of a city, is not now law, if it ever was.   (Grant on Corporations, 422; Claridge *v.* Evelin, 5 Barn. & Ald. 81.)

Women.   Here another rule of the statute excluding women is the rule of the common law.   In the case before noticed, under the charter of Trinity Church, New Rochelle, the admission of votes by females was deemed improper.

In general, women cannot be corporators, although in some hospitals they may be so ; and there is one instance in the books, of a corporation of brethren and sisters invested with municipal powers to a certain extent.   (Grant on Corporations, p. 6 ; Palmer's Reps. 77; Sutton Hospital Case, Coke's Rep. vol. ix. part 10.)

Proxies. Voting by proxy is scarcely ever allowable, except in cases of the right being expressly given by charter or prescription, and in the case of peers in the House of Lords. Personal presence is essential.   (Rex *v.* Ellis, 17 State Trials, 822.)   The language of Chancellor Walworth in Phillips *v.* Wickham (1 Paige, 598), is decided and comprehensive upon this point. See also the case of the Dean and Chapter, Sir John Davies' Rep. 129, and Taylor *v.* Griswold, Supreme Court of New Jersey (2 Green's Rep.), deciding, that it required express legislative authority to authorize a corporation to make a by-law admitting votes by proxy. See also Kent's Comm., vol. ii. p. 229.

§ 14. *When Held.* "Such election shall be holden immediately after morning service." (§ 1 of Act of 1813.) Of course the service should take place. It may be doubted whether an election, without such service being held, would be valid. In the absence of express authority all that can safely be said is, that it would be very inadvisable to omit it.

Notice not Essential. It is customary and expedient to give notice of the stated election two Sundays previous; but the statute does not direct any notice, and an election is good without it. The parishioners are assumed to know the day in Easter-week selected. (Wilson *v.* Dennison, Ambler's Rep. 182.)

§ 15. *Presiding Officer.* The rector, or if there be none, or he be absent, one of the church-wardens or vestrymen, shall preside, and receive the votes of the electors, and be the returning officer. (§ 1 of Act of 1813.)

In The People *v.* Peck (1 Wendell, 604), it was declared, that no one but the persons designated under another section (elders or church-wardens), could preside at an election, if present. The appointment of others, when one of the class were present, was illegal, and vitiated an election.

It is to be noticed that the language in relation to the presiding officer is peculiar. "The rector, or if there be none, or he be absent, one of the church-wardens or vestrymen, shall preside, and receive the votes of the electors, and be the returning officer."

The class is designated out of which the presiding officer, in absence of a rector, shall be chosen. No order of presiding is declared. If any warden or a vestryman preside, the course is regular. But if a claim is made by a warden over his brother-warden, or over vestrymen, the only mode seems to be, to settle it by the votes of those present. The custom has been for a warden to preside; but my opinion is, that the voters present may choose any one of the designated classes to do so. In the absence of express regulation, this right is an incident to every corporate or associated body. (Wilcox on Corporations, 1-59.)

The presiding officer is to receive the votes, and make the return. By force of this language, its accepted construction, and general law, he is the judge of qualifications of the voters. There is no appeal to the meeting from his decision. The Supreme Court, on application, determines the validity of the election, and the propriety of admitting or rejecting votes.

It is sufficient to notice here that it is an inflexible rule, that the Court will not set aside an election unless the result would have been changed, had the decision of the presiding officer been correct. (31 N. Y. Rep. 550.)

The rector or presiding officer has a vote as a member; but there is no provision allowing a casting or double vote, upon an equal division.

A plurality of votes is insufficient. A majority of all the votes is necessary, that is, a majority of the legal votes, cast for an eligible person.

In Claridge v. Evelyn and others (5 Barn. & Ald. 81), an infant had received a majority of the votes cast for the office of Clerk of the Court of Requests. The voters for him were informed of his disqualification. The plaintiff received a minority of votes. The Court held, that the votes for the infant were thrown away, and that the plaintiff had been duly elected, receiving a majority of votes really cast.

So in Rex v. Hawkins (10 East, 218), it is ruled, that if the incapacity is discovered before the election is closed, the voters may cast their votes anew, for some one qualified. But if they do not, the voice of such as do vote prevails.

If the assembly is properly convened, and votes are cast, but the majority neglect to vote, yet the election will be valid. Their neglect is considered as equivalent to an assent to the decision of those who do vote. (Rex v. Foxcroft,

2 Burrows, 1020; Crawford *v.* Powell, 2 Burrows, 1016; Goslin *v.* Vesey, 7 Queen's Bench, 439; Also Regiua *v.* The Mayor of Leeds, 7 Adol. & Ellis, 963.)

The case of Goslin *v.* Vesey, *ut supra*, contains a summary of the whole law.

It seems to me that these cases warrant the conclusion, that a blank vote is not to be counted. See, especially, the reasoning in Goslin *v.* Vesey.

By our statute, for the first election the decision is to be by a majority of voices, that is, of voters. For the subsequent elections, there is no similar phrase. The common-law rules will therefore control.

As to the persons eligible, as there is no special provision, it may be sufficient to say, that they may be chosen, who are competent to choose. The qualifications of an elector are the qualifications of the officers. (Wilcox on Corporations, § 480.)

After the ballots have been received without challenge or objection, the right to inquire into the character of the voters ceases. The duty is then to count the votes, and return the number received, and the names of the parties having the greater number. (People *v.* White, 11 Abbott, 168.)

The judges at an election set forth in their certificate, that one set of candidates had a majority of the votes cast, but that after the result had been declared, satisfactory evidence was produced to them, that part of such votes were illegal; and that setting them aside, the other set of candidates were elected, which they therefore certified to be the result. It was held, that the certificate destroyed itself, and that the first set of candidates were to be deemed elected. (Hart *v.* Harvey, 32 Barbour's Rep. 55.)

It was ruled that the inspectors as judges must decide when the vote is offered; and the decision then made, if in favor of receiving the vote, is final. From the necessity of the case, a decision cannot be delayed until after the vote is deposited in the box. How are the inspectors to know which of the ballots should be withdrawn?

In general, a certificate of election is *prima facie* evidence of the right of the parties to the office; but not where the facts stated show they were not elected.

§ 16. "The presiding officer shall enter the proceedings in the book of the minutes of the vestry, and shall sign his name thereto, and offer the same to as many of the electors present as he shall think fit, to be by them also signed and certified."   (§ 1 of Act of 1813.)

§ 17. "The church-wardens and vestrymen, to be chosen at any of the said elections, shall hold their offices until the expiration of the year for which they shall be chosen, and until others be chosen in their stead."   (Ibid.)

This provision must be considered in connection with the second section of the Act of April 16, 1844, chap. 158. Whenever there shall have been an omission or neglect of any church, etc., at their stated annual meeting, to choose any of the trustees, church-wardens, vestrymen, or other officers, such church, etc., shall not be deemed or taken to have been thereby dissolved; but the trustees, church-wardens, vestrymen, or other officers then in office at the time of such omission, shall be deemed and taken to be the legal officers of such church, etc., and shall continue to hold their offices nutil others be chosen in their stead: *Provided*, that elections to supply such omissions shall be made within one year after their occurrence respectively.

It may be considered, I think, that the *omission* spoken of in this last act, may signify as well an omission to elect on the stated day, although the meeting for that purpose is held, as an omission to hold any election.

The following case, which occurred in 1863, led to a consideration of these provisions. At an annual election of the vestry of an Episcopal Church, the full number of vestrymen was duly elected, and one of the former wardens. There was a tie vote between the other former warden and a stranger.

Now, cases of a similar character may easily be supposed. If a given number of the old vestrymen receive a majority of legal votes, and the election fails as to the rest, as by reason of a tie, or that none of them have a majority of the votes cast, the other vestrymen are ascertained and continue. If they hold over, the vestry is complete, neither exceeding nor falling short of the prescribed number.

And so in cases under sections 3 and 6 of the General Act of 1813, if one or two persons of the class to be elected are old trustees rechosen, and no election takes place as to the others or other, the persons holding over are definite and known.

But suppose a definite number of vestrymen, being new persons, are duly chosen, there is no mode pointed out of settling who of the old vestrymen hold over. The number must not exceed eight, and the body should, if practicable, be kept complete. So if a third person was chosen warden, or a third person a trustee, of the class under section 6, the like difficulty would exist.

Both provisions cited admit of the construction, that if the election fails as to a single vestryman or trustee, it fails wholly, and all the former officers hold over until a new election within the year. This construction is not reasonable, as it would defeat the express will of the corporators as to those whom they have actually chosen. Hence, it seemed to the writer, that where the statute could be observed and reconciled with that will, it might legally be done; and hence, that in the case stated, the election as to the vestrymen and the old warden was valid, and that the other former warden held over.

But in the other cases above suggested, I do not see how the consequence is to be avoided, that if there is a failure even as to one, when seven new vestrymen are duly chosen, there is no election, and the old vestrymen hold over. I speak without confidence where is no guide in any authority of which I am aware.

There is no rule of the common law by which a person elected continues in office after the expiration of the term limited by law. Charters or special statutes provide frequently for this. (The People *v.* Tiernan, 8 Abbott, 359.) There are cases, however, in which the rights of third persons are involved, in which an officer is deemed to continue in his functions.

A party claiming to hold over under such a provision, must, upon a *quo warranto*, show specially, or plead, that no one has at any time been chosen to succeed him. It is not enough that an attempt has been made to choose a new trustee and failed, if there was time after such failure to have had an election, when a choice might have been made. (The People *v.* Phillips, 1 Denio, 388.)

§ 18. The church-wardens and vestrymen shall have power to call and induct a rector to such church or congregation, as often as there shall be a vacancy therein. (§ 1 of Act of April 5, 1813.)

In this provision, the call or election, and communication to the party, is the presentation of the English law.

The induction of that law consists of some act giving the party possession of the glebe and parsonage if any, the use and control of the church edifice to a certain extent, and reception of rents and income given for the support of a rector for the time being. The clerk is not complete incumbent till after induction, or as the common law calls it, corporal possession. It is an act of a temporal nature. It is so, although it is an act of spiritual persons about a spiritual matter. It instates the party in full possession of the temporalities. And the parson may maintain an action of trespass on the glebe land, although he has not taken actual possession of it. (Bulwer *v.* Bulwer, 2 B. & Ald. 470.)

But with us, such an action could only be maintained by the corporation in its corporate name, through the trustees. This is distinct from the right of enjoyment, which is in the minister.

Under section 21 of this chapter (*post*), I have examined minutely the points as to a rector's interest in, and possession of, the property belonging to a church.

§ 19. "No meeting or board of such trustees shall be held, unless at least three days' notice thereof shall be given in writing, under the hand of the rector, or one of the church-wardens." (§ 1 of Act of 1813.)

Perhaps this does not interfere with the right of a vestry to pass a by-law or order fixing stated days for a vestry meeting. Of such days the members are chargeable with notice, although it is a custom to give the special notice even in such cases. (Wilcox on Corp., § 59; Wilson *v.* Dennison, Ambler's Rep. 82 ; 4 Barn. & Cress. 441 ; Smith *v.* Lane, 21 N. Y. Rep. 296.) It is very common for vestries to fix upon some special days for their meetings. But at least, if anything of moment is contemplated, it is prudent to give the notice.

§ 20. " No such board shall be competent to transact any business, unless the rector, if there be one, and at least one of the church-wardens, and a majority of the vestrymen, be present." (§ 1 of Act of 1813.)

1. Thus far, the provision is very explicit. For the constituting of a legal board, competent to act, there must be present the rector, a warden, and a majority of the vestrymen. There are thus three integral parts of the body, which personally, as in the case of the rector, or by representation, as in the cases of the wardens and vestrymen, must attend.

2. *Vacancy.* In case of there being a vacancy by death, resignation, or otherwise, of both the wardens, no legal meeting can be had or act performed. An election to fill the vacancies must be had. The statute provides for this conveniently.

And so if the vestrymen are reduced below five in number.

But I am inclined to think, that if the defect is in the number of vestrymen, still leaving five, and the board is otherwise competent, the power of the vestry is unimpaired.

The statute requires only *a majority of the vestrymen to be present.* No doubt a majority of those to be elected, the full number of eight, is intended ; not a majority of those surviving or remaining. (Rex *v.* Morris, 4 East, 26 ; Rex *v.* Thornton, Ibid. 307 ; Rex *v.* Miller, 6 T. R. 278.)

Even if the phrase, " for the time being," is used in a charter, a majority of surviving members of a definite class is not enough. And in the leading case of The King *v.*

Devonshire (1 Barn. & Cress. 609), the words, "remaining and surviving," used in a charter, were held to mean only, " for the time being."

A careful examination of Chief Justice Abbott's opinion in this last case, and of The King *v.* Bellringer (4 T. R. 810), stated by him, will, I think, warrant the position that five vestrymen will be enough, where there are vacancies as to the others. His language is, " That The King *v.* Bellringer had decided, that where an election is to be made by a body consisting of a definite number, a good elective assembly cannot be had without the presence of such a number of persons as will constitute a majority of the entire definite number, although the number present may constitute a majority of the entire number existing. From the time of The King *v.* Bellringer, this has been taken as a general and established rule of corporation law."

The converse of the proposition, I take it, must be true. If a majority of the definite body when full, is present, it must be sufficient. Yet it would be prudent to fill up the vacancies before any important act is performed.

3. It is quite clear that no act is technically legal, unless had at a meeting thus composed of a rector, (if one,) a warden, and a majority of vestrymen. Yet, for current and ordinary business, not affecting property or rights, a custom has arisen of transacting it at an irregular meeting, and obtaining a subsequent approval.

4. *Equality of Votes.* But what are the positions of rector, wardens, and vestrymen when thus assembled?

The right of presiding is vested in the rector by another clause; or if there be none, in a church-warden. With this qualification, I consider every thing integral and distinctive, to be lost. The vestry is a board of trustees established by statute, and governed by its prescriptions or general principles of law. The members are then upon an equality of power as to every corporate resolution or act, except as to a casting vote in the presiding officer, if the view of that provision, taken hereafter, is correct. (See § 21, *post.*)

I cite some pertinent authorities : —

Thus in the case of St. Mary's Church, Philadelphia, (7 Serg. & Rawle, 517,) the trustees of a church consisted of three clerical and eight lay members. The Court say : "When legally assembled, the majority of voices govern; but every integral part must be present at a corporate assembly, by a majority, at least, of its proper members; though the major part of all present when assembled are competent to do a corporate act.

So in Beck *v.* Hanson (9 Foster's N. H. Rep. 213), by the charter of Portsmouth, the board of aldermen and board of councilmen formed, in their joint capacity, a body called the City Council. And a majority of each board was to constitute a quorum for business; that is, business in its own chamber. Each board voted separately to meet in convention on a given day to choose city officers. A minority of the board of aldermen appeared. But the members of the Common Council and this minority made a majority of the whole number of both boards. They chose an officer by a majority of voters present, and the election was held valid. After the agreement of the aldermen to meet, it was not necessary that a majority of them should appear.

See the case of The King *v.* Brower, 1 Barn. & Cress. 492, commented upon in Whiteside *v.* The People, 26 Wendell, 643.

In Ex parte Rogers (7 Cowen's Rep. 527), the question arose under the following statutory provision : "There shall continue to be appointed two officers, by the name of Canal Appraisers, who, being associated with any acting canal commissioner, shall be the appraisers of damages in the cases hereafter specified." (Laws of 1825, chap. 275.)

Mr. Young was a canal commissioner, and Messrs. Wood and Selden, appraisers. They met, heard witnesses, and discussed the merits of an application for damages, and separated. On coming together subsequently, Mr. Young refused to act, and declared himself no longer a member. The two appraisers assessed the damages at a certain sum, and signed a certificate thereof. On motion for a mandamus, the Court held the proceeding valid, and granted a peremptory mandamus for payment.

In a note by Justice Cowen, a number of cases are cited. He says : " Yet in several cases (indeed, this is generally so, 1 Barn. & Cress. 492), the requisite parts being present, they constitute one body, each individual having but a single vote ; the integral part, composed of the lesser number, being in this way within the power of the more numerous, for want of an absolute veto. Thus in the case of mayor and aldermen, when all are assembled, the vote of the mayor, one of the integral parts, weighs no more than that of a single alderman."

He then notices the cases in which a mayor, after business had begun, left the meeting. In the instances in which it has been held, that an election after he withdrew was void, it was plain, that the charters made it essential that he should be present at the consummation of the act.

So in relation to dean and chapter. It is a body corporate spiritual, consisting of many able persons in the law, namely, the dean who is chief, and his prebendaries; and they together make the corporation. (Burns' Ecc. Law, 2-92.) It is not a perfect corporation without the dean. (Ibid. 94.) Yet it is certain the dean is one, and but one member of the body corporate. (Ibid. 117.)

Under particular local statutes, questions as to the negative power of a dean arose. See particularly the case of the Cathedral Church of Carlyle, stated fully in 2 Burns, 113, where it is shown, that such a power is contrary to the general law of the land, and must be most expressly conferred.

At page 117, is an opinion of a very able advocate and two learned counsel, which was acquiesced in : " That by the general rule of law, in all corporations aggregate, the act of the major part shall bind the whole ; for it is said, *ubi major pars ibi totum.* But though the law was so in the case of corporations aggregate, yet as in those corporations there is generally a chief member of the corporation, as dean and chapter, master and fellows, mayor and commonalty, the consent of the head member has, by many local statutes, been made necessary in corporate acts.

Hence it was found necessary, in order to prevent confusion, by an act of Parliament to abrogate all private local statutes in every such corporate body, which were contrary to the said rule of the common law. And therefore the act of 33d Henry 8th, declares, that every rule or statute made or to be made, whereby any grant, lease, gift, or election by the majority of a corporation, shall be let or hindered, shall be absolutely void and of no effect. A presentation by the major part must bind the lesser; otherwise differences in the body could never be terminated, nor could any corporate act be done without the assent of the dean.

5. The rector has not power to terminate or adjourn a vestry meeting after it has been convened and business is before it. This belongs to the majority of those assembled, himself included.

Thus in Stoughtou v. Reynolds (2 Strange, 1045, and Fortescue's Rep. 168), Mr. Stoughton moved for a mandamus to the chancellor of the diocese to admit him as churchwarden of the Parish of All Souls. The chancellor returned that he considered Mr. Stoughton not to have been chosen, but some one else. The action was for a false return. It was found by special verdict, that the vicar had the nomination of wardens. That on the regular appointed day for choosing, the vicar nominated Mr. Lowth, and the parishioners the plaintiff. That upon a dispute arising, whether the parishioners could choose the plaintiff, the vicar adjourned the meeting to the next morning; but that part of the parish stayed behind and elected him. The other party chose another person the next day. The question was, whether the vicar who presided could, *ex mero motu*, adjourn the election of wardens without any previous notice or consent of the meeting; and after the persons present had elected one, could proceed to elect another.

It was held by the King's Bench, that the adjournment was void. All the judges concurred. Lord Hardwicke said, that admitting the vicar had the power of presiding, it did not follow that he had the power of adjourning.

In Baker & Downing v. Wood (1 Curtis' Rep. 552), Sir

Herbert Jenner comments upon this case, stating it very fully, and says: " Most undoubtedly in such circumstances, there is no authority for the power assumed and exercised by the chairman in that case. It was calculated to put an end to the privilege possessed by the parishioners of selecting a person for church-warden, and to put a stop to all discussion at a meeting called for the purpose of an election."

After citing the case of The King *v.* The Commissary of the Bishop of Winchester (7 East's Rep. 573), he says : " To the extent to which this case goes, it supports the authority of the case of Stoughton *v.* Reynolds, that the chairman, as such, has not the power to adjourn the vestry at any time, and under any circumstances he may think proper."

Reference is then made by the learned judge to the case of The King *v.* The Archdeacon of Chester (1 Adol. & Ellis, 342), as decisive of certain points. A vestry being to be held in Manchester for the election of church-wardens, notice was given that the meeting would be held at the parish church, but that if a poll was demanded, it would be adjourned to the Town Hall.

After a show of hands, a poll was demanded, and the chairman adjourned to the Town Hall, without taking the sense of the meeting. It was held, that the proceeding was regular, no business having been interrupted, and the adjournment being part of the original appointment.

So in Downing *v.* Wood *ut supra,* the original notice apprised the parties of an adjournment upon a certain event occurring, and such adjournment was entirely reasonable and convenient.

And so in The Queen *v.* Doyly (4 Perry & Davison's Rep. 58), the power to adjourn a poll to a more convenient time and place, when it has been demanded, is recognized to be in the chairman, of course the rector, when present.

In such cases, the power is for the better furtherance and proper exercise of the business to be done, not the breaking up of a business properly commenced before the proper body.

6. It follows from these principles and authorities, as I apprehend, that a rector cannot, by withdrawing from a vestry once duly constituted, prevent its finishing business entered upon, or from entering upon business.

It is quite clear, that if his continued presence is essential, as an integral member, for every act while considered and until decided, so is that of one warden and five vestrymen. The power to arrest action by withdrawing is as absolute in a warden, or in vestrymen reducing the number below five, as in the rector.

In The King *v.* Norris (Barnardiston's Rep. 385), the charter made it necessary for the mayor to be present at an assembly for admitting freemen. At such a meeting he was present, and admitted one freeman. A list of others was delivered in, when he left the assembly, and would not admit them. After his departure they were admitted, and it was held good.

It is true this case is questioned in Rex *v.* Butler, 8 East, 393, and Rex *v.* Gaborian, 11 East, 87. In these cases, the assent of the mayor to the election of an officer was made indispensable.

This case of The King *v.* Norris is cited with approbation in the case of Whiteside *v.* The People, 26 Wendell, 643, in the Court of Errors.

There are other authorities proceeding upon the principle that by unequivocal language of statute or charter, the consent of the head officer (the mayor generally), was made essential to the consummation of the act. These cases are stated in Justice Cowen's note, before referred to in Rogers' case, (*ante*, p. 73). It cannot, I think, be said, that the provision now considered positively requires the continued presence of the rector or a warden for every act, thus substantially giving him a veto upon the proceedings.

Upon the whole, I consider the true conclusion to be, that when once a vestry is fully assembled, a rector, a warden, and five vestrymen, it becomes a massed assembly, governing itself by the rules of common law in analogous cases; that the right of presiding is a privilege and a duty. If vacated wilfully or not from necessity, it cannot dissolve the vestry, or make its action illegal.[1]

7. The statute empowers a warden to call a meeting. But if so convened, and the rector refuse to attend, intentionally to defeat or prevent the consideration of a measure within the province of the vestry to act upon, what, if any, is the redress?

In the English cases, in which the power to convene is lodged in a head officer, and his presence is indispensable to constitute the body, his obstinate refusal to convene it, or to attend, is an abuse of power, a neglect of a trust which the King's Bench will punish, and compel him to do it by mandamus, and will allow a criminal information to be filed against him.[2]

But even if any similar resort to a civil tribunal were possible in our country, it is most earnestly to be deprecated and sedulously avoided. The authorities cited show, however, in what light the law regards the wilful neglect of one intrusted with somewhat of a public duty. It is a criminal offence.

I do not doubt that such a course on the part of a rector, deliberately persisted in, after notice of a meeting, and the subject to be considered, would afford ground to apply to the ecclesiastical authority for its consent to his dismissal, under the Canon of the General Convention.

Questions have also, in my experience, arisen, as to the extent of the duty of a rector to put questions for the decision of the vestry. There can be no doubt of his obligation to do this, in every case of a proposition properly within the province of a vestry to act upon. It is, on the other

---

[1] In the *Parish Hand-Book*, p. 27, is a statement that the rector has sole power to call the vestry together, to preside over its deliberations, and to dissolve it. Dr. Hawks' *Constitution and Canons*, and Hoffman's *Law of the Church*, are referred to for this proposition. Certainly neither of the passages referred to, warrant the statement. In one particular, the statute is the reverse. A warden may call a meeting.

[2] See the cases cited, Wilcox on Corporations, § 94 ; Rex *v.* Gaborian, 11 East, 87, note ; Rex *v.* Church-wardens of St. Mathews, 8 Barn. & Adol. 907 ; Rex *v.* Church-wardens of St. Bartholomew, 2 Barn. & Adol. 506.

side clear, that he is not bound to put questions or resolutions tending to censure or criminate himself. When acts or resolutions are proposed hostile to the rector, as under the Canon respecting a dissolution of the connection, or where a vestry is authorized to present, the body acts of necessity as warden and vestrymen, not as the strict integral body. (See Hoffman's "Law of the Church," p. 323 – 5.) There may possibly be resolutions of neither character, as to which good sense and mutual forbearance must be the guide.

In closing this important branch of the subject, I beg to remark, that clergymen too often forget the new and peculiar relation in which they place themselves, when the church they belong to has been incorporated under the statutes of the State. Whenever the provisions of such statutes expressly, or by necessary implication, govern his relations with a vestry, or a congregation, or otherwise, they form the absolute law for him.

§ 21. "Such rector, if there be one, and if not then the church-warden present, or if both the church-wardens be present, then the church-warden who shall be called to the chair by a majority of voices, shall preside at every such meeting or board, and have the casting vote." (Section 1 of Act of 1813.)

Here again, the English rule is observed. The rector, the *præses ecclesiasticus*, has the right to preside. A warden only presides when there is no rector.

I have entered largely under the preceding section (§ 21), upon the subject of the rights, powers, and duties of a rector, in connection with a vestry, and its convening and acting.

Casting Vote. The clause respecting a casting vote was examined in the case of the Church of the Atonement, in November, 1866.

The author's opinion was asked upon the following case: There being no rector, the senior warden was, at a meeting of the vestry, called to the chair. A resolution to call the Reverend Mr. R. as rector was offered. The two wardens and eight vestrymen were present. Five voted in the affirmative. Five, the presiding warden included, voted in the negative. That officer declared the resolution lost. It was claimed that it had been carried, because the presiding officer had no right to vote at all, except in the case of an equal division resulting from votes not including his own.

The author's opinion was, that by the true construction of the statute, a warden, by presiding, did not lose his privilege of voting as a member; and the phrase in the statute therefore meant a casting vote in the sense of a double vote. Numerous authorities were cited.

As the case went to the Supreme Court, and the most of the authorities were referred to by the learned judge, the author's opinion is not further stated.

The question came before the Supreme Court at Special Term (Judge Gilbert), in Remington *v.* The Rector, etc., of the Church of the Atonement, in January 1867. The learned judge, after stating the facts, and citing the statutory provisions as to the election of church-wardens and vestrymen, their becoming trustees, and the above-quoted section, proceeded: —

The question then is, What is the legal signification and effect of the phrase, " and have the casting vote?" Does the calling of a church-warden to the chair annul, for the time being, his right as a constituent member of the corporate body, or absolve him from the execution of any trust or duty devolved upon him as such member? No authority for such a proposition was cited, except the learned treatise of Mr. Cushing on Parliamentary Practice. This author does indeed, in his commentary on the Practice of Legislative Assemblies, in the absence of express regulations, sustain the portion of the relator's counsel. But he shows at the same time, that the reasons for such practice are peculiar to that kind of assembly. In the English House of Commons, the Speaker never votes but when there is an equality without his casting vote, which in that case creates a majority; but the Speaker of the House of Lords has no casting vote. His vote is counted with the rest of the House; and in the case of an equality, the noncontents or negative voices, have the same effect and operation as if, in fact, they were a majority. (1 Bl. Com. 181, n.)

The practice in the Congress of the United States, and in the Legislature of this State, is different. Neither the Vice-President of the United States, nor the Lieutenant-Governor of this State as presiding officer of the Senate, has any vote, unless the votes be equally divided. The Speaker of the House of Representatives of the United States, and of the Assembly of this State, each have a vote. The rule of the common law applicable to corporations, however, is uniform and well settled, and it is applicable to religious societies incorporated under our law. They do not belong to the class of ecclesiastical corporations, in the sense of the English law, but are civil corporations, governed by the ordinary rules of the common law. (Robertson *v.* Bullions, 1 N. Y. Rep. 25.) In corporations consisting of an indefinite number, a major part of those who are existing at the time is competent to do the act. But when the body is definite (as it is in this case), there must be a major part of the whole number, *for it is a special appointment.* (Rex *v.* Varlo, Cowp. 250; Rex *v.* Bellinger, 4 T. R. 810; Kernan, 504; 6 Vin. 269; 2 Kent's Com. 293.) This rule of the common law has been expressly declared by statute. (2 R. S. 555, § 27; Horton *v.* Garrison, 23 Barb. 176.)

As a majority of the vestry did not vote in favor of calling the relator, he was not, therefore, called or elected, unless the statute, giving the chairman a casting vote, is to be construed as meaning a vote only in case of a tie arising upon the votes of the other members.

The plain reading of the statute does not admit of such a construction. It first vests the power of election in a body of which the chairman is a constituent member. This is a grant to every such member of a right to vote.

It then contains another grant of power *to the presiding officer, virtute officii,* in the words, " he shall have the casting vote." What is the legal effect of the latter grant? By the common law, a casting vote sometimes signifies the single vote of a person who never votes but in the case of an equality; sometimes the double vote of a person who first votes with the rest, and then, upon an equality, creates a majority by giving a second vote.   (1 Bl. Com. 181, n.; Jac. Law Dic. Parliament, 7.)

I think that in the statute under consideration, the term "casting vote," is used in the latter sense.   (1 Bl. Com. 478, n.; Cowp. 377.)   It is true that a double vote is not allowed in corporate meetings except by express statute (Anon. Lofft, Rep. 315; 15 Vin. 214); but that it ought to be allowed where the statute is clear, cannot be doubted. In Rex *v.* Giniver, 6 T. R. 732, a charter had been granted creating a corporation, and giving *the bailiffs and aldermen,* or *a major part of them,* power to choose a senior bailiff.   A by-law was passed, *giving* to the senior bailiff the casting voice, in cases where in the election of bailiffs, aldermen, or other officers, the voices should happen to be equal.   The Court held the by-law void, because it was contrary to the constitution of the charter; but it was tacitly conceded that if the provision of the by-law had been incorporated in the charter, the senior bailiff would have had, in the case of an equality of votes, a double vote.   Lord Kenyon, Ch. J., and Lawrence, J., expressly asserted that such would have been the effect of the by-law if it had been valid.   (See, also, Rex *v.* Bumpstead, 2 B. & Ad. 699.)

It appears from the evidence that the chairman voted with his colleagues, and that the votes were equal.   He must be deemed also to have given the casting vote.   His declaration that the vote was lost, was equivalent to that, and it would not be strictly correct unless it should be so regarded. But if the foregoing views are correct, it is immaterial whether he declared the resolution lost, upon the fact that the votes were equal, or whether he gave a casting vote. Upon the vote actually taken, the resolution to call the relator failed, for lack of a majority of the votes of all the members of the vestry entitled to vote.   If the chairman voted twice, it was *lost* by reason of a majority voting against it.

It follows, therefore, that the respondents are entitled to judgment with costs.

§ 22. The general statutory powers which this church possesses in common with other religious bodies, incorporated under the Act of 1813, and its amendments, are stated in chap. 16, *post*. There are, however, some special rules and modifications, growing out of the ecclesiastical system of the church, which require notice.

§ 23. *Rights in Property.* The distinctions between the rights of the rector and of the vestry as to the property of the corporation, or the use of the church edifice and appurtenances, is in several cases difficult to be drawn.

The title, the legal fee, and the right to occupy the premises, is generally and exclusively in the trustees, namely, the vestry. The right to take and appropriate all the rents and profits of land and the income of personal estate, is in the same body.

If, however, a conveyance or a bequest has been made, appropriating rents or income to the support of a rector distinctly and exclusively, he has the right to them, unless by consent he has qualified such right. This is the case with the property given to St. Andrew's Church, Richmond. By a conveyance, the rents and profits of certain real estate were to be applied to the use and support of the rector of the church for the time being. It was considered that a call and acceptance vested the right absolutely in the rector, but the opinion was also given, that a call reserving a certain sum out of such rents, for the support of services at a chapel, duly accepted in writing, bound a new rector. It was recommended to have the call, with its condition and acceptance, recorded on the minutes, and signed.

A call generally specifies the salary to be paid; and under the 8th section of the Act of 1813, it is paid out of the revenues of the church. This, as before shown, does not prevent an action to recover the amount. But the rector is, in this respect, in the same position as a sexton or organist, engaged for a fixed compensation. The funds of the church are responsible, and the vestry liable, to the same extent and no further, in each case. There cannot be, rightly, any preference in payment, should there arise a deficiency.

There are some questions connected with the ownership and use of the church edifice and particular portions of it, of moment, and not clearly defined.

By the English law, the title to the church edifice is ordinarily vested in the parson or rector. Yet the possession and control is in the minister and church-wardens. " All persons," says Sir John Nicholls, " should understand that the sacred edifice of the church is under the protection of the ecclesiastical laws, as they are administered in these courts; that the possession of the church is in the minister and church-wardens ; that no one has a right to enter it when it is not open for divine service, except under their permission and with their authority." (Jarratt *v*. Steele, 3 Phillimore's Rep. 167.)

Yet a private right of property may, by such law, exist in an individual, in a portion of the edifice, such as an aisle. Thus, Bishop Gibson states, that an aisle which has, time out of mind, belonged to a particular house, and been repaired by its owner, is part of his frank tenement, and the parson or ordinary cannot meddle with it.[1] And so it was held in Cowen *v*. Prym, cited by Burns.[2] But this right may not be conferred by any grant from an ordinary. It is attached to the ownership of a house by presumption, and it may be assumed that it does not exist in our country.

By Canon 85 of the Canons of 1603, the church-wardens or questmen shall take care and provide that the churches be well and sufficiently repaired, and so from time to time kept and maintained ; that the windows be well glazed, and that the floors be kept paved, and every and all things in au orderly and decent sort, as best becometh the house of God, and is prescribed in a homily to that effect. The like care they shall take that the church-yards be well and sufficiently repaired, fenced, and maintained, with walls, rails, or pales, as have been in such places accustomed, at their charges unto whom by law the same appertaineth.

In general, the fences and inclosures are kept in order at the expense of the parishioners, who may be proceeded against in the spiritual courts for neglect of the duty.

[1] *Codex*, p 197.   [2] *Ecc. Laws*, vol. i. p. 362.

We have before seen that the title to the property of the church vests in the corporate body, so that an action connected with it cannot be brought in the name of the trustees. But they are expressly empowered to repair and alter the edifice, etc., and as agents and representatives of such corporation, the possession and control, maintaining in proper order, direction of reparation, etc., devolves upon the vestry as trustees. Such duties as the English Canon before cited impose upon the wardens or questmen, are performed by the vestry, through persons employed by them.

In relation to property, and the more extensive term temporalities, the law, when a church has accepted an act of incorporation, is clear. Every ecclesiastical rule is superseded by the statutory rule, where one is expressed, and there is any inconsistency in the provisions.

There is no inconsistency when the minister has, for religious or ecclesiastical purposes, a limited and particular possession and control.

Dr. Hawks has a long and able note upon this subject. He discusses it chiefly in connection with the office of institution, — as to what rights the instituted rector acquires, and what the wardens and vestrymen, the *quasi* patrons, relinquish.

(1.) He considers that the rector may not be dismissed without the concurrence of the ecclesiastical authority under Canon 33 of 1832.

(2.) That he has exclusive power over the church edifice as to granting or refusing its use for public worship. He deduced this from the nature of the pastoral charge, the cure of souls, and the absolute necessity, that he to whom the charge of watching over them is committed should teach himself, or select those who may teach in his absence.

The Church interdicts other clergymen from interfering with his charge. No clergyman could, under Canon 31 of 1832, officiate in his parish without his express consent. *A fortiori*, the Church will not allow the laity to interfere.

(3.) He then examines the question, in whom resides the power of directing the use of the church at other times and for other purposes, than during public worship on appointed days. He argues strongly from the institution office, and the delivery of the keys accompanying it, that the rector has, in these cases also, exclusive authority.

It seems to me impossible to deny the force of this reasoning. But it may be added, that the conclusion is almost equally clear, when the institution office has not been used. The delivery of the keys is no more than a token of the reception, by the parish or church, of the party as its priest and rector; and he receives the keys of God's house as a symbol and pledge of his assumption of the office and its duties.

I have frequently stated the opinion, that the call, acceptance, and entering upon the duties of a rector (without any special restrictions agreed upon), as fully establishes the relation between a rector and the parish, as the institution office does. The learned Justice Emmott, of the Supreme Court, adopted this view.[1]

We may, I think with confidence, conclude, that whether the institution office has been used or not, the right to allow any other clergyman of the Church to officiate in the church edifice, belongs exclusively to the rector.

This is English law; this is general Ecclesiastical law. This is deducible from our canons and offices as our own Ecclesiastical law. This is not inconsistent with the statutes granting incorporation and vesting title and property in the vestry as trustees. The statutes contemplate temporalities, and their management. A canon provides for the case of there being no rector.

But the members of the congregation have rights in the matter. As members of the Protestant Episcopal Church, they are entitled to have "the office of public preaching, and ministering the sacraments in the congregation, performed by one lawfully called and sent to execute the same;"[2] with the exposition of what is such a call contained in our standards. They have a right to demand that a minister "do so minister the doctrine, sacraments, and

<hr>

[1] Youngs *v.* Ranson, 31 Barbour, 19.   [2] Article 23.

discipline of Christ, as the Lord hath commanded, *and as this Church hath received the same*, according to the commandments of God." [1] The vow of the rector becomes the right of the congregation. These rights are violated, if any one is allowed to officiate, who (I take strong cases) should teach an anti-Trinitarian doctrine,[2] or the Romish doctrine concerning purgatory, pardons, worshiping and adoration of images or relics, or the invocation of saints.[3] We may add (which was undeveloped when the Articles were framed), the dogma of the Miraculous Conception.

But what is the redress?

It is quite clear that the vestry or congregation have no right to select any one without the rector's assent. And from the nature of the right, its necessary exclusive character, the vestry cannot forcibly interfere, as by closing the doors. I apprehend this is one of the cases in which the application for a dissolution of the pastoral connection would be proper; or the case might be so grievous as to demand a presentment. It is part of the English law, that for any irregularity in the conducting the services, the churchwardens may complain to the ordinary. (Burns' Ecc. Law, vol. i. p. 170; Lord Stowell, 1 Lee's Rep. 129; 2 Haggard's Rep. 25.)

Use of Sacred Buildings. But there is not an unrestricted liberty in rector, or vestry, or congregation, to use the church edifice on other days or other occasions than for worship. By the consecration office, the edifice is separated from all unhallowed, ordinary, and common uses, and (as an interpretation of this language) is " dedicated to the service of the Lord, for reading His holy Word, for celebrating His holy sacraments, for offering to Him the sacrifices of prayer and thanksgiving, for blessing the people in His name, and for the performance of all other holy offices ; " the supplications which follow referring to baptism, confirmation, the holy communion, marriage, the hearing and preaching of the Word in the church, also illustrate the question. *All other holy offices* must mean all offices of that nature prescribed or

----

[1] The Ordering of Priests. [2] Article 1. [3] Article 22.

permitted in the formularies, as catechizing, the burial service, the ordering of priests, etc. And what is thus ennmerated defines all the cases that are permissible, and excludes everything else.

Thus fairs, commencements, public gatherings for charitable, or even religious purposes, not strictly prescribed Church purposes, are inevitably and clearly forbidden. An election of wardens and vestrymen is, in a general sense, secnlar, but yet is purely for Church purposes. By accepting an act of incorporation, requiring an election to be held in the church, the congregation consent to such a use, and the object partakes of an ecclesiastical character.

It deserves notice, that while by the English law, a schoolhouse cannot be erected on ground consecrated for a burialground, a vestry-room may be, at least when no bodies have been interred. (See *post*, chap. 19, § 8.)

Music. Some points may be considered as clear npon this subject. The selection of an organist, of singers or members of a choir, is almost universally left to the rector; and the rubrical direction in the selections, that the minister, with snch assistance as he can obtain from persons skilled in music, shall give order concerning the tunes to be sung, indicates this to be the views of the Church, to some extent at least. It may be considered, that not only the choice of the tunes, bnt of the music generally, is left with the minister; but the negative, at least, npon the selection of the singers, etc., is with him.

Yet it is clear that as to salary, terms of employment, and numbers to be employed, the vestry collectively possesses the power. Contracts which affect the revenues or property of the church, can only be made by that body.

In a case within the writer's knowledge, where the snbject of these relative rights was discussed between a rector and the other members of the vestry, an adjustment was made, by which the period of employment, the number of persons to be employed, and the salaries, were determined at a vestry meeting, and the selection of persons and other regulations was left to the rector. This is the actual, legal, and canonical position; this, certainly, is the most expedient and ecclesiastical.

The English law leaves the erection of an organ, and the employment of organist and others, to the incumbent, at least, with the consent of the ordinary; but if any expense of putting it up or maintaining it is incurred, there must be a rate levied at a vestry meeting of the parishioners. The control of the organist is with the minister. (Burns' Ecc. Law, vol. i. 374, a, b.)

Assistant Minister. Assistant ministers are sometimes found necessary or important in parishes. Not unfrequently, they are needed when the Mother Church has established a chapel of ease.

They answer to the curates of the English law in general; in particular cases, to the coadjutors. The latter term was not limited to bishops, but extended to assistants of an incumbent, in case of insanity or infirmity. The bishop appointed a licensed curate to perform the duties.[1]

The principle of this regulation is found in Sub. 3 of § vi. Canon 12, of the Digest. If a minister neglect from inability, or any other cause, to perform the regular services, the bishop may open the doors to any regular minister of this Church.

The curates of the English law were appointed by the incumbent, unless the appointment was vested in others by *deed* or prescription. The better opinion seems to be, that a curate cannot be removed except for cause shown, during the term of his employment.[2]

In the case of the Church of St. Esprit, 1864, the following view was presented.

" Assistant ministers have been known in our Church for a long period. They are noticed in colonial charters. That to Trinity Church authorized the vestry to appoint an assistant from time to time."

Upon the election of a minister unto a church or parish, a certificate is given, the form of which is prescribed in

---

[1] Burns' *Ecc. Law*, vol. L p. 429.

[2] *Ibid.*, vol. ll. p. 56, *et seq.*

Canon 12, part 1, of the Digest: " We, the church-wardens *(or in case of an assistant minister),* we, the rector and church-wardens, do certify that —————— —————— has been duly chosen rector, *or,* assistant minister, etc." The second section of the same Canon recognizes such a minister. And the institution office provides for the institution of a rector or assistant minister.

" After a careful consideration of the questions submitted, I am of opinion —

" That the decision of the necessity or utility of an assistant minister to perform duties in the parish, rests in the vestry collectively, as well as the terms and period of employment, and the salary or compensation to be allowed.

" That the selection of the person cannot be made without the assent of the rector. This seems plainly deducible from the able argument of Dr. Hawks, before referred to. The guidance of the parish in spiritual matters, is committed to the rector by his call.

" And I am inclined to think, that the concurrence of a warden and a majority of the vestrymen, in vestry assembled, is necessary. The rector would thus have what is equivalent to a veto in the selection, and the vestry a consenting voice. I regard this result as most consonant to true ecclesiastical principle, and most consistent with our peculiar laws and canons."

While the statutes of incorporation vest powers over the temporalities in the vestry, as trustees, and an aggregate body, there are several points in which ecclesiastical rules and principles have an influence. There are some duties and powers, which are given more particularly to some members of this body. We have seen that there are some such in the rector. There are also some vested in the church-wardens.

Church-wardens. It will be useful to advert briefly to their position in the English law.

By several Canons of 1603 (18, 19, 85, 90, 111), the church-wardens or questmen are to enforce the keeping of good order during public service, to prevent idle persons frequenting the church-yard or porch, to keep peace during any meeting of the congregation. In the visitations of bishops and archdeacons, they were to present the names of all who had behaved rudely or disorderly in the church.

Church-wardens are described as ancient officers annually chosen, to look to the church, church-yard, and things that belong to both; to provide what is necessary for the performance of divine service, and to observe the behavior of the parishioners, concerning such faults as belong to the ecclesiastical jurisdiction.

They are directed, by Canon 89 of 1603, to be chosen by the joint consent of the minister and parishioners; but if they cannot agree, then the minister chooses one, and the parishioners the other.

But it is said, that of common right every parish ought to choose its own church-wardens, which right can only be overthrown by a contrary custom. *(Dawson v. Towle, Hale, Ch. Baron, Hardress' Rep.* 378.) Church-wardens are lay incorporations, and for many purposes they are temporal ministers and officers, as appears by many acts of Parliament concerning the poor, maimed soldiers, etc. Of common right, every parish ought to choose its own church-wardens, but a custom may be alleged.

Lord Stowell (1 Lee's Rep. 129) thus states their office and duties: "I conceive that their duties were originally confined to the care of the ecclesiastical property of the parish, over which they exercised a discretionary power for certain purposes. In all other respects, it is an office of observation and complaint, but not of control, with respect to divine worship." So it is laid down by Ayliffe in one of the best dissertations on the duties of church-wardens, and in the Canons of 1591. In these, it is observed, that the church-wardens are appointed to provide the furniture of the church, the bread and wine of the Holy Sacrament, the surplice, and the books necessary for the performance of divine worship, and such as are directed by law; but it is the minister who has the use. If, indeed, he err in this respect, it is just matter of complaint, which the church-wardens are bound to attend to; but the law would not oblige them to complain if they had a power themselves to redress the abuse. In the service, the church-wardens have nothing to do but to collect the alms at the offertory; and they may refuse the admission of strange preachers into the pulpit; for this purpose they are authorized by the Canon: but how? When letters of orders are produced, their authority ceases. Again, if the minister introduces any irregularity into the service, they have no authority to interfere, but they may complain to the ordinary of his conduct. I do not say there may not be cases where they may not be bound to interfere. They may repress, and are bound to repress, all indecent interrupting of the service by others. They have the custody of the church under the minister; if he refuses access to the church on fitting occasions, complaint must be made to higher authorities."

In Bennet *v.* Bousher (2 Haggard's Rep. 25), articles were exhibited by a church-warden against an incumbent for frequent irregularities in the performance of divine service, and neglect of parochial duties.

The church-wardens were to be chosen in Easter-week, and to continue in office until their successors were sworn.

In an action of trespass for assault and battery, against a church-warden, the plea was, that the plaintiff had his hat on during divine service; that he desired him to take it off, and on his refusal, took it off and delivered it to him. The Court held, that the plea was good, all concurring, except Twisden, J. (Cited Gibson's Codex, 29; 2 Keble, 124.)

In the late case of Wall *v.* Lee (36 N. Y. Rep. 14), a person behaving rudely in a Roman Catholic church, the priest officiating took measures to have him removed; and it was held, that an action of assault would not lie. He was the proper person to keep order, having charge of the church under the bishop.

Force enough could be used to remove any one disturbing a religious meeting.

Before concluding this chapter, I would call attention to the repeated efforts made in our Convention, to obtain a change in the statute law as to the incorporation of churches.

In the year 1860, a committee before appointed reported to the Convention a series of amendments. They were chiefly these : —

Requiring that not less than ten persons belonging to the congregation should assemble in order to become incorporated.

The persons entitled to vote at such first election were declared to be the following : —

(1.) " Those who have been baptized in the Protestant Episcopal Church ; or who shall have been received therein, either by the rite of confirmation, or by receiving the holy communion."

(2.) " Those who have purchased or hired and paid for a pew or seat in such church, or shall have contributed in money, not less than two months next prior to such meeting, to the support of such church or the minister thereof."

Some changes in detail were made of no importance to be noticed here.

So persons entitled to vote at ensuing elections were those qualified for the first election, and who should have belonged to such church or congregation for twelve months immediately preceding the election. To the clause requiring the presence of a rector for the transaction of business, if there be one, was added, —

" *Provided*, however, that if the rector be absent from the State, and shall have been so absent for over four calendar months ; or, if the meeting shall have been called by the rector, and he be absent therefrom, the board shall be competent to transact all business, if there be present one church-warden and a majority of the laymen ; *except* that no measure shall be taken for effecting a sale or disposition of the real property, nor may any sale or disposition of the capital or principal of the personal estate of such corporation be made, nor any act done which shall impair the rights of such rector."

In the Convention of 1862, the following report was made : —

The Committee heretofore appointed upon the subject of amendments to the Act for the incorporation of churches, and instructed by the last Convention to submit the amendments then adopted to the bishop and standing committee of the Diocese of Western New York, and, when concurred in by them, to take measures for procuring the enactment of the same, respectfully report, —

That a communication, with a copy of the act as proposed, was sent to the Bishop of Western New York, and by him submitted to the standing committee; that committee adopted a report of a sub-committee to the following effect : —

" That in some important features the amendments proposed would be prejudicial to the interests of the Diocese.

" In clause one of section one, it is proposed that not less than *ten* male persons of full age shall at any time be competent to meet for the purpose of incorporating themselves as a parish. Such a provision in this diocese would, in the case of many prosperous missionary stations, if it hitherto had been in force, have entirely defeated the organization of the parish. We suggest that the word *six* be substituted for ten.

" In clause five, subdivision three, the corporators are required to elect eight vestrymen. We suggest that it be altered so as to give the option of choosing not less than four, nor more than eight; so that in small parishes, where there may not be the larger number of suitable men to act in that station, the smaller may be adopted.

" The tenth clause requires a notice to be given for two Sundays next previous to the day fixed, but omits stating the time. We suggest that ' immediately after morning service,' be added, as is done in the second clause of section first.

" In the ninth clause, where it is required that eight vestrymen shall be elected, we would substitute the words, ' not less than four, nor more than eight,' so as to be in harmony with the proposed alteration of the third division of the fifth clause.·

"The fifteenth clause allows the transaction of business, if the rector and one warden and three vestrymen are present. We suggest it would be better to require the presence of one half the vestrymen and one warden.

"We advise the entire omission of the eleventh clause, that declares the board, once duly organized, competent to transact business, although members may have withdrawn, leaving perhaps less than one half of the trustees present. The adoption of that clause, it appears to your committee, would open the door to many contingent evils.

"With these alterations, your committee advise the concurrence of the standing committee in the proposed amendments."

The alterations thus adopted by the standing committee of Western New York, precluded the committee from taking measures to procure the adoption of the act by the legislature.

An act was, however, introduced into the Senate, embodying these alterations, except that for a valid meeting of a vestry, a majority of the vestrymen, instead of half, as had been suggested, was required.

The proposed act had also a further provision, to the effect, that the number of vestrymen might, at any time, be increased or diminished, so however, as never to be less than four, nor more than eight, by a vote of the vestry, if confirmed by a vote of the members of the congregation qualified to vote at an election for wardens and vestrymen; and the mode of procuring and recording the vote of both vestry and congregation was provided.

It is understood that the committee of the Senate to which the bill was referred, adopted the act as thus varied by the Western Diocese, except in one important particular. The fifteenth section was altered so as to read thus: "No such board shall be competent to transact any business, unless the rector, if there be one, *or* one of the church-wardens, and not less than a majority of vestrymen be present." The present act is : "Unless the rector, if there be one, *and* at least one of the church-wardens, and a majority of vestrymen be present."

It is understood that a distinguished member of the Senate, and a member of this Convention, had prepared amendments to the bill as reported, which, while restoring the language of the present act in the clause above quoted, enabled a vestry to transact any business in the absence of the rector, after due notice to attend for some consecutive meetings. These views, it is also understood, did not meet the approval of the Bishop of Western New York, who, at the request of the standing committee, represented their views. The matter ended with the report not being acted upon.

It will be seen from this statement that a material difference (perhaps the only material one) between the act adopted by this Convention and that approved by the standing committee of Western New York, relates to the number of vestrymen, which, by the plan of the latter, may be eight or not less than four, with the power in the congregation, however, to increase or diminish the number chosen. It will be recollected, that in the proposed amended act adopted by the Convention of 1859, there was the same provision as to the number of vestrymen, without any clause as to the congregation changing the number. That provision seems not very important, as the number could, under the clauses as originally shaped by this Convention, be varied by the congregation at any annual election. In 1861 this Convention revised the act they had before approved, and strong objections were made to this provision. The committee, to which that Convention referred the subject, restored the number eight, as now required by law, and the Convention of 1862 approved and adopted it.

As to the other very important matter of the action of a vestry in the rector's absence, it is quite clear that the change, suggested in the report of the committee of the Senate, has never met any approval of the Convention. But the provisions snggested, where the rector is persistently absent, were reported upon favorably by the committee which submitted the act to the Convention of 1860.

That committee reported a clause, that if the rector shonld have neglected to attend two vestry meetings, notified to be held at an interval of ten days, and shall be absent at a third meeting held within three months after such neglect, and after ten days' notice of the same, served personally upon him, the service so made and certified by the clerk, then snch board might transact any business, one warden and a majority of the vestrymen being present. The Convention, however, did not approve of this portion of the report, and adopted a provision almost identical with that sanctioned by the Convention of 1862, as to the circnmstauces under which, and the extent to which, the vestry might act in the rector's absence.

In the Convention of 1864, some further, but no definite action was taken, and the committee was continned.

In 1865, and again in 1866, the committee was continned with the powers conferred in 1863 and 1864.

In the course of this proceeding, the present writer had commnnications with the late Bishop Delancy, and a personal interview with him, in which he expressed himself strongly against the policy of any attempt to get a change in the law, and that the Church had better endure its existing defects or inconveniences. He had spent some time in Albany, engaged in the passage of an act for the Parochial Trnst Fund, and watched the movements as to the amendments of the incorporating act. His opinion was decided that we ran a great risk of changes being introduced, radically affecting the ecclesiastical character and polity of the Church, or leading to an abandonment of the advantages of an incorporation.[1]

---

[1] An act is now (March, 1868,) before the Legislature upon this subject, which, if passed, I shall be able, I presume, to place in a note.

*image
not
available*

island of Manhattan, New Netherlands, written by Jonas Michælius, from which it appears that he was the first minister in this city.

The letter was found at the Hague in 1858, and a copy was sent to this country by Mr. Murphey. He considers the evidence of its authenticity to be ample. In this letter the writer speaks of having established the form of a church, "and as Brother Sebastian Crol very seldom comes down from Fort Orange, because of his directorship of the fort and trade there, it had been thought best to choose two elders for my assistance, and for the proper consideration of all such matters as might occur."

He also observes, " that although our small consistory at the most, when Brother Crol is down here, has not more than four persons, all of whom, myself excepted, have public business to attend to, yet I hope to separate the ecclesiastical from the civil matters, so that each one will be occupied with his own matters."

The letter is very interesting. The passage as to the Indians is eloquent with religious earnestness. I do not know that any of the learned of the Dutch Church have followed up the traces afforded by this letter. Who was Brother Crol, and who were the two others that formed the single consistory of the colony in 1628 ?

The system in respect to the settlement of ministers is shown in the case of the Reverend Dr. Megalopensis. He was invited by the patroon of Renssaerlerwick to become their pastor. As the Classis of Amsterdam was the ecclesiastical superior of all the Dutch colonial clergy, it was necessary to obtain its assent to the arrangement. He appeared before the committee *ad res externas* of that Classis, and a formal call was attested by the Classis. The Amsterdam Chamber claimed the right of approving this instrument. The patroon asserted a power in the matter. After some difficulties and reservations of rights, the appointment was made.

By one of the articles of the Freedoms and Exemptions, granted by the Directors of the West India Company, with the sanction of the States-General, the 19th of July, 1640, " no other religion shall be publicly admitted in the New Netherlands except the Reformed, as it is at present preached and practised by public authority in the United Netherlands; and for this purpose the Company shall provide and maintain good and suitable preachers, school-masters, and comforters of the sick." [1]

By the seventh of the conditions offered by the city of Amsterdam to emigrants, approved by the Directors of the West India Company the 12th July, 1656, "the city was to cause to be erected about the market, or some other convenient place, a public building suitable for divine service; also a house for a school; and shall have a house built for a minister."

" The city shall provisionally provide and pay the salary of a minister and school-master, unless their High Mightinesses or the Company shall direct otherwise." [2]

The national religion, thus established, found an uncompromising defender in Governor Stuyvesant. Strong, decided, and inflexible in his character, with great energy and vigorous sense, his antipathy to New Englanders, to the populace, and to Dissenters, was vehement, and was not allowed to sleep. In 1656 he issued a proclamation forbidding preachers, not having been called thereto by ecclesiastical or temporal authority, from holding conventicles not in harmony with the established religion as set forth by the Synod of Dort, and here in this land, and in the Fatherland, and in other reformed churches, observed and followed. " A penalty was imposed upon every unlicensed preacher for violating the ordinance, and upon any one who should attend." [3]

Again, as respects the Lutherans, they were refused permission to worship in a church of their own. The Lutheran congregation at Amsterdam sent out a minister to organize a church. The Classis wrote, that the Company's intention was to permit every one to have freedom within his own

---

[1] Documents of Colonial History. *Holland Documents,* vol. i. p. 123.
[2] *Ibid.,* p. 620.   [3] *Ibid.,* p. 617.

dwelling, to serve God in such a manner as his religion requires, but without authorizing any public meetings or conventicles.[1]

It is somewhat surprising that the spirit of intolerance was developed with greater severity against the Quakers, both in Massachusetts and the New Netherlands, than against any other class.

The punishment of Hodgson for preaching at Hempstead, has not often been exceeded for severity or circumstances of ignominy. The history of the struggle at Flushing in favor of Townsend, who had held meetings of Quakers at his house, is creditable to the spirit and sense of the inhabitants of that town. Tobias Feake, the schout, was degraded from his office, and sentenced to pay a heavy fine or be banished, for framing a strong and well-written protest against the proceedings of the Governor.

Again in 1663, a severe persecution was had against John Bowne, also of Flushing, who had attended the meetings in the woods, and finally joined the Society. He was imprisoned, fined, and proving contumacious, banished and shipped to Amsterdam.

The authorities there disapproved of the proceedings of the Governor, and rebuked him for them. In a paper marked with wisdom and policy, they tell him: "That though it is our anxious desire, that similar and other sectaries might not be found among you, yet we doubt extremely the policy of adopting vigorous measures against them. The consciences of men ought to be free so long as they continue moderate and peaceable. Such have been the maxims of prudence and toleration by which the magistrates of this city (Amsterdam) have been governed; and the consequences have been that the oppressed and persecuted from every country have found among us an asylum in distress. Follow in the same steps, and you will be blessed."

The letter of instructions to Andreas Druyer, commander and schout, of the 26th of December, 1673, after

---

[1] Documents of Colonial History. *Holland Documents*, vol. 1. p. 684.

the reconquest, directs, " that the pure, true, Christian religion, according to the Synod of Dort, should be taught and maintained in all things as it ought, without suffering the slightest attempt to be made against it by any other sectaries.[1]

By the 8th Article of the Surrender to the English in 1664, the Dutch were to enjoy the liberty of their consciences in divine worship and church discipline. (Smith's "New York," p. 20.)

It has been questioned whether this Article was not confined personally to the then inhabitants ; and it was urged that at any rate it was annulled when the province was restored to the English upon the peace of 1674, without any condition.[2]

It is stated by Lieutenant Governor Colden, in a letter of the 7th of December, 1763, that four charters had been granted by the Governors to churches, besides those of the Church of England ; all to Dutch churches. That there had been a strenuous effort made in 1759, to procure a charter for the Lutheran Church, which had been renewed in 1763, and was submitted to the Lords of Trade for decision. The Reformed Dutch churches united in the attempt.[3]

One of the four charters mentioned to have been granted to Dutch churches, was that to the minister, elders, and deacons of the Reformed Protestant Dutch Church of the city of New York, by Governor Fletcher, on the 11th of March, 1696, the third year of William. Another was granted to the church in Albany on the 10th of August, 1720, as appears by an Act of February 2, 1798, reciting it. From an Act of the 29th of April, 1786 (1 Greenleaf, 275), I am led to suppose that a third was to the Dutch Church at Flatbush. I am not able to trace the fourth.

§ 2. *Charter of* 1696. The charter of 1696 to the church in New York is of interest, if viewed only as an historical

---

[1] Documents of Colonial History. *Holland Documents,* vol. ii. p. 618; *Ibid.,* 692; under Colve, Governor.

[2] Letter of Governor Colden, *Documents,* vol. vii. p. 586.   [3] *Ibid.*

document. But as the basis and muniment of the Dutch Church in many particulars, it is of much importance.

It recited that the minister, elders, and deacons, and other members in communion of the said Dutch Protestant congregation, in our said city of New York, have built a church, with a cemetery, etc., in Garden Street, of said city, and are seised in fee of a certain messuage, etc., and also of the Manor of Fordham. It set forth a petition that they might be incorporated, and made capable of holding and enjoying such property by incorporation of the members of the said Dutch Protestant congregation, in our city of New York, by the name of " The Minister, Elders, and Deacons of the Reformed Protestant Dutch Church, of our city of New York."

" Being willing, in favor of the pious purposes of our loving subjects, to secure to them and their successors the liberty of worshiping God according to the constitutions and directions of the Reformed Churches in Holland, approved and instituted by the National Synod of Dort.

" We ordain, etc., that no person within our said city of New York, in communion of the said Reformed Dutch Church, be molested or called in question for any difference in opinion in matters of the Protestant religion, who does not actually disturb the civil peace of our province."

It is then stated that the Reverend Hendricus Selyns was the then minister of such church, and others named were the elders and deacons. It then provided that the said Hendricus Selyns, Nicholas Bayard (and others named) the present minister, elders, and deacons, and all such others as now are or hereafter shall be admitted into the communion of the said Reformed Dutch Church, in our city of New York, shall be from time to time, and at all times, a body corporate and politic in fact and in name, by the name of " The Minister, Elders, and Deacons of the Reformed Protestant Dutch Church of the city of New York." By the same name they were to have perpetual succession, etc.

They were authorized to have, take, acquire, possess, and purchase lands, tenements, and hereditaments, or goods and chattels, and the same to lease, grant, alien, sell and dispose of at their own will and pleasure, as other our liege people, or any corporation or body politic within our realm of England or this our province, may lawfully do.

The *habendum* is: "Unto them the said minister, elders, and deacons of the Reformed Protestant Dutch Church, of the city of New York, and their successors. In trust to the sole and only use and benefit, and behoof of them, the minister, elders, and deacons, and other members in communion of the said Reformed Protestant Dutch Church, in the city of New York, and their successors forever.

"And for the better ordering and managing the affairs of the said corporation and successors, there shall be four elders and four deacons from time to time constituted, elected, and chosen out of the members of the said Dutch Church, inhabitants in our said city of New York, for the time, in such manner and form as is hereinafter expressed; which persons, together with the minister for the time being, shall apply to take care for the best disposing and ordering the general business and affairs of and concerning the lands and hereditaments herein mentioned to be granted."

The elders and deacons named in the act were to continue in their offices until the second Sunday of November next ensuing.

Power was given to the minister for the time being, or in his absence by sickness or otherwise, to the first elder for the time being, to give order for the assembling of the elders and deacons, to consult on the business of the church.

Yearly and every year on the third Tuesday of October, at the said church, the elders and deacons of the said church, with the approbation and consent of the members of the said church for the time being, shall nominate and appoint such of their members of the said church that shall succeed in the office of elders and deacons for the year ensuing.

Provision was made for filling vacancies. The presentation, patronage, advowson, after the decease of the said first minister, was vested in the elders and deacons of the said Reformed Protestant Dutch Church, and their successors forever, provided they bore due allegiance to the crown.

Power was also given to the minister, with the consent of the elders and deacons, or any four of them, as need shall require, to nominate one or more able ministers, lawfully ordained according to the constitutions of the church aforesaid, to be preachers and assistants to the said minister and his successors, to aid in divine offices. Likewise to appoint a clerk, school-master, bell-ringer, a sexton, and such other officers as they stand in need of. Power was also given to the minister, elders, and deacons, with the consent of the members in communion of the said church, or the major part of them, to make rates or assessments upon all and every the members in communion of the said church, for the raising moneys for the yearly stipends and salaries of the aforesaid officers of the said church, and for repairing the church, church-yard, and other things necessary, belonging to the said church.

Other provisions are made for carrying this power of rating property into effect.

By another clause, authority is given to the ministers, elders, and deacons, together with the members in communion of the said church, inhabitants, from time to time inhabiting and to inhabit in our said city of New York, that they or the greater part of them, (whereof the minister, elders, and deacons, and the major part of the members in communion of the said church shall be part), shall have power to choose, nominate, and appoint so many of our liege people as they shall see fit, and shall be willing to accept the same, to be members of the said church and corporation and body politic.

Power is also given to make and ordain rules and ordinances for the good discipline and weal of the members of the said church and corporation, not repugnant to the laws of England or the constitutions and decrees of the Synod of Dort.

The Earl of Bellemont accused Governor Fletcher of having received a bribe for granting this charter. His statement is, that he applied to the Rev. Mr. Selyns for an inspection of the minutes of the church to prove this; that it was refused until the sanction of the consistory was given; that it was finally obtained, and he transmits a copy.[1] The copy is not among the documents printed. But it seems satisfactorily clear that it did not make out the charge, for a short time after the Earl of Bellemont transmitted a long list of charges against Fletcher for mal-conduct, and this is not one of them.[2]

There is also a strong tribute to Fletcher from the church-wardens and vestry of Trinity Church, as being the principal promoter of the English Church, and speaking of the irreconcilable aversion Lord Bellemont had to him.[3]

The Lords of Trade heard Fletcher upon the charges, and found him guilty upon some, particularly of encouraging piracy.

Whatever may have been the offenses of which Colonel Fletcher was guilty, yet in this transaction, the church stands, upon the evidence, absolved from any complicity, and the charter as unstained in its origin as it is perfect in law.

We find by this charter that the church in Garden Street had been erected. The history of these church edifices is thus stated: "The first place of worship was a loft over a mill erected in 1626, on the arrival of Dominie Jonas Michælius. In 1633, a barn-like structure was put up in Broad Street, between Bridge and Pearl. In 1642, Kieft erected a new church within the fort, contrary to the wishes of the people. This was of stone, seventy-five feet long by fifty wide.[4] This continued until 1741. The church in Garden Street was built about 1694, the Middle Dutch Church in 1729, and the North Church in 1769."

In common with others, the Dutch ecclesiastical author-

---

[1] *Colonial Documents*, vol. iv. pp. 426–27. [2] *Ibid.* p. 488. [3] *Ibid.* p. 526.
[4] See Father Jaques' *Novum Belgium* (New York, 1862), p. 25 and note, p. 10 ; Broadhead, vol. i. pp. 243, 336.

ities had a controversy with Lord Cornbury (1704). Contrary to the express terms of the charter of 1696, that the minister, with the consent of the elders and deacons, should nominate and appoint the school-masters, he attempted to forbid their exercising their office without his license. The attempt was defeated.[1]

§ 3. *Will of Harpending.* To understand an important point in the legal position of the Dutch Church in colonial days, as well as now, the will of John Harpending must be noticed.

It was dated in May, 1723, and by it he devised and bequeathed to the ministers, elders, and deacons of the Reformed Protestant Dutch Church, of the city of New York, and their successors forever, all, etc. (the Shoemaker's field), to have and to hold unto them, the said ministers, elders, and deacons of the said Reformed Protestant Dutch Church, of the city of New York, and their successors, for the payment of the salary and maintenance of the respective minister or ministers, which, from time to time, shall be duly called to the ministry of the said church, and to no other uses.

The sole management and direction of the property was to be in the elders of the church for the time being, or whom they shall appoint, " to account to the minister or ministers, elders, and deacons of the Reformed Protestant Dutch Church, of the city of New York, for the time being, and to them only."

We notice that the word *ministers* is used.

Even as early as 1652, Drisisus and Megapoliensis were colleagues at New Amsterdam. Two or more ministers to a church or congregation — a collegiate pastorate — is part of the order of the Church.

Harpending was a deacon of the church in 1694, and is a grantee in a conveyance as early as 1675.[2]

---

[1] History of the *School of the Dutch Church*, pp. 56, 57. The author's grandfather, Nicholas Hoffman, was a deacon in 1773, and one of the school committee.

[2] Hoffman's *Law of the Corporation of New York* vol. ii. p. 218.

§ 4. *Act of* 1753. An act was passed on the 12th of December, 1753, entitled "An Act to enable the minister, elders, and deacons of the Reformed Protestant Dutch Church, of the city of New York, to sell and dispose of their lands in Westchester, commonly known by the name of the Manor of Fordham; and also for granting unto them some further liberties and privileges, for the better management of their affairs, and the well ordering or governing of their said church." [1]

This act recited the 8th Article of the Surrender of 1664: " The Dutch shall enjoy the liberty of their conscience in divine worship and church discipline, and their own customs concerning their inheritances." I omit the recitals as to the will of one Steenwyck, under which the Manor of Fordham is alleged to have been held, as not material to any purpose.

This act recited the charter of 1696, and the erection of a church, with a cemetery, and a church-yard, and the seisin of the Manor of Fordham, with some leading points of the charter. It recites the building of another church, by means whereof they have been obliged to keep generally three, and sometimes four, ministers to perform divine service in their sanctuaries, and that they were desirous of selling such Manor of Fordham, etc.

The charter of 1696 was, in every article, matter, power, and privilege, approved, ratified, and confirmed, as fully and amply as if the same were therein repeated.

" And the said ministers, elders, and deacons, shall, by virtue hereof, have the care and management of both the said churches, or such others as they may hereafter think proper to build; and provide for the ministers and officers thereof.

"And on the days of election appointed by the charter, and according to their usual custom to elect, choose and appoint such further and greater number of elders, deacons, and other officers as shall be necessary and convenient ; which

---

[1] *Journals Legislative Council*, vol. ii. p. 1145; Van Schaick edition of the Laws, vol. i. Approved by the King in Council, 25th February, 1755.

said elders and deacons, etc., so to be chosen from time to time, are hereby added to, and declared to be, part of the said body politic, and shall have full power to act with them in their respective stations."

The annual income of lands to be held was increased to £1000. It was made lawful for the said minister, elders, and deacons, and their successors, to alter and enlarge their said churches, and to purchase and build more churches, houses, and gardens, for their ministers for the time being.

There was an unusual clause in this act, preventing its going into effect until it received the royal sanction.[1]

It received such sanction at a council 25th February, 1755.

§ 5. *Constitution of* 1777. The 35th, 36th, 38th, and 39th Articles of the Constitution of 1777, are hereafter quoted fully. (*Post*, chap. 5.) The charters to the Dutch churches were, with others, preserved in force.

§ 6. *Act of* 1783. By an Act of the 25th February, 1783, (1 Greenleaf, 629,) " to incorporate the minister, elders, and deacons, of the Reformed Protestant Dutch Church in Tappan, or town of Orange, of Orange County," a deed of 1729 was recited granting a lot of land, and the erection of a church for public worship therein, according to the usages and customs of the Reformed Dutch churches of the United Netherlands in Europe. The desire of the petitioners to be incorporated was then stated. And it was enacted, That S. B., the minister, T. B., etc. elders, and A. and B., deacons of the same church, and their successors, elected, chosen or appointed, according to the mode practised in, or by, the Reformed Protestant Dutch churches or congregations, be, and they are hereby, made and constituted a corporation and body politic, in law and fact, to have continuance forever, by the name, style, and title of " The Minister, Elders, and Deacons of the Reformed Protestant Dutch Church of the town of Orange, in Orange County."

The title of the original patentees who conveyed in 1729, was declared to be vested in the corporation thus created.

---

[1] Hoffman's *Laws of the Corporation*, vol. i. p. 28. The People *v.* Trinity Church, 22 N. Y. Rep. 44.

The second section gave them power, by the name aforesaid, to have, take, receive, acquire, purchase, and possess, lands, tenements, hereditaments, and goods and chattels, as any person or persons, or any corporation or body politic could, can, or lawfully may do, to the annual value of five hundred pounds, equal to eleven hundred and eleven ounces, and one ninth part of an ounce, of Seville pillar or Mexico plate, and no more; and the same lauds, tenements, hereditaments, goods, chattels, and appurtenances to lease, demise, alien, bargain, sell and dispose of, at their own will and pleasure.

And by section 5, power was given to the said minister, elders, and deacons, and their successors, from time to time, to elect from among themselves, a president, treasurer, clerk, and such other officers as they shall stand in need of, and the same at their pleasure to remove, change, or continue.

§ 7. *Act of March,* 1784. On the 17th of March, 1784, (Laws, chap. 9,) an act was passed "to remove doubts which may have arisen respecting the charter rights of the minister, elders, and deacons, of the Reformed Protestant Dutch Church, of the city of New York, in consequence of the late invasion of the State." It referred to the charter of William, of the 11th of May, 1696, as having been suspended by the war: "In order, therefore, to put the said corporation in the same state of activity which they enjoyed at the commencement of the said war," it was enacted, "that the said charter, and all and singular the rights, estates, powers, liberties, franchise, and immunities, thereby granted and confirmed, and which the said corporation and the members thereof did actually hold, exercise, and enjoy, on the 11th of April, 1775, by virtue of the said charter, or by virtue of any act of the legislature of this State, whilst the same was the Colony of New York, shall continue to be and continue in full force and virtue, to all intents and purposes whatever, notwithstanding any nonuser or misuser thereof, or any part thereof, between the 18th of April, 1775, and the day of passing this act."

"The minister, elders, and deacons, who, from an adherence to the cause of their country, were compelled by the British army to leave the said city, or such of them as since the evacuation of the said city, returned thereto, shall be the minister, elders, and deacons of the Protestant Reformed Dutch Church, of the city of New York, until others shall be elected or appointed in their stead, according to the said charter."

By the second section, the power given by the charter to make rates and assessments upon members in communion, to pay the salaries and stipends, repairing the church, etc., was stated; that such power had never been exercised, and the present minister, elders, and deacons, were willing to surrender the same. It was then enacted that such power should not thereafter be exercised, but should be abrogated and annulled.

It should be observed that this power to assess was a branch of the power of taxation, which a governor could not grant by charter. The Act of Assembly of 1704, conferred it upon Trinity Church, which was not given by its charter of 1697.

§ 8. *General Act of* 1784. The legislature of the State, on the 6th of April, 1784, passed a General Act for the incorporation of religious societies. It was applicable to every denomination, and prescribed one course for all.[1] Its material provisions are stated, *ante*, chap. 3, § 2.

§ 9. *Act of March*, 1788. These provisions being found inappropriate to the Dutch churches, a statute was passed on the 7th of March, 1788, reciting that by the usages of the religious societies commonly known by the appellation of the Reformed Protestant Dutch churches or congregations, the minister or ministers, elders, and deacons for the time being, have the management of the temporalities of the respective congregations, and the said congregations cannot avail themselves of the benefit intended by the Act of 6th April, 1784, without departing from such usage long

---

[1] Laws, 1784, chap. 18.   [2] Laws, 1788, chap. 61.

established. That the congregations had petitioned the legislature for an alteration.

It is not necessary to transcribe the section enacted, as it was in substance the same as the second section of the Act of 27th of March, 1801, and the second section of the present Act of 1813. But the second section of the Act of 1801 contained this clause: "*Provided, always,* that nothing therein contained shall be construed in any manner to impair or alter the rights of any chartered churches within this State."

From an Act of the 29th of April, 1786 (Laws, chap. 54, § 5), it appears, that there were trustees of the Reformed Protestant Dutch Church of Flatbush. They were authorized to sell portions of their real estate, not exceeding six acres, for an academy.

§ 10. *Act of February,* 1792. By an Act of the 11th February, 1792 (2 Greenleaf, chap. 11), the trustees of the Reformed Protestant Low Dutch Church, at New Utrecht, in King's County, were authorized to sell certain lands, not exceeding twenty-six acres, for the advancement of the interests and prosperity of the said church.

§ 11. *Act of February, 1st,* 1798, *Albany.* By an Act passed February 2, 1798 (Laws 1798, chap. 7), entitled "An Act concerning the charter to the minister, elders, and deacons of the Reformed Protestant Dutch Church, in the city of Albany," it was recited, that they and their predecessors, and the other inhabitants of the city of Albany, communicants or members of the Reformed Protestant Dutch church or congregation, had been incorporated by letters-patent or a charter under the Great Seal, dated the 10th of August, 1720; that it was granted thereby, that the minister, elders, and deacons for the time being, should be the consistory of such church, and although it was granted that the consistory could call more than one minister to officiate in the said church, and that there should be no preëminence in that office, yet doubts had arisen whether, in case of a plurality of ministers, more than one of them could, at the same time, be a member of the consistory. That the charter was also unprovisional as to the right to elect more than four elders and four deacons.

That it had been requisite to have two ministers for the church; and an additional church, or place of public worship, had lately been erected.

It was enacted that in the case of a plurality of ministers in the said church or congregation, only the minister who shall at any time preside in the consistory, shall, for the time being, be considered a member of the said consistory; that they should severally be president by turns, in such manner as should be ordained by the consistory. *Provided,* that nothing in the act should be construed to abridge the powers and privileges of any of the ministers, respecting the exercise of Christian discipline in such church, according to the rules of Church government, ratified in the Synod of Dordrecht, in the year 1618 and 1619, and adopted by the General Synod in New York on the 10th of October, 1792. That four elders and four deacons of the said church or congregation, in addition to the present members, might be elected equally, as if it had originally been granted by the said charter that eight elders and eight deacons might have been elected; and provision was then made as to the mode of electing. That four elders and four deacons, with the president for the time being, should form a consistory to transact business. In case the minister whose turn it shall be to preside, shall neglect or be unable to attend such meeting, it shall be lawful for any other minister of the said church or congregation, or in case all the ministers be absent, then for the senior elder of the consistory, to preside at such meeting. *Provided,* that when a senior elder shall so preside, four elders and four deacons, exclusive of the president, shall be requisite to form a consistory.

§ 12. *Act of 15th February,* 1800, *New York.* By an act of the 15th February, 1800 (Laws, chap. 4), it was provided as follows: " An Act to amend the Charter of the Reformed Protestant Dutch Church in the city of New York: Whereas, the day appointed by the charter of the Reformed Protestant Dutch Church, of the city of New York, for the election of elders and deacons, hath become inconvenient for that purpose —

" Therefore, etc., That the elders and deacons of the said church shall annually hereafter be elected on the second Thursday of January; that the elders and deacons now in office shall continue until the third Sunday inclusive, next after the day of election; and their successors in like manner, until the third Sunday after the first annual election day after that election.

" And whereas the said charter does not provide for supplying vacancies in said offices, which may happen by resignation or declining an election, Therefore, That if any of the said elders or deacons shall resign, or any one elected shall decline the office for which he shall have been elected, then, and in either of these cases, an election shall be held to fill such vacancies in the manner provided by the said charter to supply a vacancy in said offices by death or removal."

§ 13. *Act of April* 9, 1819. By an act of April 9, 1819 (Laws, chap. 129), it was made lawful for the religious corporation in the city of New York, known as the minister, elders, and deacons of the Reformed Protestant Dutch Church, of the city of New York, and their successors, to hold real and personal estate of an annual value or income not exceeding £5,000, anything in the original charter or of any law of this State contained to the contrary notwithstanding. *Provided*, that the said property shall be such only as may be necessary for the purposes of the said religious incorporation.

§ 14. *Act of April* 7, 1819. *General Synod.* By an act passed April 7, 1819 (Laws, chap. 110), the General Synod of the Reformed Dutch Protestant Church was created a body politic and corporate, by the name and style of the General Synod of the Reformed Protestant Dutch Church, with power to take, purchase, and hold real and personal estate, and to sell and convey the same, the yearly value not to exceed $10,000, and the same shall not be appropriated to any other than religious and charitable uses and purposes.

The regular members were empowered to choose a president, three directors, and a treasurer of the corporation, and to make by-laws relating to the management and disposition of their property, the duties of such officers, and the duration of the offices.

The legislature could alter and repeal this act.

In the year 1839 the church in Lafayette Place was erected; that in Ninth Street in 1837; and that in Fifth Avenue in 1854. A chapel was built in 1864 in Forty-eighth Street.

§ 15. *Act of* 1813. The existing law for incorporating such churches is as follows (Sess. 36, chap. 69, § 2): "The minister or ministers, and elders and deacons, and if during any time, there shall be no minister, then the elders and deacons during such time, of every Reformed Protestant Dutch church or congregation now, or hereafter to be established in this State, and elected according to the rules and usages of such churches within this State, shall be trustees for every such church or congregation; and it shall be lawful for the said trustees, if not already incorporated, to assemble together as soon as they shall deem it convenient, and execute under their hands and seals, a certificate certifying the name or title by which they and their successors forever, as a body corporate by virtue of this act, shall be known and distinguished; which certificate, being duly acknowledged or proven as aforesaid, shall be recorded by the *Clerk* of such county,[1] in a book to be by him provided as aforesaid; and such trustees and their successors shall thereupon, by virtue of this act, be a body corporate, by the name or title expressed in such certificate. It shall be lawful for the trustees of any such church or congregation, elected by virtue of any former law of this State, by writing under their hands and seals, to be proved, acknowledged, and recorded as aforesaid, to declare their intention not to continue any longer a body corporate; and thereupon, such body corporate shall cease, and all the estate, real and personal, held by them, shall pass to, and be

---

[1] Register of the City and County of New York.

vested in, the trustees of such church or congregation made a body corporate in the manner above directed. *Provided, always,* that nothing herein contained shall be construed in any manner to impair or alter the rights of any chartered churches within this State."

There could be no necessity or convenience in changing the chartered name of the Dutch Church in New York; and I am informed the provision of the act to that effect was not resorted to.

The consistory of the Dutch Church is analogous to the vestry of the Episcopal Church.

§ 16. On the 14th of February, 1816, an act was passed (Laws, chap. 6), "Concerning the Reformed Protestant Dutch churches in Albany." It recited that the congregations had been divided into two congregations, and the minister, elders, and deacons of one had been incorporated under the existing law, by the name of "The Second Reformed Protestant Dutch Church in the city of Albany," and were desirous of obtaining the rights and privileges, which were granted by charter to the minister, elders, and deacons of the Reformed Protestant Dutch Church in the city of Albany.

It was then enacted, that the minister, elders, and deacons of the aforesaid Second Congregation, and their successors in office, be a body politic and corporate, by the name of the "Minister, Elders, and Deacons of the Second Protestant Dutch Church in the city of Albany;" to have and enjoy the like rights, powers, and privileges, and be subject to the like responsibilities, restrictions, and government as are granted by, and expressed in, the original charter to the said minister, elders, and deacons of the Reformed Protestant Dutch Church in the city of Albany, and the several acts of the legislature confirming or amending the same.

All *bond fide* contracts or conveyances made by, to, or with such Second Reformed Church, in their corporate name, should be binding upon the parties and privies, the same as if made subsequent to the passage of the act.

The division between the churches of tne real and personal estate was confirmed.

Each of such churches was to have four elders and four deacons, to be elected at the time and in the manner prescribed by the charter.

§ 17. *Act of April,* 1835. On the 15th of April, 1835, an act was passed entitled, "An Act to amend the Charter of the Minister, Elders, and Deacons of the Second Protestant Reformed Dutch Church in the city of Albany." (Laws, 1835, chap. 90.)

The provisions of the first seven sections relate exclusively to that church ; and it is not deemed necessary to cite them, except that by the sixth section, the said church was to be known thereafter, in its legal corporate capacity, as "The Second Reformed Protestant Dutch Church in the city of Albany."

And by the seventh section, the mode of electing the members of the consistory of the said church shall not hereafter be controlled or regulated by the charter thereof ; but the said members of the consistory shall hereafter be elected according to the rules and usages of the Reformed Protestant Dutch churches within this State.

The eighth section is as follows : —

§ 18. "Any of the churches in this State in connection with the Reformed Protestant Dutch Church, whose temporal affairs are under the management of a consistory, or board of officers, elected or chosen from such persons only as are in communion with the said church, may, if the said consistory or board so determine, at any time hereafter, confide the management and care of the temporal concerns of said church, to a board of trustees, not less than seven, nor more than nine in number." (§ 8 of Act of April 15, 1835, chap. 90.)

(2.) Such determination shall be reduced to writing, and signed by the president and secretary, or clerk of such board, with the seal of the corporation (if any) thereto affixed, and shall be acknowledged by said president, before some person authorized to take the acknowledgment of deeds, and be recorded in the office of the *County Clerk of the County*, in which such church shall be situated, in the book of records relative to religious incorporations, or other proper book of records. (Ibid.)

(3.) Thereupon such proceedings shall be taken for the election of the said board of trustees; and they shall be chosen, on the same notice, in the same manner, out of the same body, by the same persons; shall have their election certified in the same manner, continue in office for the same term, their successors be elected in the like manner, and shall have, possess, and enjoy the same rights, powers, and privileges, and be subject to the like obligations, and shall act in concurrence with the consistory of such church in the choice of ministers, and in all respects be a board of trustees, with the same rights and powers, and have the like control of the property and temporal affairs of the church, as the board intended to be constituted by the previous sections of this act. (Ibid.)

§ 19. (1.) If the said board of trustees that may so be elected by any other church in communion with the Reformed Dutch Church, shall deem it necessary or proper to change the corporate name of said church to that of a Reformed Dutch Church, with such further designation as may be necessary in consequence of the change effected in its organization, by the election of a board of trustees as aforesaid, they shall be at liberty so to do, and certify their determination in proper form, under the signature of the president, which shall be acknowledged by him before some officer authorized to take the acknowledgment of deeds, and be recorded in the same manner as the certificate referred to in the last section. (Ibid. § 9.)

(2.) And thereupon such corporation shall be known and distinguished by the corporate name and style that may have been determined upon, and expressed in said certificate. (Ibid.)

§ 20. Any church in connection with the Reformed Protestant Dutch Church in this State, the choice or election of the members of whose consistory is not subject to the ecclesiastical rules or jurisdiction of said church, may, at any time, on the determination and resolve of said consistory to that effect, be made subject to such rules and jurisdiction; and thenceforth the choice of members of such consistory shall be made in accordance with such rules and the practice of the said Dutch Church. (Ibid. § 10.)

§ 21. The following rules or regulations are pertinent to the present work. They are taken from the Constitution. (Edition 1840.)

The elders and deacons, together with the minister or ministers, if any, shall form a consistory, and the minister shall preside at all consistorial meetings; but in the absence of a minister, the consistory may appoint one of the elders to be their president, *pro tem.*; and it shall be competent to the several consistories to prescribe the mode and time of calling their meetings. If there be a plurality of ministers, they shall preside in rotation. (Art. II. § 1.)

The elders, with the ministers of the Word, constitute what, in the original articles of Church government, is properly called the consistory. But as the deacons have always in America, where the congregations were at first very small (see Synod of Dort, Art. 38), been joined with the elders, and wherever charters have been obtained, are particularly named, as forming with them one consistory, it is necessary to define their joint as well as respective powers. From the form of their ordination, it is evident that to the elders, together with the ministers of the Word, is committed the spiritual government of the church, while to the deacons belong the obtaining of charitable assistance, and the distribution of the same for the relief and comfort of the poor. When joined together in one board, the elders and deacons have all an equal voice in whatever relates to the temporalities of the church, to the calling of a minister, or the choice of their own successors, in all which they are considered the joint and general representatives of the people; but in admitting members to full communion, in exercising discipline upon those who have erred from the faith, or offended in morals, and in choosing delegates to attend the Classis, the elders, with the ministers, have alone a voice.

No consistory shall be constituted in any place, without the previous advice and concurrence of Classis.   (Ibid. 3.)

Elders and deacons shall be chosen annually, and the result of such election shall be published in the church or place of worship of the congregation three successive Sabbaths previous to their ordination, to the end that all lawful objections to such ordination may be offered to, and duly considered and adjudicated by, the consistory.   (Ibid. § 4.)

A majority of the consistory, regularly convened, shall be a quorum for the transaction of business; and in a like manner a majority of ministers and elders, and also a majority of deacons so convened, shall be a quorum respectively.   It shall be competent for the consistory, when an election shall have been omitted at the usual time, to appoint another time for that purpose on an early day, giving the like notice as herein above prescribed, and in like manner for filling vacancies which may occur.   (Ibid. § 4.)

§ 22. *General Remarks.* In considering the legal position of the Dutch Church, we are struck with the strong features of permanence and consistency which it exhibits from its foundation, particularly from its charter of 1696.

And its resemblances to the frame of the charter of Trinity Church of 1697, is very marked.

(1.) There was one minister recognized, and there was a right to call other ministers as assistants. So there was one rector of Trinity Church, and a right to nominate assistants.

(2.) I have no doubt that under the charter of 1696, new congregations could be formed worshiping in new edifices, but retaining their connection with, and subordination to, the ecclesiastical authority of the church of the charter. That church in local habitation was the church in Garden Street, perhaps also the church in the Fort.

(3.) The Act of 1753 explicitly sanctions the spread of

the same church, — that particular corporate church, into several congregations, in distinct edifices. The governing power remained the same in substance and form. There was allowed an increase in the number of the persons constituting such governing power.[1]

(4.) There is another analogy to English law and to the charter of Trinity Church. It was a right clearly incident to every parish or mother church to have what are called chapels of ease. They were simply places of worship for convenience of parishioners. They were component parts of the mother church.

The worshipers in the chapels had all the rights of the worshipers in the parish church, and were subject to the same duties. The rector of the parish governed the chapels. He had curates under him, but wholly subordinate. Here I believe there is a difference. The collegiate ministers are on an equality, except as some presidency is conventionally provided.

With this qualification the congregations in William Street, Lafayette Place, and Fifth Avenue, are precisely in the same legal position as the chapels of St. Paul and St. John are to Trinity Church. In each case, one corporation established them as its own branches. One corporation governs them. The worshipers in each are members of the same corporation, are entitled to votes according to the rules of the corporation, and have all the same equal privileges, unless modified by consent.

(5.) But the English law recognized what are called parochial churches or chapels; and here the position of Trinity Church in its contests, and of the Dutch Church, is singularly alike.

These parochial chapels are those which by deed or prescription have become, though within the parish bounds, separated from the parish church, with a separate rector, separate rights of ministrations, baptisms, sepultures; neither owing duty to, nor sharing in the privileges of, the parish church.

---

[1] Dr. DeWitt's Evidence in Marselus *v.* The Dutch Church, 1859.

Now this is exactly what Trinity Church has asserted with unanswerable force, as to all the churches separately organized and incorporated in the city of New York, denying that the members of such separate organizations and corporations could have a right to vote for vestrymen of Trinity Church. This is precisely what the Reformed Dutch Church insist upon. I quote from the answer of that church to the complaint of the Rev. Mr. Marselus, in the Supreme Court. It is very striking : —

"Edifices were built for the accommodation of the members of the corporation, being members in communion with the said church so incorporated, and as congregations not separating themselves from the said corporation, but continuing members thereof. They deny that the congregation forming the church at Greenwich, after it became a separate congregation, continued to be a part or members of the corporation of the defendants; but that they organized themselves into a separate consistory and congregation, *and into a separate corporation,* under the general law of the State."

We may almost suppose ourselves reading the masterly argument of the late David D. Barnard in the Trinity Church case.[1]

I am not aware that any minister of a separate church, organized and incorporated, has demanded to share in the revenues of Trinity Church, as a minister in the parish. The claim would be upon the same footing as to its legality as the claim of the separated members to vote. But in the case of the Dutch Church, the question has arisen, and been decided in the Court of Appeals. (The Attorney-General, *ex rel.;* Marselus *v.* The Minister, etc., 1867.)

The relator was the pastor of the Reformed Dutch Church situated at Greenwich, in the city of New York. This had become a separately organized church in 1803, with the assent of the Classis, the proper ecclesiastical authority, and had become incorporated under the statute of the State then in force. It had a distinct pastorate and consistory. Its

---

[1] Letter to Senator Brooks. Albany, 1857.

pastors were not known or recognized as ministers of the collegiate pastorate of the church under the charter.

The information set forth the position of the relator as a minister of the Dutch Church generally, and pastor of the church at Greenwich by regular succession. It set out the will of one Steinwich, the questions arising upon which are not of importance here. Also, the will of Harpending, before quoted; that a very large amount of rents and profits derived from the property had been received by the defendants; that such reception was in trust for the benefit of a class of ministers, of which the relator was one, and claiming an application of a proper portion to his maintenance.

The judge at Special Term held, that the devise of Harpending was exclusively for the benefit of the ministers of the church of the defendants. He says: " At this time the defendants being incorporated by the name of ' The Minister, Elders, and Deacons of the Reformed Protestant Dutch Church, of the city of New York,' and these words being used in the will to describe the only body for whose exclusive benefit the devise was made, and to whom alone, by express direction, there was to be any accountability for the income of the property shown, that the donor intended that body alone to have the right to the income of his property without accountability to others, whether of the same communion of faith or not."

The Court at General Term concurred in this view.

Another point decided at General Term was, that the devise was void under the Statute of Wills of Henry VIII., and the trusts fell with it. The plaintiff could not claim as *cestui que trust*, when a will erecting the trusts was invalid.

The title to the real estate rested upon the adverse possession of 140 years, which was enough, whether a claim was made under a void conveyance, or without any proper title at all. The presumption of a grant from the true owner was to be made. (Harpending *v.* The Dutch Church, 16 Peters, 455; Humbert *v.* Trinity Church, 22 Wendell, 485.)

In the Court of Appeals, the case was heard April, 1867, and decided in July of that year.

The opinion of the Court, delivered by Judge Grover, may be thus summarily stated.

That the claim was, that the relator, and all other ministers of the Dutch Reformed Church, engaged in ministering in churches in the city of New York, in communion with the Protestant Reformed Dutch Church, were entitled to payment of their salaries, in whole or in part, out of the income of property in the hands of the defendants, derived under the will of one Steinwich of 1684, and of one Harpending of 1723.

If the facts of being a minister of the church designated, and officiating in a church in the city of New York, and being in communion with the Dutch Reformed Church, gave a legal right to such payment, the case of the relator was made out.

He notices the difficulty of the Attorney-General sustaining the action upon the theory of the plaintiff, but assumes that it may be sustained.

The question was, whether the trusts created by the wills were in favor of one particular church, represented by the defendants, or whether they were in favor of all the officiating clergy of the denomination, from time to time officiating in the city of New York.

When Steinwich made his will, there was but one such church in the city. It was unincorporated, and known as the Nether Dutch Church.

The devise of Steinwich was to the elders or overseers of the Nether Dutch Reformed congregation, within the city of New York, for the proper use and behoof of the minister of the Nether Dutch Reformed congregation, within the city of New York, for the support and maintenance of their minister, ordained according to the Church orders of the Netherlands, etc.

The question was not whether the will was valid, but it was, to whom did Steinwick intend to give the property, and on what trust? The facts before stated left no doubt upon this point.

If the will, and the deed executed pursuant to its directions, conveyed a title, that title and the trust was acquired by the parties for the benefit of this particular congregation. If no title was acquired, no trust was created, and the relator, of course, had no claim on the property or income.

The charter of 1696 is then stated. After an examination of its provisions, it was concluded, that this particular church alone was incorporated; that by the clause, " those in communion with the Protestant Reformed Dutch Church," was meant members of this particular church; that the charter did not create a denominational corporation, embracing all the churches or congregations that might exist thereafter in the city of New York.

The will of Harpending of 1723 is then noticed. It followed from the previous positions stated, that if the will was valid, the title vested in, and the trust was for the benefit of this Protestant Reformed Dutch Church.

It was wholly immaterial whether the will was valid or not, because if valid, the whole beneficial interest vested in this particular church.

It is noticed that a colonial act authorized the corporation to apply its income to the building or repairing of churches. This it had done, governing all by the same officers as one church, preserving all in the same corporation.

The case showed that the income largely exceeded what was necessary to pay the ministers employed, and the question was, — What should be done with the surplus?

After referring to the course in the English Court of Chancery of a charitable scheme upon the doctrine of *cy pres*, where the intent cannot be literally or fully carried out, the Court say, that our courts will only give effect to the intention of donors when intelligently expressed and in accordance with the rules of law. A substantial defect will not be supplied.

The property was devised to the defendants; and so far as the parties before the court were concerned, it must be conceded that they held the legal title. The surplus, after discharging the trust charged upon the fund, belonged to the defendants, to be used for any purpose authorized by their act of incorporation. The judgment was affirmed.

In the case of the Dutch Church in Garden Street *v.* Mott (7 Paige, 77), the bill was to compel a purchaser to accept a conveyance of the Garden Street property sold to him. The deed of the corporation of New York to Bayard, and the deed by him to Van Cortlandt and others, of February, 1691, for the use of the minister, elders, and deacons of the Low Dutch Church, and of their successors forever, and for no other use or uses. The charter of 1696 is stated, and that it was granted to enable the corporation to hold this property to the uses for which it had been conveyed, and by which it was confirmed to them. The presumption, after the lapse of one hundred and fifty years, was, that the trustees, Van Cortlandt and others, had conveyed the legal title. But independently of this presumption, the Act of 1801 (1 R. L. 1801, p. 339, § 4) was operative to transfer the legal estate from the heirs of the trustees to the church when incorporated, although no conveyance had been executed.

There could be no doubt that previous to the separation of the complainants from the collegiate churches, in 1812, the legal, as well as equitable title, was vested absolutely in the corporation, and no violation of the trust could revest any title in the heirs of Bayard, or of the original trustees, although a breach of trust might form a proper ground for an application by the corporators, or by the Attorney-General, to compel the due execution of the trust.

The complainants became separately a distinct church, and were separately organized and incorporated in 1812, and the corporation of the collegiate churches gave them a lease for 999 years with certain restrictions and conditions. After the destruction of the edifice by fire, in 1835, the absolute title in fee was conveyed in consideration of the sum of $100,000.

The rule of the common law giving corporations the unlimited right of alienation, and the restrictions upon the alienation of Church property by statutes in England, were noticed. The supposition that these restrictions existed here, led to the enactment making the sanction of the Chancellor necessary to a sale. There was no doubt that the intention of the legislature was to give to every religious corporation an unlimited power to convey any real estate held by them in trust for the corporators, provided the previous consent of the Chancellor, and a direction for the proper application of the proceeds was obtained.

I am not aware of anything else in our laws or decisions peculiarly applicable to the Dutch Church; and I have deemed it useful to comprise in one chapter all that I have found so peculiar.

At the meeting of the General Synod of the Church in June, 1867, an elaborate and able report was submitted, upon a proposition for a change of the ecclesiastical and corporate name of the church. It closed with a series of resolutions. The first was: That the General Synod proposes to the Classis, the amendment of the first section in Article 5, chap. 2, of the Constitution, by appending to it the following sentence: "The body thus formed shall be called the General Synod of the Reformed Church in America."

Embarrassed with considerations arising from the frequent use of the term, "Reformed Dutch Church," in the Constitution and Formularies, and coming to the conclusion not to expunge the term absolutely, the following resolutions were adopted: —

" 2. *Resolved*, That the Synod propose to the Classis, the adoption of the following prefatory note, with a view to its incorporation into the Constitution.

" In the year 1867, the Reformed Dutch Church which is named in the following pages, dropped from its ecclesiastical name the word 'Dutch,' which was first formally assumed therein in the year 1792, and added the words 'in America,' so that the said church might thenceforth be known as the Reformed Church in America; yet in order that the absolute identity of the Reformed Church in America with the Reformed Dutch Church might be subject to no possible doubt or dispute, it was also ordained that the epithet 'Dutch' should be retained in all those places in the Constitution in which it had previously been used, but should be inclosed in brackets, to indicate the purpose of the church to discourage the ecclesiastical and popular use of that word as a part of its name."

(2.) A third resolution was as follows : —

3. "*Resolved*, That the General Synod proposes to the Classis, the further amendment of the Constitution by prefixing thereto a title in the terms following : 'The Constitution of the Reformed Church in America, known for a time as the Reformed Dutch Church, and also designated in the Act of Incorporation, passed by the legislature of New York April 7, 1819, as the "Reformed Protestant Dutch Church," embracing the Catechism, the Compendium, the Confession of Faith, the Canons of the Synod of Dordrecht, and the Liturgy.'"

A committee was appointed to consider the details of the civil legislation which the proposed change of name may make necessary, and to report on the same at an adjourned meeting of the Synod.

In the historical notice which accompanied these resolutions, the fact was stated, that the designation Dutch was unknown to the Hollanders, who would be as slow to call themselves Dutch as to call themselves Russians. The Church of Hollanders was of *Nederlanche.* Particular congregations might be termed *Nederduitsche.* The Hollanders who brought their Church to this country were members of the "Reformed Church of the Netherlands." The change took place after the English conquest.

The charter to the church in New York is referred to. It will be seen that the other charters, and the statute of 1753, use the title "The Reformed Protestant Dutch Church." (*Ante*, § 4.)

This view of the original true title of the church is confirmed by the Article of Freedoms and Exemptions of 1640, before cited. (*Ante*, § 1 of this chapter.)

THE TRUE REFORMED CHURCH.

The churches or congregations in this State, in connection with the church which has styled itself "The True Reformed Church in the United States of America," may incorporate themselves in the mode prescribed in and by the second section of the act entitled, "An Act to provide for the Incorporation of Religious Societies," passed April 5, 1813. § 1 of Act of April 21, 1825. Laws, chap. 303.)

CHAPTER VI.

In chapter 1, I have stated the history of the Acts of the Colonial Assembly passed in 1693, and subsequent years, for settling a ministry in four counties, and the efforts of the Presbyterians, particularly at Jamaica, to have the amount levied under those laws, applied to the support of a minister of their own. These efforts were finally successful at that place, and through a judicial decision. It was shown, that with the exception of the violent and unwarrantable conduct of Lord Cornbury, the course of the Governors, particularly of Governor Hunter, had been moderate and legal. It was also noticed, that while charters, four in number, had been granted to Dutch churches, none had been given to any other denomination.

In 1719, 1721, and 1759, applications were made to the Governors, on behalf of Presbyterians in the city, for acts of incorporation. That of the last date was referred by Governor Delancy to the Lords of Trade. In July, 1765, they wrote to Governor Moore, that his Majesty had been pleased to refer to them for consideration the petition of the present ministers of the Presbyterian Church in the city of New York, praying to be incorporated by a charter under the seal of the province, for the purposes set forth in such petition. Referring to a similar application made to Lieutenant Governor Delancy, and to the proceedings had thereon, they required him to submit the petition to the Council and to report in the fullest manner, the present state of this Protestant establishment, the proceedings upon the former petition, and the reasons why it was not complied with, and his opinion whether there were reasons against granting the request.[1]

Iu July, 1767, the Lords of Trade made a report to the Committee of the Privy Council on Plantations, stating, that they had considered the petition of the ministers, elders, deacons, and trustees of the Presbyterian Church in the city of New York, for a charter to create them a body politic and corporate, according to the Westminster Confession of Faith, catechisms and directions. They state that many proceedings had been had before the Couucil in New York, touching an application there for such a charter. In consequence they had directed the Governor to report such proceedings, and his views upon the whole subject. That he had doue so, and that a copy of his report was annexed.[2] That it stated a poiut of great weight aud importance, namely, whether his Majesty, consistent with the obligation he is under by his coronatiou oath, founded ou the Act of the 5th of Queen Anne, cap. 5, entitled "An Act for securing the Church of England as by law established," could create such an establishment in favor of the Presbyterian Church as was uow requested. They proceed: "That is a question of too great importance for us to decide, but we are of opinion, that independeut of this objection, it is not expedient, upon priuciples of general policy, to comply with the prayer of the petition, or to give the Presbyterian Church of New York any other privileges or immunities thau it is entitled to by the laws of toleration.[3]

On the 4th of May, 1775, the Earl of Dartmouth writes to Governor Tryon thus: "The only difficulty or doubt which has occurred is, whether such charters would not have an effect to create an establishment inconsisteut with the priuciples of the law of England; and it was the more necessary to attend to this, as it was first started by the Council of New York, upon the application made in 1766. If, however, upon consideration of the cases in which the request was now made, the law servants of the King in the

---

[1] *Colonial Documents*, vol. vii. p. 846.   [2] I have not been able to find it.
[3] *Colonial Documents*, vol. vii. p. 948.

Province and the Council shall be of opinion that they are free from any difficulty of this nature, it was the King's pleasure that he do grant such charter."[1]

What would have been the result of this relaxation of the former view of the Lords of Trade, we can only conjecture. The strife of the Revolution quickly ensued, and prevented any further effort for the attainment of the object.

It appears that as early as 1719, a piece of ground was conveyed to Dr. John Nicholl, Patrick McKnight, Gilbert Livingstone, and Thomas Smith, and a church was built upon it. This was the church in Wall Street, west of Nassau Street, as is shown upon Lyne's map of 1728, and a church continued on that site until 1848.

On the 10th of March, 1730, the persons in whom the legal title was then vested, conveyed the property to the moderator of the General Assembly of the Church of Scotland, the commissioner thereof, the moderator of the Presbytery of Edinburgh and others, as a Committee of the General Assembly. On the 15th of August, 1732, the Church of Scotland, by an instrument, under the seal of the General Assembly, and signed by various members and officers, declared, that it should be lawful for the Presbyterians then residing, or that should thereafter be resident in or near the city of New York, or others joining with them, to convene in the aforesaid church for the worship of God, and for the dispensation of the gospel ordinances, fully and freely at all times, they maintaining such edifice and appurtenances at their own charge.[2]

Between 1732 and 1766, a conveyance must have been made by the trustees in Scotland to trustees in New York.

On the 25th of February, 1766, a conveyance was made by the Mayor, Aldermen, and Common Council of the city of New York, to John Rodgers and Joseph Treat, present ministers of the English Presbyterian Church, in the said city, William Smith and others, the then elders, John Stephens and Peter Riker, the then deacons, and Thomas

---

[1] *Colonial Documents*, vol. viii. p. 572.
[2] Smith's *History of New York.*

Smith, Peter R. Livingston, and others, the *present trustees* of the said church. The petition of such parties is recited. It is stated, that although the petitioners were already possessed of a convenient and spacious edifice for the public worship of Almighty God, yet by their great growth, that building was rendered incapable of containing their congregation, and the cemetery was too small for the burial of the dead. They refer to the grant of the burial-ground to Trinity Church, and of a number of lots to the Reformed Dutch at a reasonable rate, and they suggest the triangular piece of ground adjoining the Vineyard, as suitable for their purposes.

The grant was made to the petitioners as trustees, upon condition of their erecting thereupon an edifice or church for the worship of Almighty God, or to use the same or part thereof for a cemetery; and they shall not appropriate, apply, or convert the same forever thereafter to private secular uses. There was reserved an annual rent of forty pounds to the corporation. There was a clause of reëntry upon breach of either of these conditions.

Between the 6th day of April, 1784, and the 31st of August of that year, the church was incorporated by the name of the First Presbyterian Church of the city of New York, under the General Act of said 6th of April, 1784.

On the 31st of August, 1784, the survivors of the trustees in the grant of 1766, conveyed the premises adjoining the Vineyard, to the corporation of the First Presbyterian Church in the city of New York.

By an Act of March 6, 1793 (3 Greenleaf, 51), the corporations of the First Presbyterian Church in the city of New York was authorized to take and hold real estate, to a value not exceeding the sum of six thousand dollars annually.

On the 23d of September, 1795, the corporation of New York released to the corporation of the First Presbyterian Church in the city of New York, the sum of eighteen pounds, fifteen shillings, part of the rent reserved in the deed of 1766.

An act was passed on the 17th of February, 1809, entitled, " An Act for the separation of the First Presbyterian Church of the city of New York." It states that the body possessed three places of public worship, and that a separation would be conducive to their interest. It was enacted, that it should be lawful for the said church to become two or more distinct and separate congregations, and to incorporate themselves severally under the act to provide for the incorporation of, etc., but not without the consent of the majority of the pew-holders and stated hearers. They were authorized to execute all proper conveyances, to vest part of the real and personal property in trustees.

The approval of pew-holders and stated hearers was obtained, and a division took place.

It appears that the First Presbyterian Church became again incorporated, and by the same name, on the 1st of May, 1809, under the General Act then in force of 1800.

The members of what was commonly known as the Brick Church, erected on the site adjoining the Vineyard, became also incorporated at the same time, with the title of " The Corporation of the Brick Presbyterian Church, in the city of New York." And by an indenture of the 29th of May, 1809, the premises were conveyed by the trustees of the First Presbyterian Church to the trustees of the Brick Church.

The third of the churches mentioned, appears to have been what was known as the Rutgers Street Church.

In the year 1837, negotiations were had for the sale and surrender to the corporation of New York, of the lease held by the Brick Church. Application was made to Vice-Chancellor McCoun for his approval, under the statute. He considered that a conditional order could be made without an actual contract being entered into with any intended purchaser. The Court could approve and confirm a sale on the terms suggested, by a subsequent order.

Nor was it a decisive objection that the church had not selected a new site for their edifice.

The objections also of pew-holders, could not avail against

the application. The order could be made without prejudice to the legal rights of pew-holders in the new building.

But the special character of the deeds of transfer to the vault-holders, gave them an interest in the land, and not merely a qualified privilege to construct a vault. The enjoyment was restricted to below the surface. There could be no building above ground. The petition was dismissed.

In 1854, the opinion of Judge Bronson, Mr. Charles O'Connor, and Mr. George Wood was taken, and they concurred in holding, that the premises could be sold for any purposes which were of a public nature, such as a mint, post-office, or court-house. The uses for which an alienation was prohibited were *private*, as well as secular uses.

In 1856 the property was sold by the church to private individuals. The approval of the Supreme Court was obtained for a sale, subject to the restrictions in the grant, in February, 1853.

The case of The People *v.* Wood and others, commissioners of the sinking fund, was, in the course of the proceedings, brought before Mr. Justice Duer and the present writer. Some points of importance were agreed upon.

That although the commissioners of the sinking fund were entitled to the rent reserved in the grant to the church, this had not carried any right of property, or other right than perhaps an action for breach of covenant to pay rent. The right to reënter for breach of the covenant not to alien for certain purposes, did not pass by a grant of the rent. The title — the possibility of reverter, if it might be so termed — remained in the corporation. But the assent of the Commissioners of the sinking fund was highly desirable if not essential.

The cause did not come to a decision, in consequence of the point being started, that the assent of one board was passed in one year, and of the other in a succeeding year. The Supreme Court subsequently held this to be illegal.

The sale was finally consummated. The church conveyed subject to the covenants. The corporation released and confirmed to the purchaser, and the commissioners of the sinking fund agreed to and ratified it. The assent of the vault-holders was also obtained.

Act of 1867. A General Act was passed on the 30th of March, 1867 (Laws, chap. 206), by which the Presbytery of New York (of which the Reverend John M. Krebs is stated clerk), in connection with the General Assembly of the Presbyterian Church in the United States of America, having designated from its membership the following persons, namely, John M. Krebs, etc., etc., citizens of the United States, to be trustees in their behalf, the said trustees and their successors to be from time to time appointed by said Presbytery, are hereby created a body politic and corporate by the name of " The Trustees of the Presbytery of New York."   (§ 1.)

The said Presbytery shall, in law, be capable of taking for religious and charitable purposes, by gift, devise, bequest, grant, or purchase, and of holding, conveying, and otherwise disposing of the same from time to time, all real and personal estate now held for the benefit of the said Presbytery, or which hath been or may hereafter, for the purposes of the said Presbytery, used in the promotion of its charitable or religious purposes, be given, devised, bequeathed, or granted to the said corporation by their name, or to the said Presbytery, or for the charitable and religious uses thereof, or which may in any manner have accrued, or shall accrue from the interest, income, or use of such real or personal estate. *Provided,* that the yearly income received from the property of the said corporation shall not exceed ten thousand dollars.   (Ibid. § 2.)

The management and disposal of the affairs and property of the said corporation shall be in the hands of the said trustees and their successors in office from time to time; and which trustees shall hold their offices at the pleasure of the said Presbytery; and all vacancies shall be filled by them.   (Ibid. § 3.)

The said corporation shall possess the general powers, rights, and privileges, and be subject to the liabilities and provisions contained in the 18th chapter of the first part of the Revised Statutes, so far as the same are applicable; and also subject to the provisions of chapter 360 of the Laws of 1860.   (Ibid. § 4.)

The last-mentioned act restricts the power to devise to one half the person's property in certain cases.

CHAPTER VII.

THE FRENCH CHURCH.

§ 1. By an act of the 19th June, 1703, the ministers and elders for the time being, of the French Protestant Church in the city of New York, were authorized to build a larger church.

The act enabled them to sell the church and ground occupied by them in Petticoat Lane. The proceeds were to be applied to the purchase of a larger piece of ground within the city, and to erect a church and dwelling-house for a minister.

The habendum was, " To have, hold, and use for the use and interest aforesaid, by the name of the Minister and Elders of the French Protestant Church in the city of New York, to them and their successors forever."

The fourth section authorized them to collect, from among the members of the congregation, the sums required for the maintenance and reparation of the church, dwelling-house, and other things appertaining thereto. But no one was compelled to contribute.

CHAPTER VIII.

THE LUTHERAN CHURCH.

As early as 1673, certain members of the Lutheran Church petitioned the Governor (Anthony Colve), in their own, and in the name of the congregation of the Augsburg Confession at Williamstaat (Albany), for the free exercise of their religious worship. The petition was granted, on condition of their conducting themselves quietly, without giving offense to the congregation of the Reformed Religion, which is the State Church.[1]

In Lieutenant Governor Colden's letter to the Board of Trade, of December, 1763, he adverts to the favor felt towards the Lutheran congregations, and their efforts to obtain a charter of incorporation in 1759. He states the Council had agreed to grant it, but Governor Delancy, finding many similar applications from other dissenting congregations, opposed it until the views of the Lords of Trade were ascertained. Such applications had been renewed, and were also submitted.

The edifice was, it appears, at first without the gate, but in a petition of the church (about 1684, as I judge), it is stated, that they had been obliged by Governor Colve to tear the edifice down. They had got a patent for a piece of ground within the gate, which was mislaid.[2]

The edifice long remained on the corner of Broadway and Rector Street.

In the case of Knistern v. The Lutheran Churches of St. Johns and St. Peters (1 Sandf. Ch. Rep. 440), the history of the Lutheran Churches in this State, and the statement

[1] *Colonial Documents*, vol. ii. p. 617.
[2] *Documentary History of New York*, vol. iii. p. 484.

of the peculiar dogmas of faith absolutely held, are to be found at length. It is shown that the great formulary is the Augsburg Confession of Faith.

The Lutheran missionary, Dr. Muhlenbergh, writes in 1750, that the Lutheran Church in the city of New York, had been built and dedicated with their own mites and friendly aid from Europe, for an Evangelical Lutheran congregation, according to the unaltered Augsburg Confession.   (1 Sandf. Ch. Rep. 521, *note.*)

In Miller *v.* Gable (2 Denio, 492), the doctrines of the Lutheran and Calvinistic Churches arc also discussed, with historical notices of the churches in this city.

CHAPTER IX.

§ 1. THE proceedings in the Colony in respect to Roman Catholics are very striking. Robert Livingston, in a letter to Governor Fletcher of the 14th of February, 1695, speaks of the generosity of the people to a papistical governor who never did, or meant them good, and of their neglect of one of their own religion with whom Heaven had blessed them.[1]

In 1696, a list of the Roman Catholics and reputed Papists in New York, was transmitted to England, with a statement that they had all been disarmed. The Mayor, by command of the Governor, made a return of all in the city, amounting to ten.[2]

The instructions to the Earl of Bellemont of 1667, directed him to permit liberty of conscience to all persons except Papists.

On the 31st of July, 1700, an act was passed against Jesuits and Popish priests. It enacted that every Jesuit and seminary priest, or ecclesiastical person, made or ordained by any authority derived or pretended to be derived from the Pope or See of Rome, then residing within the province, should depart therefrom on or before the 1st of November ensuing. Any such person preaching, or teaching others to say popish prayers, masses, granting of absolution, or celebrating or using any other of the Romish ceremonies and rites of worship, shall be deemed an incendiary and disturber of the public peace, and an enemy to the true Christian religion.

Severe penalties were imposed upon any Jesuit or Popish

---

[1] *Colonial Documents,* vol. iv. p. 98. [2] *Ibid.* p. 166.

priest remaining in the province. An exception was made as to shipwrecked persons, but they were compelled to leave within a limited time.

§ 2. It appears that St. Peter's Church and St. Patrick's Cathedral had been incorporated jointly under the Act of 1813. An act was passed April 11, 1817 (Laws, chap. 205), stating this fact, and the desire of the petitioners that distinct acts of incorporation should be passed for each of them, for which the sanction of the legislature seemed necessary.

It was enacted, that the members of the religious society of Roman Catholics, belonging to the congregation of St. Peter's Church, in the city of New York, should be, and were thereby constituted a body corporate and politic, by the name and description of "The Trustees of St. Peter's Church in the city of New York."

They were authorized to take and hold all that portion of the joint property which belonged to such church, whether given, granted, or devised to the same, or to any other person for its use. Also to take and hold lands and tenements, the annual income of which should not exceed $10,000, whether the same be by gift, grant, or bargain and sale, and to purchase and hold personal estate, whether by gift, grant, or bargain and sale, bequest, or otherwise; and to give, grant, devise, lease, or dispose of as they should think best for the advantage of the church. *Provided*, that nothing should authorize them to sell real estate without the sanction of the Chancellor, according to the eleventh section of the act "to provide for the Incorporation of Religious Societies."

The Roman Catholic Bishop in the city of New York, for the time being, was to be *ex officio* the president of the board of trustees; but in case of his death or absence, the board could appoint a chairman *pro tempore*.

The trustees were to be nine in number. Provision was made for the first election, and division into classes, holding for one, two, and three years respectively.

The elections for trustees after the first election, were to be held on Easter-Monday in every year, between the hours of eleven o'clock in the forenoon and three o'clock in the afternoon, by ballot, at such place and under such directions as the board of trustees, or a majority of them, should agree upon; whereof due notice was to be given three Sundays successively in said church, during divine service, and immediately preceding such election.

Three trustees were to be elected at such election, to supply the place of the three whose term expired.

The electors were to possess the same qualifications as were requisite at the first election. These were : —

The being male persons of full age belonging to the said church, being pew-holders, or stated hearers, and contributing to the said church not less than four dollars annually, in quarterly payments, and not more than six months in arrear.

It was made the duty of the trustees to keep a book to register all the names of the electors so qualified, and to produce such book at the elections, in order to test the qualifications of the electors in case the same should be questioned.

If any vacancy in the office of trustee should happen by resignation, death, or otherwise, the remaining trustees might make temporary appointments until the next annual election, which appointments shall then fill such vacancies to the end that no elector may give more than one vote in the same year, except he is a trustee and votes to supply a vacancy.

Power was given to appoint a treasurer and clerk, and to elect two auditors to state the situation of the funds.

The trustees of St. Peter's Church were made jointly liable with the trustees of St. Patrick's Cathedral, for the debts which the trustees of St. Peter's had before contracted, and the property and revenue of each of the churches was to remain liable for the liquidation of the same. Annual accounts should be mutually rendered, and the surplus funds be so applied.

By section fifth, it was made lawful for the trustees of St.

Peter's, at the call of any two of such trustees, to meet together for the purpose of transacting the business of such society; of the time and place of such meeting, notice shall be given to all the said trustees, at least one day before such meeting, except in cases of emergency. If five of the trustees attend, they shall form a quorum or board, and shall have power, by a majority of votes, to make, ordain, and establish such rules, orders, and regulations for the management of the temporal concerns of the said congregation, and for the government of the schools attached to the said church, as they should deem proper. *Provided,* that the same be not repugnant to the laws or constitution of this State or of the United States. *Provided, also,* that the trustees shall not enter into any expenses other than the ordinary and necessary contingent expenses without the consent of the trustees of St. Patrick's Cathedral in the city of New York, until the final extinguishment of the debts of the church.

By the seventh section, in case of a dissolution by reason of any non-user, the society might be re-incorporated under the law of the State, and all the property should vest in the new corporation.

By the eighth section, the joint incorporation of St. Peter's Church and St. Patrick's Cathedral was dissolved. But all grants or gifts made for the benefit of St. Peter's Church in the city of New York, and all acts of the legislature for the benefit thereof, were ratified and confirmed.

An act was passed April 14, 1817 (Laws, chap. 239), incorporating separately "The Trustees of St. Patrick's Cathedral, in the city of New York." Its provisions are the same as the Act of April 11, just cited.

§ 3. By an act of April 3, 1821 (Laws, chap. 237), the act as to the congregation of St. Peter's Church, of April 11, 1817, was amended as follows: From and after the passing of this act, it shall be the duty of the joint treasurer, for the time being, of St. Peter's Church and St. Patrick's Cathedral, duly appointed under the by-laws of such corporations, to keep a book to register all the names of electors qualified to vote at elections for officers under the act hereby amended; and it shall be the duty of the said joint treasurer to give to every person duly qualified, a certificate of such fact, which shall bear date within six months prior to the election, and shall be full and conclusive proof of the qualifications of the person named therein to vote at such elections.

By the second section, a penalty was imposed for refusing the certificate without sufficient and legal cause.

"And whereas, under the act hereby amended, notice of the said elections is required to be given in the church, and during divine service; and whereas such arrangement is offensive, and disturbs the harmony of divine worship, therefore —

"Be it enacted, that the notification of all elections under the said act hereby amended, shall be in writing, signed by the Catholic Bishop for the time being, the president *ex officio* of the board of trustees of said church, and shall be put up in a conspicuous place in the porch of the said church, for three Sundays successively immediately preceding such election."

§ 4. We may here notice the Act of April 9, 1855 (Laws, chap. 230): "An Act in relation to conveyances and devises of estates for religious purposes." It was enacted, that no interest in property, real or personal, should be conveyed, or descend to any ecclesiastic or his successor; that none but legally incorporated religious societies within this State could take grants, or devises of real property, dedicated or appropriated, or intended to be dedicated or appropriated, to the purposes of religious worship.

Other provisions were made as to property theretofore given to any ecclesiastic for such purposes, and its vesting in the church or congregation when incorporated, provided it became incorporated before the death of the person in whom it was vested.

There are other provisions of this statute not deemed necessary to be cited, as the act itself was repealed by a statute of April 8, 1862. (Laws, chap. 147.)

An important statute was passed on the 25th of March, 1863. It is entitled "An Act supplementary to the Act entitled 'An Act to provide for the Incorporation of Religious Societies,' passed April 5, 1813."

§ 5. *Act of* 1863. (1.) "It shall be lawful for any Roman Catholic church or congregation, now or hereafter existing in this State, to be incorporated according to the provisions of this act." (§ 1 of an act passed March 25, 1863.)

(2.) "The Roman Catholic Archbishop or Bishop of the Diocese in which such church is erected, or intended so to be, the Vicar-General of such Diocese, and the pastor of such church for the time being, respectively, or a majority of them, may select and appoint two laymen, members of such church, and may, together with such laymen, sign a certificate in duplicate, showing the name or title by which they and their successors shall be known and distinguished as a body corporate, by virtue of this act; which certificate shall be duly acknowledged or proved in the same manner as conveyances of real estate." (Ibid.)

(3.) "One of such certificates shall be filed in the office of the Secretary of State, and the other in the office of the Clerk of the County in which such church may be erected or intended so to be; and thereupon such church or congregation shall be a body corporate, by the name or title expressed in such certificate, and the persons signing the same shall be the trustees thereof." (Ibid.)

(4.) "The successors of any such Archbishop, Bishop, Vicar-General, or Pastor, respectively, for the time being, shall by virtue of his office, be the trustee of such church, in place of his predecessor, and such laymen shall hold their office respectively for one year, and whenever the office of any such layman shall become vacant by death, removal, resignation, or otherwise, his successor shall be appointed in the same manner as herein provided for his original selection." (Ibid.)

(5.) "The trustees of every such church or congregation, and their successors, shall have all the powers and authority granted to the trustees of any church, congregation, or society, by the fourth section of an act entitled, 'An Act to provide for the Incorporation of Religious Societies,' passed April 5, 1813; and shall also have power to fix or ascertain the salary to be paid to any pastor or assistant pastor of such church." (Ibid. § 2.)

(6.) "But the whole real and personal estate of any such church, exclusive of the church edifice, parsonage, and school-houses, together with the land on which the same may be erected, and burying-places, shall not exceed the annual value of income of three thousand dollars." (Ibid.)

(7.) "Nothing herein contained shall be held or taken to repeal, alter, or impair the effect of chap. 360 of the laws of 1860." [That law of 1860 prohibited a devise or bequest by a person having a husband, or wife, child, or parent, to any benevolent, charitable, literary, scientific, religious, or missionary society or corporation, in trust or otherwise, of more than one half part of his or her estate, after the payment of his or her debts; and such devise or bequest shall be valid to the extent of one half and no more. (§ 1.)]

(8.) All laws and parts of laws inconsistent with such act were repealed. (§ 2.)

§ 6. The trustees of any church incorporated under this act, are required to exhibit upon oath to the Supreme Court in the judicial district in which such church is situated, and in every three years, an inventory of all the estate, real and personal, belonging to such church, and of the annual income thereof; which inventory shall be filed in the office of the Clerk of the county in which such building is situated. (Ibid. § 3.)

§ 7. Whenever any church incorporated under this act shall be dissolved by reason of any non-user, or neglect to use any of the powers necessary for its preservation, or otherwise, the same may be re-incorporated in the mode prescribed in this act, within six years from the date of such dissolution; and thereupon all the property, real and personal, belonging to such dissolved corporation at the time of its dissolution, shall vest in such new corporation. (Ibid. § 4.)

§ 8. All conveyances to any church incorporated under this act, of any real estate heretofore appropriated to the use of such church or the congregation thereof, or intended so to be, are duly confirmed and declared valid.

In the case of McCaughall *v.* Ryan (27 Barbour's Rep. 376), there was a devise made in 1862, as follows: " I give, devise, and bequeath all the rest and residue of my personal estate, and all my real estate, which I shall own or be possessed of at the time of my death, unto the Right Rev. Bishop Hughes, of the city of New York, in trust for the use and benefit of the Roman Catholic Church of the State of New York."

It was held to be an attempt to create an express trust more extensive than what was permitted by the Revised Statutes, and was void.

CHAPTER X.

THE REFORMED PRESBYTERIAN CHURCH.

§ 1. *Act of* 1860. (1.) The members of the religious society now belonging, or who at any time hereafter shall belong, to the congregation of the Reformed Presbyterian Church, in the city of New York, from and immediately after the passage of this act shall be, and are hereby constituted, a body corporate and politic, in fact and in law by the name, style, and description of "The Consistory of the Reformed Presbyterian Church in the city of New York," and the said consistory shall be the present minister, elders, and deacons of the said congregation, for the time being, and their successors." (Act of March 24, 1860, Laws, chap. 98.)

(2.) They shall, by and in their name aforesaid, have, hold, enjoy and possess all and singular, the rights, liberties, privileges, and powers as trustees, and be subject to the like duties as are mentioned and described in and by the act entitled, "An Act to provide for the Incorporation of Religious Societies," passed April 5, 1813, and to hold property in the manner particularly mentioned in and by the same act; the rents, issues, and profits whereof, shall not annually exceed the whole sum of five thousand dollars. (Ibid.)

(3.) "*Provided*, that they shall not at any time determine or alter the minister's salary, or the annual rent of pews in the church, but that the same shall always be subject to the vote of the congregation, anything in the said act to the contrary notwithstanding." (Ibid.)

§ 2. (1.) The minister or ministers, and elders and deacons, and if during any time there shall be no minister, then the elders and deacons during such time, of every

Reformed Presbyterian church or congregation, elected according to the rules, constitution, and usages of the Reformed Presbyterian Church, now or hereafter to be established within this State, shall be the trustees for such church or congregation. (§ 1 of Act of April 12, 1822, Laws, chap. 187.)

(2.) It shall be lawful for said trustees, if not already incorporated, to assemble together as soon as they shall deem it convenient, and execute, under their hands and seals, a certificate stating the name and title by which they, and their successors in office forever, by a body corporate, by virtue of this act, shall be known and distinguished. (Ibid.)

(3.) Such certificate shall be duly acknowledged or proved in the manner directed by the " Act to provide for the Incorporation of Religious Societies," with regard to the certificates of other religious societies, incorporated under the said act, and shall thereupon be recorded by the Clerk of the County in which such church or congregation is established, in the book by him provided according to the directions of the aforesaid act. (Ibid.)

See, as to the officers who may take the acknowledgment and as to recording in the Register's office, when the church is in the city of New York, *ante*, chap. 4, § 8.

(4.) Such trustees and their successors shall thereupon, by virtue of this act, be a body corporate by the name or title expressed in such certificate, and such trustees and their successors so elected and incorporated by and in such name or title, shall have, hold, possess and enjoy, all and singular, the rights, liberties, powers, and privileges, and be subject to all the duties and limitations of trustees, mentioned and prescribed in and by the act to which this act is supplementary, and may hold property in the manner and to the amount prescribed with regard to religious societies under that act. (Ibid.)

(5.) *Provided*, That they shall not at any time determine or alter the minister's salary, or the annual rent of pews, but that the same shall be always subject to the vote of the congregation, anything in this act, or in the act to which this is snpplemeutary, to the contrary notwithstanding. (Ibid.)

§ 3. (1.) "When any Reformed Presbyterian church or congregation shall, by resolution duly passed at a meeting of such church or congregation, determine that the deacons of such church or congregation shall be the trustees of such church or congregation alone, then it shall be lawful for the deacons of every such church or congregation now or hereafter to be established in this State, to be the trustees of every such church or congregation ; *provided*, that they shall have been elected according to the rules, constitution, and usages of the Reformed Presbyterian Church, and are actually engaged in the exercise of their office in said church or congregation." (§ 1 of Act of April 7, 1866, Laws, chap. 447.)

(2.) " And it shall be lawful for the said trustees, if not already incorporated, to assemble together, and proceed to incorporate themselves in the mode prescribed in and by the act entitled ' An Act for the Incorporation of Religious Societies,' passed April 5, 1813, and an act entitled ' An Act supplementary to an Act entitled " An Act to provide for the Incorporation of Religious Societies, passed April 5, 1813," passed April 12, 1822.' " (Ibid.)

This act of April 12, 1822, is cited, *ante*, § 2.

CHAPTER XI.

THE ASSOCIATE REFORMED CHURCH OF NEW YORK.

§ 1. THE Associate Reformed Church in this country originated in the union of two bodies of Scotch Presbyterians known as the Associate and the Reformed Presbyterian Churches. This union was accomplished in 1782. In 1855 there was a general Synod of the Presbyteries in the Western States, including three particular Synods at the West, and a separate Synod of New York. In that year, the Synod of New York united as a particular Synod with the general Synod of the West. This then became the supreme, judicial, and legislative body of the Associate Reformed Church.

By an act of the legislature of 1836 (p. 776), "the trustees of the Theological Seminary of the Associate Reformed Church," were created a body corporate, and the election of the trustees of such corporation was vested in "The Associate Reformed Synod of New York at their annual meeting."

This Synod was a particular Synod composed of several Presbyteries. Presbyteries consist of all the ministers within a certain district, each accompanied by a ruling elder commissioned by the Sessions.

The Associate Reformed Church was a Presbyterian Church, adhering to a government by ministers of equal grades, and ruling elders chosen by the congregation.

The union which was effected in 1782, was not concurred in by all the members of the two churches. Many preserved a distinct organization as the Associate Church. Negotiations for that purpose resulted in a union of these churches, and the formation of a General Assembly embracing the particular Synods and Presbyteries of the Associate and Associate Reformed Churches.

Upon a *quo warranto*, to test who were properly chosen trustees of the Seminary, it appeared that the relators were chosen by a body of persons undoubtedly members of the church before the last union, but who acceded to it, and the defendants were elected by a body who dissented from such union.

It was held, that plaintiffs had the better title. That such a union as had been effected had not destroyed the church membership, or extinguished the church office in the church which still subsisted. The separate organization was retained. Particular synods were not merged in the united church. (Mr. Justice Emmott in The People *ex rel.* Geam *v.* Farrington, 22 N. Y. Rep. 294.)

The case of The Associate Reformed Church *v.* The Trustees of the Theological Seminary (3 Green's Ch. Rep. of New Jersey, p. 79), was cited and distinguished. The General Synod of the Associate Reformed Church in 1822 formed a union with the General Assembly of the Presbyterian Church, by which it surrendered its separate existence and became merged in the latter body. This involved the transfer to the latter of the library and funds of the seminary which was under its charge, and was not then incorporated. A considerable portion of the Associate Reformed Church refused the connection with the Presbyterian Church, and adhered to their peculiar tenets and distinct organization. They proceeded by bill in the church name against the Princeton Seminary, to which the property had been transferred. The Chancellor held, that the merger in the Presbyterian Church of the majority, did not extinguish the body they had left, if there remained any constituents to continue that body. It was a breach of trust to devote the property which had been given for the supply of the ministry of the Associate Reformed Church to the use of another denomination. (See as to this, in our State, *post,* chap. 22, § 4.)

CHAPTER XII.

THE METHODIST EPISCOPAL CHURCH.

§ 1. THE corporation of the Methodist Episcopal Church in the city of New York, shall be, and are hereby authorized to continue to elect nine trustees of the said corporation, in the same manner as if that number of trustees had originally been named in the certificate of incorporation; and such trustees shall be classed, or continue to be classed, in the manner prescribed by the sixth section of this act. (§ 14 of Act of April 5, 1813, chap. 60.)

§ 2. *Act of April* 5, 1867. By an act of the 5th of April, 1867 (Laws, chap. 265), the presiding elder and a majority of the district stewards, appointed, according to the discipline of the Methodist Episcopal Church, residing in any ecclesiastical district in this State, erected by an annual conference of said Church as a presiding elders district, may make, sign, and acknowledge, before some officer competent to take the acknowledgment of deeds, and file in the office of the Clerk of any county in such district, and a duplicate thereof in the office of Secretary of State, a certificate in writing in which shall be stated the corporate name of such corporation; the names, residences, and official relation to the district of the persons signing such certificate; the number of trustees not less than three, nor more than nine, who shall manage the property and affairs of said corporation for the first year, and their names; and in which certificate it shall be further stated in substance, that the object of such corporation is to secure the benefits of this act. (§ 1 of Act of April 5, 1867, Laws, chap. 265. "An Act to authorize the formation of corporations to secure parsonages and other property for the use of presiding elders of the Methodist Episcopal Church.")

§ 3. When such certificate shall be filed as aforesaid, the persons who shall have made, signed, and acknowledged the same, and their successors, shall be and become a body politic and corporate, by the name stated in such certificate; and such corporation shall have succession, and possess the general powers conferred on corporations by the 18th chapter of the first part of the Revised Statutes of this State; and shall also have power to take by gift, grant or purchase, any estate, real or personal, for the use of, and as a residence for the presiding elder, for the time being, of such district, and his successors in office; and from time to time, to sell and convey the same, and reinvest the proceeds thereof for a like purpose, as the trustees of such corporation, with the approval of the annual conference having jurisdiction over the district, may direct; but the annual income or value of such real and personal estate shall not exceed five thousand dollars.   (Ibid. § 2.)

§ 4. Any real estate heretofore conveyed for the use of, or as a residence for a presiding elder of any such district and his successors in office, may be conveyed by the trustees holding the title thereof, to a corporation formed as aforesaid, for the district in which such estate is situated; whereupon the title thereto shall vest in such corporation, for the purposes defined by this act.   (Ibid. § 3.)

§ 5. The district stewards of any presiding elders district, at their annual meeting, may appoint, from time to time, trustees for any such corporation within their district to supply the places of those whose terms shall expire, and to fill any vacancies in the number of such trustees; and trustees of any such corporation shall respectively hold their offices for one year, and until others are appointed in their places.   (Ibid. § 4.)

In The People *ex rel.* Goffin *v.* Steele and others, trustees (2 Barb. Superior Court Rep. 397), members of three Methodist churches had become incorporated under the General Act, and built a meeting-house and parsonage in 1839.   They were admitted into connection with other churches of the denomination by the presiding elder of the district, and agreeable to their discipline, received from him a preacher. For about eight years they received annually from the Conference a preacher, appointed by the Bishop. In 1847, their preacher, having been suspended by the authorities, the congregation determined to stand by him. They notified the Bishop that they did not desire a preacher to be appointed by him; and. agreed to continue the former as their pastor.

The Bishop appointed the relator to the station. He was refused admittance into the church by the trustees, and a mandamus was issued and return made.

The facts were made out of their professing to be members of the Methodist Church, and subject to its discipline and order. It had no independent organization.

The cardinal rule of the itinerancy of preachers was stated and dwelt upon, and the equally settled rule that the appointment of preachers to the stations vested in the Bishop. The opinion of Judge Edmonds is very full and interesting upon these points.

The question of the propriety of the writ of mandamus in such a case was carefully examined. A peremptory writ was issued in favor of the relator.

CHAPTER XIII.

§ 1. ALL deeds or declarations of trust of real or personal estate, heretofore executed and delivered to any person or persons in trust, or for the use and benefit of any meeting of the Religious Society of Friends, and the trusts thereby created or declared, shall be valid; and the legal estates may be transmitted, and the trusts so created or declared may be continued and pursued so long as may be required for the purposes of the trusts, by conveyances from the trustees appointed by such meeting, and by conveyances by them to others appointed in like manner, or otherwise, according to the direction of such meeting. (§ 1 of Act of April 17, 1839, Laws, chap. 184.)

§ 2. (1.) Trusts of real or personal estate for the benefit of any meeting of the religious Society of Friends may be hereafter created for the use of such meeting, according to the regulations and rules of discipline of said society; and the legal estate of any property so held in trust, shall be vested in the trustees and in those to whom the said property may be conveyed in trust by the appointment of any such meeting, so long as may be required for the objects and purposes of such trusts. (Ibid. § 2.)

(2.) Nothing contained in this act shall be so construed as to impair or diminish the rights of any person, meeting, or association of persons, claiming to be a meeting of the religious Society of Friends, which such person, or meetings, or association of persons, claiming to be a meeting as aforesaid, hold either in law or equity to or in any real or personal estate, held in trust for the use and benefit of any meeting of the said religious society, at the yearly meeting held in the city of New York, in the month of May, in the year of our Lord one thousand eight hundred and twenty-eight. (Ibid.)

(3.) No such real or personal estate shall be held in trust for any meeting of such society, the annual value or income of which shall exceed five thousand dollars. (Ibid.)

CHAPTER XIV.

THE SHAKERS.

§ 1. ALL deeds of trust in relation to real and personal estate executed and delivered prior to the first day of January, 1830, to any person in trust for any united society of the people commonly called Shakers, shall be valid and effectual to vest in the trustees the legal estates and interests to be conveyed by such deeds, to and for the uses and purposes declared therein, or declared by any declaration of trust, executed by such trustees in the same manner and to the same effect, as before the first day of January, 1830.

(2.) And such legal estates and trusts may be continued so long as may be required for the purposes of the trust by conveyances from the trustees named in such deeds, to other trustees appointed by such society, and by conveyances from them to others appointed in like manner. (§ 1 of Act of April 15, 1839, Laws, chap. 174.)

By an Act of April 1849 (chap. 373), the provision contained in subdivision 2 above, was amended so as to read as follows: " And all the legal authority with which the original trustees were vested by virtue of their appointment and conferred powers, shall forever descend in regular succession to their successors in office and trust, who, in conformity to the constitution of said society, have been duly chosen and appointed."

§ 2. (1.) Trusts of real and personal estate for the benefit of any united society of the people called Shakers, may hereafter be created for the use of the members of such society according to the religious constitution of such society, and the legal estates of any property so held in trust, shall be vested in the trustees and in those to whom such property may be transmitted in trust by the appointment of any such society, so long as may be required for the objects and purposes of such trusts. (Ibid., amended by Act of April 10, 1852, chap. 203.)

(2.) " No society shall become beneficially interested in any real or personal property, or acquire any equitable right or interest in any such property, either directly or indirectly, the annual value or income of which after deducting necessary expenses, shall exceed twenty-five thousand dollars, on pain of forfeiture of the privileges conferred by this act." (Ibid.)

In the Act of 1839 it was five thousand dollars.

(3.) " Nor shall any trustee be a trustee of more than one such society at the same time." (Ibid.)

§ 3. " The word ' society ' for the purposes of the preceding section, shall be construed and understood to mean, and includes all persons of the religious belief of the persons called ' Shakers,' resident within the same county." (Ibid. § 3.)

These statutory provisions relative to the Quakers and Shakers are referred to in McCaughall *v.* Ryan, 27 Barbour, 376, to strengthen the argument, that no devises, even for religious purposes, creating trusts not within the provisions as to trusts in the Revised Statutes, are valid. Trusts of real estate for pious and charitable uses, are prohibited by the Revised Statutes.

CHAPTER XV.

INCORPORATIONS GENERALLY UNDER SECTION THREE.

§ 1. *First Election of Trustees.* "It shall be lawful for the male persons of full age, belonging to any other church, congregation, or religious society, now or hereafter to be established in this State, and not already incorporated, to assemble at the church, meeting-house, or other place where they statedly attend for divine worship, and by plurality of voices to elect any number of discreet persons of their church, congregation, or society, not less than three nor exceeding nine in number, as trustees, to take the charge of the estate and property belonging thereto, and to transact all affairs relative to the temporalities thereof." (§ 3 of Act of April 5, 1813, chap. 60.)

The male adults are to assemble, and at the usual place of worship. The phrase "belonging to," is explained more fully in an ensuing section as to voters, *post*, § 4.

§ 2. *Notice of Election.* "The minister of such church, congregation, or society, or in case of his death or absence, one of the elders or deacons, church-wardens or vestrymen thereof, or for want of such officers, any other person being a member or a stated hearer in such church, congregation, or society, shall publicly notify the congregation of the time when, and place where, the said election shall be held, at least fifteen days before the day of election.

(2.) "The said notification shall be given for two successive Sabbaths, or days on which such church, congregation, or society shall statedly meet for public worship, preceding the day of election." (Ibid.)

§ 3. "On the said day of election two of the elders or church-wardens, and if there be no such officers, then two of the members of the said church, congregation, or society, to be nominated by a majority of the members present, shall preside at such election, receive the votes of the electors, be the judges of the qualifications of such electors, and the officers to return the names of the persons who, by plurality of voices, shall be elected to serve as trustees of the said church, congregation, or society." (Ibid.)

If persons answering to the description of elders or church-wardens are present, they must preside, and a nomination and presiding of any others is illegal.

The case of The People *v.* Peck (11 Wendell, 604), establishes this. In that case, the minister had nominated as moderator and clerk, persons not so qualified, persons qualified being present. It was held to be illegal. There was in the case some evidence of a dissent to this course. But I doubt whether the consent of the majority of those present would have been sufficient to justify the choice of any one out of the appointed class of elders, if present; or members, if elders are not present.

It was also held, that the legislature did not mean one of the clergy to preside. Although a minister in the Baptist Church is called an elder, he was not within this clause of the statute.

The fact that the certificate states that the presiding officers were chosen by a plurality of votes, does not negative the fact that they were *nominated* by a majority of the members present, which the statute requires. No objection having been made, it would be presumed, in the absence of evidence to the contrary, that the directions of the act had been observed. (Methodist Church *v.* Picket, 23 Barbour's Rep. 436.)

§ 4. "At such election, every male person of full age, who has statedly worshiped with such church, congregation, or society, and has formerly been considered as belonging thereto, shall be entitled to vote." (§ 3, *ut supra.*)

The choice is decided by a plurality of voices. (Ibid.)

In The People *v.* Tuthill (31 N. Y. Rep. 550), the phrase " stated attendance on divine worship," used in the seventh section, received a judicial construction. It means, regular attendance at the stated times of worship, as established in the church or congregation, as distinguished from irregular or occasional attendance. This attendance must be personal, and cannot be supplied by another. The regular attendance of a wife, or member of his family, is not sufficient. And no amount of contribution can be accepted in lieu of such stated personal attendance. I presume the language used in this section must receive the same construction.

The clause, "and has formerly been considered as belonging thereto," has not been, I believe, judicially interpreted. As no period for the stated attendance on worship is fixed for the first election of trustees, and the conjunction *and* is used, something else is plainly intended. Belonging to the church or congregation, implies, I apprehend, conformity to its doctrines, worship, and discipline. This should be made out satisfactorily to the presiding officers. There might be, for example, a society formed but a month previous, and persons worshiping for the whole period. Yet that would not complete the qualification. Adherence to the tenets and order of the body would amount to belonging to it. Still, a regular attendance on the public services may be deemed presumptive evidence of such belonging or adherence until disputed.

§ 5. " The said returning officers shall immediately thereafter *(after the election),* certify under their hands and seals, the names of the persons elected to serve as trustees for said church, congregation, or society; in which certificate the name or title, by which the said trustees and their successors shall forever thereafter be called and known, shall be particularly mentioned and described." (§ 3, *ut supra.*)

For the form of such certificate, see Appendix.

§ 6. "Said certificate, being proved or acknowledged as above directed, shall be recorded as aforesaid." (Ibid.)

See *ante,* chapter 4, § 8, as to the acknowledgment, proof, place of record, etc. In the city of New York, the Register's office is now the place of recording.

§ 7. "And such trustees and their successors shall thereupon, by virtue of this act, be a body corporate, by the name or title expressed in such certificate." (Ibid.)

The creation of the corporation, therefore, essentially depends upon the sufficiency of the certificate, of its acknowledgment or proof, and its being duly recorded.

The Methodist Episcopal Church *v.* Picket (19 N. Y. Rep. 482), is important upon the subject of the certificate. In that case it merely set forth, that agreeably to a law of the State of New York, of the 5th of April, 1813, the male members of the Methodist Episcopal Church at, etc., agreeably to public notice given, met at, etc., on, etc., at their meeting-house; and by a plurality of votes chose R. J. and O. B. to preside, and then proceeded to the choice of five trustees. On canvassing the votes, it was found, that the following persons were duly elected, namely, Richard Jones, etc. We, the returning officers, do certify that R. J., etc., were legally elected trustees for the Methodist Episcopal Church, in the village of Lyons, agreeably to said statute passed April 5, 1813.

The Court held, in the first place, that to establish a corporation *de facto* against one who had recognized its corporate character by dealing with it, it was sufficient to show the existence of a law authorizing the formation, proceedings taken in professed compliance with such law, and acts of subsequent user.

It held also, that the certificate did substantially conform to the provisions of the statute. The Court adopted the views of the Supreme Court.

§ 8. "The Clerk of every county, for recording every certificate of incorporation by virtue of this act, shall be entitled to seventy-five cents, and no more." (§ 3, *ut supra.*)

It was before shown that in the city of New York, the recording must be done in the Register's office. (*Ante,* chap. 4, § 8.)

§ 9. (1.) "It shall be lawful for any two of such trustees, other than the trustees mentioned in the past section of this act, or their successors, at any time, to call a meeting of such trustees." (§ 5 of Act of April 5, 1813, chap. 60.)

(2.) " A majority of the trustees of any church, congregation, or society mentioned in this act, being lawfully convened, shall be competent to do and perform all matters and things which such trustees are authorized or required to do and perform."   (Ibid.)

(3.) " All questions arising at such meeting shall be determined by a majority of the trustees present; and in case of an equal division, the presiding trustee shall have a casting vote."   (Ibid.)

The trustees are not duly convened unless notice is given to every one of them of the meeting called; or unless a by-law or rule has appointed fixed days for a meeting, of which all are legally bound to take notice. (*Ante*, chap. 4.) When duly convened, there must be a majority of the whole present; and a majority of such majority can decide.

I have not found any provision as to the choice of the presiding trustee.   No doubt the corporation could regulate this matter by a by-law.   If there is none such, the trustees present may choose him.

The direction of these matters is with the members of the church, who could establish rules; and I think the trustees themselves may do so.   (Wilcox on Corporations, p. 42.)

The presiding trustee is not deprived of his regular vote, because of presiding, and I apprehend the clause as to a casting vote may operate to give him a double vote, in the case when the equality is produced by his own regular vote. (See *ante*, chap. 4, § 16.)

The trustees, in order to bind the society by any act in their power to perform, must meet as a board, so that they may have each other's views, and deliberate and decide the questions before them.   The separate action of the trustees individually without consultation, although a majority should agree upon a measure, would not be a lawful act.   (Commeyer *v.* United German Lutheran Churches, 2 Sandf. Ch. Rep. 186.)

§ 10. (1.) *Tenure. — Classes. — Vacancies.*   The trustees first chosen according to the third section of this act, shall continue in office for three years from the day of their election.   (§ 6 of Act of April 5, 1813, Laws, chap. 60.)

(2.) Immediately after their election, the said trustees shall be divided by lot, into three classes, numbered one, two, and three; and the seats of the members of the first class shall be vacated at the expiration of the first year, of the members of the second class at the expiration of the second year, and the members of the third class at the expiration of the third year, to the end that the third part of the whole number of trustees, as nearly as possible, may be annually chosen.   (Ibid.)

(3.) The said trustees, or a majority of them, shall, at least one month before the expiration of the office of any of such trustees, notify the same in writing to the minister; or, in case of his death or absence, to the elders or church-wardens; or, in case there shall be no elders or church-wardens, then to the deacons or vestrymen of any such church, congregation, or society, specifying the names of the trustees whose time will expire.   (Ibid.)

(4.) And the said minister, or, in case of his death or absence, one of the said elders or church-wardens, or deacons or vestrymen, shall, in manner aforesaid, proceed to notify the members of the said church, congregation, or society, of such vacancies, and appoint the time and place for the election of new trustees to fill up the same, which election shall be held at least six days before such vacancies shall happen; and all such subsequent elections shall be held and conducted by the same persons, and in the manner above directed, and the result thereof certified by them; and such certificate shall entitle the persons elected to act as trustees.   (Ibid.)

(5.) And in case any trustee shall die or refuse to act, or remove within the year, notice thereof shall be given by the trustees as aforesaid, and a new election appointed and held, and another trustee be elected in his stead in manner aforesaid.   (Ibid.)

§ 11. *Voters at Subsequent Elections.* (1.) "No person belonging to any church, congregation, or society intended by the third section of this act, shall be entitled to vote at any election succeeding the first, until he shall have been a stated attendant on divine worship, in the said church, congregation, or society, at least one year before such election; and shall have contributed to the support of such church, congregation, or society, according to the usages and customs thereof." (§ 7 of Act of April 5, 1813.)

(2.) The clerk of the said trustees shall keep a register of the names of all such persons as shall desire to become stated hearers in the said church, congregation, or society, and shall therein note the time when such request was made; and the said clerk shall attend all such subsequent elections, in order to test the qualifications of such electors, in case the same should be questioned. (Ibid.)

The case of The People *v.* Tuthill (31 N. Y. Rep. 550), was before referred to (*ante*, § 4), as interpreting the phrase " stated attendance of divine worship." It must be regular personal attendance. That of a wife or other member of the family would not suffice. So it was decided that the contribution prescribed must be according to the usages and customs of the society, which implied that such contributions must be of a vital and substantial character. Contributions, however regular or large, could not give a right to vote without the stated personal attendance.

The register is not conclusive. It does not prevent an inquiry into the qualifications of a person offering to vote. Parol evidence to this point is admissible. It is *prima facie* proof of the right of one registered. (The People *v.* Peck, 11 Wendell, 605.)

§ 12. " Nothing in this act contained shall be construed or taken to give to any trustee of any church, congregation, or society, the power to fix or ascertain any salary to be paid to any minister thereof; but the same shall be ascertained by a majority of persons entitled to elect trustees, at a meeting to be called for that purpose; and such salary, when fixed, shall be ratified by said trustees or a majority of them, by an instrument in writing, under their common seal; which salary shall thereupon be paid by the said trustees out of the revenues of such church, congregation, or society." (§ 8 of Act of April 5, 1813.)

I have before noticed, that this section is not applicable to the Protestant Episcopal Church; but that the vestry fix the salary. I apprehend that it is also inapplicable to the Dutch Reformed Church.

In the case of Erbagh *v.* The German Reformed Church (3 E. D. Smith, 30), the suit was by a minister against the corporation, alleging a call in 1844 at a fixed salary, and rendition of services until January, 1846. That the defendants had executed three bonds to him, two in June, 1845, and one in January, 1846. Before the call, the Chancellor, reversing a decree of the Assistant Vice-Chancellor, had determined that the board of trustees which called the plaintiff was the lawful board of the corporation. A surrender of the temporalities had then been made to such board by the adverse party. Upon an appeal, this decree of the Chancellor was reversed.

It was decided, that the bonds executed before the reversal, for the salary, were valid and binding, and the one made subsequently was not so.

It was also held, that the statute as to fixing the salary was complied with under the following circumstances. Notice of making the call was published from the pulpit, and a meeting for that purpose of the congregation called. At such meeting the call was approved; and was ratified by the trustees on the same day. The call contained the amount of salary to be paid to the minister.

The clause as to payment out of the revenues of the church was noticed. It was considered to be directory, and a neglect to comply with it could not vitiate a contract otherwise valid, and upon which the minister could sue.

In The German Reformed Church *v.* Basche (5 Sandf. Sup. Ct. Rep. 666), a minority of the trustees and other officers, in communicating to the defendant his election, undertook to fix his salary, no vote of the congregation having been taken. It was held void. It was also held, that the salary must be confirmed by the trustees. "It was the right, if not the duty, of the trustees, to withhold their assent, where there was reason to believe that the employment of the individual selected by the majority of the congregation, be he orthodox or not, will destroy the harmony of the church." Lawyer *v.* Cipperly, 7 Paige, 381, was cited.

§ 13. *Increase or Reduction of Trustees.* The ninth section of an act entitled "An Act to provide for the Incorporation of Religious Societies," passed April 5, 1813, is hereby amended so as to read as follows : —

"And be it further enacted, that whenever any religious corporation within this State, other than the chartered corporations, shall deem it necessary, and for the interest of such religious corporation, to reduce, *or to increase,* their number of trustees, it shall and may be lawful for any such religious corporation to reduce, *or to increase,* their number of trustees at any annual meeting; provided that such reduction *or increase,* shall not be such as to leave a less number than three, *or a larger number than nine* trustees, in any one of the said religious corporations; *provided, that a notice of at least two weeks shall be given at a regular meeting of such society, of the time and place of holding any meeting at which such reduction or increase may be proposed.*" (§ 1 of Act of April 6, 1866, Laws, chap. 414.)

The amendments are shown in the passages italicized.

I presume that this section is not applicable to the Protestant Episcopal churches, nor to those of the Dutch Reformed.

§ 14. (1.) "If any church, congregation, or religious society now, or hereafter to be incorporated, according to the provisions of the third section of the act hereby amended, shall neglect or omit, or have neglected or omitted, at their stated annual elections, to choose any one of the three classes of trustees as mentioned in the sixth section of the said act, the said church or congregation, or religious society shall not be deemed or taken to be thereby dissolved; but the trustees then, or now already chosen, shall continue to hold their offices until others be chosen in their stead." (§ 1 of Act of February 15, 1826, Laws, chap. 47.)

This clause introduces the important point of a holding over of old trustees until the choice of new trustees, which was omitted in the sixth section of the Act of 1813. (See, as to this rule, *post*, chapter 16, §§ 15, 16, where the subject is examined at length.)

(2.) " Whenever such neglect or omission shall happen through defect of due notice or otherwise, the trustees of said church, congregation, or society, or a majority of them, shall immediately thereafter give notice thereof in writing to the minister, or in case of his death or absence, to the elders or church-wardens; and in case there shall be no elders or church-wardens, then to the deacons or vestrymen of any such church, congregation, or society." (Ibid.)

(3.) " And the said minister, or in case of his death or absence, one of the said elders or church-wardens, deacons, or vestrymen shall, in the manner prescribed in the third section of the said act, proceed to notify the members of the said church, congregation, or society, of such neglect or omission, and appoint the time and place for the election of new trustees to remedy the same; of which election at least fifteen days' notice shall be given in the manner aforesaid." (Ibid.)

(4.) " The said election shall be held and conducted by the same persons, in the same manner, and the result be certified in like manner, as is prescribed in and by the sixth section of the act hereby amended, and shall have the same force and effect as elections held under and by virtue of said section, and not otherwise." (Ibid.)

There are some decisions under this third section, of a general character, and of great importance.

Thus the case of Petty *v.* Tooker (21 N. Y. Rep. 267), arose under this section, and related to a church originally Congregational, attempted to be changed into a Presbyterian. The action was ejectment to recover the church property.

It was decided, all the judges concurring —

That congregations formed under the third section, have no denominational character, and none can be engrafted on them. The legal character is not affected by the ecclesiastical connection, doctrines, rites, or modes of government of the church formed by the corporators.

That persons, otherwise qualified, do not lose their right as corporators to vote at elections, by reason of their having individually or collectively renounced the doctrine or ecclesiastical government professed and recoguized by the religious body, in whose worship and services the corporate property has been employed.

The title of the trustees to office and control of the property is not impaired by a change as to doctrine or church goverument, on their part, or on the part of those by whom they are elected. They are to determine who shall conduct the religious exercises. The only restraint is the power of the corporators to fix the salary of the person employed.

They have also the power to make such regulations as to the renting and occupation of pews, as to exclude persons holding obnoxious opinions, from becoming attendants upon public worship, and thereby obtaining a right to vote.

In this mode only, or by express condition in a grant of property, can its use be restricted to the support of any particular form of religious belief or ecclesiastical organization.

The comment of Mr. Justice Selden upon the seventh section, requiring a member to be a stated attendant for a year, is, that under it the society has obviously, through its trustees, full power to determine what persons it will thus admit to membership. The trustees can regulate the renting of pews, and could adopt such regulations as that no pew could be rented originally, or assigued to a new occupaut, without a previous consent.

All who had been stated attendants upon the services of the preceding year, were legal voters. Nothing else was required. As they who adhered to the Presbyterian forms and faith were prohibited from voting, the election was void, and no rights were acquired under it.

So in Burnet *v.* The Associate Reformed Church (44 Barbour's Rep. 252), land had been conveyed to trustees in trust to and for the uses and interests of the religious society denominated the Associate Reformed Church, of the town of Seneca, for building a church on said lot, or for a burying-ground. Another deed gave land in trust for the same society by name. And a third deed conveyed other land to the same trustees, "for a parsonage, and nothing else."

It was decided that the trustees held the property for the use of the society, that is, of the corporators entitled to vote at the election of trustees, a majority of whom had control of the property, and decided the ecclesiastical relations, and the character of the doctrines taught from the pulpit.

If a religious society separate from the denomination with which it was before connected, and connect with another, the trustees can call a minister of such other denomination, and exclude all others.

The trust deeds did not make the holding of the property to depend upon adherence to any particular tenets, or form of church government.

See further upon this point, *post*, chapter 23. "The Interposition of Civil Tribunals."

The trustees do not form the corporation. The body of members, those entitled to vote, constitute the corporate body. The trustees are the agents or officers of the corporation in like manner as the directors of a bank or insurance company, clothed with certain powers, derived from statutes, or necessarily incident to powers so conferred. (The People *v.* Fulton, 11 N. Y. Rep. 94.)

CHAPTER XVI.

GENERAL PROVISIONS APPLICABLE TO ALL INCORPORATIONS UNDER ACT OF 1813, AND ITS AMENDMENTS.

§ 1. *Common Seal.* The trustees of every church, congregation, or society hereinbefore mentioned, and their successors, shall have and use a common seal, and may renew and alter the same at their pleasure. (§ 4 of Act of April 5, 1813, chap. 60.)

The common law intended by a seal an impression upon wax or wafer, or some other tenacious substance, capable of being impressed. This remains the general rule of law in this State. (Warren *v.* Lynch, 5 Johns. Rep. 239.) Such law is applicable to deeds and private instruments still. Instruments of a public character with a stamp impressed upon the paper are made valid by special acts.

From the various passages of Scripture cited by Chancellor Kent and others, referred to by Calmet,[1] the conclusion seems to be, that the seal, at least such as was used on letters, as in Esther viii. 10, were raised inscriptions or marks upon clay or metal. Wax was unsuitable to the warm climates of the East.

§ 2. *Power to take the Property.* (1.) The trustees are authorized and empowered to take into their possession and custody all the temporalities belonging to the said church, congregation, or society, whether the same consist of real or personal estate, and whether the same shall have been given, granted, or devised, directly to such church, congregation, or society, or to any other person for their use. (§ 4, *ut supra.*)

(2.) " And (*are authorized and empowered*) to recover, hold,

---

[1] *In verbo,* and see Title *Books.*

and enjoy all the debts, demands, rights and privileges, and all churches, meeting-houses, parsonages, and burying-places, with the appurtenances, and all estates belonging to such church, congregation, or society, in whatever manner the same may have been acquired, or in whose name soever the same may be held, as fully and amply, as if the right or title thereto had originally been vested in the said trustees." (Ibid.)

These clauses of the section relate to property, real or personal, held by the congregation or church, or by some person as trustee or for its use, prior to its incorporation.

In the Act of the 6th of April, 1784, the clause above marked (1), was enacted, with this addition: "And although such gift, grant, or devise, may not have been strictly agreeable to the rigid rules of law, or might, on strict construction, be defeated by the operation of the Statutes of Mortmain."

The fourth section of the general revised Act of March 27, 1801 (Laws 1801, chap. 69), was the same as the section in the act of 1784.

The Chancellor, in The Dutch Church in Garden Street *v.* Mott (7 Paige, 77), cites this provision of the Act of 1801, as authorizing the trustees of that church, incorporated in 1696, to take and hold land given to trustees for the use of the church or congregation in 1691. He considered that after the lapse of 140 years, the legal presumption would be, that a conveyance had been made, but independently of that, this provision of the Act of 1801 (he might have said of 1784) transferred the legal title to the corporation. See also, The Baptist Church *v.* Wetherell, 3 Paige, 298.

The case of Jackson *v.* Hammond (2 Caines' Cases in Error, 33), is undoubted law, so far as it settled that a devise to a secular incorporated body, in trust for the minister of an unincorporated church, was invalid. It is certainly not law in deciding that the fourth section of the Act of 1784 did not cure the objection, if the church became incorporated under that statute. The construction that the section related only to personal property was erroneous. To this,

Justice Duer alludes in the case of Ayres *v.* The Methodist Church, 3 Sandf. Sup. Ct. Rep. 351.

§ 3. *Trustees to Sue and be Sued.*   The trustees may, by their corporate name and title, sue and be sued, in all courts of law and equity.   (§ 4, *ut supra.*)

In the case of The Reformed Dutch Church *v.* Veeder (4 Wendell, 494), a grant had been made to individuals for the use of the church.   It was subsequently incorporated. An action in the corporate name for rent was sustained.

In The People *v.* Fulton (11 N. Y. Rep. 94), it was held, that an action under statute for forcible entry and detainer, could not be supported in the name of the trustees, but must be in the name of the corporation.   The title was in that body, not in the trustees, who were only the agents or officers having control and possession, but not the title.

Religious incorporations, when bringing an action, must show themselves to be incorporated.   But, by statute (2 R. S. 458, § 3), it is not necessary to make this proof on the trial, unless there is a plea of no incorporation in abatement or bar.   This statute seems general, as to all corporations created under any statute of the State.

In the matter of The Methodist Episcopal Church *v.* Ticket (23 Barbour, 486), it was allowed, that when a corporation brings an action, the fact of a legal incorporation must be proven.   The certificate showed an act of incorporation in 1826.   It was proven that certain persons were trustees in 1850; that the society had a place of worship. A subscription paper had been circulated to raise funds to remove the old, and erect a new house.   The defendant had subscribed.   The evidence, it was held, warranted the conclusion, that the society had acted as a corporation since the date of the certificate.

In The Trustees of the Methodist Episcopal Church *v.* Stewart (27 Barbour, 553), it was held, that a trustee could not be sued by his co-trustee as a trespasser, in respect of the property of the society, until he had been divested of his character as trustee.   His possession is that of his co-trustees, and his right equal to that of others.

§ 4. *Authority to purchase and hold Lands.* (1.) "The trustees are also authorized to purchase, take, and hold other real and personal estate, and to demise, lease, and improve the same, for the use of such church, congregation, or society, or for other pious uses, *so as* the whole real and personal estate of any such church, congregation, or society (certain exceptions are specified), shall not exceed the annual value of three thousand dollars." (§ 4 of Act of 1813.)

(2.) It shall be lawful for each and every of the religious incorporations created, or to be created within the city of New York, in pursuance of this act, or of the act hereby amended, to take and hold real and personal estate of the annual value and income of six thousand dollars, anything contained in the fourth section of the act hereby amended, to the contrary notwithstanding. (§ 3 of Act of March 5, 1819, chap. 33.)

(3.) It shall be lawful for every religious corporation created by letters-patent, under the great seal of the Colony of New York, to have, hold, and enjoy lands, tenements, goods and chattels, of the yearly value of three thousand dollars, although the letters-patent by which such corporation was created, shall contain a clause or clauses, restraining and limiting the annual revenue and income of such corporation, to a sum less than the said three thousand dollars. (§ 12 of Act of April 5, 1813, chap. 60.)

Acquisition by Deed. The leading case of Tucker *v.* St. Clement's Church (3 Sandf. Sup. Ct. Rep. 242, affirmed in 4th Selden, 558, n.), was as follows : —

The church was incorporated in 1830, under the first section of the Act of 1813. By a deed dated in 1843, premises in the city of New York (subject to a lease for life) were conveyed to "the Rector, Church-wardens, and Vestrymen of St. Clement's Church," being the corporate name. *Habendum* as follows: "To have and to hold all the above-mentioned and described premises, with the appurtenances, unto the said party of the second part, their successors and assigns forever, upon condition that the rents, issues, and profits of the premises hereby granted and conveyed, and in case the same shall be sold, the interest, income, or dividends of the money for which the same shall be sold, shall be applied by the said parties of the second part to the maintenance and support of the minister for the time being of the said church, and for no other purpose whatsoever."

The Court held, Mr. Justice Duer delivering the opinion, —

That a corporation, if unrestricted by law or charter, has a capacity to take and dispose of real estate, the same as a natural person; and that it was not to be doubted, that it could hold lands as a trustee.

That where the purposes for which it may hold real estate are enumerated in its charter, the maxim *expressio unis est exclusio alterius*, is to be applied, and the specification is construed as a prohibition of all that it does not embrace. It can hold lands for the purposes specified, and for none other.   (Jackson *v.* Hartwell, 18 Johnson's Rep. 422; 1 R. S. 602, §§ 1 and 4.)

The right to take and hold lands was co-extensive with, and for the same purposes as that to demise and lease them; and the trusts were of the same character.   The use specified in the conveyance must be one of the purposes for which the society was incorporated, and to which the trustees might lawfully apply the property if generally conveyed to the corporation.

Within the most strict rules of interpretation, the phrase of the statute, "to take and hold for the use of the church and other pious uses," the support of a minister of the church was plainly within the meaning.

Again it was held, that the power of a religious corporation to hold lands upon a trust of this description was not forbidden by the Revised Statutes as to trusts.   The act for the incorporation of religious societies, far from being repealed, was in fact reënacted in that revision.

This case was affirmed in the Court of Appeals; and I apprehend that nothing in the subsequent cases in that court (Levy *v.* Levy, 33 N. Y. Rep. 97 ; Bascom *v.* Albertson, 34 ibid. 584,) affect this decision.

It may be observed that the learned justice who decided the case of St. Clement's Church gave the opinion in the case of Ayres *v.* The Methodist Church (3 Sandf. Sup. Ct. Rep. 351), the leading case in overturning the old doctrine of charitable uses. He insists, with unanswerable force, that there is no inconsistency between the decisions.

The law as laid down in the case of St. Clement's Church, was recognized in Williams *v.* Williams, 8 N. Y. Rep. 525.

Devises to Incorporations. It is a question which has arisen, and may arise again, in connection with colonial charters, and incorporations under the successive general acts, to what extent and under what circumstances devises to religious corporations were valid. I believe the following propositions can be sustained, and will tend to determine the point in particular cases.

(1.) As matter of history, we are to conclude, that the statute of Elizabeth did not create a new law upon the subject of charitable uses. It created a new and ancillary jurisdiction to execute them. It left the authority of the Court of Chancery over them, as it before existed. It defined what should be deemed charitable uses, and so far guided and controlled the courts.

(2.) The Statutes of Mortmain, which were passed before 1664, were in force in the Colony and State, until the general repealing act of all English statutes, by the Act of the 27th February, 1788.

The clause in the Act of April 6, 1784, before cited, appears to be a legislative recognition of the prevalence of such statutes, or some of them.

The charter to Trinity Church of 1697 gives authority to take and acquire lands of a certain value, the Statute of Mortmain and any other statute to the contrary notwithstanding.

Mr. Justice Duer in The Methodist Church *v.* Ayres (3 Sandf. Sup. Ct. Rep. 351), refers to the clause in the Act of 1784 as establishing the force of such statutes.

Numerous judges in the late cases speak of the general repealing Act of 1788, as repealing the Statutes of Mortmain, thus conceding their prevalence before.

One observation is of much importance: "The alienations in mortmain, before the statute 9 George II., were never made void, so as to let in the grantors or their heirs at law; but a right was given to the mesne Lords, or the King, to seize them as forfeited. Therefore, if they remitted this right, the alienation was good. Dispensations by license to hold in mortmain then arose." (Wilmot's Opinions, p. 2, and the statutes and cases cited in Wright *v.* The Methodist Church, Hoffman's Rep. 253.)

The statute of 9 George II. (1734), the crowning Statute of Mortmain, created a new rule. It is hereafter shown that it was not of force in the colony.

The statutes commencing with Magna Charta (9 Henry III. cap. 36, A. D. 1224), and ending with 23 Henry VIII. cap. 10, 1531, are cited in Burns' Ecclesiastical Law, p. 317, *a.* They were all in force in 1664, and certainly were not inapplicable to our colonial situation and circumstances. The early statutes were directed against ecclesiastical corporations. Chief Justice Wilmot says that the prohibition was extended to all lay and secular corporations as well as religious, by the act of 7 Edward I. cap. 2. (Wright *v.* Trustees, etc., *ut supra.*)

(3.) The Statute of Wills, 32 Henry VIII., a branch of the law of mortmain in one particular, was in force in the colony, until superseded by our Statute of Wills of the 3d of March, 1787. (1 Greenleaf, 385.)

The statute of Henry VIII. — the act of our State of 1787 — the statute in the revision of 1813, and in the previous revisions, — all contained the clause which excepted from the power to devise, a devise to bodies politic and corporate. In the revision of 1830, a change was made, by which a corporation was made incapable of taking by devise, unless expressly authorized by its charter or by statute. (2 R. S. 57, § 3.) The restriction upon the power of the devisor to grant, was changed into an incapacity of the devisee to take, except as provided.

(4.) The statute of 43 Elizabeth is treated as prevailing, by Justice Duer in Ayres *v.* The Methodist Church; by the Court in Andrews *v.* The Bible Society, 4 Sandford, 186; by Justice Comstock in Beekman *v.* Bonser, 23 N. Y. Rep. 307; by Justice Wright in Levy *v.* Levy, 33 N. Y. Rep. 110; and by Justice Porter in Bascom *v.* Albertson, 34 N. Y. Rep. 603.

A careful examination of the opinion of Denio, Justice, in Williams *v.* Williams (4 Selden, 525); of Justice Selden in Owen *v.* The Missionary Society (14 N. Y. Rep. 384), will show that nothing said by these learned judges is hostile to this proposition.

And the true view is, that this statute did not merely create an inquisitorial commission and a new remedy, but legalized a variety of specific charities; defined what should be regarded as charities, and brought such within the jurisdiction of the Court of Chancery. The commission fell into disuse. The charities of the statute were enforced in equity. The law in every particular, except the special mode of enforcement, was applicable to the situation of the colony. The opinion of Chancellor Jones in the Orphan Asylum case (9 Cowen, 437), as to its operation, has stood the test of every examination.

When we examine this famous statute, either as an epitome of the former law, or as defining what it shall be for the future, there is scarcely an object in its enumeration which was not necessary or important to be promoted in the very infancy of a colony. The remedy was local, and even that remedy soon became obsolete in England.

(5.) Another consideration appears to me to be of much force. Many of the statutes of mortmain, prior to that of 9 George II., were particularly directed against gifts in support of Papistical and Romish doctrines. They were in fact offsprings of the Reformation. The statute of 1 Edward VI. cap. 14, respecting Chantries Collegiate, with its noble preamble, is preëminently so. Any conveyance or devise for the support of a priest to continue an *obit* or *anniversary* forever, was declared absolutely void. The Chantries were little chapels or altars in a church, endowed with revenues for the maintenance of a priest to pray for the soul of the founder and deliverance from purgatory. Anniversaries and obits were the offices used on such occasions, the former every day, and the latter at the end of the year.[1]

Under this statute various cases were decided separating the good from the superstitious use. Thus in the Cloth-workers' case (Moore's Rep. 654), there was a devise of land, to give £3 6s. to the poor, a provision for an obit, and the remainder to maintain the edifices and ornaments of the church. Adjudged that the king should not have the land, because where good uses are mixed with an *obit, anniversary, light* or *lamp,* the land is preserved for the good uses, and the gift *for superstition* is nought. See also Comberton's case and Rosse's case, cited Hoffman's Chan. Rep., 250, 251.

Now in the year 1700 the Colonial Assembly passed the severe act against Jesuits and Popish priests before cited. (*Ante,* chap. 9, § 1.) It is reasonable to conclude that if the opinion had not been that such acts as we have noticed were in force, the legislature would have carried out their hostility to the Papists by reënacting them. Manifestly such statutes would be deemed applicable to the situation of a colony, where such hatred of Romish doctrines and observances existed.

(6.) Between the 43 of Elizabeth (1602), and the 9 of George II. (1734), devises for purposes within the first-named act were valid. No point is better settled than this, that the statute of Elizabeth operated as a partial repeal of the exception in the Statute of Wills of Henry VIII. and enabled a devisor to limit and appoint lands for any object enumerated, or within the intendment of the act. (Grant on Corporations, p. 115, and the several cases cited in Wright *v.* The Methodist Church, Hoffman's Ch. Rep. 262.)

(7.) But the act of 9 George II. (1734) prohibited alienations (devises among them) to bodies corporate, or any charge upon land for the benefit of any charitable use, unless by deed executed twelve calendar months before the

---

[1] Burns' *Ecclesiastical Law,* vol. i. p. 58.

death of the donor and grantor, and enrolled in the enroll-
ment office of the Court of Chancery within six months
after its execution. Every gift, etc., not so enrolled was
absolutely void.

This act could be taken advantage of by heirs. One evil
leading to its passage is recited, as being the disinheritance
of heirs.

But the decision of the Master of the Rolls in The Attorney General *v.* Stewart (2 Merivale's Rep. 143), that this
statute did not extend to Granada, or any other colony, seems
to me unanswerable. "In its causes, its objects, its provisions, its qualifications, and its exceptions, it is a law wholly
English ; calculated for purposes of local policy ; complicated
with local establishments ; and incapable, without great
incongruity, of being transferred as it stands, into the code
of any other country."

See also The Mayor of Lyons *v.* The East India Company,
Moore's Privy Council Rep. vol. i. p. 175.

Again, as a general rule, it may be stated, that the colonies of England had the common law for their government,
and such statutes, particularly if amendatory, as were in
force at the time of their being planted, and were not inapplicable to their situation.

And it may be regarded as a rule that statutes subse-
quently passed, did not extend to a colony, particularly after
it has a legislature of its own, unless expressly so declared.
(Kent, vol. i. p. 472; Chalmers' Opinions, vol. i. p. 194;
Smith's History of New York, vol. 1, p. 243 ; Bogardus *v.*
Trinity Church, 4 Paige's Rep. 178.)

I conclude that under the statute of Elizabeth, from the
time that the English acquired the colony in 1664 (with the
slight interval from 1673 to 1674), devises to religious corporations for their proper purposes, were valid, and continued to be so until the passage of the Statute of Wills of
March 3, 1787.

Next, by force of the fourth section in the successive
statutes for incorporating churches, devises made to a
church or congregation previous to its incorporation became
valid, and vested when it became incorporated.

And as to devises after the incorporation of a church, and after the Act of March 3, 1787, to such corporations, they were absolutely void. And this continued to be the law until the Act of 1860, hereafter noticed.

It is fully settled, that the general words in statutes for the incorporation of religious societies, enabling them to take, receive, purchase and acquire, and hold real estate, are not sufficient to authorize the taking by devise so as to repeal the Statute of Wills. (McCartee *v.* The Orphan Asylum, 9 Cowen; Downing *v.* Marshall, 23 N. Y. Rep. 383; s. c. 24 Howard's Pr. Rep. 10.) This rule applies to the same and similar language in royal charters.

Lastly, it must be considered as finally determined, that the law of charitable uses, either as found in the common law, whatever that was, or in the statute of Elizabeth, has no force in the State of New York; clearly none since the Revised Statutes of 1830. All that exists of that law is to be found in special charters, or special or general acts of the legislature. (Levy *v.* Levy, 33 N. Y. Rep. 77; Bascom *v.* Albertson, 34 ibid. 584; Goddard *v.* Pomeroy, 36 Barbour, 540.)

In the case of McCaughall *v.* Ryan (27 Barbour, 376), there was a devise in 1842 of all the testator's real and personal estate, to the Right Rev. Bishop Hughes of the city of New York, in trust for the use and benefit of the Roman Catholic Church of the State of New York. The Bishop, in 1846 and 1850, conveyed the premises, by separate parcels, to the defendants. In 1853, the legislature vested in the plaintiff all the title of the State to the property acquired by escheat.

It was held to be an attempt to create a trust more extensive than the Revised Statutes permitted, and to be void.

Mr. Justice Emmott, dissenting from the views of Mr. Justice Strong in that particular, held, that a corporation sole was not known to our law. The title, Right Rev. Bishop Hughes, was a *descriptio personœ*. If he took at all, he took as trustee upon the trusts of the will. If they were void, the devise must fail altogether. The Roman Catholic

Church in the State of New York, was not a corporation, nor a person in whom the title might vest, passing through the trustee.

The Court concurred in holding that the trusts were against the Revised Statutes, and the will void. The plaintiffs recovered.

And in King *v.* Rundle (15 Barbour, 139), it was decided, that a direction in a will to sell lands and pay over the avails to a corporation for purposes and trusts, which involved a perpetuity, was invalid.

The provision of the Revised Statutes so often referred to is, "that the corporation must be expressly authorized by its charter or by statute to take by devise." The evident meaning is, that in judging of the validity of a devise to a corporation, the intent of the legislature to enable it to take by devise is not to be collected from probable reasoning, but that the necessary authority must be given in terms so clear and positive, as not to admit of any other construction. (Ayres *v.* The Methodist Church, 3 Sandf. Sup. Ct. Rep. 360 ; McCaughall *v.* Ryan, 27 Barbour, 377.)

Act of April 13, 1860. By an act passed April 13, 1860, entitled "An Act relating to Wills" (Laws of 1860, chap. 360), it is provided : "No person having a husband, wife, child, or parent, shall, by his last will or testament, devise or bequeath to any benevolent, charitable, literary, *religious,* or missionary society, association, or corporation, in trust or otherwise, more than one half of his or her estate, after payment of his or her debts ; and such devise or bequest shall be voted to the extent of one half and no more.

"All laws and parts of laws inconsistent with this act are hereby repealed."

This act was modelled upon an act of April 17, 1848, entitled, "An Act for the Incorporation of Benevolent, Charitable, Scientific, and Missionary Societies." (Laws, 1848, chap. 319.) It prohibited, when there was a wife, child, or parent, gifts by devise of more than one quarter of the party's estate. It did include in its enumeration religious societies or corporations. And it also directed, that the devise must have been made two months before the death of the testator.

It may be a question whether, as to the societies named in the Act of 1848, this provision is repealed. The author presumes it is so. But as *religious* societies are for the first time mentioned in the Act of 1860, which does not contain such clause, it cannot be in force as to them.

In Beekman *v.* The People (27 Barbour's Rep. 304), the Act of 1848 was commented upon, and considered as the latest legislation upon the subject of mortmain.

§ 5. *Repairing and Altering.* "The trustees are authorized to repair and alter their meeting-houses, and to erect others if necessary; and to erect dwelling-houses for the use of their ministers, and school-houses, and other buildings for the use of such church, congregation, or society," (§ 4 of Act of April 5, 1813.)

The repairing and altering of churches is thus placed in the hands of the trustees; and no act or assent of the corporators is necessary.

The clause as to erecting other churches if necessary, is very broad. It comprises, of course, the case of a new erection on the same ground, when a former edifice has been destroyed or become decayed. It has been also held, that the trustees have power to remove the church from one lot to another, or from one village to another, without application to the court for permission. (Matter of the Second Baptist Society, 20 Howard Pr. Rep. 324.)

It might seem to warrant the building of additional churches; but as another statute gives the authority to erect chapels, etc., it is needless to resort to this clause for power. (*Post,* chapter 18.)

By the English law, if a church be so much out of repair, that it is necessary to pull it down; or is so little, that it needs to be enlarged, the major part of the parishioners, with the consent of the Ordinary, and meeting upon due notice, may make a rate for new building and enlarging the church. The church-wardens are to take care that public notice be given in the church for a general vestry of the whole parish for that purpose; which notice should be attested and preserved, as the foundation of all the subsequent proceedings. At the time and place, the minister and church-wardens should attend; and when the parishioners are assembled the minister is to preside. He or one of the church-wardens, or such person as shall be appointed by them, ought to enter the orders of the vestry, and then to have them read and signed. Then a petition to the Ordinary is to be made for a faculty. He cites the parties concerned to show cause, and in his discretion grants the faculty. (Burns' Ecc. Law, vol. i. p. 357.)

The erection of dwelling-houses for the use of the minister, and of school-houses, is subservient to the authority to acquire and hold land. It cannot authorize the purchase of land for such purposes beyond the limit prescribed as annual income.

§ 6. *Powers of Trustees.* Such trustees shall have power —

(1.) To make rules and orders for managing the temporal affairs of such church, congregation, or society.

(2.) To dispose of all moneys belonging thereto.

(3.) To regulate and order the renting of the pews in their churches and meeting-houses.

(4.) And the perquisites of the breaking of the ground in the cemetery, or church-yard, and in the said churches and meeting-houses, for burying of the dead.

(5.) And all other matters relating to the temporal concerns and revenues of such church, congregation, or society. (§ 4 of Act of 1813.)

The power to make rules or by-laws for carrying out the objects of a corporation is incident to its creation, without formal words conferring it. (19 Wendell, 37.) But two great rules of law must be observed.

The by-laws must be consistent with the provisions of the charter, and necessary or convenient to carry out the purposes of its creation; and must not be at variance with the law of the land.

A provision of the Revised Statutes of New York expresses the rule. "A corporation has power to make by-laws, not inconsistent with any existing law, for the management of its property, and the regulation of its affairs." (1 R. S. p. 600.)

I cite a few cases exemplifying this power.

In The King *v.* Beton (Burrows' Rep. 2260), the freemen of the town entitled to votes and town privileges, were by charter and settled usage, those entitled by birth, servitude, or election in a certain manner. Full power was given to make by-laws for the good government of the corporation. An ordinance was adopted, that persons might be admitted (not entitled by birth or servitude, or elected in the mode prescribed,) upon payment of the sum of ten pounds, or less under certain circumstances. On *quo warranto* against the mayor and town clerk, it was held, that this by-law was an alteration of the constitution given by the Crown, and void.

In The Commonwealth *v.* Cain (5 Serg. & Rawle, Penn. Rep. 510), the charter of a church corporation authorized the minister, church-wardens, and vestrymen to make rules, by-laws, and ordinances, and transact everything requisite for the good government and support of the church, and directed also, that the election of ministers, etc., should be conducted according to certain rules; one of which was, that no persons were to vote, except those who had been regularly admitted and members of the church for twelve months previous to the election. A by-law, enacting that no member whose pew-rent was in arrear for a longer time than two years should be entitled to vote for officers, was held valid.

In Taylor *v.* Griswold (2 Green's N. Jersey Rep. 223), the Chief Justice said: "The incidental power of making by-laws is limited not only by the terms of the charter, but by the spirit and design of the charter, the purpose for which it was created, the object which the Crown or the Legislature had in view, and the general principles and policy of the common law." A by-law authorizing a vote by proxy, was void without legislative sanction.

See also The Vestry of St. Luke's *v.* Mathews, 4 Dess. Rep. S. C. 578.

By-laws, duly passed under a law of the legislature conferring the power to make them, and properly relating to corporate purposes, have the same force as if they were enacted by the legislature. (McDermott *v.* The Board of Police, 5 Abbott's Rep. 422; Brick Presbyterian Church *v.* The Mayor, etc., 5 Cowen, 388.)

§ 7. *Appointment of Clerk, etc.* " The trustees may appoint a clerk and treasurer of their board, and a collector to collect and receive the said rents and revenues, and may regulate the fees to be allowed to such clerk, treasurer, and collector, and them or either of them may remove at pleasure, and appoint others in their stead. Such clerk shall enter all rules and orders made by such trustees, and payments ordered by them, in a book to be provided by them for such purpose." (§ 4 of Act of 1813.)

In the case of The South Baptist Church *v.* Tracy, April 5, 1842, before the author as Assistant Vice-Chancellor, the defendant was sued as treasurer, for an account, and to compel the surrender of books in his hands. He insisted that he was still the lawful treasurer, not having been legally removed ; and also that he was a creditor. The first question was, whether the resolution of removal had been legally passed. The act authorized a removal at the pleasure of the trustees. The Court thought, that it would be difficult to imagine a case in which that power could be interfered with, however wantonly exercised. The case cited from Hopkins' Rep. 279, treated the power as arbitrary, but did not question its existence.

It was said that the resolution was not legally passed, because two of the trustees were not eligible ; or if eligible, had forfeited their places by leaving the church and connecting themselves with another.

It was held, that under the sixth section, strictly considered, no qualification was prescribed, and one who had never been connected with the church might be chosen. But if this section was to be explained by the third, then it was only necessary to be "a discreet person of the church, congregation, or society." The party had continued to pay for a pew, and occasionally occupied it, though generally he worshiped at another place, and meant at an ensuing day to leave the church altogether. He was considered as not having ceased to be a trustee.

It was held also, that if this was doubtful, yet the certificate of election was, as to such collateral matters, conclusive. (Trustees *v.* Vernon Society, 6 Cowen, 23; All Saints Church *v.* Lovell, 1 Hall's Rep. 198.)

§ 8. *Reduction of Trustees.* Whenever any religious corporation within this State, other than the chartered corporations, shall deem it necessary and for the interest of such religious corporations, to reduce their number of trustees, it shall and may be lawful for any such religious corporation to reduce their number of trustees at any annual meeting. *Provided,* that such reduction shall not be such as to have (*leave*) a less number than three trustees in any one of the said religious corporations. (§ 9 of Act of April 5, 1813.)

It may be doubted whether this provision is applicable to Episcopal churches organized under the first section of the statute. Two wardens and eight vestrymen are the trustees of such a church, and are part of its settled ecclesiastical organization. Neither does it seem applicable to the Dutch Reformed Church and its peculiar system.

The chartered corporations referred to in this section are, no doubt, the corporations which had received charters under the colonial Governors, or by special statutes. The number of trustees, etc., must be governed by the provisions of such charters.

§ 9. (1.) The treasurer of any religious corporation singly, or the trustees, or persons entrusted with the care and management of the temporalities of any church or religious society already incorporated, by virtue of any act of the legislature, or which may hereafter be incorporated in the cities of New York, Albany, or Schenectady, or a majority of them respectively, shall, once in every three years, and between the first day of January and the first day of April, triennially, to be computed from the first day of January last, exhibit upon oath to the Chancellor, or to one of the justices of the Supreme Court, or any of the judges of the Court of Common Pleas, in the county where such church, congregation, or society shall be situated, an account and inventory of all the estate, both real and personal, belonging at the time of making such oath, to the church, congregation, or society, for which they respectively are trustees or managers as aforesaid, together with an account of the annual revenue arising therefrom; and if any such trustees or persons entrusted as aforesaid, shall neglect to exhibit such account and inventory for the space of six years after the expiration of every three years as aforesaid, and shall not then exhibit the same, and procure a certificate to be endorsed thereon by the Chancellor or judge, that he is satisfied that the annual revenue arising from the real and personal estate of such corporation does not, nor has not for the six preceding years, exceeded the sum which by law it is allowed to receive, then such trustees or persons entrusted as aforesaid, shall cease to be a body corporate. (§ 10 of Act of April 5, 1813.)

(2.) In every case where it shall appear from such account and inventory that the annual revenue of any such church, congregation, or religious society in either of the said cities, exceeds the sum which, by virtue of any charter or law, they may or can respectively hold and enjoy, it shall be the duty of the Chancellor, justice, or judge, before whom the same shall be so exhibited, to report the same, together with such account and inventory, to the legislature at their next meeting. (Ibid.)

§ 10. Every corporation of any church, congregation, or religious society heretofore made in pursuance of any law of this State, and in conformity to the directions contained in this act, shall be, and the same is hereby established and confirmed, and such corporation shall be deemed to have commenced from the time of recording such certificate as aforesaid. (§ 13 of Act of April 5, 1813.)

§ 11. In case of the dissolution of any such corporation, or of any corporation hereafter to be formed in pursuance of this act, by reason of a non-compliance with the directions herein contained, the same may be re-incorporated in the manner prescribed in this act, at any time within six years after such dissolution; and thereupon all the estate, real and personal, formerly belonging to the same, shall vest in such corporation, as if the same had not been dissolved. *Provided*, that in such case the said account and inventory required to be exhibited by such corporation, in the cities of New York, Albany, and Schenectady, shall be exhibited within one month after such re-incorporation, and triennially thereafter as above directed.   (Ibid.)

§ 12. *Certain Neglects no Dissolution.*   No religious corporation shall be deemed to be dissolved for any neglect hitherto to exhibit an account or inventory of its real or personal estate and the annual income thereof, or for having held, or hereafter holding, elections of church officers on days before or after any movable feast observed by such church, the intervening time between such elections being more than a solar year.   *Provided*, that such account or inventory shall be exhibited within two years after the passing of this act, and that previous public notice be given to the congregation of the time and place for holding such elections.   (Ibid. § 15.)

§ 13. Whenever any religious corporation shall be dissolved by reason of any non-user or neglect to exercise any of the powers necessary for its preservation, it shall be lawful for the religious society which was connected with such corporation to re-incorporate itself in the mode prescribed by this act; and that thereupon all the real and personal property which did belong to such dissolved corporation at the time of its dissolution, shall vest in such new corporation for the said society.   (Ibid. § 16.)

§ 14. Whenever there shall have been any omission or neglect of any church, congregation, or religious society, at their stated annual meetings, to choose any of the trustees, church-wardens, vestrymen, or other officers, according to the provisions of the act hereby amended, such church, congregation, or religious society shall not be deemed or taken to have been thereby dissolved; but the trustees, church-wardens, vestrymen, or other officers, then in office at the time of such omission, shall be deemed and taken to be the legal officers of such church, congregation, or society. *Provided*, that elections to supply such omissions shall be made within one year after the passing of this act. (§ 2 of Act of February 15, 1826, chap. 47.) See next section.

§ 15. *Omission to Elect.* Whenever there shall have been any omission or neglect of any church, congregation, or religious society, at their stated annual meeting, to choose any of the trustees, church-wardens, vestrymen, or other officers, such church, congregation, or religious society shall not be deemed or taken to have been thereby dissolved; but the trustees, church-wardens, vestrymen, or other officers, in office at the time of such omission, shall be deemed and taken to be the legal officers of such church, congregation, or society, and shall continue to hold their offices until others be chosen in their stead. *Provided*, that elections to supply such omissions shall be made within one year after their occurrence respectively, or within one year after the passage of this act. (§ 3 of Act of 1844, chap. 158. " An Act to amend an Act entitled, ' An Act to provide for the Incorporation of Religious Societies,' passed April 5, 1813.")

§ 16. No church or religious society now incorporated shall be deemed dissolved, nor shall any of its rights or privileges be impaired or affected by reason of the trustees, or other persons entrusted with the management of its temporalities, having omitted to exhibit an account and inventory of the real and personal estate belonging to such church or society, or of the annual revenue or income arising therefrom. And any forfeiture incurred by reason of any such omission is hereby waived and discharged; and no such account or inventory shall hereafter be required from any incorporated church or religious society, unless the annual income of its property shall exceed six thousand dollars. (§ 1 of Act of March 30, 1850, chap. 122.)

The subject of a dissolution of a corporation under the preceding sections presents several points, some of difficulty.

Suppose the case of an election wholly omitted on the appointed day, and none held within the ensuing year, is the corporation *de facto* dissolved, so that it could be taken advantage of collaterally; so that a deed to it by its corporate name would not take effect.

There is a class of cases holding that certain acts of omission, misuser, or abuse of powers and franchises furnish grounds for a judicial declaration of forfeiture and dissolution, but do not of themselves produce such effect.

Thus in Kondon *v.* Vanmore (12 Modern, 274), a charter was granted upon a condition which the corporation neglected to perform, to the public inconvenience. It was held, that it could be repealed by *scire facias*.

So in The King *v.* Pasmore, 3 T. R. 242, an abuse of the powers of the corporation justified a repeal of the charter by *scire facias*, which was declared to be the only way of taking advantage of it.

In our own courts, the cases of The People *v.* Runkle, (9 John. Rep. 147); The Attorney-General *v.* The Bank of Niagara (Hopkins' Rep. 301); Slee *v.* Bloom (5 Johns. Ch. Rep. 379); and The Trustees of Vernon *v.* Hills (6 Cowen, 23), are leading cases. They establish the general rule, that for mis-user or non-user of franchises, there must be a judgment of forfeiture.

Still, where the language of a statute is, that upon the omission of an act prescribed, the corporation " shall be deemed dissolved," or " shall cease to be," or " shall not be deemed dissolved," provided an act is done within a certain time, it does not seem certain that these authorities apply. And particularly is the doubt increased if the neglect is of an act essential to keep up the corporate existence.

In The Corporation of Bunbury (10 Modern, 346), the Court say : " If a Mayor be not chosen at the time prescribed by the charter, and there be no provision for the old

Mayor continuing on until a new one is chosen, the corporation is dissolved, and cannot proceed to a new election."

In Phillips *v.* Wickham (1 Paige's Rep. 590), the Chancellor held, that if a corporation consists of several integral parts, and some of those are gone, and the remaining parts have no power to supply the deficiency, the corporation is dissolved.

If the corporators have the power in themselves to supply the deficiency in their body, their rights are not extinguished, but only dormant. If, however, that power is gone, and they cannot act until the deficiency is supplied, the corporation is dissolved. In the language of Lord Macclesfield, "this is not a forfeiture by non-user, but is a consequence of law. The corporation is dead, and not barely asleep."

It may be argued, that the power of self-continuance is a common law attribute of a corporation, and while there are corporators, the power of choosing officers resides in them. But when the legislature fixes a time for an election, and specially extends that time with a provision that the corporation shall not be deemed dissolved, if an election is had within the extended time, the inference is very strong, that it will be dissolved if wholly neglected beyond such time.

The provisions of the Act of 1844 (*ante,* § 15), contemplate, by the most natural version, an omission to choose any of the trustees, etc., — an omission to hold an election. But I apprehend that this is not the only case provided for. If there should be a tie vote upon a whole ticket, the election would fail. There would be an omission to choose, and the former trustees would hold over until an actual election had within a year. In the case of St. Philip's Church, April, 1863, such a state of facts occurred, and the above was the conclusion of Mr. Dunscomb and the author.

Another case may occur. The choice may be perfect as to a certain number of trustees. Suppose five vestrymen were duly chosen, and three not. There would be an omission to choose some trustees. The language is, " An omission to choose any of the trustees, vestrymen, etc." The statute in its terms seems to include such a case.

But here some distinctions naturally arise. If, in the case supposed, the five persons chosen were former trustees, (vestrymen, for example, reëlected), the remaining three of the old vestrymen hold over until an election within the year. And so if a lesser number chosen were former members. But suppose five or a lesser number duly chosen are new members, how is it to be determined which of the old members hold over, so as to form the board or vestry, and legally to exercise the powers ?

The fixed number of trustees should be kept up to preserve the corporation in its integrity. There ought not to be less than the prescribed number, although a less number may act. The advantage of the judgment of all is contemplated. There cannot lawfully be more than the defined number.

If, then, some new members are elected, but there is no election as to the residue, the election, I apprehend, wholly fails. There is an omission to elect the whole body, and no mode of selecting some of the former to unite with the new members is provided. There must be a new entire election, and all the old trustees hold over.

The same line of reasoning applies, if some of the old members are rechosen, some new ones are elected, but a failure to elect the full number. It is impossible to say who of the old members are to be retained to complete the body.

§ 17. *Change of Day of Elections.* It shall be lawful for the members of any church, congregation, or society, qualified to vote for trustees, wardens, or vestrymen, or a majority of them, at any stated annual meeting of the said members, to appoint and fix any day in the ensuing year as the day on which the election of officers of such church, congregation, or society, shall be had ; and the elections held on that day shall be as valid to all intents and purposes, as if the same had been made on the day formerly appointed for that purpose.

And in case elections shall not be held on the day so appointed, it shall be the duty of the trustees, church-wardens, or vestrymen, then in office, to give the notice prescribed in the first section of this act, and to proceed according to the provisions thereof, to an election to supply all vacancies then existing.   (§ 3 of Act of February 15, 1826, chap. 47.)

The first section of this Act of 1826 is cited *ante*, chapter 15, § 14.

§ 18. *Change of Name.*   (1.) Any religious corporation incorporated under the laws of this State, may make the application for a change in its corporate name in the manner provided in the act entitled, " An Act to authorize Persons to change their names," passed December 14, 1847, which application shall be made to any of the officers designated in the first section of the said act within the county in which said corporation was so originally incorporated, and is to be located, and upon such proceedings, may obtain an order authorizing the assumption by such corporation of a new name, and upon fully complying with the requirements of the said act, shall be known by such new and assumed name, and by no other. (§ 1 of Act of June 4, 1853, chap. 323. " An Act to authorize Religious Corporations to change their names.")

(2.) The officer to whom such application shall be made shall also be authorized to grant an order allowing any such religious corporation to assume such other and new name, not previously assumed by any other existing religious corporation, on being satisfied by the petition presented to him therefor, verified by oath or affidavit, that the name of such corporation, by reason of the change of its location or place of worship, or of the name of the place in which its place of worship is situated, or any other change in the circumstances with reference to which its name was adopted, has become incongruous or inconvenient, or that the location or character of such corporation will be more correctly or effectually designated by such change of name." (Ibid. § 2.)

The Act of December 14, 1847, referred to in the above cited act, is chapter 463 of the laws of that year.

The officers to whom the application is to be made are, the county judge of the county in which the applicant resides, or a justice of the Supreme Court residing in such county, or in the city of New York, to a justice of the Supreme Court residing therein, or any justice of the Superior Court, or a judge of the Court of Common Pleas in such city.   (§ 1 of the Act of December 14, 1847.)

The application must be by petition, setting forth the grounds for the desired change, and be verified by affidavit annexed to or endorsed thereon.   It is presumed that the affidavit of one of the officers will be sufficient.

In the case of The Church of the Atonement, December, 1866, an opinion was given under this statute to the following effect: —

An attempt had been made to incorporate the church by the name of The Milnor Memorial Church of the City of New York, in November, 1865.   But the certificate had been recorded in the clerk's office of the city of New York, instead of the register's office.   There was no corporation created.   Recording in the wrong office was the same as not recording at all.

Proceedings had been taken, and an order obtained, to change the name to that of The Church of the Atonement. But the Act of 1853, authorizing a change of name, required that the new name should be one not previously assumed by any other existing religious corporation.   There had been a church incorporated with the same title in 1860. It had not in fact acted since 1862.   But it was considered that this fact of non-user did not render the corporation extinct, but there must be a judicial declaration of forfeiture. (Kent's Comm. vol. ii. p. 312, Marginal; Wilcox on Corporations, § 807 ; Attorney-General *v.* Bank of Niagara, Hopkins' Rep. 361 ; Trustees of Vernon *v.* Hills, 6 Cowen, 23.) The provisions of the Code, §§ 430, 431, were founded upon this principle.

As there was no valid incorporation originally, from the nullity of the record, the proceedings and order to change the name were also null.   They were also void because of the existence of a corporation with the same name.

The suggestion was made that the members select some new title, and proceed to incorporate themselves anew, as if nothing had taken place. Strong reasons existed against their retaining the first name. These reasons had induced the change.

§ 19. *Sale of Real Estate.* "It shall be lawful for the Chancellor of this State, upon the application of any religious corporation, in case he shall deem it proper, to make an order for the sale of any real estate belonging to such corporation, and to direct the application of the moneys arising therefrom by the said corporation, to such uses as the same corporation, with the consent and approbation of the Chancellor, shall conceive to be most for the interest of the society to which the real estate so sold did belong. *Provided*, that this act shall not extend to any of the lands granted by this State for the support of the gospel." (§ 11 of Act of April 5, 1813.)

This provision is found for the first time in the Act of March, 1806. (4 Webster and Skinner, 360.)

The Supreme Court, since the amendment of the Constitution in 1846, had succeeded to this power of the Chancellor, and it is exercised by one of the judges.

By the 30th section of the Code, as amended in 1851, jurisdiction is vested in the county courts, as to the sale or mortgaging of real property of a religious corporation situate within the county, and of the disposition of the proceeds thereof.

It is recommended in the present state of the law, not to apply to the Court of Common Pleas in the city of New York, as a county court within this provision of the Code.

A question has arisen whether this provision is really a restriction upon an otherwise absolute power of alienation, appurtenant by the common law to a corporation, or whether it is a relaxation of statutory restraints upon such alienation. In DeRuyter *v.* The Trustees of St. Peter's Church (3 Barb. Ch. Rep. 222), Chancellor Walworth thought the statutes of England restricting alienations by ecclesiastical corporations were in force here, and only alienations by leases for three lives or twenty-one years could be made until the Act of 1806.

The language of that act is *almost* precisely the same as that of the present act.

But notwithstanding the high authority of the Chancellor, this proposition may be doubted. It may be questioned whether such laws were applicable to our situation. The want of a bishop to give a license is an argument against their prevalence. The general professional opinion has been, that the provision is really a restriction upon the absolute common-law right of alienation.

In that case, there had been a special Act of 1817, incorporating St. Peter's Church, in the city of New York, and the right of selling was conferred in nearly the identical terms used in the General Act.

It deserves notice also, that many special statutes were passed before 1806, authorizing religious corporations to sell their real estate. (See Act of 1803, chaps. 66, 67; of 1804, chap. 52 and chap. 53.)

In Wyatt *v.* Benson (23 Barbour's Rep. 327), it was held, that the application for the approval of the Court of a sale of real estate could only be made by the corporation. The legally elected trustees had no power to institute or carry on proceedings for this purpose without the consent of the majority of the corporators.

The corporation is composed of every member of the congregation qualified to vote. The control of the temporal affairs was intended to be placed in the hands of the majority of the corporators.

An order of sale, made on the petition of the trustees, if not executed, may be revoked by the Court. It is its duty to do so when a sale is against the views of a large majority of the members.

The question of the propriety or expediency of a sale, cannot be submitted to an arbitrator, nor to any other tribunal or body than the Court.

Nor are corporators bound by the decision of an arbitrator as to who are legally elected trustees.

The case arose under the third section. All the reasoning of the Court is founded upon the language used in it and on some special clauses concerning the particular church, as the 11th and 14th sections of the act. It was the case of a Methodist Episcopal Church.

In the matter of St. Ann's Church (14 Abbott, 424), it was held at Special Term (Emmott, Justice), that the vestry or trustees of a church may apply to the Court to be allowed to sell or mortgage its real property, without an express vote of the congregation. They represent the corporation, are its managing agents, and may act as fully as the directors or agents of an ordinary corporation may act on its behalf. This was the case of an Episcopal Church.

In the Baptist Society of Canaan (20 Howard's Pr. Rep. 324), it was also held, that the trustees could make the application. These cases are referred to and approved in The Madison Avenue Baptist Church v. The Baptist Church in Oliver Street (Abbott's Rep. vol. i. new series, p. 214).

In the case of Bowen v. The Irish Presbyterian Church (6 Bosworth's Rep. 245), it was held, that a religious corporation has power to make an executory contract to sell real estate subject to the action of the Supreme Court, to be conveyed when the authority of the Court was obtained. If such authority is obtained, on due petition for that purpose, the contract will be binding upon the corporation, without further ratification by it.

It is not essential that an order be obtained before an agreement is made. Its confirmation by the Court is sufficient.

In making a sale of real estate, the corporation does not act in a ministerial capacity only, executing merely the mandate of the Court.

The fee was vested in the corporation, not in the trustees as trustees.

It is indispensable to obtain an order sanctioning a sale, but such order is permissive, not mandatory. It does not compel the corporation to sell.

It is the preferable mode of conducting a sale, *first*, to

negotiate and agree upon the terms, and then to lay the agreement before the Court and obtain its approval, an authority by order to convey, and directions as to the application of the purchase-money.

The production of an instrument under the corporate seal, and signed by the proper officers, is *primâ facie* evidence of its due execution by the body, and raises a presumption that it was duly authorized by the competent power.

When the rights of the purchaser have become so far fixed, that he holds an agreement duly executed by the corporation, and the sanction of the Court has been obtained, he can be compelled to pay for the land, and his title to a conveyance is clear, unless and until by some proceeding to which he is a party, that sanction, if it be revocable, is revoked.

In Lovett *v.* The German Reformed Church (12 Barb. Rep. 67), the trustees who had been recognized by the Chancellor as the legal trustees while his decree stood unreversed, executed a mortgage upon property of the church with the approbation of the Chancellor. The decree was afterwards reversed, and the adverse set of trustees held to be the legal trustees. The mortgage was however sustained. They were trustees *de facto*, and their dealings with third persons for a valuable consideration were valid.

The case of The Madison Avenue Baptist Church *v.* The Baptist Church in Oliver Street (1 Abbott's Rep., new series, p. 214), involved some important questions.

The action was to recover possession of a parcel of ground in Madison Avenue. The plaintiffs had erected a church edifice on the ground and occupied it as a place of worship. In 1862 proceedings took place for a union of the congregation of this church with that of the congregation known as the Baptist Church in Oliver Street. By the terms of union, the Madison Avenue Church was to convey its real and personal property to the Oliver Street Church, the members of the former to become members of the latter, the services to be held in the Madison Avenue Church. The trustees of the Oliver Street Church were to resign, and an election to be held by the united congregations. Measures were to be taken to change the name to that of the Madison Avenue Baptist Church. The real and personal property of both churches was to be liable for the debts of both.

A petition was presented by the trustees of the Madison Avenue Baptist Church to the Supreme Court, setting forth this agreement, and stating the inability of the church to pay their liabilities, or meet their expenses. It stated the plan and terms agreed upon by a joint committee of both churches, and that at a meeting of the congregation of the Madison Avenue Baptist Church duly convened, the plan was approved, and the trustees authorized to petition the Court for an order sanctioning the conveyance as agreed upon; also that the report had been adopted by the congregation of the Oliver Street Church.

The petition also stated that the latter church owned property to the amount of from fifty thousand to sixty-five thousand dollars over its indebtedness, which would be applicable to the indebtedness of the Madison Avenue Church. That a portion of the pew-holders had consented to the transfer of the property, and the residue were in favor of the union.

Upon this petition an order was made authorizing and directing the trustees of the Madison Avenue Baptist Church to convey the property to the Baptist Church in Oliver Street.

On the trial a deed for the property was offered in evidence, also the fact of the union of the two congregations in public worship; the petition and order for the change of the corporate name of the Oliver Street Church to that of the Madison Avenue Baptist Church. The judge rejected the evidence and rendered judgment for the plaintiffs.

On appeal to the General Term, it was held —

(1.) That the Supreme Court had the power to make an order for such a conveyance upon the considerations expressed and moving it.

(2.) That the application for the order by the trustees was warranted by the direction given by the corporators, and was the same as if the members had signed the petition. The cases holding that the trustees could apply without a previous vote of the corporators were cited, and without disapproval. Any opposition on the part of corporators would be attended to.

(3.) It was unnecessary for the order to direct the application of the money arising from the sale. The consideration of the conveyance was the agreement to assume the plaintiff's debts, to unite in forming one church organization, to adopt the plaintiff's corporate name, to sell their own property, etc.

That in Wheaton *v.* Gates, Judge Denio had held, that the Court had no authority to originate any scheme, or to execute any enterprise determined on by the corporation, but only to allow or disallow the application of the moneys to such purposes as the corporation should represent to be most for the benefit of the society. Besides, the order for a sale might be made separately from the order directing the application of the proceeds, citing The Matter of the Presbyterian Church, 3 Edw. Rep. 155.

(4.) That the objection that the transaction had produced a dissolution of the plaintiff's corporation, and not a continuance of it for the purposes of its organization, was not tenable.

A new trial being ordered, upon that trial testimony was adduced to the point of the amount of debt, and other matters of fact not necessary to be noticed.

One ruling of the judge recognized a well-settled and important point of law. At the meeting which ratified the agreement for a union, etc., only twenty corporators were present, far less than a majority, and it was insisted that a majority must be present. But the Court held, that where the corporators are of an undefined number, such as may assemble upon a regular call of all, will constitute a quorum for the transaction of business; and a majority of such quorum can pass a resolution, or take other action.

Wheaton *v.* Gates, which is referred to in the foregoing case, is reported 18 N. Y. Rep. 395. It was decided, that the Court could make a provisional order giving liberty to the corporation to sell its real estate for a certain price, and for a legitimate purpose. But it had no power to authorize a sale for the purpose of closing up the society, and distributing the proceeds of the property among the corporators.

Mortgages. Chancellor Kent considered, that although the statutes spoke of *sales* of real estate only, yet that a mortgage being a conditional sale in substance, was within it. Applications and orders for leave to mortgage have been numerous. One, before so eminent a lawyer as Chancellor Jones, was within the author's personal knowledge.

In The South Baptist Society *v.* Clapp (18 Barbour's Rep. 35), it was noted, that the execution of a mortgage upon taking a conveyance of land, to secure part of the purchase-money, did not need the assent of a judge. The trustees could execute it. The statute was only applicable when the church was owner of the real estate.

In the case of St. Peter's Church (3 Barbour's Ch. Rep. 122), the corporation having become insolvent, owing a large sum besides the mortgages on their property, conveyed it to trustees, the appellants, for payment of its debts ratably. After a full examination, and a change of his opinion expressed at a prior stage of the case, the Chancellor held the conveyance to be legal and operative. The decision was affirmed in the Court of Appeals. (3 Comstock's Rep. p. 238.)

In Manning *v.* The Moscow Presbyterian Society (27 Barbour, 52), it was held, that a corporation could mortgage its property to secure payment of a debt created by advances for its use, without an order of the Court. A mortgage was not a sale, either in the ordinary or strict legal sense.

But with respect, this seems a very doubtful point, and is certainly a dangerous rule. The term sale, used in a statute of the date of 1806, conveys the idea of a transfer of title. This was the original theory of a mortgage in the law. The mortgagee could take possession. The owner of the equity of redemption, after forfeiture, could not maintain ejectment against the mortgagee or any one holding under him. He had only the right to redeem in equity. So formerly the mortgagee could bring an ejectment, though this is now prohibited by the Revised Statutes. (Pell *v.* Ulmar, 18 N. Y. Rep. 112.)

If the decision in this case of Manning is correct, then almost every guard against alienation and perversion is lost. The mortgage for a debt, one preferred for example, among many, involves the power to sell, which may soon be necessary, and divert the property to other uses. Our courts hold, that a sale shall not be authorized except for the attainment of the identical or similar religious purposes for which the property was originally acquired, and to which it was consecrated. This object will be effectually defeated. It is surely enough to allow a conveyance in a case of entire insolvency, for the proportionate discharge of every debt.

CHAPTER XVII.

CHAPELS, ASSOCIATE CHURCHES, ETC.

§ 1. The second section of the act entitled " An Act to amend the Act entitled ' An Act to provide for the Incorporation of Religious Societies,' passed April 5, 1813, and the several acts amendatory thereof," passed March 30, 1850, is hereby amended to read as follows : —

(1.) *Chapels, etc.* " Whenever any religious corporation, incorporated under the act to provide for the Incorporation of Religious Societies, passed April 5, 1813, or by any special charter, shall deem it necessary or expedient for the accommodation of its members, in consequence of their number, or dispersed habitations, or otherwise, to increase the facilities of public worship, the vestry or trustees thereof may purchase and hold grounds in the same village, town or city, and may erect thereon suitable associate houses, or churches, or convenient chapels.

(2.) *School-houses.* And also, at the same time or thereafter, may purchase and hold other grounds for the purpose and erecting thereon suitable school-houses for Sunday or parochial schools, for the said associate meeting-houses or churches or chapels ; or may hire and purchase and hold any such grounds with suitable buildings already erected thereon, for the like purpose, notwithstanding any restriction contained in the said act, or in any such charter.

(3.) And the persons statedly worshiping in any such associate meeting-house or church, or in said chapel, may, with the consent of the vestry or trustees of such corporation, be separately organized and incorporated. (§ 1 of Act of March 30, 1850, as amended by Act of April 10, 1860, chap. 235.)

§ 2. (1.) Any religious corporations incorporated under the several acts to provide for the Incorporation of Religious Societies, passed April 6, 1784, March 27, 1801, April 5, 1813, or by any special charter made or granted before or after July 4, 1776, may purchase and hold grounds in the same village, town, or city, in which the church edifice belonging to such corporation is situated, for the purpose of erecting, and may erect and maintain thereon free churches or chapels.

(2.) *School-houses.* — *Residences.* And also, at the same time or thereafter, may purchase and hold other grounds for the purposes of erecting, and may erect and maintain thereon suitable school-houses, for Sunday or parochial schools, of the said free churches or chapels; and residences for the clergy and teachers in charge of or employed in such churches, chapels, or schools.

(3.) *Mission Houses.* — *Hospitals.* And also mission-houses for the temporary accommodation and relief of the poor, and free hospitals and asylums for the relief of the sick, aged, and indigent, and dispensaries of medicine for the poor.

(4.) Or may hire and purchase and hold any such grounds with suitable buildings already erected thereon, for the like purposes, notwithstanding any restrictions contained in the said act, or in any such charter.

(5.) *Control of such Chapels, etc.* And the vestry or trustees of such religious corporation may take the control and management of such free churches or chapels, schools, or mission-houses, asylums, dispensaries, and hospitals, and may appoint and employ clergymen, teachers, and others, officers, or persons to take the charge and management thereof. (§ 1 of Act of April 23, 1867, Laws, chap. 634. An Act to authorize the Erection of Free Churches and Chapels in certain cases.)

§ 3. The seats and pews in every church or chapel, erected by any religious corporation under the provisions of this act, shall be forever free for occupation and use during public worship, to all persons conducting themselves with propriety, and under such rules as may be established therefor by the parent church; and no rent charge, or exaction shall ever be made or demanded for such occupation or use. (Ibid. § 2.)

§ 4. Persons attending public worship in such churches or chapels, or otherwise claiming in any manner to be connected therewith, shall not, by reason of such attendance or claim of any kind, be entitled to vote at the annual elections for church-wardens or vestrymen or trustees, of the religious corporation by which such churches or chapels shall have been erected and maintained; and shall not have any right, claim, or demand, as corporators in said parent church. (Ibid. § 3.)

Chapels erected under the Act of 1860, (cited *ante*, § 1,) are substantially the chapels of ease of the English law. (See *ante*, chapter 2.) They may be free, or with purchased and hired pews, as the vestry shall decide. And they may be separately organized and incorporated, with the assent of the vestry or trustees. Then, of course, all connection with the parent church ceases.

The chapels so formed under the Act of 1867 must be upon the free principle. They are governed by the vestry or trustees. But by express provision, the members or worshipers are excluded from voting, or exercising any rights as corporators in the parent church.

CHAPTER XVIII.

FREE CHURCHES.

§ 1. (1.) Any seven or more persons of full age, citizens of the United States, and a majority of them being residents of this State, who shall associate themselves for the purpose of founding and continuing one or more free churches, may make, sign, and acknowledge, before any officer authorized to take the acknowledgment of deeds of land to be recorded in this State, and may file in the office of the Secretary of State, and also of the Clerk of the county in which any such church is to be established, a certificate in writing, in which shall be stated the name or title by which such society shall be known in the law, the purpose of its organization, and the names of seven trustees, of whom not less than five shall be persons not ministers of the gospel or priests of any denomination, to manage the same.

(2.) Such certificate shall not be filed unless with the written consent and approbation of a justice of the Supreme Court of the district in which any such church shall be intended to be established, or in the city of New York, of a judge of the Superior Court of the said city, to be endorsed on such certificate. (§ 1 of Act of April 13, 1854, Laws, chap. 218. " An Act for the Incorporation of Societies to establish Free Churches.")

§ 2. Upon the filing of such certificate, the persons named therein and their successors, being citizens of the United States, and residents of this State, shall be a body politic and corporate, with all the rights, powers, and duties, and subject to all the restrictions and obligations, and other provisions, so far as the same may be applicable, and consistent with this act, specified and contained in the act entitled,

"An Act for the Incorporation of Benevolent, Charitable, Scientific, and Missionary Societies," passed April 12, 1848, and the act amending the same passed April 7, 1849, except that the limitation in the first of said acts of the value of the real estate that may be held by any society in the city or county of New York, incorporated under this act, shall not be applicable to any church edifice erected or owned by such society, or the lot of ground on which the same may be built, and except that the provision in the first of the said acts, in relation to the personal liability of the trustees, shall be applicable only to the trustees who have assented to the creation of any debt. (Ibid. § 2.)

§ 3. Any vacancies occurring in the said board of trustees shall be supplied by the remaining trustees, at any legal meeting of the members; but there shall always be at least five members of the board who are not ministers of the gospel or priests of any denomination. (Ibid. § 3.)

§ 4. (1.) The seats or pews in every church building, or edifice owned or occupied by any corporation organized under this act, shall be forever free for the occupation and use, during public worship, of all persons choosing to occupy the same, and conducting themselves with propriety; and no rent, charge, or exaction, shall ever be made or demanded for such occupation or use.

(2.) *Sale of Real Estate.* "Nor shall any real estate belonging to any such corporation, be sold or mortgaged by the trustees thereof, unless by the direction of the Supreme Court, to be given in the same manner, and in the like cases, as provided by law in relation to religious incorporations." (Ibid. § 4.)

§ 5. The second section of the Act of 1854 above cited, makes free churches subject to the provisions of the Act of April 12, 1848, and of the amendatory Act of April 7, 1849, as far as the same are applicable and consistent with such Act of 1854. That act was entitled "An Act for the Incorporation of Benevolent, Charitable, Scientific, and Missionary Societies."

Corporate Powers. The second section of that Act of 1848

created a corporation; gave succession, the right to sue, the liability to suits, the use of a common seal, and the power to alter it.

To hold Real Estate. It gave also the power of taking, receiving, purchasing, and holding real estate for the purposes of their incorporation, and for no other purpose, to an amount not exceeding fifty thousand dollars in value, and personal estate, for the like purposes, to au amount not exceeding seventy-five thousand dollars in value; but the clear annual income of such real and personal estate was not to exceed ten thousand dollars.

The limitation as to value in this second section is abrogated in the Act of 1854, so far as regards the church edifice erected or owned by the society, or the lot of ground on which the same may be built.

§ 6. *By-Laws.* The second section of such Act of 1848 gives power also to make by-laws for the management of its affairs, not inconsistent with the constitution or laws of this State, or of the United States, and to elect and appoint the officers and agents of such society, for the management of its business, and to allow them a suitable compensation.

These provisions seem to be applicable to the free churches established under the Act of 1854.

The third section of this Act of 1848 is, I apprehend, not applicable. The trustees of free churches form the corporation, and vacancies are supplied by the remaining trustees. The succession is thus continued.

Elections. I apprehend that the fourth section is applicable. The trustees of free churches can appoint days for filling vacancies by a by-law, and if there is an omission to choose at the time appointed, "it shall be lawful on any other day to hold an election for trustees, directors, or managers in such manner as may be directed by the by-laws of such society."

A by-law may then clearly appoint certain days for an election to fill vacancies, and may also provide, that if no choice is made on such days, an election may be held on other subsequent specified days.

§ 7. *Name.* The fifth section prohibiting the adoption of a name already attached to another corporate body may be assumed to be applicable.

§ 8. The sixth section of the Act of 1848 is as follows: "Any corporation formed under this act shall be capable of taking, holding, or receiving any property, real or personal, by virtue of any devise or bequest contained in any last will or testament of any person whatsoever, the clear annual income of which devise or bequest shall not exceed the sum of ten thousand dollars. *Provided*, that no person leaving a wife, or child, or parent, shall devise or bequeath to such institution or corporation more than one fourth of his or her estate, after payment of his or her debts; and such devise or bequest shall be valid to the extent of such one fourth.

"And no such devise or bequest shall be valid in any will which shall not have been made and executed, at least two months before the death of the testator."

Thus, under the second section of the Free Church Act of 1854, adopting the provisions of the Act of 1848, and under the second section of that act, incorporated free churches may take and hold, by purchase in its technical sense, real and personal estate, and in respect to the edifice and ground on which it stands, without a limitation as to value. And again, under the sixth section of such Act of 1848, above cited, they are made capable of taking by devise or bequest, provided the income does not exceed ten thousand dollars; but subject to the provision, where there is a wife, child, or parent. Then the devise or bequest might be for the one fourth of the testator's estate, but no more.

But we are to consider the effect of the act "relating to Wills," passed April 13, 1860 (chap. 360), whether it applies to free churches. By that act, "no person having a husband, wife, child, or parent, shall, by his or her last will and testament, devise or bequeath to any benevolent, charitable, literary, scientific, *religious*, or missionary society, association, or corporation, in trust or otherwise, more than one half part of his or her estate, after the payment of his

or her debts; and such devise or bequest shall be valid to
the extent of one half, and no more."

All laws and parts of laws inconsistent with such act
were repealed.

Now the Act of 1854 has only adopted the Act of 1848, as
amended in 1849. The effect is the same as if all those
provisions not inapplicable, were transferred literally into its
text. Then comes the comprehensive statute of 1860, using
for the first time, the term *religious*, as well as benevolent,
etc. There can be little doubt, I presume, that it extends
to free churches.

There is one point, however, perhaps doubtful. The sixth
section of the Act of 1848 made it necessary that the devise
or bequest should be executed two months at least before
the testator's death. The Act of 1860 omits this provision
entirely. Now as the Act of 1848 did not extend to religious
.incorporations at all, and the Act of 1854 extended it to free
churches solely, other *religious* corporations really take by
force of the Act of 1860, and it may be concluded that this
two months' clause does not prevail as to devises to them.

Perhaps the better opinion is, that the Act of 1860, as it
is the last, and very comprehensive revision of the whole
subject-matter, has superseded the two months' provision, as
to all the societies or corporate bodies enumerated in it.

§ 9. *Liability for Debts.* The seventh section of the Act
of 1848 is as follows: "The trustees of any company or corporation organized under the provisions of this act, shall be
jointly and severally liable for all debts due from said company or corporation, contracted while they are trustees;
provided such debts are payable within one year from the
time they shall have been contracted, and provided a suit for
the collection of the same shall be brought within one year
after the debt shall become due and payable."

The second section of the Act of 1854 has this clause as
to such liability: "And except that the provision in the
first of such acts" (that above quoted), "in relation to the
personal liability of the trustees, shall be applicable only to
the trustees who shall have assented to the creation of any
debt." See Eaton *v.* Aspinwall, 6 Duer's Rep. p. 176.

§ 10. The eighth section provides, that all institutions formed under the act, together with their books and vouchers, shall be subject to the visitation and inspection of the justices of the Supreme Court, or by any person or persons who shall be appointed by the Supreme Court for that purpose; and it shall be the duty of the trustees, or a majority of them, in the month of December in each year, to make and file in the county clerk's office, where the original certificate is filed, a certificate under their hands, stating the names of the trustees and officers of such association or corporation, with an inventory of the property, effects, and liabilities thereof, with an affidavit of the truth of such certificate and inventory, and also an affidavit that such association or corporation has not been engaged, directly or indirectly, in any other business than such as is set forth in the original certificate on file.

§ 11. Each corporation formed under this act shall possess the general powers conferred by, and be subject to, the provisions and restrictions of the third title of the 18th chapter of the first part of the Revised Statutes. (Ibid. § 9 of Act of 1848, 1 R. S. 599.)

§ 12. In chapter 17, §§ 2 – 4, I have transcribed the sections of the Act of April 23, 1867. A religious corporation may purchase and hold grounds for the purpose of erecting free churches with school-houses and residences. The seats must be free. The corporation erecting the churches, govern and regulate them entirely, and the worshippers are not to vote or have right as corporators in the parent church.

The system of free churches, under the Act of 1854, has made it necessary to have some special regulations in the Protestant Episcopal Church in New York.

A new clause was adopted providing, that "a church or congregation incorporated under any law of the State of New York, other than the General Act of 1813, and the amendments, applying for admission into union with the Convention of this diocese, shall submit to the Convention, or a committee appointed by its authority, the certificate or Act of Incorporation, or a copy of the same duly certified,

and shall also comply with the requirements of section 2 of
this Canon." (Canon 4, § 4, of Diocese of N. Y., ed. 1864.)

That section prescribes that every incorporated church,
applying for admission into union with the Convention of
the diocese, shall produce to the Convention a certificate
of the Bishop, or, in case of his absence, or of a vacancy in
the Episcopacy, of the major part of the standing committee, that he or they approve of the incorporation of such
church.

To entitle a church to admission into union with the
church in this diocese, it shall be required that the vestry
submit to the Convention, or to a committee appointed by
its authority, the certificate of incorporation duly recorded,
or a copy thereof certified by the clerk of the county, or by
the officer whose duty it is or may be made by law, to record
certificates of incorporation of religious societies in the
county in which such church is situated. (Canon 4, § 1, as
amended in 1866.)

Every church or congregation incorporated since April,
1813, or hereafter to be incorporated under any law of the
State of New York, other than the General Act for the incorporation of churches, passed April, 1813, and its amendments, shall be entitled to appoint lay delegates to the Convention, not exceeding three in number, who shall have
been connected with the said church or congregation for at
least twelve months previous to the election ; to be chosen
by the male members of full, legal age, of the church or
congregation, who shall have been connected therewith as
stated worshipers, for the space of one year previous to the
election.

The time, place, and manner of holding such election, and
the notice for holding the same (which shall be ten days at
the least), shall be fixed by rules or by-laws, made by the
trustees of such church or congregation, or by the members
of the same, qualified as aforesaid, at a meeting duly convened.

A written certificate of the appointment of such delegates
signed by the minister, if there be one, or by the presiding

officer at a meeting of the congregation by which they were appointed, and by the clerk or secretary, is to be presented to the Convention, declaring that such persons have been duly chosen lay delegates by such church or congregation, are members of the same, and have been such members for twelve months preceding; and further, that all the requirements of the Canon, and of the general rules or laws governing the election, have been duly observed.

No other certificate or evidence of the appointment, shall be allowed or received.

The secretary of the Convention shall record, in the book mentioned in the preceding section,[1] all certificates that shall be transmitted to him in accordance with the second section of Canon 30 of the General Convention of 1832, being Canon 12, §§ 1, 2, title 1 of the Digest, and also all certificates that shall be transmitted to him by the bishop of the diocese, of the settlement of any minister in any church or congregation, incorporated since April, 1813, or hereafter to be incorporated, under any law of the State of New York, other than the General Act for the Incorporation of Churches, passed April, 1813, and its amendments, which has been or may hereafter be admitted into union with the church in this diocese; *Provided*, that such certificate be such as is required in Canon 12, § 1, title 1 of the Digest, except that the same may be signed by the presiding and recording officers of the body electing the minister; and *provided further*, that the Bishop shall have endorsed on such certificate, that he is satisfied that such minister is a qualified minister of this Church.

A question was submitted to the writer in 1867, which led to the following opinion. It related to St. Matthew's Free Church in the Ninth Ward of the city of Brooklyn.

The church was organized some time prior to its incorporation, with a rector, wardens, and vestrymen, and the seats were free. Its title was, "The Free Church of St. Matthew's."

On the 20th of June, 1859, the members became incorpo-

---

[1] Section 1, Canon 11.

rated, by the name and title of "The Rector, Church-wardens, and Vestrymen of the Free Church of St. Matthew in the Ninth Ward of the City of Brooklyn." The certificate was recorded on that day.

The incorporation was expressly under the General Act of 1813 and its amendments, not under the Act of 1854, as to the incorporation of free churches.

On the 1st of November, 1859, a conveyance was made of the lots on which the church edifice stands, to "The Rector, Wardens, and Vestrymen of the Free Church of St. Matthew."

(1.) Independently of the question arising under the deed, I do not doubt that the vestry possesses the power of making the church a pay church as it is termed, selling or renting the pews, fixing a rate upon them, etc., in the usual mode. The statutes confer this authority fully upon the vestry as trustees, and the mere designation of "Free" in the title, cannot take away or abridge this power. It would be advisable to get the consent of a majority of the congregation, that is, of those entitled to vote for wardens and vestrymen, to the change.

(2.) "I think also, that under the cases of Robertson *v.* Bullions (11 N. Y. Rep. 243), and Petty *v.* Tooker (21 N. Y. 26), the title to the property granted by the deed of November, 1859, will not be impaired by the alteration. There is not a word in the conveyance making the grant conditional upon the church remaining a free one. The land is given to a church or corporation whose pews were then free, but in subordination to the legal power to change the system, and selling or leasing them.

"To guard, however, against any difficulty, I would advise, that after the change is made, a release be obtained from the grantor, reciting the alteration and confirming the grant."

The Act of April, 1854, covers the case of every denomination of Christians who may wish to establish Free Churches under it. But not a word connects its provisions with any church or body of Christians.

The ecclesiastical organization, the faith, worship, and discipline, to be observed, is necessarily left to the trustees. This is so because no one of the attendants upon the services have the slightest voice or power as a corporation or otherwise. The whole corporation centres in the trustees. They fill up vacancies. The third section of the Act of April 12, 1848, is inapplicable of course.

The authority upon this subject thus necessarily inferable, involves among other things the selection of the rector or minister.

The right to take and hold real estate is conferred by the second section of the Act of April 12, 1848. It is " for the purposes of the Incorporation, and for other purposes." The great purpose is to keep the sittings free in the church, but by means of trustees who are to *manage the same*. To vest a power of nomination or creation of agencies in a class of other persons, infringes upon this exclusive authority to manage the church.

While everything pertaining to the church, except what belongs to the ministerial functions of the pastor, is within the province of the trustees, and must be controlled by them, yet the pastor and communicants can suggest agencies of action to the trustees, and with their consent carry them out. Either by by-laws or special resolution this can be done. But ultimate and supervisory control must rest in the trustees.

CHAPTER XIX.

BURYING-GROUNDS, CEMETERIES, VAULTS.

§ 1. *Act of April* 11, 1842. *By Religious Corporations.*
(1.) Any incorporated religious society within the city of
New York which, having exhibited the account and inventory required by the tenth section of the act entitled " An
Act for the Incorporation of Religious Societies," has not
since purchased or acquired lands or tenements within this
State, may hereafter purchase, acquire, and hold land
within the city and county of New York, or in any neighboring county of this State, or any estate or interest in such
land, for the purpose of a burial-place or cemetery.

(2.) And may erect thereon a suitable edifice, in which to
perform the religious services usual on the burial of the
dead.

(3.) And also necessary buildings for the residence and
accommodation of grave-diggers and keepers of the ground.

(4.) And whilst and so long as such land shall not be appropriated and applied to any other purpose, such corporation shall not, by reason of the purchase or acquisition thereof, become bound or liable again to exhibit an account or inventory of its estate, unless it shall subsequently purchase
or acquire other lands or tenements within this State.   (§ 1
of Act of April 11, 1842, Laws, chap. 153.)

(5.) *Misapplication of Land.* If any land, so to be purchased or acquired by any such religious corporation, shall
be subsequently appropriated or applied to any use or purpose other than as is hereby authorized, every such corporation which shall so otherwise appropriate or apply the same,
or suffer it to be so otherwise appropriated or applied, shall
thenceforth be subject to the provisions of the tenth section

of the above-mentioned act,[1] in the same manner as if this act had not been passed.   (Ibid. § 2.)

§ 2. The authority given by the act concerning the acquisition of burial-places by religious corporations in the city of New York, passed April 11, 1842, to purchase, acquire, and hold land for the purpose of a burial-ground or cemetery, and to erect thereon suitable buildings for purposes connected with the burial of the dead, is hereby extended to religious corporations in every part of the State; and such purchases heretofore made, or hereafter made in the city of New York, or elsewhere, and the erection of buildings thereon, as authorized by the said act, are hereby confirmed and declared valid, notwithstanding any restriction contained, or supposed to be contained in the act to provide for the Incorporation of Religious Societies, passed April 5, 1813, or in any special charter of such corporation.   (§ 3 of Act of March 30, 1850, Laws, chap. 122.)

§ 3. *When may be Mortgaged.*   It shall not be lawful for any church or religious association to mortgage any burying-ground used for the interment of human remains, for the use of which they shall have received compensation, without the previous consent in writing of three fourths in number of the congregation or society of such church or corporation; which consent shall be proved or acknowledged in the same manner as deeds are now required by law to be proved or acknowledged, and shall thereupon be recorded in the office of the register of the city, or clerk of the county in which such burying-ground is situated.   (§ 1 of Act of April 11, 1842, Laws, chap. 215.)

§ 4. *Removal of Bodies.*   It shall not be lawful for any person or persons to remove any dead body or human remains from any burying-ground for the interment of which compensation shall have been received by any church or religious corporation, or by any officer or officers thereof; and which shall have been used for that purpose during the last three years, with the intent to convert the said burying-ground to any other purpose, without having first obtained

---

[1] Section 10 of Act of 1818, *ante*, chap. 14, § 9.

the consent in writing of three fourths in number of the congregation or society of such church or corporation; and which consent shall be proved or acknowledged, and recorded in the manner prescribed by the first section of this act, before any such removal shall be commenced or attempted. (Ibid. § 2.)

§ 5. Any person offending against any of the provisions of the second section of this act, shall, upon conviction, be adjudged guilty of a misdemeanor, and shall be punished by imprisonment in a county jail not exceeding six months, or by a fine not exceeding five hundred dollars, or by both fine and imprisonment, in the discretion of the Court. (Ibid. § 3.)

§ 6. The title to every lot which shall have been used by the inhabitants of any town in this State, as a cemetery or burying-ground, for the space of fourteen years next and immediately before this title shall take effect (December 4, 1827), shall be deemed to be vested in such town, and shall be subject in the same manner as other corporate property of towns, to the government and direction of the electors in town meeting. (1 R. S. 1830, p. 360.)

§ 7. The trustees of every religious incorporation under the Act of 1813, have power to make by-laws as to the perquisites for breaking the ground in the cemetery or church-yard, and in the said churches and meeting-houses for burying the dead. (§ 4 of Act of April 5, 1813.)

It can scarcely be doubted that a general power to take and hold lands for the use of a church or congregation, or other pious uses, would authorize the application of such land for the purpose of burying. This seems to be implied in the clause cited. It would seem that portions of the land adjoining the church was intended. Further legislation authorized the purchase of ground elsewhere.

§ 8. *Associations.* Any number of persons residing in this State, not less than seven, who desire to form an association for the purpose of procuring and holding lands to be used exclusively for a cemetery or place of burial for the dead, may meet at such time and place, as they or a majority of them may agree, and appoint a chairman and secretary by a vote of the majority of the persons present at the meeting, and proceed to form an association by determining on a corporate name by which the association shall be called and known; by determining on the number of trustees to manage the concerns of the association, which number must be not less than six nor more than twelve.

They thereupon may proceed to elect, by ballot, the number of trustees so determined on; and the chairman and secretary must immediately after such election divide the trustees by lot into three classes: those of the first class to hold their office one year, of the second class two years, and the third three years.

The meeting must also determine on what day in each year the future annual election of trustees shall occur. (§ 1 of Act of April 27, 1847, chap. 133. An Act authorizing the Incorporation of Rural Cemetery Associations.)

§ 9. The chairman and secretary of the meeting shall, within three days after such meeting, make a written certificate, and sign their names thereto, and acknowledge the same before an officer authorized to take the proof and acknowledgment of deeds in the county where such meeting was held.

Such certificate must state the names of the associates who attended such meeting, the corporate name of the association determined upon by the majority of the persons who met, the number of trustees fixed on to manage the concerns of the association, the names of the trustees chosen at the meeting and their classification, and the day fixed on for the annual election of trustees.

Which certificate it shall be the duty of the chairman and secretary of the meeting to cause to be recorded in the clerk's office of the county in which the meeting was held,[1] in a book to be appropriated to the recording of certificates of incorporation. (Ibid. § 2.)

§ 10. Upon such certificate duly acknowledged as aforesaid being recorded, the association mentioned therein shall

---

[1] It is presumed in the Register's Office in New York.

be deemed legally incorporated, and shall have and possess the general powers and privileges, and be subject to the liabilities and restrictions contained in the third title of the 18th chapter of part first of the Revised Statutes. (Ibid. § 3.)

§ 11. (1.) The affairs and property of such associations shall be managed by the trustees, who shall annually appoint from among their number a president and a vice-president, and shall appoint a treasurer and secretary, who shall hold their places during the pleasure of the board of trustees; and the trustees may require the treasurer to give security for the faithful performance of the duties of his office. (Ibid. § 3, as amended by Act of April 16, 1852, Laws, chap. 280.)

(2.) The trustees may fill any vacancy in the office of president or vice-president, occurring during the year for which they hold their office. (Ibid. § 2.)

§ 12. *Land may be taken for Cemeteries.* (1.) Any association incorporated under this act may take by purchase or devise, and hold, within the county in which their certificate of incorporation is recorded, not exceeding two hundred acres of land; to be held and occupied exclusively for a cemetery for the burial of the dead. (Ibid. Law of 1847, § 4.)

(2.) Such land or such parts thereof as may from time to time be required for that purpose, shall be surveyed and subdivided into lots or plats of such size as the trustees may direct, with such avenues, paths, alleys, and walks as the trustees deem proper; and a map or maps of such surveys shall be filed in the clerk's office of the county in which the land shall be situated. (Ibid.)

(3.) And after filing such map the trustees may sell and convey the lots or plats designated on such map, upon such terms as shall be agreed upon and subject to such conditions and restrictions, to be inserted in or annexed to the conveyances, as the trustees shall prescribe. The conveyances to be executed under the common seal of the association, and signed by the president or vice-president and the treasurer of the association. (Ibid.)

(4.) Any association incorporated under this act may hold personal property to an amount not exceeding five thousand dollars, besides what may arise from the sale of lots or plats. (Ibid.)

(5.) It shall be lawful for such association to agree with the person or persons from whom cemetery lands may be purchased, to pay for such lands, or the purchase price thereof, any specified share or portion, not exceeding one half the proceeds of all sales of lots or plats made from such lands; in which case, the share or portion of such proceeds so agreed upon, not exceeding one half thereof, must be appropriated and applied to the payment of the purchase-money of the lands so acquired, and the residue thereof must be appropriated to preserving, improving, and embellishing the cemetery grounds, and the avenues and roads leading thereto, and to defraying the incidental expenses of the cemetery establishment. (Laws of 1853, chap. 122.)

(6.) In all cases where cemetery lands are purchased and agreed to be paid for in the manner referred to in the last preceding section, the prices for lots or plats specified in the by-laws, rules and regulations, first adopted by any such association, cannot be legally changed without the written consent of a majority in interest of the persons from whom the cemetery lands were purchased, their heirs, representatives, or assigns. (Ibid.)

§ 13. All lots or plats of ground designated on the map filed as aforesaid, and numbered as separate lots by the incorporation, shall be indivisible, but may be held and owned in undivided shares. One half at least of the proceeds of all sales of lots or plats shall be first appropriated to the payment of the purchase-money of the lands acquired by the association, until the whole purchase-money shall be paid; and the residue thereof, to the preserving, improving, and embellishing the said cemetery grounds, and the avenues or roads leading thereto, and to defraying the incidental expenses of the cemetery establishment.

And, after the payment of the purchase-money, and the

debts contracted therefor, and for surveying and laying out the land, the proceeds of all future sales shall be applied to the improvement, embellishment, and preservation of such cemetery, and for incidental expenses, and to no other purpose or object.   (Ibid. § 7, as amended by Act of April 14, 1852, chap. 280.)

§ 14. Any association incorporated pursuant to this act, may take and hold any property, real or personal, bequeathed or given upon trust, to apply the income thereof, under the direction of the trustees of such association, for the improvement or embellishment of such cemetery, or the erection or preservation of any buildings, structures, fences, or walks, erected or to be erected upon the lands of such cemetery association, or upon the lots or plats of any of the proprietors; or for the repair, preservation, erection, or renewal of any tomb, monument, grave-stone, fence, railing, or other erection in or around any cemetery lot or plat ; or for planting or cultivating trees, shrubs, flowers or plants in or around any such lot or plat, or for improving or embellishing such cemetery, or any of the lots or plats in any other manner or form, consistent with the design and purposes of the association, according to the terms of such grant, devise, or bequest.   (Ibid. § 9.)

§ 15. The cemetery lands and property of any association formed pursuant to this act, shall be exempt from all public taxes, rates, and assessments; and shall not be liable to be sold on execution, or be applied in payment of debts due from any individual proprietors.   But the proprietors of lots or plats in such cemeteries, their heirs or devisees, may hold the same exempt therefrom so long as the same shall remain dedicated to the purposes of a cemetery ; and during that time, no street, road, avenue, or thoroughfare shall be laid through such cemetery, or any part of the lands held by such association, for the purposes aforesaid, without the consent of the trustees of such association, except by special permission of the legislature of the State.   (Ibid. § 10.)

§ 16. Whenever the said land shall have been laid out in plats or lots, and said lots or plats shall have been transferred to individual holders, and after there shall have been an interment in a lot or plat so transferred, such lot or plat from the time of such first interment shall be forever thereafter inalienable, and shall, upon the death of the holder or proprietor thereof, descend to the heirs at law of such holder or proprietor, and to their heirs at law forever. *Provided,* nevertheless, that any one or more of such heirs at law may release to any other of the said heirs at law, his, her, or their interest in the same, on such conditions as shall be agreed on and specified in such release; a copy of which release shall be filed with the town clerk of the town, or the register of the city, within which such cemetery shall be situated.

And, *provided further,* that the body of any deceased person shall not be interred in such lot or plat, unless it be the body of a person having at the time of such decease, an interest in such lot or plat, or the relative of some person having such interest, or the wife of such person, or her relatives, except by the consent of all persons having an interest in such lot or plat.   (Ibid. § 11.)

§ 17. Any person who shall wilfully destroy, mutilate, deface, injure, or remove any tomb, monument, grave-stone, building, or other structure, placed in any cemetery of any association incorporated under this act, or any fence, railing, or other work for the protection or ornament thereof, or of any tomb, monument, or grave-stone, or other structures aforesaid, or of any plat or lot within such cemetery, or shall wilfully destroy, cut, break, or injure any tree, shrub, or plant within the limits of such cemetery, shall be deemed guilty of a misdemeanor; and such offender shall also be liable in an action of trespass, to be brought in all such cases in the name of the association, to pay all such damages as shall have been occasioned by his unlawful act or acts.   Such money when recovered, shall be applied by the trustees to the reparation or restoration of the property so destroyed or injured.   (Ibid. § 8.)

§ 18 (1.) The annual election for trustees to supply the place of those whose term of office expires, shall be holden on the day mentioned in the certificate of incorporation, and at such hour and place as the trustees shall direct; at which election shall be chosen such number of trustees as will supply the places of those whose term expires. (Ibid. § 5.)

(2.) Such trustees shall have the power, by a resolution of a majority of all of them, to change the time for the annual election of trustees as fixed in the act of incorporation; but no such resolution shall take effect until sixty days after the same has been published six successive weeks, once in each week, in some newspaper published in the city or county where the association is situated, and a copy of such resolution, certified by the president and secretary, shall have been filed in the office of the clerk of the county where the certificate of incorporation is recorded. (Ibid., as amended by Act of April 5, 1860, chap. 163.)

(3.) The trustees chosen at any election subsequent to the first shall hold their places for three years, and until others shall be chosen to succeed them.

(4.) The election shall be by ballot, and every person of full age who shall be proprietor of a lot or plat in the cemetery of the association, containing not less than ninety-six square feet of land, or if there be more than one proprietor of any such lot or plat, then such one of the proprietors as the majority of joint proprietors shall designate to represent such lot or plat, may, either in person or by proxy, give one vote for each plat or lot of the dimensions aforesaid; and the persons receiving a majority of all the votes given at such election, shall be the trustees to succeed those whose term of office expires. But in all the elections after the first, the trustees shall be chosen from among the proprietors of lots or plats. (Ibid. § 5, as amended in 1860.)

(5.) The trustees shall have power to fill any vacancy in their number occurring during the period for which they hold their office. Public notice of the annual elections shall be given in such manner as the by-laws of the corporation shall prescribe. (Ibid.)

§ 19. (1.) The trustees at each annual election shall make report to the lot proprietors of their doings, and of the management and condition of the property and concerns of the association.

(2.) If the annual election shall not be held on the day fixed in the certificate of incorporation, the trustees shall have power to appoint another day, not more than sixty days thereafter, and shall give public notice of the time and place at which the election may be held, with like effect as if holden on the day fixed in the certificate. The office of trustees chosen at such time to expire at the same time as if they had been chosen on the day fixed by the certificate of incorporation. (Laws of 1847, chap. 133, *ut supra*, § 6.)

§ 20. (1.) The trustees may fund any outstanding indebtedness of the association, for lands purchased for cemetery purposes, or for moneys actually expended in preserving, improving, and embellishing the cemetery grounds, and may provide for the payment of such funded debt. Whenever such trustees, by a vote of two thirds of all the trustees elected, may desire to fund such indebtedness, they are required to ascertain the amount of obligations outstanding for the purchase-money of the lands acquired by the association, and for preserving, improving, and embellishing the cemetery grounds; and thereupon, with the consent of any creditor to whom the indebtedness or any part of it, may be due and owing, the said trustees may issue certificates for the amount thereof in sums of one hundred dollars each, payable at such time, and drawing such interest as may be agreed upon, in satisfaction and discharge of such indebtedness, or such part of it; but no certificate shall be issued for any fractional part of one hundred dollars, nor drawing any higher rate of interest than seven per cent. per annum.

(2.) The certificates must be sealed with the corporate seal of the association, and signed by the president and treasurer thereof, and shall be deemed personal property and transferable by delivery, unless otherwise provided on their face, and an exact and true account of the number and amount thereof, the persons to whom issued, the time of maturity, and the rate of interest, must be accurately entered on the books of the association. (Laws of April 5, 1860, chap. 163, § 1.)

§ 21. The trustees shall keep a distinct and separate account of the certificates issued for the purchase of lands acquired by the association, and the certificates issued for debts incurred in improving and embellishing the cemetery grounds, in the cemetery books; and it shall be their duty at least twice in each year, to apply the proceeds of all sales of lots or plats in redemption of such certificates, one half for the redemption of certificates issued for said purchase-money until the whole are redeemed, and the residue thereof for the redemption of certificates issued for debts incurred as aforesaid, and upon such redemption, the trustees must cancel the certificates on their books and destroy the certificates returned. (Ibid. § 2.)

§ 22. Until the certificates are redeemed, the holders of the same shall be entitled to vote at all elections and business meetings of the corporation, one vote for each and every certificate of one hundred dollars, held by such voter. None of the provisions shall be construed to create a lien upon lots or plats belonging to individual proprietors, within the cemetery limits; nor shall any other or greater liability be created by the certificates against the association or trustees issuing them, than may be necessary to enforce the faithful application of the proceeds of sales, in the redemption of such certificates in the manner specified. (Ibid. § 4.)

§ 23. It shall not be lawful for any rural cemetery hereafter incorporated under the act hereby amended to take by deed, devise, or otherwise, any lands in the counties of Westchester, Kings, or Queens, or set apart any ground for cemetery purposes therein, without the consent of the board of supervisors of said county first had and obtained, as provided for by this act; nor shall it be lawful for any person or incorporation, not incorporated under said act, to take as aforesaid, or set apart or use, any land or ground in either of said counties for cemetery purposes, without the consent of the board of supervisors of such county first had and obtained, in like manner as provided for in this act.

And such board of supervisors in granting such request, may annex thereto such conditions, regulations, and restrictions as such board may deem the public health or the public good to require. (§ 1 of Act of April 15, 1854, Laws, chap. 238. An Act to amend an Act passed April 14, 1852, entitled An Act further to amend the Act entitled, An Act authorizing the Incorporation of Rural Cemetery Associations, passed April 27, 1847.)

§ 24. Nothing contained in the preceding section shall prevent any ecclesiastical corporation now organized in either of said counties, from using any burial-ground now belonging to it within such county, as it has been heretofore accustomed. (Act of April 15, 1854, chap. 238.)

§ 25. Any cemetery association or other incorporation, desiring to use any lands for cemetery purposes, in either of said counties, or to take a conveyance thereof, must cause notice to be published in the county in which such lands are situated, of their intention to apply to the board of supervisors of such county, stating the time at which such application will be made for the consent mentioned; such notice must contain a brief description of the lands for which such consent is asked, and also their location and the number of acres. At such meeting, upon due proof of the publication of the notice required, the applicants, and remonstrants, if any, may be heard in person and by counsel; and thereupon, if the board of supervisors grant the consent, it shall be lawful for such corporation to take and hold the lands designated in such consent, not exceeding two hundred and fifty acres in any county. (§ 2 of Act of April 14, 1852, chap. 280.)

§ 26. The board of supervisors of each of said counties (Westchester, Kings, and Queens), is authorized to make, from time to time, such regulations as to the mode of burials in any cemetery within their bounds, as they may judge the public health or public decency to require, and such regulations must not be disobeyed. (§ 3 of Act of April 15, 1854, chap. 238.)

§ 27. *Act of May 7, 1847.* The legal voters of any incorporated village, at any meeting thereof lawfully convened, may, by resolution, direct the trustees of such village to purchase suitable land for a burying-ground of such village, or land in addition to any burying-ground already owned, upon such terms and conditions, not inconsistent with certain provisions hereinafter stated, as such meeting shall prescribe; but the whole expense of purchasing such ground or additional lands in any village, fencing the same, and putting it in proper condition to be used as a burying-ground, shall not exceed twenty-five hundred dollars, unless the population of the village shall exceed four thousand persons, nor more than four thousand dollars in any case. And the title of such burying-ground, when so purchased, shall be vested in such village, by its corporate name, and shall be inalienable except to individuals for the purpose of interments. (§ 1 of Act of May 7, 1847, Laws, chap. 209, as amended by Act of April 2, 1864, chap. 117. "An Act in relation to Cemeteries, in incorporated villages.")

§ 28. No such resolution shall have any force or effect, unless it shall provide for imposing, levying, and collecting a general tax upon the taxable property in such village sufficient to pay all the expenses of such purchase, and fencing the lands so purchased, and putting them in a proper condition to be used for a burying-ground, to be levied and collected within one year, or in equal portions within three years, from the time of the adoption of such resolution, which, so far as respects the levying and collecting of such tax, shall not be altered. And every such tax shall be collected in the manner, and within the time specified in this section, and when so collected shall be applied to the purpose in this section specified, and to no other. (Ibid. § 2.)

§ 29. No such resolution for the purchase of a burying-ground, and for imposing, levying, and collecting such tax, shall be passed at any such meeting, by virtue of the provisions of this act, unless notice of an intention to move for the adoption of such a resolution at such meeting, be given previous to holding the same, by publishing such notice at least once in each week, for four successive weeks, in a newspaper published in the village in which such meeting is to be held, or in case no newspaper be published in such village, by posting up such notice in at least ten public places in such village, at least thirty days before the time of holding the meeting. And before any such resolution is adopted, proof by affidavit of publishing or posting such notice as required, must be filed with the trustees of the village. (Ibid. § 3.)

* 30. The trustees of such village shall make such ordinances from time to time as they think proper, not inconsistent with the laws of the State, or of the United States, in respect to such burying-grounds, the conveyance of lots therein to individuals for the purpose of interments, as to interments in such lots or portions of such ground not so conveyed, and the management of such ground; and may enforce such ordinances by penalties not exceeding twenty dollars, to be sued for and recovered with costs, in the corporate name of the village, for its use, in any court having jurisdiction thereof. (Ibid. § 4.)

§ 31. Such burying-ground shall be laid out in suitable lots pursuant to the ordinances of such trustees, and they may on such terms and conditions as shall be prescribed, and for such prices as shall be agreed to by them on behalf of such village, convey any of such lots to individuals, for the sole purpose of making interments therein, by conveyances which may be acknowledged and recorded as other conveyances of real estate, and which shall be recorded by the clerk of such village in a suitable book to be kept by him; but no such conveyance shall be executed for any such lot until the price thereof shall be paid to such village. (Ibid. § 5.)

§ 32. It shall be the duty of the trustees of every village in which there shall be a burying-ground, purchased by means raised by a general tax upon the taxable property in such village, to reserve a reasonable portion of such ground for the interment of strangers, and other persons, who may die in such village under such circumstances that it would be unreasonable to require payment for the privilege of making such interment. (Ibid. § 6.)

§ 33. It shall be the duty of the trustees of every village in which there shall be a burying-ground so purchased, to cause an accurate record to be kept of every interment therein, and the time when made, and the name, age, and place of birth, of every person buried therein, when these particulars can be conveniently ascertained, and such record shall be so kept as to show the lot and part of the lot in which each interment shall be made. (Ibid. § 7.)

§ 34. A general tax not exceeding one hundred and fifty dollars in any one year may be imposed, levied, and collected on the taxable property in any village owning a burying-ground, for the purpose of improving the same; such tax shall be imposed in the manner prescribed by law for imposing such general taxes in each village as are now authorized by law to be imposed thereon for village purposes, and when collected, shall be applied to improving such burying-ground. (Ibid. § 8.)

§ 35. *Private Cemeteries.* Private or family cemeteries may be incorporated in the manner hereinafter prescribed, (§ 1 of Act of April 1, 1854, Laws, chap. 112. "An Act for the Incorporation of Private and Family Cemeteries.")

§ 36. Any number of persons desirous of availing themselves of the provisions of this act may purchase or set off for a private cemetery, land to the extent of not more than three acres, and after inclosing the same, shall cause to be published in a newspaper printed in the county where the land is situated, or if there be no newspaper printed in that county, then in one printed in an adjoining county, a notice that a meeting of the proprietors of the land so purchased or set off, will be held at a time and place designated, such notice to be published at least once in each week for six weeks successively next previous to the time of meeting. Such meeting shall consist of not less than seven of such proprietors, and shall then and there elect not less than three of their number as trustees to manage the affairs of the corporation for five years; and in case of the death or resignation of either of said trustees, the surviving or remaining trustees shall be authorized to fill the vacancy for the residue of the term, from the members of the corporation; and at the end of the said term new trustees shall be chosen in the same manner. (Ibid. § 2.)

§ 37. The chairman and secretary of the meeting shall make a written certificate and sign their names thereto, and acknowledge the same before an officer authorized to take the acknowledgment of deeds, containing the names of said trustees, and the title of said corporation, and a description of the land, and shall file the same in the office of the clerk of the county in which the land so set apart is situated ; and thereupon the said proprietors shall be deemed legally incorporated, and shall possess the general powers, and be subject to the general liabilities which corporations by law possess and are subject to.

A certified copy of such certificate shall be evidence in all courts and places, of the formation of such corporation. (Ibid. § 3.)

§ 38. No cemetery shall be established under this law that shall not be inclosed by a suitable fence or wall, nor shall such cemetery be hereafter located at a less distance than one hundred rods from any dwelling-house, without the written consent of the owner or owners thereof. (Ibid. * 4.)

§ 39. Every person who shall pull down or deface any fence, monument, or stone, in or about any private cemetery incorporated under this act, shall forfeit to the said corporation a sum not exceeding five hundred dollars for each offense, to be recovered in a court of record ; and such offender shall be adjudged guilty of a misdemeanor. (Ibid. § 5.)

§ 40. Cemeteries, which have been heretofore used for private or family interments, may be incorporated under the provisions of this act, subject to the provisions and conditions therein prescribed. (Ibid. § 6.)

§ 41. *Birds in Cemeteries.* Any person who shall kill or wound, or trap any bird, within any public cemetery or public burying-ground, or who shall destroy any bird's-nest, or remove the eggs or the young birds therefrom, shall be deemed guilty of a misdemeanor, punishable by a fine of five dollars for every bird killed, wounded, or trapped, and for every bird's-nest destroyed, or eggs or young birds removed, recoverable in any justices' court within the county where the offense has been committed, to be sued for by any person making the complaint. The penalty to go towards the support of the poor of the county. (§ 1 of Act of July 21, 1853, Laws, chap. 629. " An Act for the Protection of Birds in Public Cemeteries.")

§ 42. Any person who shall knowingly buy or sell any bird which has been killed or trapped, or shall have such birds on sale, shall be deemed guilty of a misdemeanor, punishable by a fine of five dollars for every bird bought, sold, or on sale, to be recovered and to be disposed of in like manner as provided for in the first section of this act. (Ibid. § 2.)

§ 43. *Removal of Bodies.* Every person who shall remove the dead body of a human being from the grave or other place of interment, for the purpose of selling the same, or for the purpose of dissection, or from mere wantonness, shall, upon conviction, be punished by imprisonment in the State Prison, not exceeding five years, or in a county jail not exceeding one year, or by a fine not exceeding five hundred dollars, or by both such fine and imprisonment. (2 R. S. 688, § 13.)

§ 44. Every person who shall purchase or receive the dead body of any human being, knowing the same to have been disinterred contrary to the provisions of the preceding section, shall, upon conviction, be subject to the same punishment in the said section specified. (Ibid. § 14.)

§ 45. Every person who shall open a grave or other place of interment with intent —

(1.) To remove the dead body of any human being, for the purpose of selling the same, or for the purpose of dissection; or,

(2.) To steal the coffin, or any part thereof, or the vestments, or other articles interred with any dead body, shall, upon conviction, be punished by imprisonment in a State prison not exceeding two years, or in a county jail not exceeding six months, or by fine not exceeding two hundred and fifty dollars, or by both such fine and imprisonment. (Ibid. § 15.)

Church-Yards. The consecration of churches is of the

most remote antiquity. It is said, that Euginus, a Greek, and the first who styled himself Pope, directed it in the year 154. The Emperor Justinian prescribed a form of consecrating the place where a church was to be erected. The consecrated ground was to be marked out. The constitutions of Otho and Othobon were very decisive upon this head.[1]

In 1712 a form of consecrating churches, chapels, and church-yards, was agreed upon by convocation, and is to be found in Burns, vol. i. p. 327, etc. The form for a church-yard is either when it is consecrated at the same time as the church, or separately. Our own office of consecration is for a church or chapel only. Church-yards have, however, been consecrated in our country.

When a church-yard has been enlarged, there is a new consecration of the additional part.[2]

By Canon 85 of 1603, the church-wardens or questmen shall take care that the church-yards are well and sufficiently repaired, fenced, and maintained with walls, rails, or pales, as hath been in each place accustomed, at their charges unto whom by law the same appertaineth. And by virtue of their office, they are bound to see that the foot-paths are kept in proper order, and the fences in repair. (1 Curtis' Rep. 621.)

These duties fall with us upon the vestry, in its collective capacity.

In the case of The Rector and Church-wardens of St. Johns v. The Parishioners thereof (24 Eng. Law & Eq. Rep. 595), it was held, that nothing but an act of Parliament would enable the Court to apply consecrated ground to secular purposes, however advantageous to the public or the parish.

And in Campbell v. The Parishioners of Paddington (24 Eng. Law & Eq. Rep. 597), Dr. Lushington repeated this proposition, but held that a vestry-room might be erected in a consecrated burial-ground, where no bodies had been interred. The uses were of a religious nature.

---

[1] See Burns' *Ecc. Law*, vol. i. p. 323, etc.   [2] Gibson's *Codex*, p. 190.

The case of St. George's, Hanover Square, *v.* Stewart, was cited, where a prohibition was granted against building a school-house on consecrated ground.

A church-yard adjoining the church has become so associated in our minds with ancient custom and religious thoughts, that we look upon it as the most fitting place for the last sleep of relatives and friends. "God's Acre" of the parish church was not merely the ground on which the building stood, but the consecrated soil around it, in whose bosom the worshipers reposed when their prayers and praises were hushed in death.

Yet it is certain that the earliest places of burial were without the walls of cities. It is said that Cuthbert, Archbishop of Canterbury, brought over from Rome the custom of burying in and near churches, about the year 750. (Burns, vol. i. p. 256.)

The practice of burying in churches is said to be prior to that of burying in church-yards, or places adjoining, but the privilege was reserved for persons of preëminent sanctity of life. It is much discountenanced by the present policy of the Church, as injurious to the stability of the fabric, and the health of parishioners.[1]

The learned Bingham shows clearly that the fact of the early Christians meeting at times in cemeteries for public worship, fails to prove that they buried in churches, or even in cities. Generally the graves and monuments of the martyrs are spoken of as being without the walls, and churches were often built over them.[2]

It is singular, that the burying in ground adjoining churches began in connection with the introduction into the Romish Church of prayers for the remission of the pains of the departed. It is stated that the practice of burying in remote places continued to the age of Gregory the Great, when the monks and priests beginning to offer prayers for the souls of the dead, procured leave, for their greater ease and profit, that liberty of sepulture might be in churches, or places adjoining them.

---

[1] 3 Phillimore, 849; 4 Haggard, 174.   [2] See vol. viii. p. 94, etc.

The parishioners have in England a right to be buried in the parish church-yard, without paying any fee except from immemorial custom.

"About the year 650, spaces of ground adjoining the churches were carefully inclosed, and solemnly consecrated and appropriated to the burial of those who had been entitled to attend divine service in those churches, and who now had become entitled to render back unto those places their remains to earth, the common mother of mankind, without payment for the ground which they were to occupy, or for the pious offices which solemnized the act of interment."[1]

The right of a parishioner to burial in the church-yard of his own parish church, was so exclusive that it was against law to bury any stranger therein, except with the permission of the church-wardens, and perhaps the incumbent. It might interfere with the room necessary for the interment of parishioners.[2]

In our State and churches, no such right exists in parishioners. The trustees may adopt by-laws for regulating the mode, time, and fees for interments, whether in the church-yard proper, or in ground purchased under the statute before cited. (*Ante,* § 1.)

Vaults. The trustees may allow the erection of vaults, upon such conditions as they shall think proper.

The law of England appears to be that a faculty, as it is termed, for the erection of a vault, will be granted only upon the assent of the rector, church-wardens (and ordinary, if it is to be in the chancel). It must be limited like a faculty for pews, to the use of the family, "so long as they continue parishioners and inhabitants;" and the Court must be satisfied, that it is not likely to be prejudicial to the parish.[3]

In the case of Windt *v.* The German Reformed Church (4 Sandf. Ch. Rep. 471), the subject of the rights of vault-holders was discussed. The defendants, a corporation, bought lots in 1823, and used them for a burial-ground.

---

[1] Per Lord Stowell, in Gilbert *v.* Buzzard, 3 Phillimore, 349.

[2] Burns, vol. 1. 258.

[3] Burns' *Ecc. Law*, vol. 1. p. 278 *a*, etc.

No instrument of any kind was executed by them, giving a right of burial. Upon allowing graves to be opened, and bodies deposited, a certain fee was charged. In 1846, they had obtained an order from the Vice-Chancellor, allowing them to sell the lots, and had purchased some others for burying at Brookwick, Long Island. The plaintiffs, relatives or representatives of buried persons, sought an injunction to restrain the removal of the remains.

. It was held, that there was no title to the land occupied by the body interred. There was a right to have it undisturbed, so long as the cemetery continued to be used as such, and also the right, in case the land was sold, for secular purposes, to have such remains removed, and properly deposited in a new place of sepulture.

The restrictions of the Act of 1842, before cited, were then noticed, and it was suggested whether the Court now possessed (under the section relating to the sanction of a sale) any control over the subject, in reference to the previous use of the ground for burying, "where the requisite consent of three fourths had been obtained to a sale or mortgage."

Where vaults or burying lots have been conveyed by religious corporations, some rights of property are conferred upon the purchasers. This was the case with the instruments executed by the corporation of the Brick Presbyterian Church. (3 Ed. Ch. Rep. 155.)

In that case, the form of the instrument transferring the ground for a vault was such as to transfer a title to the soil without restriction or limitation. The Vice-Chancellor held, that the property could not be sold without the consent of the vault-holder.

It subsequently became common to grant only the use and occupancy of the space allotted, so long as the corporation continued to occupy the edifice and grounds, for religious purposes.

In the case of Richards *v.* The Northwest Protestant Dutch Church (32 Barbour, 42), the subject was considered. The owner of a vault was treated as possessing a similar right to that of the owner of a pew. It was a right to the use and exclusive possession of the space, for burying purposes, so long as the property remained unchanged and devoted to religious objects. If the soil was sold with the sanction of the Court, the right or easement was terminated.

In 4 Bradford's Reports, 503, is an opinion of S. B. Ruggles, Esquire, as referee in the matter of widening Beekman Street. His report to the Supreme Court was confirmed, and payment for vaults directed in conformity to it.

The case arose upon the petition of the corporation of the Brick Presbyterian Church, stating an award of commissioners of estimate and assessment for widening Beekman Street, awarding $28,000 for a piece of land taken. That the piece comprised vaults for the burial of the dead, in which various individuals claimed certain rights of interment, and the use thereof as vaults. That subject to such rights, the church was entitled to the whole amount.

The order of reference was to ascertain the parties interested in the fund, and in what proportions.

The referee noticed the form of the instruments, and the decision of Vice-Chancellor McCoun, 3 Edw. Ch. Rep. 155, respecting them. They conferred a title to the land, and not merely an easement in it. They conveyed, however, a base fee and not a fee-simple absolute. It was the quality of the fee, the restrictions upon the usufruct, the enjoyment for only one specific purpose, that rendered it less valuable.

The cost of a vault of equal dimensions in Greenwood Cemetery, and the cost of removing the remains, formed the basis of the valuation which the referee adopted.

We notice that here the land was taken for public purposes in exercise of the right of eminent domain. The case of course is different where the property is voluntarily sold by the corporation.

The form of the instrument given by St. Thomas' Church in the city of New York was as follows: " Received, etc., being the purchase-money for the use of Vault No. —, built upon the premises held by St. Thomas' Church, in the city and county of New York, situate in Houston Street in said city. In consideration whereof, the said St. Thomas' Church doth agree and covenant with the said ——————————— his heirs, executors, and assigns, that he or they shall have the sole right to the use of said vault, as a family vault, so long as the said corporation shall continue, unless such use shall be prohibited by the corporation of the city."   It was sealed.

The church applied for an order authorizing a sale of the whole property.   Justice Bonney considered that the grants amounted to demises, for rent paid in advance, of the use of portions of such real estate, and were legal under section 4 of the Act of 1813.   And the Court was bound in allowing a sale, to protect the equitable rights of the vault-holders. An order was entered for a sale, "subject to the rights of such vault-holders as shall not release."

Negotiations for a settlement ensued, in which many vault-holders agreed to take a sum about one half of the value of the parcels of ground occupied by the vaults.   The case has not gone further in the courts at present.

We thus see that the question of strict law is not yet decided ; that is, whether the corporation, the consent of the Supreme Court being had, could make a good title and the vault-holders be compelled to look to the proceeds or the body for indemnity, or whether the release of the vault-holders was essential.   I refer now to the case of instruments like that given by St. Thomas' Church.

That the corporation can, under the power to lease their property, lease for the term of their continuing a corporation, which may be in perpetuity (equivalent as to quality of estate to a sale), is not perhaps quite clear.   If the instrument was simply a covenant, the remedy would be an action for its breach, and damages.

Coffins.   In our country, the habit of inclosing the body of the dead in a coffin is so universally prevalent, that it may be said to attend the right of interring in a particular place. Yet at former periods it was a right of no absolute character.   "Some *involucra* or coverings," says Lord Stowell,[1]

---

[1] Gilbert *v.* Buzzard, 3 Phillimore's Rep. 335.

"have been necessary in all civilized and Christian countries; but chests or trunks containing the bodies, descending along with them to the grave, and remaining there till their own decay, cannot plead either the same necessity or the same general use. In our own country, the use of coffins is extremely ancient, though most probably, by no means general; they are not *nominative* or directly required by any authority whatever; and it is to be observed, that in the Funeral Service of the Church of England, there is no mention — indeed, there is rather a studious avoidance of any mention — of coffins. It is, throughout the whole service, the *corpse* or the *body*. Funerals were anciently *coffined*, or *unconfined*, and were charged for accordingly. From which I might venture to draw the conclusion, that even at that time (1627), it was recognized as not unjust, that where the deceased, by the use of a coffin, took a larger occupancy of the ground, he should compensate the parish by an increased payment."

CHAPTER XX.

BEFORE the Reformation, no seats were allowed nor any distinct portions of the church assigned to particular parties, except in some exceptional cases for great persons. The seats were movable, and the property of the incumbent, and old wills are found disposing of them.[1]

It is stated that the earliest date of a pew now to be found in England is in Geddington, Northamptonshire, in 1602.

But in the time of Bishop Owen, of Hereford, they had become so frequent as to be the subject of an Article of Visitation : "Are all the seats and pews so ordered, that they which are in them may kneel down in time of prayer, and have their faces up to the holy table ? "

Generally the seats in churches were to be built and repaired, as the church was to be, at the general charge of the parishioners, unless any particular person be chargeable to do the same by prescription.[2]

Although the freehold of the body of the church be in the incumbent, and the seats thereof be fixed to the freehold, yet because the church is dedicated to the service of God, and is for the use of the inhabitants, and the seats are erected for their more convenient attendance on divine service, the use of them is common to all the people that pay to the repair thereof. Every person who settles as a householder has a right to call on the parish for a convenient seat.[3] It is clearly the law that a parishioner has a right to a seat without paying for it.[4]

The incumbent has no authority in the seating and arranging the parishioners, beyond that of an individual mem-

---

[1] Hook's *Dict.*, Tit. Pews.
[3] 1 Consis. Rep. 196.
[2] 3 Burns, 358.
[4] *Ibid.* 317.

ber of the vestry; it is not the vicar, but the vestry, which appropriates the seats, the general superintendence being with the ordinary.[1] The latter may grant a pew to a particular person while he remains in the parish, or there may be a prescription; but as to personal property in a pew, the law knows no such thing. (3 Phillimore, 16.) The appropriation of pews is generally made by the church-wardens under the directions of the ordinary. For that purpose they are his officers. (1 Phill. 316; 1 Haggard, 394.)

The earliest notice I have found of a parliamentary sanction for the selling or renting of pews, is in the Act of 58 George III., cap. 45, (1818). By the 75th section, a part of the sittings, not less than one fifth of the whole, were to be marked with the words, " Free Seats," and reserved for the use of poor persons resorting thereto, upon whom no rent was to be charged. Subscribers, being parishioners, were to have the choice of pews at the rate fixed by the commissioners. Church or chapel-wardens were not to let or sell any pews or seats to others than parishioners during their continuing inhabitants of the parish.

By the charter of Trinity Church of 1697, this practice is recognized and regulated. The church-wardens were only to dispose of a pew or place to an inhabitant, unless the vestrymen consented. And in 1748, directions were given as to letting pews in St. George's chapel.

Dr. Berrian gives the form of an assignment of a pew in Trinity Church. The burden of repairing it was upon the assignee, and it was to revert, if he ceased to be an inhabitant of the city. (" History of Trinity Church," etc., 26.) At page 338 is a list of the grants or patents for pews sold.

The rights of a pew-holder in a pew under the general law, and under the language of all the instruments given by churches, which have fallen under my notice, is an incorporeal hereditament. It is more than an easement. It is connected with the land, and has some of the qualities of realty. It passes to the heir at law. (3 Kent's Comm. 402; McKnabb v. Pond, 4 Bradford's Rep. 7, Surrogate's Court,

---

[1] Tattersall v. Knight, 1 Phillimore, 233.

New York.)   It requires a writing to pass the title as an interest in land.   (Viele *v.* Osgood, 8 Barbour's N. Y. Rep. 130 ; St. Paul's Church *v.* Ford, 34 Barbour, 16 ; and particularly, The First Baptist Church *v.* Bigelow, 16 Wendell, 28.)

The usufructuary right is a right to some extent, in the soil, as well as in the structure upon it.   This enables the holder to sustain ejectment or trespass *quare clausum fregit*, as was held in Shaw *v.* Beverige, 3 Hill's N. Y. Rep. 26 ; and is laid down by Chancellor Kent (3 Comm. 402), and by Chancellor Walworth (3 Paige's Rep. 302).   This distinguishes our law from the English, under which such an action could not be supported, because the freehold is in the incumbent.

This right in the soil is attached to the pew.   It gives, indeed, no power to dig a vault under it without consent. It is subject to the paramount ownership of the trustees, to be exercised in cases of necessity, of important improvements, or a legalized sale.

It is quite clear, that in the State of New York, a pew-holder has no such right to a pew, or the ground on which it stands, as will prevent a sale of the church edifice and soil, if the assent of the Supreme Court is obtained.   A sale or permanent lease of a pew is subject to this condition. The purchaser takes with presumptive knowledge of, and assent to, the same. (Wheaton *v.* Gates, 18 N. Y. Rep. 395.)

The Church of the Ascension (when in Canal Street), was, it may be said, completely destroyed by fire.   The vestry determined against rebuilding on the same site, and upon moving to the present situation on Fifth Avenue.   The pew-holders were settled with, by allowing all who purchased pews in the new building, the amount they had paid in the former, as part of the purchase-money.   Mr. Peter A. Jay was the legal adviser.

So in the case of the Church of the Incarnation, where a sale was made under the statute, of the building and ground, and the present new church was built, precisely the same course was adopted.

In the case of Trinity Church, when the present edifice was erected, the subject was much considered. The edifice was nearly unfit for public worship, and its entire demolition was necessary in order to erect a larger one, fitted to accommodate worshipers. The case might fairly be considered as one of a destruction from necessity. Mr. G. C. Verplank gave an opinion, denying the legal rights of the pew-holders; but by an arrangement, the old pew-holders were allowed an abatement on the price of new pews.

Let it be granted, that this course was not in consequence of a legal obligation; yet it is of so strong an equity, that it has been made an express statutory provision in the State of Maine.

" When a meeting-house is altered or rebuilt, pews must be assigned to the former pew-holders, conformable, as nearly as practicable, to those before held by them." (Tyler's Am. Ecc. Law, § 339, and statute cited.)

The following is a review of the leading authorities in the State of New York.

In Freligh *v.* Platt (5 Cowen, 494), all that is material is the language of the Court, that a pew-holder has a limited usufructuary right. If the house be burned or destroyed, the right is gone.

In Henry *v.* St. Peter's Church (2 Edw. Rep. 608), the resolution was to take down the old church, and erect a new one of an enlarged size and accommodations. The Vice-Chancellor refused to interfere by injunction. If the complainant had any right, it could be settled afterwards, when he came to demand a pew in the new church. There was no ground to interfere with the trustees' power of alteration for the general benefit.

In the Matter of the Brick Church (3 Edw. Rep. 156), it was held, that the right of a pew-holder was limited in duration, to continue so long as the church edifice stands; his right is subordinate to the right of pulling down and removing. A pew-holder, if a corporator, will be so still after a change of location. The order for a sale of the property could be made without prejudice to the legal rights of pew-holders in the new building.

When the present Brick Church was erected in Fifth Avenue, the same course as to owners of old pews purchasing in the new building was pursued, and a valuation allowed, as in the cases of the Churches of the Ascension and Incarnation.[1]

In Morrison *v.* St. Peter's Church (7 Legal Observer, 361), the trustees had adopted a plan of altering and extending the church, which considerably changed the situation of the plaintiff's pew, in regard to the pulpit and chancel, but did not interfere with his possession. The Court said: Everything granted to him by the instrument remained. If the value of the pew was depreciated, it was a contingency to which he was liable; the trustees being in the exercise of an undoubted power, and acting in good faith.

The case of Shaw *v.* Berige (3 Hill's Rep. 26), has been before noticed for the point decided. The general doctrine of the right of a pew-holder being subservient to the paramount right of the trustees or corporation, is recognized.

In the case of the Reformed Dutch Church (16 Barbour, 237), the law was stated that the trustees could no more sell a pew so as to give an absolute title to the purchaser without an order of Court, than it could sell the church edifice without it. The title conferred is the right to occupy the pews for the purposes of public worship.

Voorhies *v.* The Presbyterian Church (17 Barbour, 103 ; 8 Barbour, 135), is the strongest positive decision in our books. The edifice was in a ruinous and dangerous state. The trustees rebuilt it except the walls. They changed the inside so that the pulpit was placed in the situation of the plaintiff's pew. It was held, that they had a right to do this, and the party was without a remedy. "If, in doing this (*rebuilding*), the pews are necessarily destroyed, the pew-holders cannot sustain trespass or ejectment."

In Cooper *v.* The First Presbyterian Church, etc. (32 Barbour, 222), Mr. Justice Bokee entered largely upon the

---

[1] Mr. Daniel Lord has informed me, that he believes this was not considered a strict legal right, but a matter of equity and propriety.

questions. He recognized the principle of several Massachusetts cases, as to the right of changing or taking down the church building. In case of a destruction from necessity, no compensation could be demanded; but if done for reasons of convenience or propriety, it could be.

The case arose upon a motion for an injunction by pewholders to restrain the removal of pews, and erecting of slips or other structures in their place.

The learned judge, after observing that the question of important alterations should be decided by a majority of the members assembled, adds : " No one would be driven from the church, but a seat or occupancy during public worship (which is all any one possessed), would be provided ; and if as good and equally commodious, although of a different form, no claim for damages could be sustained."

The leading cases in Massachusetts are, Kimball *v.* Rowley, 24 Pickering, 347; Gay *v.* Barker, 17 Mass. 435; Gordon *v.* Waddell, 9 Cushing, 508; Facet *v.* Boylston, 19 Pick. 361.

In Gay *v.* Barker, it was held, that a parish may take down the church edifice, and rebuild on the same ground, or may alter the shape and form, to make it more convenient. If in doing so, the pews are destroyed, the parish must provide an indemnity on just and equitable principles.

" Unless the edifice is unfit for public worship, and so old and ruinous as to render its entire demolition necessary, a pew-holder would be entitled to indemnity for the destruction of his pew. But if the parish abandon the edifice, when it continues fit for public worship, and erect a new one on a different site, it does not subject itself to any liability to a pew-holder, unless it does it maliciously."

This passage is from Mr. Tyler's work (" Ecclesiastical Law," section 445), and seems to be a correct statement of the result of the Massachusetts cases.

The case of Kellogg *v.* Dickenson (18 Vermont Rep. 266), may be also usefully referred to. If a church edifice is taken down from necessity, because it has become ruinous and unfit for the purposes of worship, no compensation is to be made. In other cases of alterations, it must be.

Mr. Buck of Boston, has lately published a work on the ecclesiastical law of Massachusetts; and he states the law on this head to be, " that no compensation is given where the house is taken down on account of its permanent unfitness for public worship. Otherwise, if it is temporarily unfit, and does not require entire demolition." (p. 140.)

In Wheaton *v.* Gates (18 N. Y. Rep. 396), Judge Denio thus states the rules: " If the edifice were destroyed, or if it became permanently unfit for the purposes of public worship, the rights of pew-holders ceased. I do not say what interests they would retain in case of extension and costly reparations, and great changes not destroying the identity of the building; for that question is not before us. Where the edifice was reasonably capable of further use as a church, the interests of the pew-holders would, no doubt, be a subject to be considered by the Court." This was said in reference to an application for a sale. " But if overruling considerations existed, rendering it expedient upon the whole matter, that a sale should take place, the interests of owners of pews would necessarily be destroyed."

From these authorities we may conclude: That when a removal has been decided upon, and has been sanctioned, as when an approval by the Court to a sale has been obtained, the rights of a pew-holder *stricti juris* are terminated. The situation of a church edifice as to its fitness for worship has not a decisive, and may not have any influence upon the question.

When an absolute, utter demolition has taken place, whether it has proceeded from the fall of the building, from decay, entire destruction by fire, or a justifiable tearing down on account of decay and danger, and a rebuilding on the site, it is probable, the rights of pew-holders are also at an end. But it must be noticed that there is not a case in our State deciding the point distinctly. There is as much indirect authority supporting some right in the pew-holder, as against it. " While the house remains, the right to the pew is absolute." And see the cases before the Vice-Chancellor, before cited.

In the case of St. George's Church, Stuyvesant Square, several important questions arose. An opinion was taken from the writer and Mr. S. Cambreling. The main facts were as follows : —

St. George's Church was erected out of funds of the corporation, and cost about $275,000. The vestry affixed a price or valuation on each of the pews, except two specially reserved. The amount of such valuation was $115,856. They were sold upon permanent leases at such prices, subject to such rent or assessment as the vestry might impose. Many pews were purchased, down to the fire in 1805; others were leased from year to year at fixed rates. The form of the transfer of pews sold was as follows : —

" Know all men by these presents, that we, the Rector, Church-wardens, and Vestrymen of St. George's Church, in the city of New York, in consideration of the sum of ——— dollars, paid to us by ——— ——— of said city, the receipt whereof is hereby acknowledged, have granted and sold, and by these presents do grant and sell, unto the said ——— ———, all that certain pew in said Saint George's Church, in the city of New York, fronting on Sixteenth Street and Rutherford Place; such pew being known and numbered —. To have and to hold the same unto the said ——— ———, his heirs and assigns, *so long as the said church edifice shall endure*, subject to such annual rent as we, or our successors, shall from time to time, impose on the said pew. *Provided*, that if, at any time, default be made in the payment of such rent for the space of two years, it shall be lawful for us and our successors to reënter on the said pew, and sell and dispose of the same in like manner as if these presents had never been made or executed, rendering the surplus moneys, after deducting all the arrears of rent then due with interest thereon, and all costs and charges attending such sale, to the said ——— ———, his heirs or assigns. *Provided, also*, that no alteration shall be made in the said pew hereby granted, and that no assignment or sale of the same shall be valid and effectual without the consent of the said church thereunto obtained."

The church took fire in November, 1865. The roof, galleries, pews, floor, stairs, doors, and windows were destroyed, except those of the two vestry-rooms, which were damaged. The main outer walls remained standing, although greatly damaged on the inner face. The stone work around the windows and doors was injured so as to be unfit for use, and the wall between the porch and the body of the church was so damaged that it had to be removed. The stone towers were damaged, but capable of being repaired.

The amount insured upon the church was $70,000, which was collected. The cost of rebuilding was stated at $164,-000. Contributions had been made to $70,000, without any conditions as to the appropriation of the new pews. The contributions were in part from persons who held deeds for their pews, and partly from others.

At the time of the fire, there had been 101 pews

deeded, of the price of . . .	$54,900
And not deeded " "	60,950
	$115,850

To pay for the reparations of every kind, about $24,000 was required beyond the insurance money and contributions.

The following opinion was given : —

Upon the case submitted to us by the vestry of St. George's Church, and the questions annexed, we reply —

1. The vestry, without the sanction of the parishioners, had the right to decide upon the propriety of rebuilding the church in its former situation, and upon the plan of rebuilding. We do not consider that the vestry was under any legal obligation to the pew-holders by deed, to rebuild. Their duty embraced the whole body of worshipers, and to carry out great religious purposes. But having so decided, and without a dissenting opinion, they were authorized to adopt a plan varied or otherwise, and to apply the insurance money and other funds within their control to the object.

2. The parties who merely rented pews from year to year,

the time having expired, have no claims upon the corporation, and are under no obligations to it. We do not see that any question can arise as to this class.

3. We understand that some of the contributors are not pew-holders. We consider that the contributions made by them impose no legal obligation on the vestry to transfer to them pews or seats.

4. As to the pew-holders under the instruments of transfer from the vestry —

(1.) We do not think that any separate right has accrued to such pew-holders, by reason of their subscriptions or donations towards the erection of the new edifice, upon the facts in the case. The pew-holders who have not subscribed and they who have, are, in relation to the corporation, upon the same legal footing.

(2.) We understand that the pews on the floor and in the galleries, will be the same substantially as before; that the pews will respectively actually occupy the same, or nearly the same, site as before, or with immaterial deviations.

An occupant of a former pew can be reinstated in the same or nearly the same position.

We are of opinion, that upon the new edifice being completed, the rights are so far revived, as that the pew-holder should be entitled to occupy, upon the same terms as before, a pew in the same position as his former pew, or as nearly conformable to that position as can be; but this upon the condition of his paying the cost of reconstructing the pew, or such cost, after deducting a proportion of the insurance money, if the vestry shall think proper, but is not legally bound, to allow.

A resolution of the vestry recognizing this right, and for ascertaining the estimated cost, is suggested.

Mr. Cambreling and myself concur in the conclusion, that the relations of the parties ought to be settled upon equitable principles, and these are what we have above stated. In my individual opinion, the Courts would declare the same to be matters of law.

New York, January, 1867.

A paper accompanied this opinion in which all the above cited authorities were noticed. The paper proceeded as follows : —

"We may now examine particularly the contract in this case between the corporation and the pew-holder. The latter is entitled to hold the pew 'so long as the church edifice shall endure.'"

What is the just construction of this stipulation?

Certainly an injury to other portions of the edifice, reparable out of adequate funds of the corporation, would not impair his right. Equally clear is it, that a partial destruction whether of pews or other portions, which the insurance money could fully repair, would not have such an effect. The duty so to apply the insurance money is plain. The pew-rent paid by a pew-holder went into the fund, out of which the premium as well as other charges were paid.

Suppose a destruction by fire of a certain number of pews and no insurance. If the pew-holders offered to reconstruct them, it is impossible that the trustees could legally refuse permission, exacting of course conformity in materials, etc. But the corporation has not insured the pew from destruction or injury in favor of the holder; nor is there any stipulation to that effect. Yet the trustees would be bound to replace the pew for the corporate religious purposes. The principle then of a total demolition of the edifice terminating all rights, leads to the conclusion, that a partial destruction modifies them. So in the case supposed, the trustees replacing the pews destroyed, would have a right, and as we think in equity would be bound, to proffer them to the holders of the destroyed pews, they paying the cost of reparation.

If this was refused, the right and title of the holder would cease, and the title of the corporation become absolute.

It seems to us, that these just and most equitable principles may fairly be elicited from the authorities, as the law to govern the case supposed.

The application of such principles in the present instance is varied by the reception of the insurance money.

The pew-holders may, with much apparent equity, ask, that a proportion of this money should be applied to the replacement of the pews. Thus, the whole cost is to be $164,000, and the insurance money is $70,000. The separate cost of reconstructing the pews should be ascertained. What proportion that bears to the whole cost, is the proportion of the insurance money to be allowed. But we think that in strictness, the actual cost of reparation may be imposed without such allowance or appropriation of part of the insurance money.

Each holder of the 191 pews, held under the permanent leases, will thus be chargeable with a definite sum, not personally, but as a condition of his right to retain the site and reoccupy the new pew upon it. We have no doubt of the power of the vestry to allow this amount as payment in whole or in part of the contribution of a pew-holder.

CHAPTER XXI.

DISTURBANCE OF RELIGIOUS WORSHIP.

§ 1. (1.) No person shall willfully disturb, interrupt, or disqniet any assemblage of people met for religious worship, by profane discourse, by rude and indecent behavior, or by making a noise, either within the place of worship, or so near to it as to disturb the order and solemnity of the meeting.

(2.) Nor shall any person, within two miles of the place where any religious society shall be actually assembled for religious worship, expose to sale or gift, any ardent or distilled liquors, or keep open any huckster shop in any other place, inn, store, or grocery, than such as have been duly licensed, and in which such person shall have usually resided or carried on bnsiness,

(3.) Nor shall any person within the distance aforesaid, promote, aid, or be engaged in any racing of any animals, or in any gaming of any description.

(4.) Nor shall any person obstruct the free passage of any highway to any place of pnblic worship, within the distance aforesaid. (1 R. S. 674, § 64. Edmonds' edition.)

§ 2. Whoever shall violate either of the provisions of the foregoing section may be convicted summarily before a jnstice of the peace of the county, or any mayor, recorder, alderman, or other magistrate of any city, where the offense shall be committed, and on such conviction, shall forfeit a snm not exceeding twenty-five dollars, for the benefit of the poor of the county. (Ibid. § 65.)

§ 3. It shall be the duty of all sheriffs and their deputies, coroners, marshals, constables, and other peace officers who may be present at the meeting of any assembly for religious worship, which shall be interrupted or disturbed in the manner herein prohibited, to apprehend the offender, and take him before some justice of the peace, or other magistrate authorized to convict as aforesaid, to be proceeded against according to law.   (Ibid. § 66.)

§ 4. All judges, mayors, recorders, aldermen, and justices of the peace, within their respective jurisdictions, upon their own view of any person offending against the provisions of this article, may order the offender into the custody of any officer in the preceding section named, or of any official member of the church or society so assembled and disturbed, for safe keeping, until he shall be let to bail, or a trial for such offense be had.   (Ibid. § 67.)

§ 5. If any person convicted of any of the offenses herein prohibited shall not immediately pay the penalty incurred, with the costs of the conviction, or give security to the satisfaction of the officer before whom the conviction shall be had, for the payment of the said penalty and costs, within twenty days thereafter, he shall be committed by warrant to the common jail of the county, until the same be paid, or for such terms not exceeding thirty days, as shall be specified in the warrant.   (Ibid. § 68.)

§ 6. Whenever complaint shall be made to any justice of the peace, mayor, recorder, or alderman, of a violation of either of the provisions contained in the last three articles, relative to profane swearing (the 6th), the disturbance of religious meetings, or the observance of Sunday (the 8th), or when any such violations shall happen in the presence of such officer, he shall cause the offender to be brought before him, and shall proceed summarily to inquire into the facts; and if the person charged, be found guilty, a record of his conviction shall be made and signed by such officer, before issuing any process to enforce the same; which conviction shall be final, and shall not be reëxamined upon the merits in any court.   (Ibid. p. 676, § 73.)

§ 7. No prosecution shall be maintained for any of the violations specified in the preceding section, unless the same be instituted by the actual issuing of process to apprehend the offender, or by his actual appearance to answer the complaint within twenty days next after the offense committed. (Ibid. p. 677, § 74.

§ 8. Upon a conviction being had for any of the offenses in the last three articles specified, where no other special provision is made for the collection of the penalties incurred, the magistrate, before whom the same is made, shall issue an execution to any constable of the county, commanding him to levy the said penalties and the costs of the conviction, by distress and sale of the goods and chattels of the offender; and in case sufficient goods and chattels cannot be found, then to commit such offender to the common jail of the county, for such time as shall be specified in the said execution, not less than one day, nor more than three days. (Ibid. § 75.)

§ 9. Within thirty days after any such conviction shall be had, the magistrate making the same, shall cause to be filed in the office of the clerk of the county, a certificate of such conviction, briefly stating the offense charged, the conviction and judgment thereon, and if any fine has been collected, the amount thereof, and to whom paid. (Ibid. § 76.)

§ 10. In all prosecutions for any of the offenses specified in the last three articles, the like fees shall be allowed and taken, as in civil suits before justices of the peace, which shall in no case exceed five dollars, and be paid by the party offending, over and above the penalties incurred; but in case of the imprisonment of the offender, no charges or fees shall be allowed. (Ibid. § 77.)

In The First Baptist Church *v.* The Schenectady, etc., Railroad Company (5 Barbour's Rep. 79), it was held, by Harris, Watson, and Parker, Justices, at General Term, that an action would lie on behalf of a religious corporation against a railroad company, for running their cars, blowing off steam, ringing bells, and making other noises in the vicinity of a church, during public worship on the Sabbath, by which the congregation was so annoyed as to depreciate the value of the house of worship. The depreciation of the property for the purposes to which the owner had devoted it, was enough.

But in The Trustees of the First Baptist Church, etc. *v.* The Utica, etc. Railroad Co. (6 Barbour's Rep. 313), before Justices Cady, Willard, and Hand, the reverse was decided. That the corporation could not sustain such an action, the damages being too remote. If they could not recover on the ground of injury to property, they could not at all. The molestation was to the worshippers. What was authorized by the legislature could not be a nuisance. Even if it were a public nuisance, an individual attendant could not sue. He received no special damage.

In Owen *v.* Hinman (1 Watts & Serg. 548), the action was by a member of a Presbyterian Church, complaining of the defendant interrupting his religious worship by loud singing and talking. The Court held such an action would not lie. The plaintiff claimed no property on the building or a pew in it. There is no damage to his property, health, reputation, or person. The injury complained of, if against the will of the officers of the church, is in the nature of a nuisance or injury to them, and it is for them to seek redress. It is well known that the property of our churches and meeting-houses, and the superintendence of the congregations, and the right to control and regulate them, and to prevent improper intrusion or interference, is vested uniformly in some corporation or trustees, in whom is placed the power to enforce the will of the owners.

Under the clause of the statute marked *ante,* § 4, it was decided in Farrell *v.* Warren (3 Wendell, 253), that a justice of the peace, etc., could, upon his own personal view of an offense committed against the act, put the offender in custody of a constable, without issuing a warrant.

In proceeding under the statute against a disturber of a religious meeting, it is not necessary that process should actually issue. The main purpose of the 7th section was to limit the time within which proceedings must be commenced; but parties may voluntarily, within that time, as in other cases, appear and join issue, or confess the complaint. (Foster *v.* Smith, 10 Wendell, 377.)

A person arrested as an offender under the act by warrant, must be carried before the magistrate who issued such warrant.   (The People *v.* Fuller, 17 Wendell, 211.)

The justice cannot, on the return of process personally served, proceed to hear the proofs, and convict the party, without a personal appearance.   He must be brought before him.   (Bigelow *v.* Stearns, 19 Johns. Rep. 39.)

The following points were established in the case of Wall *v.* Lee, 34 N. Y. Rep. 141, Court of Appeals.

A person disturbing a religious meeting during services, may be removed from the building by the application of force sufficient to effect that purpose.

To justify such a removal, and the force necessary to effect it, it is not requisite that the disturbance should be willfully made.

If the proceeding was under the statute against a person as a disturber, then the willfulness of the act must be stated and proven.

But in every congregation assembled for religious purposes, there must necessarily exist the power to preserve order and to expel any one guilty of a disturbance, and who should persist in it so that worship could not be conducted in an orderly and proper manner.

In Roman Catholic churches the appropriate person to preserve order is the priest.   He can call upon others to aid him.   The defendant was such a priest, and had tried to remove the plaintiff.

CHAPTER XXII.

THE DISMISSAL OF MINISTERS.

THE important point of the dismissal of ministers is much influenced by the special regulations of different denominations. These will be noticed to some extent in considering the subject.

We should, however, first recollect the decided assertion of the permanence of the relation of rector and parish found in the English law. The tie cannot be broken except by judicial sentence or resignation to, and acceptance by, the Ordinary.[1] It is stated by Bishop Gibson that the Ordinary is not bound to accept, but is the judge of the motives for the application, and that there is no remedy if he will not accept, more than if he will not ordain.[2]

The eloquent language of Lord Stowell[3] as to the relation of husband and wife, may well be applied here. "When people understand that they must live together, except for a few reasons known to the law, they learn to soften, by mutual accommodation, that yoke which they know they cannot shake off. They become good husbands and good wives, from the necessity of remaining husbands and wives, for necessity is a powerful master in teaching us to bear the duties it imposes." See also a striking passage in Hume's "Essay on Polygamy and Divorce," Essay 19.

The following are the strong expressions of the Rev. Mr. Thatcher of Massachusetts. No description of men under

---

[1] Burns' *Ecclesiastical Law*, vol. iii. p. 540, etc.

[2] *Codex*, p. 822. Marchioness of Rockingham *v.* Griffith, 3 Burrows, p. 543. As long ago as the year 740, it was declared that priests be neither constituted to any church, nor ejected from it, without the authority and consent of the Bishop. Eggbright's Exceptions, Johnson's Laws, etc., vol. i. p. 158.

[3] Evans *v.* Evans, 1 Haggard's Cons. Rep. 36.

the government of Jews, Turks, or Pagans, were so badly off as the clergy of New England, on the supposition that the power of dismission lies with the people.[1]

§ 1. The Supreme Court of Massachusetts thus declares the law of that State: "It has been the uniform opinion of all the judges of the higher courts, that where no tenure was annexed to the office of a minister by the terms of settlement, he did not hold his office at will, but for life, determinable for some good and sufficient cause, or by the consent of both parties.[2]

But the Courts have sanctioned such special contracts, and also modes of effecting a dissolution plainly agreed upon. Where no special contract existed, the Cambridge platform had prescribed that there must be the sanction of a council, and the Courts have recognized this rule of the Church.[3] The nature of these councils will be found in Bucks' "Mass. Ecc. Law," p. 211, etc. I refer to a few authorities as to the office of these councils.

They are distinguished as *ex parte* and mutual councils. It is only when a mutual council has been proffered and declined, that an *ex parte* council can be called. Such refusal must be positive and unconditional. (Thompson *v.* Rehoboth, 7 Pick. 163; Whitmore *v.* Fourth Cong. Society, 2 Gray, 306; Burr *v.* Sandwich, 9 Mass. 277.)

I judge that the earlier cases held, that the conclusion of an *ex parte* council duly convened, if accepted by one party, bound the other in the civil courts, much more that of a mutual council. But the later authorities appear to establish these points.

That the determination of a council is not a judgment, unless accepted by both parties, and until this has taken place, the Supreme Court has no power to enforce it It is said in one case, that there was neither common law nor equity power to enable it to do so, as the parish had not, in the opinion of the Court, upon the evidence, accepted the

<hr>

[1] Quoted Bucks' *Ecclesiastical Law*, p. 90.

[2] Avery *v.* Tyringham, 3 Mass. Rep. 160.

[3] Cochran *v.* Camden, 15 Mass. Rep. 304; Sheldon *v.* Easton, 24 Pick. 286.

resnlt.   An action, therefore, for the recovery of a sum adjudged by the council to be paid to the minister, could not be supported.   (Stearns *v.* Bedford, 21 Pick. 214.)

Again, the Court looks behind the adjudication.   It must appear: (1.) That the cause for calling the council was sufficient.   (2.) That the members were properly selected.   (3.) That they proceeded impartially, and with due respect to the rights of all parties.   (4.) That their conclusion, besides being formal and explicit, is based on grounds that will support it; and finally, that the result of a council, even thus unexceptionable, is only *primâ facie* evidence, and derives its binding force mainly from the consent of parties. (Stearns *v.* Bradford, and Mr. Bucks' Summary, Mass. Ecc. Law, p. 244.)

§ 2. *Reformed Dutch Church.*   By section 18, article 1, chapter 1, of the Constitution of the Reformed Dutch Church of North America, " for the regular dismission of a minister, who has received and accepted a call from another place," it is required, " that a neighboring minister of the same Classis to which the congregation belongs, be invited to be present and superintend the dismission of the minister from his congregation, countersign the instrument of dismission, and to deliver the same, with a report upon the subject, to the Classis, which report and document shall serve as a basis upon which the final dismission and certificate of the Classis shall be founded.

Section 10 of article 3 is identically the same as the above, omitting the words " who has received and accepted a call from another place."

The form, Appendix No. 4, states that the undersigned was present at a meeting of the Consistory of ———, on, etc., when it was resolved, that an application be made to the Classis of —— for a dissolution of the pastoral connection between the Reverend ——, and the said church ; and that the said Reverend —— declared his concurrence in such application.

I donbt, therefore, whether these provisions cover the case of a hostile dismission by the congregation with the sanction of Classis. Among the powers enumerated as belonging to Classis is that of dismissing ministers when called elsewhere.

The cases provided for, seem to be those of a voluntary resignation upon a call elsewhere, or without it, sanctioned and recorded by an ecclesiastical authority.

When any minister shall be duly convicted of any offense which implicates the purity of his clerical character, and shall, in consequence of such conviction, be suspended from his office, and the conviction and suspension shall be sustained on a final appeal, his pastoral connection with the congregation in which he was settled, shall (if the Consistory so elect), be *ipso facto* dissolved. (Art. II. § 14.)

The case of The Reformed Dutch Church of Albany *v.* Bradford (8 Cowen's Rep. 457), is an instructive decision upon this, as upon several other points.

The call of Dr. Bradford under the corporate seal, was made in 1805, and stipulated that the church would pay him the sum of fifteen hundred dollars yearly, and every year, " so long as you continue our minister in the said church, and remain unmarried," and upon his marriage, to pay the further sum of $250 annually. In 1813 the salary was fixed at $2000. It had been paid up to the 2d of December, 1820, but not afterwards. The action was for the arrears.

Proceedings had been instituted by the elders and deacons of the Consistory of the church, before the Classis for an inquiry into rumors affecting the minister's character. The Classis had met. The plaintiff, upon notice, appeared before them, took objections to the regularity of the proceedings, which were overruled, and an investigation took place as to whether the reports were of such continuance and extent, as to constitute what is called common fame. The Classis determined that they were so. The Consistory was then directed to make specfic charges against the plaintiff, with the names of the witnesses. This was done, and the charges openly read to the plaintiff, who put in a general denial of their truth, and asked for time to prepare his defense. This was granted with liberty to the Consistory to furnish other specifications and names of witnesses, serving a copy fourteen days before the next meeting of Classis appointed for hearing the cause.

After a full hearing, the Classis resolved, that the plaintiff had been guilty in repeated instances of intoxication. That he be, and he is, hereby suspended from the office of the ministry, until he shall give Classis evidence of his repentance and reformation. This was on the 27th of November, 1820.

An appeal was taken before February, 1821, to the particular Synod, which rejected it on the 16th of May, 1821. An appeal to the General Synod was also disallowed.

On the 22d of February, 1821, Classis resolved, that the pastoral connection between the parties be dissolved. An appeal was taken from this decision, ultimately to the General Synod. The appeal was sustained, on the ground that Classis could not proceed to a dissolution pending an appeal from the sentence of suspension.

But at the same time (14th June, 1821), the General Synod advised Classis to proceed to such dissolution, the appeal from the judgment of suspension being disallowed. This was done by a formal act of the 26th of June, 1821.

It was decided in the Supreme Court that the minister's salary, for the period between the sentence of suspension and that of the dissolution of the pastoral connection, could be recovered. The contract was to pay him so long as he remained their minister; not so long as he performed the duties. Savage, Ch. J. dissented.

The Court of Errors held, that the plaintiff below was not entitled to recover his salary for the period between his suspension and final dismission. The contract was to be considered as implying the actual continuous discharge of pastoral duties. If the inability arose from his own fault, he could not support his claim.

Many members of the Court, and of high authority, took a different view.

§ 3. *The Presbyterian Church.* By the regulations of the Presbyterian Church (Form of Government, chaps. xv. xvi.), there can be no removal of a pastor from one church to another, nor shall he receive any call for that purpose, but by permission of the Presbytery. The mode of procuring this is pointed out.

" And when a minister shall labor under such grievances in his congregation as that he shall desire leave to resign his pastoral charge, the Presbytery shall cite the congregation to appear by commissioners, to show cause why the resignation should not be accepted." That body passes upon the case. "And if any congregation shall desire to be released from their pastor, a similar process, *mutatis mutandis*, shall be observed."

A Presbytery consists of all the ministers, and one ruling elder from each congregation within a certain district.

By chapter 11, section 14 (Forms of Process), as soon as a minister is deposed, his congregation shall be declared vacant.

Is this to be interpreted as requiring some further official declarative act? If so, by what body? Perhaps in the sentence of deposition, a clause to that effect could be inserted. In the Dutch Reformed Church, as we have seen, dismission is a formal official act consequent upon deposition. (*Ante,* § 2.)

§ 4. *Protestant Episcopal Church.* The first regulation of the Protestant Episcopal Church upon this subject, was the canon of 1804.[1] Whenever any minister has been regularly inducted or settled in a parish or church, he shall not be dismissed without the concurrence of the ecclesiastical authority of the diocese or State; and in case of such dismission without his concurrence, the vestry or congregation of such parish or church shall have no right to a representation in the convention of the State, until they have made such satisfaction as the convention may require.

Nor shall any minister leave his congregation against their will, without the concurrence of the ecclesiastical authority aforesaid; and if he shall leave them without such concurrence, he shall not be allowed to take his seat in any convention of the church, or be eligible unto any church or parish within the States which have acceded to the consti-

<hr>

[1] *Hawks' Constitution and Canons*, p. 305.

tution of this church, until he shall make such satisfaction as the ecclesiastical authority of the diocese or State may require."

The change made in 1808 was by substituting the word *instituted* for " inducted," and adding the following clause:

" This canon shall not be obligatory upon those States or dioceses with whose usages, laws, or charters it interferes."

The canon of 1832 (Canon 33), was the same.

In the Convention of 1865, it was amended, so as to read as follows : —

" *In case* a minister, who has been regularly instituted or settled in a parish or church, be dismissed by such parish or church without the concurrence of the ecclesiastical authority of the diocese, the vestry or congregation of such parish or church shall have no right to a representation in the convention of the diocese, until they shall have made such satisfaction as the convention may require; but the minister thus dismissed shall retain his right to a seat in the convention, subject to the approval of the ecclesiastical authority of the diocese.

" And no minister shall leave his congregation against their will, without the concurrence of the ecclesiastical authority aforesaid ; and if he shall leave them without such concurrence, he shall not be allowed to take his seat in any convention of this church, or be eligible into any church or parish, until he shall have made such satisfaction as the ecclesiastical authority of the diocese may require ; but the vestry or church shall not thereby be deprived of its right to a representation in the convention of the diocese.

" This canon shall not be obligatory in those dioceses with whose canons, laws, or charters it may interfere."

There are some points of importance arising under these provisions.

The office of institution is, in the judgment of the author, not necessary to entitle the minister to the rights which he possesses by virtue of his call and admission as rector.[1]

That office contains this clause: " And in case of any

---

[1] *Law of the Church*, p. 291.

difference between you and your congregation as to a separation and dissolution of all sacerdotal connection between you and them, we, your Bishop, with the advice of our presbyters, are to be the ultimate arbiter and judge."

In Hoffman's "Law of the Church," p. 334, is a statement of a case which occurred in 1848, in New York. The standing committee (the Bishop being suspended), upon an application of a vestry, required a statement in writing of the reasons for seeking a dissolution, and a request for concurrence, holding that an absolute dismission and then a request was premature. This being laid before them, and proof of reasonable notice of its presentation being made, and the minister not appearing, it was resolved, that the concurrence of the committee as the ecclesiastical authority of the diocese be given to the dismission of the Rev. Mr. ——, from the church of ——.

Two cases in Connecticut are also noticed, in which it was decided that a formal resignation accepted by the congregation, should receive such approval. The acceptance was by the body of parishioners, at a regular meeting.

From this review of our Church legislation, it follows —

That undoubtedly, the power to dissolve the connection between minister and congregation, resides in the congregation (*or in the vestry*), with the sanction of the ecclesiastical authority.

And I cannot question, that such a dissolution, regularly made, will discharge all obligations and contracts between the parties. See *post*, chapter 23.

But what are the consequences if the dismissal is without such concurrence?

The alteration of the canon in 1865, was in consequence of a resolution instructing the committee on Canons to report such an amendment as will remove the ambiguity which exists as to the effect of a dismissal by a parish of its minister, without the consent of the ecclesiastical authority. (Reporter, p. 57.) It was stated, that cases had arisen in which the question was, Whether after such dismissal and exclusion from convention, the connection absolutely ceased? That eminent counsel had differed upon the point.

An argument upon that question (before the amendment) may be thus stated. The canon forbade the dissolution without consent, in express terms, and in an independent proposition. Then a penalty was declared, namely, exclusion from a place in convention, of the congregation acting without the concurrence. Was this — could this be anything more than the ecclesiastical punishment for the disobedience to the rule? The General Convention either could not, or deemed it unwise to go further, but left the effect of the act upon the contracts and obligations of a civil nature, for decision by the civil courts. (Hawks' Const. and Canons, 309, 310.)

To the canon of 1808, relating to Institution, was added the following: But it is to be understood that this Church designs not to express any approbation of any laws or usages which make the station of a minister dependent on anything else than his own soundness in the faith, or worthy conduct.[1]

Again in the Institution Office, after recognizing a separation by mutual consent, we find this language: "And in case of any difference between you and your congregation as to a separation and dissolution of all pastoral connection between you and them, we, your Bishop, with the advice of our Presbyters, are to be the ultimate arbiter and judge."

In Young *v.* Ransom (31 Barbour's N. Y. Rep. 49), Mr. Justice Emmot expressed the opinion, that the concurrence of the ecclesiastical authority was essential.

But it must be admitted, that the amendment of 1865 appears to recognize the power to dismiss, if the congregation are ready to submit to the penalty.

It will deserve great consideration whether this can be accepted as law (in the civil courts at least), when the pastoral relation was formed before the amendment of 1865.

In a case in Michigan in 1866, after the amendment, some questions of moment arose. The assent of the authority had been given. Hence the amendment did not influence the case.[2]

---

[1] Hawks' *Constitution and Canons*, p. 276.

[2] Journal of the Convention, 1866. Pamphlet by a former member of the vestry. Detroit, 1867.

There the vestry after requesting a resignation by the rector, which was declined, passed a resolution of dismission. The Bishop, after consulting the standing committee, approved of it. In the pamphlet referred to, a committee of the congregation state that a large majority of the pew-holders expressed their unaltered confidence in the rector. It is said that although only pew-holders and communicants were solicited, two hundred and fifty-seven names were attached to a paper containing a strong approbation of his conduct.

It deserves consideration whether the true sense of the present canon is not, that the act of dismission must be the act of the congregation or parishioners, not of the vestry.

In the case of the Rector of St. Peter's Church, Salem, Massachusetts, in April, 1865, the congregation, at the annual Easter meeting, adopted by a vote of 37 to 9, a resolution that the pastoral relation between them and the rector be dissolved, and applied to the Bishop for his concurrence. Any attempt to cast reproach upon the rector was disavowed, and the Bishop stated it would be an act of great injustice to concur.

The language of the canon as amended in 1865, gives strength to the above suggestion: "In case a minister settled in a parish or church, be dismissed by such parish or church, without, etc." The language before was, "A minister settled, etc., shall not be dismissed, without, etc." Hence the vestry as a representative of the congregation, may have been treated as competent to dismiss. But the phraseology now used seems to imply that the power is in the parish or church, parishioners or members, entitled to vote.

§ 5. *Proceedings.* Another point appears to the author to be quite clear. When the sanction of the ecclesiastical authority is sought, a duty is imposed, as well as a power conferred. It cannot concur upon any *ex parte* statements, or without an examination. The right to be heard is a common law right, and must be observed, before any penalty of any description can be lawfully inflicted. If the consequence of a dismission with concurrence is to dissolve, and discharge the civil relations and contracts of the parties, it can only be so permitted when the essential rules of the law are observed. A competent authority to hear and decide — a proper reasonable notice of the matters objected to — an opportunity to meet and reply to them, are fundamental.

The opinion of that sound lawyer and canonist, Mr. G. M. Wharton, upon the case in Michigan, was, that a vestry had no right to dismiss a rector without accusation or trial. The legislation of 1865 prevents the dismissal of a minister by a vestry with the assent of the Bishop, from being uncanonical, and relieves the parties from the penalties of the canon. I do not think, however, that it makes good a dismissal without trial, or that it dissolves the contract between him and the parish. Such a result would be a violation of general principles, and, I think, the law of 1865 should be construed in subordination to these.[1] This was given in December, 1866.

In the case before the standing committee of New York, in 1848, before noticed, a written statement of the grounds of the application was required, a copy served upon the minister with notice of the day of presenting it, and action was had upon his neglect to appear.

The subject was brought before the Convention of Ohio by the Bishop in 1865. He apprised the Convention that a particular vestry had notified him of the dismissal of their regularly settled minister, and without the consent of the ecclesiastical authority.

The committee to which the communication was referred, including distinguished lawyers, reported that they were clearly of opinion, that the action of the vestry was a violation (unintentional in their judgment) of Canon 4, title 11, of the General Convention. They had received communications which led to the belief of an accommodation being effected.

But another and very important and valuable action of this Convention was had.

---

[1] Pamphlet before quoted. At page 28 is a very sensible letter of the Rev. A. DeWolfe Howe, expressing similar views.

The Bishop in his address noticed that there had been until 1859, two canons of the General Convention relating to the dissolution of the pastoral connection. One, the existing Canon 4 of title 11, and the other of differences between ministers and their congregations; that in 1859, a substitute for this canon had been reported by the joint committee on canons, which was not acted upon, while the original canon was repealed.

The last clause of the substitute proposed, declared that it should not be binding where a diocese had made or should thereafter make provision by canon on the subject.

The Bishop forcibly points out the evil of a vestry dismissing a rector, and then asking a concurrence. The standing committee of New York, in a case referred to in Hoffman's " Law of the Church," p. 330, held that the application for concurrence must precede the act of dismission.

The Bishop then notices as a sound principle that where the rights and interests of both minister and congregation are concerned, the body to judge should be composed of clergy and laity. And he refers to the suggestion that the standing committee of a diocese would be a proper body to collect the facts and present the result to the Bishop.

The Convention acted by adopting an admirable canon which is as follows : —

§ 1. Whereas it is provided in Canon 4, title 11, of the digest of canons of the General Convention, that when a minister has been regularly settled in a parish or church, he shall not be dismissed without the concurrence of the ecclesiastical authority of the diocese; it is hereby provided that in cases of controversy between any rector or assistant minister of any church or parish which cannot be settled by the parties themselves, the said parties or either of them may make written application to the Bishop of the diocese, who shall thereupon nominate four presbyters and four laymen of the diocese, and cause a list of their names to be served upon the rector or assistant minister, and also upon the clerk or secretary of the vestry, upon one or more of the applicants on behalf of the congregation, who shall, within ten days after such service, return their respective lists to the Bishop, each party having the right of striking off the name of one clergyman and one layman ; and should this right not be exercised, or both parties strike off the same names, then the Bishop shall reduce the number in the manner above prescribed to four, three of whom shall constitute a quorum, and shall meet at such time and place as the Bishop may designate, and of which due notice shall be given to the parties concerned, in order that the grounds of the controversy may be fully stated and the case fully heard.

§ 2. If it shall appear to a majority of the board thus summoned, after a full examination of the case, that there is no hope of a favorable termination of such controversy and that a dissolution of the connection is necessary, they shall recommend to such rector or assistant minister, to relinquish his connection with such parish, on such conditions as shall appear to them proper and reasonable.

§ 3. The said recommendation shall be submitted in writing, and in duplicate to the Bishop, who, if he shall clearly disapprove of the same, may set aside said recommendation, and nominate a new board which shall proceed in the manner hereinabove mentioned, and whose recommendation and finding shall be final. The Bishop shall make known to the parties the said recommendation if not set aside, or if set aside, then the said final recommendation, within ten days after the receipt of the same, and he shall report all proceedings to the Convention at its next annual meeting, with a statement of the grounds of his action in case he shall have disapproved of the first finding in any case as aforesaid.

§ 4. Should the rector or assistant minister refuse to comply within ten days after the decision shall have been made known to him, he shall be liable to suspension from the exercise of all ministerial functions until he submit to such decision.

§ 5. And if the vestry of the church or the congregation refuse or neglect to comply on their part with the decision aforesaid, the said parish shall be prohibited from a representation in the Convention of the diocese, until they shall have performed their duty in accordance with the same.

It is submitted, that a canon framed upon the following basis, would be expedient: Making the assent of the ecclesiastical authority to the dissolution of the connection and dismission of a minister, absolutely essential.

If, upon written statements of the parties, such authority cannot produce a reconciliation, or obtain a consent to the dissolution, a commission shall be appointed of two presbyters and two laymen, to inquire and report upon the case, upon notice to both parties.

Upon the written request of either party, the ecclesiastical authority shall nominate four presbyters and four laymen, etc. [Adopting the Canon of Ohio as above.]

18

CHAPTER XXIII.

THE INTERPOSITION OF CIVIL TRIBUNALS.

In no part of the world is the great principle of the exclusive rule of the Church in matters ecclesiastical, and of the State in matters civil, more generally recognized than in the United States. The provision in the Statute of 24 Henry VIII., is almost universally admitted: "Causes spiritual must be judged by judges of the spirituality, and causes temporal by temporal judges." I cite some leading cases to show the adoption and application of this maxim.

§ 1. *Sentences.* In Den *v.* Bolton (7 Halstead's N. J. Rep. 206), the Court say : "All disputes arising in the Dutch Reformed Church respecting the validity of an appointment, or call of elders and deacons, must be referrred to the church judicatory, to which the congregation is subordinate; that is, first the Classis, next to the particular Synod, and lastly to the General Synod. At a meeting of the Classis to which the congregation, of which the Reverend Mr. Demarest was pastor, was subject, he was suspended from the ministry. The question is, Was this suspension within the jurisdiction of the Classis? It appears to be given expressly in the 39th Article. The shortness of the notice was the subject of some forcible remarks, but I find no rule in the constitution of the Church ; and of course, it is within the discretion of the Classis. The suspension, then, appears to be the judgment of a competent court, within its jurisdiction, having authority over the party and the subject, with an appeal to a higher tribunal by any one aggrieved ; from which no appeal was taken, and to which, therefore, we are bound, sitting in another judicatory, to give respect and effect, without inquiring into the sufficiency of the grounds of the sentence."

In the German Reformed Church *v.* The Commonwealth (3 Barr's Penn. Rep. 282), upon a mandamus to restore the relator to the standing and rights of a minister of the Church, the Court say: "If the relator is injured by the decree of the Consistory, his remedy is by appeal to a higher ecclesiastical court. The decisions of an ecclesiastical court, like every other judicial decision, are final, as they are the best judges of what constitutes an offense against the Word of God, and the discipline of the Church. The civil courts, if they should be so unwise as to attempt to supervise their judgments on matters which come within their jurisdiction, would only involve themselves in uncertainty and doubt. Until a final adjudication by the Church judicatories, we think the relator is without remedy by mandamus." This case indicates, that had the appellate tribunal established the right of the relator, a civil court might have been resorted to for restitution to possession of temporal rights or property.

In Harmon *v.* Desher (1 Spear's Eq. Rep., South Carolina, p. 80), the Synod of the Lutheran Church had expelled Mr. Desher, a minister. The Court observe: "He stands therefore, convicted of the offenses alleged against him, by the sentence of the spiritual body of which he was a voluntary member, and whose proceedings he had bound himself to abide by. It belongs not to a civil court to enter into or review the proceedings of a spiritual court. The structure of our government has, for the preservation of civil liberty, rescued the temporal institutions from religious interference; and on the other hand, it has secured religious liberty from the invasion of the civil authority. The judgments, therefore, of religious associations upon their own members, are not examinable here."

In Wilson *v.* The Presbyterian Church of Johns' Island (2 Rich. Eq. Rep. 192, S. C.), the distinction as to the provinces of the tribunals is thus drawn by the Chancellor: "I regret that suits relating to ecclesiastical affairs have become common in our courts, and that undefined and mistaken views have been entertained in relation to the powers of civil and ecclesiastical tribunals. I think it necessary to repeat, what other judges have thought it necessary to say, that the civil tribunals possess no authority whatever, to determine on ecclesiastical matters, on questions of heresy, or what is orthodox in matters of belief; and so the ecclesiastical authority may not entertain any civil questions or in any manner affect a disposition of property by the decisions of their judicatories. The Court cannot interfere with the determination of the majority, in any manner, except to correct a misappropriation of trust property or funds."

A very important case (Forbes *v.* Eden) was decided in the House of Lords, in 1867. It was an appeal from the Court of Sessions in Scotland, by the Rev. Mr. Forbes, minister of an episcopal congregation at Buntisland, the defendant being the Primus of the church. The question depended upon the obligation of the appellant to obey the canons adopted in 1862 – 63. He objected to the introduction of portions of the English Book of Common Prayer, particularly the Burial of the Dead, Ministration of Baptism to Infants, and the Visitation of the Sick.

The Lord Chancellor said : " That no civil court could take cognizance of the rules of a voluntary religious society made for the regulation of its own affairs, except so far as they related to collateral questions affecting the disposal of property. The appellant had not shown that he had sustained any injury for which a civil court could give redress." He proceeded to examine the ecclesiastical portion of the case, although he thought that in strictness the House was not called on to deal with it. He considered it was entirely within the competency of the Synod to enact the new canons, and they bound the appellant. The appeal was dismissed.

But while full effect is given to the sentence of an ecclesiastical tribunal, certain fundamental rules of law must have been observed; and when civil rights as to property are involved, the secular tribunals will examine so far as to see that these have been obeyed.

There must be an unquestionable jurisdiction in the tribunal over the subject-matter, and over the party.

The nature of the accusation against him must have been specified with reasonable precision, and he must have had reasonable opportunity to answer it. He must have had notice of the trial or proceeding, an opportunity to produce his own, and examine the opposing witnesses; the right to the aid of counsel.

And it is always open to impeachment as having been obtained by connivance or fraud. (Story's Conflict of Laws, chapter 15.)

The case of Brinsley *v.* Davison, 4 Scammon's Reports, 539, is valuable on this head.

When the record of a court of general jurisdiction shows either that the defendant was personally served with process, or personally appeared to the action, the defendant is estopped from showing a want of jurisdiction over him. Otherwise it is but *primâ facie* evidence of jurisdiction.

When the record shows that there was no service, personal or virtual, and no appearance, it is a nullity.

If service or appearance, other than personal is shown, it is presumptive evidence that by the laws of the State giving the judgment, jurisdiction was acquired. But this may be rebutted.

In the case of Hatcher *v.* Rochelau (18 N. Y. Rep. 86), it was held that where the Court is of a limited jurisdiction, it is enough if the record states that the process was served, and the party appeared by attorney. In the case of a court of general jurisdiction, it was unnecessary to prove services or appearance, though the defendant was at liberty to controvert the facts. It was not competent to show that the judgment was erroneous, or damages awarded were too great.

§ 2. *Pending Proceedings.* In Walker *v.* Wainwright (16 Barbour's N. Y. Rep. 486), an application was made for a perpetual injunction to restrain the defendant, a bishop of the Protestant Episcopal Church, from carrying into effect a sentence of an ecclesiastical tribunal against the plaintiff, a minister of that church. By the Court:

"The only ground on which the Court can exercise any jurisdiction in this case is, that the threatened action of the defendant may affect the civil rights of the plaintiff, for the protection of which he has a proper recourse to the civil courts. The rights here invoked for that purpose are, his exemption from taxation, and the performance of certain civil duties. Conceding (though without ruling the point) that here is ground enough for the action of the Court, it becomes material to say, that the only cognizance which the Court will take of the case is, to inquire whether there is a want of jurisdiction in the defendant, to do the act which is sought to be restrained. I cannot consent to review the exercise of any discretion on his part, or to inquire whether his judgment, or that of the subordinate ecclesiastical tribunal, can be justified by the facts of the case. I cannot draw to myself the duty of revising their action any further than to inquire whether, according to the law of the association to which the parties belong, they had authority to act at all."

In Hagar *v.* Whitehouse, Bishop of Illinois, and others (Superior Court of Chicago, 1863), Chief Justice Wilson delivered the opinion. The case arose on a motion to dissolve an injunction which restrained the Bishop and the other defendants from proceeding in the investigation of charges preferred against the complainant, a presbyter of the Church. It sought also a commission to take evidence.

Upon the statements of the bill there could be no doubt of the duty of the Bishop to proceed. Such duty was imposed upon him by the canons. It would have been incumbent upon him to do so without them. An investigation was necessary for the sake of the Church, as well of the complainant. His triers would be his peers, standing in the same church relation as himself, naturally anxious to save the Church and him from disgrace.

No civil court will interfere with the legitimate exercise of the functions of Church judicatories. A church was a voluntary association, and its constitution, laws, and canons are stipulations between the parties, defining their duties and obligations. The civil rights of the members are still protected by the civil tribunals, except so far as they have been voluntarily submitted to the adjudication of the association of which they are members.

' The courts will not interfere to prevent the association from deciding any matters which the parties have agreed to submit to their decision, except where some principle of public policy is contravened, or it is against good morals. .   .   . In no case has a civil court interfered to prevent an ecclesiastical tribunal from trying an officer of a church for the purpose of discipline, according to the canons and rules of such church. Nor does the fact that the probable sentence of the ecclesiastical tribunal may incidentally affect his civil rights, give a court of chancery jurisdiction. His rights under contract will still be vindicated in common-law courts.

Whether in the contract of a rector, it is implied that he shall do no act which, by the law of the Church, disqualifies him from officiating as rector, it is unnecessary to decide.

The results of the opinion are thus stated: That civil courts will not interfere to prevent an investigation before an ecclesiastical tribunal of a voluntary religious association, when proceeding according to its constitution, canons, or rules, and when the subject-matter and person are within its jurisdiction.

That a court of chancery will not issue a commission to take depositions to be read before tribunals not established by law.

§ 3. *Salaries and other Provisions for Support.* The effect of an ecclesiastical sentence upon civil rights is frequently tested in actions for salaries or subscriptions.

Thus in The Reformed Dutch Church *v.* Bradford, stated in full, *ante*, chap. 20, § 2, the validity and finality of a sentence of an ecclesiastical tribunal was recognized. The question upon which great differences of opinion arose among the judges was, whether the sentence of suspension in the court below being appealed from, impaired the right to the salary for the period before its affirmation. It was strongly urged that the right continued until a valid final dismission, which could only be, and actually was formally had, after the affirmance. The dismission by Classis pending the appeal from the suspensory decree, was held void by the Synod.

The majority of the Court of Errors considered that the suspension was sufficient to defeat the claim.

The peculiarity of this part of the discipline of the Dutch Church gives its strength to the argument of those members of the Court who sustained the claim for the salary in the intervening period. A formal official act of dismission is prescribed as a consequence of a conviction. But in other cases, the general doctrine of an appeal has great weight upon the question. The sentence is an absolute judicial decision, which may be reversed, but whose force and execution is only so far interfered with as is necessary to make an appeal available. Indeed, in ecclesiastical courts in England, an inhibition is necessary to stop the Court below from proceeding.

In the cases in Massachusetts, we find the claim to salary rigorously supported, unless the case is controlled by some special contract, or the dismission has been effected by the sanction of a competent mutual council. (*Ante*, chap. 20, § 1.)

In Diffendorf *v.* The Reformed Calvinistic Church (20 Johns. Rep. 12), the action was upon a subscription for the support of the minister of the said church, " so long as the Rev. *John I. Wack* is, and remains our regular preacher." *Wack* had been deposed by Classis for immoral conduct; but on appeal, the sentence was reversed. The Court held the final decision to be conclusive; that the pastoral relation had not been dissolved, and sustained the action.

I presume few lawyers would hesitate in saying that a sentence of a competent tribunal of the church with which the clergyman was connected, fairly, and on proper notice obtained, deposing or suspending him, annulled any civil contract as to salary or property, unless something of express provision controlled the point.

§ 4. *Dedication of Property in trust for Religious Purposes.* The case of the Rev. Dr. Bullions in Vermont, and our own State, is a leading case.

A will contained the following provision : " I will and devise the sum of one hundred and fifty dollars, as a donation to the Associate Congregation of Rygate, to be placed under the direction of the trustees of said society, and the interest thereof to be annually paid to their minister forever." (Smith *v.* Nelson, 18 Vermont Rep. 511.)

One branch of the proceedings related to the Rev. Mr. Pringle. This requires but little attention. The point was, that the Synod which had dissolved a Presbytery, had no jurisdiction to do so at the time. But if it had that power, it could not delegate it to others (even part of its own body), and authorize them to depose the ministers.

Now the existence and competence of jurisdiction is a prerequisite upon which a civil tribunal insists, before it will regard a sentence as of any force.

The case as to the Rev. Dr. Bullions presented the difficulties.

The Presbytery to which he was subject, pronounced a sentence of deposition on the grounds of slander and contempt of court, and contumacy. An appeal was taken to the Synod, but not duly prosecuted. However, the whole case was, by consent of the parties, brought before the Synod, where the judgment was confirmed.

The Supreme Court of Vermont entered into an examination of the proceedings of the ecclesiastical tribunals, and concluded that the deposition was illegal. The principle is thus laid down. The proceedings of the Synod of the Associate Church as a court of last resort, are not to be held conclusive when they come in question directly or collaterally in courts of law; but their regularity and effect may be examined and determined, upon the same principles which subject the proceedings of inferior courts or voluntary associations, to inquiry and adjudication."

I need advert to but one, and the strongest objection the Supreme Court acted upon.

Several members of the Presbytery which tried him had been of those slandered by him.

Dr. Bullions interposed a declinature to the jurisdiction

of the Presbytery on this ground. The Synod overruled it.
The Supreme Court of Vermont held the last decision incon-
clusive, and the objection good. Vice-Chancellor Willard,
and I consider the whole Bench of the Fourth Circuit of our
State, held the decision conclusive, recognizing the force of
the objection, but holding that by his appeal and the decision against him, he was barred. (See, particularly, Justice
Hand's Opinion, 9 Barbour's Rep. 134.)

One point much less open to doubt, was also decided in
Smith *v.* Nelson, namely: That there was nothing in the
terms of the bequest which indicated that the testator intended to make the bequest depend upon the continuance
of the society in the particular connection then existing, or
with any particular tenets.

One other point is to be noticed. Nothing can be added
by implication to the express terms of the contract between
a minister and society. But if a minister ceases to be able
to perform his duties by reason of immorality, or other sufficient reasons of his own creating, it may furnish a ground
for the parties to dissolve the relation, or for one of them to
consider it as forfeited by the other.

To make this consistent with the other points determined
in Vermont, we must understand, that the reasons for such
forfeiture must be tested upon facts and law, by trial in the
civil courts.

This case, Robinson *v.* Bullions, came before Vice-Chancellor Willard in 1850.[1] He decided —

(1.) That the property was devoted to the support of
preaching the gospel and administering the ordinances in
the congregation, according to the faith and discipline of
the Associate Church of North America; and no minister
under sentence of deposition or excommunication, could perform such services in the Associate Church of Cambridge.

(2.) That the appropriation of the property for the support of Bullions since he was deposed, was an unlawful appropriation and diversion from the purposes of the trust,
and a violation of the duty of the defendants as trustees.

[1] 9 Barbour's Sup. Court Rep. 64.

(3.) That such trustees be removed, and a new election be had, unless the complainants and those acting with them, had held an election, in which case those chosen were declared trustees.

(4.) That the complainants and those concurring with them, who adhered to the Associate Presbytery of Cambridge, as subordinate to the Associate Synod of North America, were the only members of the corporation to whom the property in question belonged, and that such property be delivered up to them.

(5.) That an account be taken and a perpetual injunction issue against the defendants, restraining the defendants from applying the avails of the property to the support or use of Dr. Bullions, during the sentence of deprivation.

The case was appealed to the Supreme Court of the Fourth Circuit (9 Barbour's Rep. 64), Justice Haud delivered a very learned opinion, in the results of which Justice Paige concurred. Justice Cady dissented on several points.

The decree of the Vice-Chancellor was reversed, except so far as it restrained the defendants from applying the property to his support or use, so long as he was under the sentence of deprivation.

(1.) All the judges concurred in holding that the sentence of the ecclesiastical tribunal deposing Dr. Bullions was conclusive, and that such a dissolution, under our decisions, discharged the civil contract. The appeal taken by him in the ecclesiastical court, and the affirmance of the judgment, was decisive as to all the objections urged against the proceedings below.

(2.) The grantor, in a deed to a religious corporation, may make a connection with a particular body or church judicatory, a condition of the grant. And the corporate or denominational name may indicate the nature of the trust, as to doctrines deemed fundamental.

(3.) But the description of the grantees, as being trustees of a church, at that time in connection with a particular Presbytery or Synod, or as having a specified person as its minister, does not amount to a condition that the church or society shall remain in connection with that particular judicatory.

Justice Cady dissented from this proposition.

An appeal was taken to the Court of Appeals (1 Kernan, 24), by the complainants. There was none by the defendants. The decree was affirmed. But great doubt is thrown upon that part of the decree which restrained the employment of Dr. Bullions, and application of the funds, to his use. This will appear from the following passages: —

" While, therefore, it is settled, as far as these parties are concerned by the acquiesence of the defendants in the decree of the Supreme Court, that the trustees had, and still have no right to employ Dr. Bullions, there is no reason for following up that error, by requiring them to account."

His deposition and excommunication had nothing whatever to do with the right of the congregation to employ him so far as the administration of the temporalities was concerned, although it might subject them, or some portion of them, to spiritual censure or ecclesiastical penalties.

And the eighth proposition of the summary of Justice Seldon is this : " That the trustees of a religious corporation in this State cannot receive a trust limited to the support of a particular faith or a particular class of doctrines, for the reasons that it is inconsistent with those provisions of the statute which gave to the majority of the corporators, without regard to their religious tenets, the entire control of the revenue of the corporation."

The second and third of his propositions illustrate this one. The society itself is incorporated, not the trustees merely ; and its members are the corporators.

The relation of the trustees to the society is not that of a private trustee to a *cestui que trust,* but they are the managing officers of the corporation and trustees, in the same sense in which directors of a bank are trustees, invested with powers conferred by statute, and with the ordinary discretionary powers of similar corporate officers.

Three judges of the Court, Gardiner, Parker, and Edwards,

concurred with Judge Selden in the eighth, as well as in the other propositions. Judge Denio dissented from it. Judge Ruggles was absent, and Judge Johnson did not take part in the decision.

Judge Allen delivered an opinion. While we do not find in it any express recognition of the eighth proposition, nor a position identical with it, the first aud second paragraphs do tend to sanction it.

Again, the seventh proposition of Judge Selden is : " That when a deed is executed to trustees for religious purposes, and the use is expressed in general, and uot in specific terms, it cannot be inferred from the religious tenets and faith of the grantee (*grantor*), that it was intended to limit the use to the support of the particular doctriues which he preferred, or the religious class to which he belonged, although if the language creating the trust be ambiguous, evideuce of the surrounding circumstances, and among them perhaps, of the faith of the donor, may be received, as in other cases, to aid in its construction."

In this proposition, I understand, all the judges concurred.

The learned judge, in a previous part of his opinion says : " I by no means deny that the grantor of property to the trustees of a religious corporation, may annex such conditions to the grant as he may choose, not inconsistent with law ; and that the trustees may take the property subject to the conditions. For instance, property may be conveyed to them, to be held so long as the society continues in a certain ecclesiastical connection, or so long as it supports a minister of a certain faith ; and this condition, if explicit and clear, would be good. An uncertain condition would be void. The title of the trustees nnder such a deed would be good so long as a majority of the corporators chose to abide by the condition ; and wheu that was departed from, their title would be forfeited. This is widely different from a trust which is to be enforced iu oppositiou to the will of the majority."

The distinction of the learned judge, I nnderstand to be, that the abaudonment of the organization or tenets indicated by a grantor as those for the support of which his property is given, works a forfeiture of the property, but that a minority cannot secure its appropriation to the designated purposes against the will of the majority of the members of the church or society.

The principles of these authorities were carried out to their fullest logical results in Gram *v.* The Prussian, etc. German Society (36 N. Y. Rep. 161, 1867). The property in question was received and held by the religious corporation, the defendants, upon trust for the support of the German Evangelical Lutheran faith, doctrine, and government, as held and practised by the German Evangelical Lutheran churches under the Synod of Buffalo and its ministers.

The defendants, the trustees of the church, had excluded the plaintiffs, being the pastor, chorister, and sexton, from the performance of their respective functions; and this was found as a fact, to have been in violation of the rules of government of the Lutheran churches, and of the rights of the plaintiffs, according to the same. But it was also found that the change had been made under the direction of a majority of the members of the church and corporation.

It was held, that the trusts were not such as could be enforced, and the complaint was dismissed.

Bascom *v.* Albertson (34 N. Y. Rep. 584), had settled, that charitable uses were not excepted from the provision in the Statute of Uses and Trusts, abolishing all trusts except as therein authorized.

The trusts were clearly not legal trusts under those provisions of the Revised Statutes. Could they be sustained under the act of incorporation?

The church was incorporated under the General Act of 1813. That act was not affected by the Revised Statutes, but remained in force. Tucker *v.* St. Clement's Church is cited. The provisions of such act are then cited in detail.

Robertson *v.* Bullions is quoted: "While the scope of the act is, that the property is to be devoted to the promotion of religion through the observance of divine worship, and the ministrations of ministers and teachers; and any

diversion from such general purpose would be an abuse of
the trust, which a court of equity would correct, yet it was
equally evident, that the statute did not contemplate a devo-
tion of such property perpetual and unchangeable, to the
support of a particular system of religious faith and doctrine, or ecclesiastical rule or discipline. . . . The idea
of such a trust necessarily implies, that if a division occurs
in the society, holding the same faith at the beginning, the
portion adhering thereto must remain the *cestuis que trust*,
to the exclusion of those who do not so adhere. This cannot be done."

All the judges of the Court, except Scrugham who did
not vote, concurred in this decision.

It may be considered as settled in our State, that if property is given to a church or congregation incorporated under our general statutes, by words vesting the title in it,
and not plainly uniting the right to hold it with the faith,
doctrine or order of any particular denomination or body, a
change in the religious tenets or church discipline held at
the time of the acquisition, will not deprive the corporation
of that property.

Thus in Bunell *v.* The Associate Reformed Church of Seneca (44 Barbour's Rep. 282), certain parcels of land had been
conveyed to the trustees of the Associate Reformed Church
of the town of Salem; one parcel in trust for the religious
society designated as the Associate Reformed Church of the
town of Seneca; another parcel for the purpose of building
a church on it, or for a burying-place; and another for a
parsonage and nothing else.

The Associate Reformed Church of the town of Seneca,
separated from the church organization with which it was
connected at the time of the grant, and united with another
denomination. Its title remained the same.

It was held, after a careful examination of the cases of
Robertson *v.* Bullions and Petty *v.* Tooker (*post*), that the
property conveyed belonged to the congregation which consisted of all the members entitled to vote at the election of
trustees, a majority of whom controlled the property, and,

us a necessary consequence, decided the ecclesiastical relations and connections of the society, and the character of the religious views, opinions, and doctrines, to be inculcated from the pulpit.

In Petty *v.* Tooker (21 N. Y. Rep. 267), the property was conveyed to the trustees of a church after it had been incorporated under the General Act. No express condition as to faith or discipline appears to have been contained in the conveyance. It seems to have been a general conveyance to the trustees for the church.

The result of the case is thus stated by Justice Parker in the case from 36 N. Y. Reports, before cited. " That case involved the inquiry, whether the trustees and a majority of the society could change from Congregationalists to Presbyterians, and retain possession of the church property against those who adhered to the faith of the founders of the church and society, and it was held without dissent, that they could."

Mr. Justice Selden, in Petty *v.* Tooker, observed, that property could be secured to the support of a particular faith or order, by having the church and lot conveyed to the society, upon the express condition that it should be forever devoted to the purposes of religion, by a congregation maintaining a certain faith, and observing certain prescribed ordinances and forms. Such a condition, if clearly expressed, would be valid, and no doubt would operate as a guaranty against any change in the religious character of the society."

This must be considered in connection with the observations of the same learned judge in Robertson *v.* Bullions, before cited. It would seem that even in such a case, there would be a forfeiture and reversion, but not that the minority adhering could secure the property for their own use.

The case of Gable *v.* Miller deserves a careful statement upon this subject. (10 Paige, 627; 2 Denio's Rep. 492.)

The questions between the parties were : —

First, whether the church property was held for the purpose of supporting the doctrines of the Reformed Protestant

Dutch Church; next, if it was also held in subordination to the ecclesiastical government of that church.

The Assistant Vice-Chancellor, before whom the cause was first heard, decided : That neither, upon the facts attending the original dedication of the church and property, nor upon any subsequent act, was there ground to determine the first question in the affirmative.

That upon the points wherein differences of views existed, or were supposed to exist, between the strictly defined tenets of the Dutch Reformed Church, and the teachings represented by the defendants, there was no evidence to show that such teachings varied substantially from those which (it was to be drawn from the evidence) were held by the original founders and donors.

Historically speaking, there were considerable differences in the dogmatic teachings of the Lutheran Church, as it was termed, and the Dutch Reformed Church, upon points of moment.

And secondly, the case was clear upon the testimony, that no inseparable connection with, or subordination to, the ecclesiastical judicatory, none making the holding of the property dependent upon it, was ever formed.

The complaint was dismissed. See the opinion, 2 Denio's Rep. p. 510.

The Chancellor differed on both points, holding —

That there was a dedication of the funds and property to the worship of God according to the Calvinistic doctrines of the Dutch Reformed, German Reformed, and Helvetic Churches; that the tenets and doctrines of these were substantially the same, and the property was for the use of those who held them. Again, that the church was under the government and discipline of the Dutch Reformed Church. That the plaintiffs as holding such tenets and recognizing such subordination were entitled.

Nothing can be more explicit than his assent to the principles of the English and Scotch cases, cited by the Assistant Vice-Chancellor, to which he adds, Dill *v.* Watson, in the Irish Exchequer, 1836. Thus, he says : " Those for whose use the donations were intended have a right to claim that the property of the church shall be applied to the worship of God, and to the propagation of the doctrines, and the administering the sacraments of the church as then established, unless the defendants can show that the trust has been changed by general consent of all persons interested therein, or that the diversion of the fund to other purposes has been so long acquiesced in as to constitute a bar by lapse of time.

The decree was reversed, and a decree was made in favor of the plaintiffs.

In the Court of Errors, the result was a reversal of the decree of the Chancellor, and affirmance of that of the Assistant Vice-Chancellor. The reporter justly observes, that it is difficult to say on what grounds a majority concurred. Perhaps the opinion of Senator Barlow is more likely to have ruled the majority than any other. That no portion of the temporalities in question appear to have been conveyed or contributed upon any trusts relating to religious doctrine or church government; but if this were otherwise, that there had been no such material deviation from the former faith or practice as would authorize the interposition of the Court of Chancery.

In ascertaining what can be supported as a valid appropriation of property under the language of the Act of 1813, " for the use of such church, congregation, or society, or other pious uses," we may clearly assume that Tucker *v.* St. Clement's Church (3 Sandf. 242; 8 N. Y. Rep. 558), is law still. The Court of Appeals sustained the Court below. The gift was of the rents, issues, and profits, or income if the land was sold, "to be applied to the maintenance and support of the rector or minister for the time being of such church, and for no other purpose."

So in Williams *v.* Williams (8 N. Y. Rep. 525), there was a gift of $6,000 to the trustees of the Presbyterian Church and congregation, in the village of Huntington, and their successors, in trust for the support of a minister of such church as now constituted.

The Court of Appeals in Bascom *v.* Albertson (34 N. Y. Rep. 599), says: " We entertain no doubt that the bequest in that case was properly upheld. It was a gift to a religious corporation legally authorized to take and hold the fund for purposes within the scope of its charter."

While thus a gift or conveyance for the use of a church, or support of a minister, and other pious purposes, a parsonage for example, are, I presume, perfectly valid within the Act of 1813, it seems to be the unavoidable result that the property will belong to the majority of the voters, although they change their doctrine and church subordination.

It appears that a mode of avoiding this result, is by a condition or trust in the grant unequivocally expressed, making the tenure of the property dependent upon the continued observance of certain doctrines or ecclesiastical organization. And even in this case, it seems, that the abandonment by the majority of the tenets and order, for support of which the property was given, works a forfeiture and reverter to the donor. The minority of the church who adhere cannot demand the property.

It may be observed, that this point has not been absolutely decided as a point essential to any decision made. The dedication of property on such conditions, is allowed and assumed to be for a pious use, within the statute, and it is validly held for these purposes, while the majority adhere to them. Why the laudable and legal intentions of the donor should be defeated, and the minority, willing to carry them out, possess no voice, is not a very satisfactory conclusion.

It is intimated, however, that a diversion to what could not in any proper sense, be considered a pious use, would justify a court in interfering.

§ 5. *Elections.* When a church or corporation takes advantage of an act of incorporation, it subjects itself voluntarily to all the provisions and regulations of such act. Any inconsistent ecclesiastical regulation becomes superseded.

Thus as to elections of the officers of such incorporated churches, whatever is prescribed in the statute must be precisely followed, and whatever is obscure or omitted, must be explained and supplied by the maxims of the civil law applicable to the subject.

It follows, that when a statute, under which an incorporation has been had, contains legislation upon the subject of elections, qualifications of voters, etc., the civil tribunals obtain cognizance of the matter.

The mode of proceeding is regulated by the four hundred and thirty-second section of the Code: "An action may be brought by the Attorney-General in the name of the people of the State, upon his own information, or the complaint of any private party, against the parties offending, in the following," among other cases: "When any person shall usurp, intrude into, or unlawfully hold or exercise any public office, civil or military, or any franchise within this State, or any office in a corporation created by the authority of this State."

In Hart *v.* Harvey (10 Abbott, 322, and 13 Abbott, 332), it was ruled, that an action for an injunction was not the mode of trying the right to an office in a religious corporation. The remedy was an action in the nature of a *quo warranto.*

In *The People on the relation of Devoe* v. *Lawrence and others*, Sept. 1866, an action was brought to test the validity of an election for vestrymen in an Episcopal Church, and a jury being waived, the judge found the facts and law, as to the parties entitled to the offices, that the defendants had intruded into, and unlawfully held the office of vestrymen; and that the relators were lawfully entitled to the same.

The course of practice in these actions under the Code is in substance the same, and governed by the same rules as prevailed under the former practice. (The People *ex rel.;* Smith *v.* Pease, 30 Barbour's Rep. 588.)

Without farther details on this subject, I refer to The People *v.* Carpenter, 24 N. Y. Rep. 86; People *ex rel.;* Smith *v.* Pease, 27 N. Y. Rep. 45.

That a mandamus may sometimes be resorted to is shown by the case of The People on the relation of Heent *v.* White, 11 Abbott's Rep. 163.

In the German Reformed Chnrch *v.* Leibert (3 Barr's Peuu. Rep. 290), the relator in mandamus had been refused admission as a voter because he was no longer a member, having been excommnnicated. A strong point was taken by the Court. It was urged that the power of the Consistory extended only to a repulsion from the Lord's Table; but to annul the right of membership, the consent of the congregation was requisite. The Court admit that this seemed to be the import of the fifth and sixth articles of the Church discipline. Assuming it to be so, the remedy was by appeal to the superior tribunal. The judge poiuts ont how that was provided for. He observes, that whether the asseut was given or not, did not appear.

APPENDIX.

———◆———

NOTE I.

The charter of May 6, 1697, was granted by Governor Fletcher upon a petition of Colonel Heathcote, and others, stating the contributions for erecting a church, etc., and provided, among other things, as follows : —

That the aforesaid church erected as aforesaid, and the ground thereto adjoining inclosed and used for a cemetery or church-yard, shall be the parish church and church-yard of the parish of Trinity Church within our said city of New York; and the same is hereby dedicated to the service of God, and to be applied thereunto (or therein,[1]) to the use and behalf of the inhabitants from time to time inhabiting and to inhabit within our said city of New York, in communion with our said Protestant Church of England as now established by law, and to no other use whatever.

Rector. "There shall be a rector to have care of the souls of the inhabitants of said parish, and a perpetual succession of rectors."

"And we create and make our trusty and well beloved the Lord Bishop of London, and his successors, rectors of the said parish, together with all the inhabitants from time to time inhabiting and to inhabit in our said city of New York, and in communion of our said Protestant Church of England, as now established by our laws, a body corporate and politic, with the powers and privileges hereafter mentioned."

Name of Body Corporate. "We constitute and declare, that our Henry, Lord Bishop of London, and his successors, and all such of our loving subjects, as now are or hereafter shall be *admitted* into the communion of the aforesaid Protestant Church of England, as

---

[1] The word in the copy in the office of Secretary of State is "therein"; in Judge Troup's copy, "thereunto."

now established by our laws, shall be, from time to time, and forever hereafter, a body politic and corporate, in fact and name, by the name of the Rector and Inhabitants of our said City of New York, in communion of our Protestant Church of England, as now established by our laws."

By that name they were to have perpetual succession, were made capable to sue and be sued, etc., "and also to have, take, possess, receive, acquire, and purchase lands, tenements, hereditaments, or any goods and chattels, and the same to use, lease, grant, demise, alien, bargain, and sell, and dispose of at their own will and pleasure, as others our liege people, or any corporation or body politic within our realm of England or this our province, may lawfully do, not exceeding the yearly value of five thousand pounds, the statute of mortmain, or any other statute law, custom, or usage, to the contrary notwithstanding."

" The said rector shall have the care of the souls of the inhabitants within the said parish, and in the communion of our said Protestant Church of England."

" The patronage and presentation of the said rectory and parish, after the decease of the first rector, shall belong to, and be hereby vested in, the church-wardens and vestrymen, or the major part of the said vestrymen, together with either of the church-wardens for the time being."

Vestry. — How Chosen. " There shall be annually, on the Tuesday in Easter week, two church-wardens and twenty vestrymen duly elected, by the majority of votes of the inhabitants of the said parish, in communion as aforesaid."

Power as to Parish Affairs. " The rector, church-wardens, and vestrymen shall make the number of the whole to be twenty-three persons; and the said vestrymen, or any eleven or more of them (whereof the rector for the time being, or his assistant or clarke by appointment, and one of the church-wardens to be two), shall, and may have and exercise the like power and authority for the ordering and regulating the affairs of the said corporation and parish of Trinity Church, as the vestry of the parish of St. Mary Bow (*within our city of London in our realm of England*), now have and exercise, relative to parish affairs; and upon the death or other voidance of any such vestryman, they, or any eleven or more of them shall, and may elect a fit person, inhabitant and householder in the said parish, to supply the same.

Pews. " The church-wardens for the time being shall not at any time dispose of any of the pews or places in pews in the said church, to any person not an inhabitant thereof, nor without the consent and allowance of the vestrymen for the time being, or any eleven or more of them.

Rates for Repairs, etc. " The said church-wardens, together with eleven or more of the vestrymen shall, and are hereby authorized, from time to time, to make rates and assessments in manner aforesaid, for repairing and amending the church, steeple, cemetery, or church-yard of the said parish, when need shall be ; the said rates to be paid to the church-wardens, and to be made, collected, confirmed, and allowed as aforesaid.

The Sole Parish Church. " We do give, grant, ratify, and confirm unto the said rector and inhabitants of our said city of New York, in communion of our said Protestant Church of England, as now established by our laws, that the said church and cemetery, or church-yard, situate, lying, and being within our said city of New York as aforesaid, shall be the sole and only parish church and church-yard of our said city of New York."

The £100 Appropriated. It was declared, that the rector of the said parish church was a Protestant minister, within the intent of the act of Assembly passed in the fifth year of the reign (1693), entitled " An Act for the Settling of a Ministry," etc. The yearly maintenance of one hundred pounds was directed to be assessed and paid to the said rector. The church-wardens and vestrymen appointed under such act, were every year to assess and collect such sum in the manner therein prescribed. They were made liable to an action of debt if they neglected it.

The said rector and inhabitants were authorized to appoint, alter, and change the days and times of meeting as they should think fit.

Admission of Members. And to choose, nominate, and appoint so many others of our liege people as they shall think fit, and shall be willing to accept the same, to be members of the church and corporation and body politic, and them into the same to admit.

Election of other Officers. " And to elect and constitute such other officer and officers as they shall think fit and requisite for the orderly management and despatching of the affairs of the said church and corporation and their successors.

To Ordain By-Laws. " And from time to time to make, ordain, constitute, or repeal, rules, orders, and ordinances for the good and welfare of the members of the said church and corporation, so that they be not repugnant to the laws of our realm of England, and of this province."

The church-wardens and vestrymen or any other persons appointed by them, might upon the Lord's day, after divine service, or at any other time, a time when they should see fit, take and receive free and voluntary gifts, alms, and contributions, and employ them towards finishing of the said church, steeple, or premises, or any other pious and charitable work, as to them should seem meet.

Habendum. "To have and to hold all and every the premises, with all and singular the rights, etc., unto them, the said rector and inhabitants of our said city of New York, in communion of the Protestant Church of England, as now established by our laws, and their successors."

"To the sole and only use of them, etc. to be holden in free and common socage as of our Manor of East Greenwich, in our county of Kent, within our realm of England; yielding yearly and every year the rent of one peppercorn, if the same be lawfully demanded."

Act of 1704. On the 27th of June, 1704, an act was passed "granting certain privileges and powers to the rector and inhabitants of the city of New York, of the communion of the Church of England as by law established."

It recited the erection of a church, and the holding the same, with a cemetery, and piece of ground adjoining; with certain powers, rights, and privileges necessary for the management of the affairs of such church. "To the end therefore that such religious work may be founded upon some lasting foundation, grow up and become fruitful to the praise and glory of God, the good example of others and the benefit of their posterity and successors," it was enacted:—

"That the rector and inhabitants of the said city of New York, in communion of the Church of England, as by law established, and their successors, shall be enabled for the maintenance and recovery of their estates, rights, and privileges, to sue and be sued, defend and be defended, by the same name of the Rector and Inhabitants of the City of New York, in communion of the Church of England, as by law established; and by the same name, they and their successors, shall have, hold, use and enjoy all their said church, burying-place, and land thereto belonging, by whatever name heretofore purchased or had, or to them given or granted; to the sole and proper use and benefit of the said rector and inhabitants, and their successors forever, in as firm and ample manner in the law, as if the said rector and inhabitants had been legally incorporated, and made capable in the law of taking, purchasing, and holding the same, at and before the purchasing and taking of the said cemetery and lands thereunto belonging."

Power to take Lands. By the second section, the said rector and inhabitants by the same name, were authorized to purchase and hold lands, tenements, etc., and to lease, demise, and improve the same, to the benefit of the church, and other pious uses, not exceeding five hundred pounds yearly rent.

They were empowered to alter and enlarge the church ; to erect a dwelling-house for the use of the rector, a vestry-room, charnel-house, and other necessaries of the said church.

Advowson. By the third section it was enacted " that the patronage and advowson of the said church and right of presentation after the death of the present rector, or upon next avoidance, and forever thereafter, shall belong and appertain to the church-wardens and vestrymen of the said church, annually elected or to be elected, by the inhabitants aforesaid, in communion as aforesaid, in manner hereafter mentioned and expressed, or to the major part of such church-wardens and vestrymen for the time being, whereof a church-warden always to be one."

Institution, etc. " Such rectors shall be instituted and inducted into the said church, in such manner, and always as shall be most suitable and agreeable to her Majesty's instructions to the Governor of this colony for the time being, and the canonical authority which the Bishop of London and his successors hath and shall have over the said church."

The £100 Appropriated. By the fourth section, the succeeding rector or incumbent of the church (after the death or other avoidance of Mr. Vesey, the then rector), and his successors forever, be, and shall be, instituted, authorized, and empowered, to have and receive the sum of one hundred pounds yearly, raised and levied upon the inhabitants of the said city, for the maintenance of a good sufficient Protestant minister, in the said city, by virtue of an act of the Assembly of the fifth year of the reign of King William and Queen Mary (1693), entitled " An Act for Settling a Minister in," etc.

Section 5 authorized the use of a common seal, and to alter, break, and new make it at discretion.

Annual Choice of Wardens, etc. And by section six, it was made lawful " for the inhabitants aforesaid to assemble and meet together on Tuesday in Easter-week annually, at the said church, to choose two church-wardens and twenty vestrymen, communicants of the said church, to serve and officiate in and for the next ensuing year, by the majority of the voice of the said communicants so met, and not otherwise.

" Such church-wardens so chosen and hereafter to be chosen annually, have, and shall have like power and authority, to do, execute, and perform their said offices respectively, as church-wardens and vestrymen in England; unless some particular difference may happen by the express power and direction of the present act of the General Assembly."

The said church-wardens, or one of them, were authorized, so often as would be needful, to call a meeting of the vestrymen of said church, to meet the rector for the time being, if any there be, and church-wardens, or one of them.

The rector and church-wardens, or one of them, and a majority of the vestrymen, were empowered to make rules and orders for managing the affairs of the church, and to have the sole disposition and ordering of all payments of the church moneys.

In case of the death of a rector, and before the church was supplied with another, the said powers were fully vested in church-wardens, by and with the advice and consent of a major number of the whole vestrymen, and not otherwise.

Power was given to the church-wardens and vestrymen, or the major part of them, whereof one church-warden was always to be one, without the rector, to establish the fees and perquisites of their rector, clerk, sexton, and all other officers of the parish, not to exceed the fees and perquisites usually taken in England.

Also to regulate the fees for breaking the church-yard, and burying the dead; but not to exceed the fees reserved in the grant of the church-yard, made by the mayor, aldermen, and commonalty of the city of New York, for the use of Trinity Church.

In case of the death of any of the church-wardens or vestrymen, within the year, it was made lawful for the inhabitants aforesaid, *in communion* as aforesaid, at any time upon such emergency, to meet at the church upon notice given by the rector, to elect and choose others, qualified as aforesaid, in their room; who were to execute the offices of such as they shall be chosen to succeed respectively, until the time of the next annual election.

By the seventh section, the rector for the time being might, upon the avoidance of such officers, appoint a clerk, sexton or sextons, who shall continue in office during their natural lives, unless they voluntarily surrender, or become incapable of serving by sickness, or other infirmity, or misbehaves; in which case the rector, with the advice and consent of the church-wardens, or one of them, and vestrymen, or major part of them, might displace or remove such officer and officers so misbehaving themselves, and not otherwise.

The powers, privileges, and liberties granted, were to be construed most favorably for the benefit of the said church.

The act was not to be construed to abridge the indulgence or liberty of conscience granted to other Protestant Christians by the act of the first year of the late William and Mary, entitled, "' An Act for exempting their Majesties Protestant subjects, dissenting from the Church of England, from the penalty of certain laws;' or by any other law or statute of the realm of England, or this plantation."

Grant of 1705. The grant of the Queen's farm and the Queen's garden of the 20th November, 1705, recite the incorporation under the Act of June, 1704, and the power to take and hold lands *to the benefit of the said church and other pious uses.*

The habendum was, " unto the said rector and inhabitants of the city of New York, in communion with the Church of England, as by law established, and their successors forever."

I have now stated all of charter or legislation which bears upon any question connected with the rights and franchises of Trinity Church, prior to the Revolution.

What are the legal conclusions ?

(1.) Trinity parish was constituted the only parish in the city of New York, and the parish was made co-extensive with the city.

At that time (1697), the city was Manhattan Island.[1] It is declared to be the sole and only parish church of our said city of New York. Various passages in the charter support this view. The petition of Trinity Church in 1813 states, that this was intended, and was the fact and law.

(2.) The Act of Assembly of June 1704, was not necessary for the incorporation, nor did it supersede the charter of 1697. The Crown charters have always, under the colonial or state systems, been upheld. The act confirmed what had been granted, with full

---

[1] The county of New York to contain all the islands commonly called Manhattan Island, Manning Island, the two Barn Islands, and the three Oyster Islands; Manhattan Island to be called the city of New York, and (*with*) the rest of the islands the county. (Act of October 1, 1691. Hoffman's Estate, etc. of the Corporation of New York, vol. ii. p. 32.) I conceive that the word *with* italicized is necessary to show the full meaning. See the Act of November 1, 1683, quoted Ibid. which appears to favor this view.

legislative authority, and added some things; and the alterations it made, being accepted, became valid. Upon one important subject, that of taxing, legislative power was probably requisite, and crown authority insufficient.

(3.) The corporators were " Henry, Lord Bishop of London, and his successors, rectors of the said parish, together with all the inhabitants from time to time inhabiting, and to inhabit in our said city of New York, and in communion of our aforesaid Protestant Church of England." The Lord Bishop of London had been before constituted the first rector.

(4.) A body was constituted to represent the corporators, con. sisting of church-wardens and vestrymen; and with the rector, to manage the affairs of the parish.

(5.) The rector was to have the care of the souls of the inhabitants within the parish. IIe, or his assistant or clerk by appointment, as a distinct, integral part of the vestry, had the power, with the wardens and vestrymen, or a warden and a majority of vestrymen, to manage the affairs. IIe, with the advice and consent of the wardens and vestrymen as specified, had the appointment of a minister to be assistant and preacher.

(6.) The patronage, donation, advowson, or presentation of a minister was vested in the church-wardens and vestrymen, or the major part of the vestrymen with one church-warden.

Therefore in the presentation of the Rev. Henry Barclay as rector to Governor Clinton, the vestry style themselves the true and undoubted patrons of the rectory of the parish of Trinity Church. The admission which properly belongs to the Bishop was delegated to the Governor. See instructions to the governors, *passim*, in " Documents relating to Colonial History," vol. iii. p. 372, *ibid.* 688. No clerk could be admitted and inducted without a certificate of the Bishop of London, of his conformity to the doctrine and discipline of the Church of England, and being of a goodly life and conversation.

(7.) The right to choose wardens and vestrymen was vested by the charter in a majority of the votes of the inhabitants of the said parish, in communion as aforesaid. In the third section of the Act of 1704, the same phraseology is used. But in the sixth section of that Act, the inhabitants aforesaid are to assemble, and to choose wardens and vestrymen, communicants of the said church, to serve, etc., by the majority of the voices of the *said communicants* so met, and not otherwise.

Yet, after careful consideration, I think that this phrase cannot receive a larger construction, than the term *in communion with*.

In chapter II. sections   , I have treated at length of the meaning of the terms " inhabitants " and " in communion with· the Protestant Church of England, as by law established ; " also the position of chapels of ease, and of independent chapels or churches organized within parish limits.   The conclusions to be drawn from these statements, I think, are these : —

(1.) As to voters, the ecclesiastical qualification being in communion was, of course, satisfied, by being a communicant, or by being baptized according to the office of the church.

(2.) The being in communion demanded an outward manifestation of conformity to the doctrine and discipline of the Church of England.

This was shown, and it was essential that it should be shown, by worshipping in the parish church, or one of its chapels, if it had any.   No one who disobeyed or neglected the express requisitions of the statutes of Edward and Elizabeth, and the Canon of 1603, could be in communion.

(3.) I think that no one was entitled to vote unless he had been assessed and paid towards the £100 for the support of the minister ; or towards the £30 for the support of the assistant and other charges ; or towards charges assessed under the general law, for repairs of the church, and what was necessary for conducting divine service ; provided any assessment or rating had been made for such purposes.   If the vestry did not assess (from having other funds, for example), this qualification would not be demanded.

(4.) But it was clearly legal for the wardens and vestrymen to pass a law fixing a money qualification by rate, or in some other mode, which should regulate the right of voting ; determining who were inhabitants in communion, responsible by the law of the land, for the support of the church.

(5.) The rector, wardens and vestrymen, were endued with all the powers vested in English vestries.   No power was more clear than the right to assess rates upon parishioners.

(6.) And as a branch of this power, and a substitute for its mode of exercise, a rent or tax could be imposed upon pews or seats, and payment of it could be legally made a qualification for voting.

(7.) Inhabitancy within the parish (the city of New York), was essential.   This meant at least, not a temporary sojourning, but residing in it as a home or permanent abode.

(8.) The power to establish chapels, with all their incidents, was plain and indisputable. The power to assent to chapels being separately organized and incorporated was clear. And equally so was the right to consent to the establishment of new churches, and their being freshly and independently organized and incorporated.

(9.) When such chapels or churches were separately organized, as they were released from their dependence upon, or subjection to, Trinity Church, so that they lost all share in participation in the property, privileges, or management thereof.

(10.) It followed, that every part of the city not occupied by churches, with their precincts, thus by consent separately organized, remained the parish of Trinity Church. The law of intrusion forbade the constitution of any new church without assent of her rector and vestry, as well as the Bishop, and permitted it with such assent.

Constitution of 1777. This was the position of Trinity Church when the Revolution took place. The Constitution of 1777 saved the charter from annulment by reason of any thing contained in it. Its property, its substantial rights, franchises and privileges remained undisturbed.

Then came the important Act of April, 1784.[1] The following is its substance : —

Section one repealed such parts of the charter of 1697 as rendered necessary the induction by a governor of a rector to the church.

It repealed such other parts of the charter and of the Act of 1704 as admitted that rights existed in the Bishop of London in and over such church. It repealed all of the charter as related to the settling of the ministry, and such law and of the law of 1693.

Every other provision of the charter and of the law of 1704, was not only not repealed, but was expressly declared not to be annulled or repealed by that act ; nor by nonuser or misuser, between the 19th of April, 1775, and the date of this Act of 1784, where not inconsistent with the Constitution of the State.

By the second section, the church-wardens and vestrymen of the said corporation or a majority of them, were invested with full power to call and induct a rector to the said church, so often as there shall be any vacancy therein. The third section is, " Whereas doubts have arisen on those parts of the said charter, and law first above mentioned (the charter of 1697 and the Act of 1704),

----

[1] Jones & Varick, i. p. 128.

which speak of inhabitants in communion of *the said Church* of England, for removal thereof;

" Be it enacted, that all persons professing themselves members of the Episcopal Church, who shall either hold, occupy or enjoy a pew or seat in the said church, and shall regularly pay to the support of the said church; and such others, as shall, in the said church, partake of the holy sacrament of the Lord's Supper, at least once in every year, being inhabitants of the city and county of New York, shall be entitled to all the rights, benefits, privileges, and emoluments which, in and by the said charter and law first above mentioned (1697 and 1704), are designed to be secured to the inhabitants of the city of New York, in communion with the Church of England."

The sixth section recited, that as doubts might arise as to the continuance, force. and effect of certain acts of the legislature while a colony, reciting them, namely, the Act of 22d of September, 1693, of 27th of June, 1704, of the 4th of August, 1705, of the 27th of July, 1721, of the 21st of September, 1744, and certain parts of the Act of the 29th of November, 1745, which granted certain immunities and privileges to the Episcopal Church in certain counties : Therefore such acts and such portions of the last-mentioned act were annulled and repealed.

By au Act of 20th of April, 1784, all the above acts with several others of a subsequent date were repealed, except this Act of June 27, 1704.

By the Act of March 10, 1788, passed on the petition of Trinity Church, it was enacted that the corporation should, and might take and use the name of " The Rector and Inhabitants of the City of New York, in communion of the Protestant Episcopal Church, in the State of New York."   All grants, deeds, and conveyances made to it between the 17th of April, 1784, and the date of this act, by its former title, were confirmed, as if the Act of 1704 had not been repealed, or as if the corporation had not been expressly named therein.

This was the legal position of Trinity Church, until the Act of January 25, 1814.

In the mean time several distinct churches had been organized and incorporated within the city, to a few of which it is of consequence to refer.

In 1793, Mr. Stuyvesant offered a conveyance of land and a contribution in money toward the erection of a church. Trinity Church agreed to raise £5,000 for the building. In 1795 Mr. Stuyvesant conveyed twelve lots of land, the present site of St. Mark's, to Trinity Church. In 1798 the opinion of Alexander Hamilton and Richard Harison was taken, and measures adopted to make it a separate church. The property was conveyed in 1799 by Trinity Church to trustees, in trust for the corporation, when the same should be formed. Church-wardens and vestrymen were chosen, and measures taken for an incorporation under the Act of 17th of March, 1795. A certificate of incorporation was filed in the county clerk's office November 22, 1799. The lots were subsequently conveyed by the trustees to the corporation.

In 1805, in consequence of doubts as to whether certain omissions had not worked a dissolution, the church was reincorporated under the Act of the 27th of March, 1801. The certificate was filed July 3, 1805.

In November, 1801, the following opinion was given : —

" In consequence of a resolution of the vestry of Trinity Church, of the 9th of November instant, we have considered the subject therein mentioned, and are of opinion, that the corporation of St. Mark's Church have no valid pretensions either at law or in equity, to any part of the property of the rector and inhabitants of the city of New York, in communion of the Protestant Episcopal Church in the State of New York ; but for greater caution, we approve of their taking a deed from the corporation of St. Mark's, in the form marked A, when the lots lately set apart for that purpose, are conveyed to the said corporation.

" ROBERT TROUP,
" ALEXANDER HAMILTON,
" RICHARD HARISON."

We here find the perfect ecclesiastical organization of a new parish within the limits of Trinity parish, by the assent of the rector and vestry of the latter. It was endowed by a grant of lands from the Mother Church, as a parochial church in England is endowed by setting apart a portion of the tithes. The separation was ecclesiastically, and when incorporated, civilly complete. The independence of Trinity Church and its rector was absolute, and it inevitably followed that any participation by its members in the franchises or government of Trinity Church, by voting for its vestrymen or otherwise, was lost, was voluntarily abandoned.

A similar course was pursued in the year 1811 in relation to St. George's Chapel. It was separately organized, incorporated, and endowed by Trinity Church. An entire independence, and consequently an entire exclusion was effected.

Act of 1814. The Act of January, 1814, may be thus analyzed: The recital referred to the Act of 17th April, 1784, " making such alterations in the charter of the corporation of Trinity Church as to render it more conformable to the constitution." That at that time Trinity Church was the only incorporated religious society of the Protestant Episcopal Church. That other societies of the same denomination have been since formed and incorporated. That the name which they were enabled to take under the Act of 1788 had now become improper, and it was prayed it might be altered, and other alterations might be made. The first section therefore enacted, that the said corporation of Trinity Church, instead of their present name, should take the name of " The Rector, Church-wardens, and Vestrymen of Trinity Church in the City of New York."

It seems to me clear that the retention of the former name would not have had the slightest effect upon any right or question connected with Trinity Church or corporation. The qualifications of members and voters would have been the same, and the exclusion of those who had joined a separate organization and incorporation would have been as certain.

But the title was undoubtedly inapt and indistinct. That of Trinity Church was peculiarly appropriate.

The *church* which it was prayed " might be made parochial and incorporate with one body politic," in the preamble to the charter of 1697, was the church then lately built on Broadway, and subsequently declared to " be the parish church and church-yard of the parish of Trinity Church, within our city of New York."

The rector, church-wardens, and vestrymen are vested with power and authority to " manage the affairs of the said corporation and parish of Trinity Church."

And this church is declared the sole and only parish church in the city of New York.

The Act of April 17, 1784, is entitled " An Act for making such Alterations in the Charter of the Corporation of Trinity Church, as to render it more conformable to the constitution of the State." And the title of the Act of March 10, 1788, is " An Act to enable the Corporation of Trinity Church in the City of New York, to assume the name therein mentioned." The title of the Act of 1814 is similar.

It seems an irresistible conclusion, that the inhabitants of the city of New York in communion of the Church of England aforesaid, must have been in the communion (members) of Trinity Church, the sole parish church. There could not have been meant an ideal abstract union with the church as a spirituality. The moment we comprehend how completely communion, in the English sense, is personal local connection with a particular place of worship, all becomes clear and definite. Inhabitants of New York, professing the faith and polity of the Church of England, were parishioners. Parishioners involved the idea and fact of a parish church. There was but one such in the city. That was Trinity Church and its chapels. Parishioners were necessarily members of Trinity Church or of its chapels. To a great extent members of the chapels were members of the mother church.

The second section defines the persons qualified to vote. There is not a single qualification among those specified, which was not equally essential and, at least, as plainly prescribed by the charter of 1697, or could have been defined and prescribed by a by-law of the corporation. "Members of the congregation of Trinity Church or any of its chapels," is neither more perspicuous or discriminating than "*inhabitants of the city, parishioners of Trinity Church,*" with the known obligations flowing from the term.

The substance of the provision as to being members for a year, could have been adopted in a by-law requiring stated attendance on public worship for that time. The limitation to male persons of full age is a rule of the common law. (Grant on Corporations, p. 5.)

The third section confirms grants of land before made by Trinity Church, or that might thereafter be made to any religious society then or thereafter to be incorporated, the value not to exceed the limit of their charter.

Now the charter had conferred unlimited power of conveying the lands held by the church. Of course this power was subordinate to any trust or purpose for which it may have acquired the particular land. We have seen that in 1798, a conveyance had been made with the sanction of Alexander Hamilton and Richard Harison, to trustees for St. Mark's Church, and when that church was incorporated, those trustees conveyed.

A statute created restriction upon the common-law right to alien, by rendering the assent of the Chancellor necessary.[1] It is

---

[1] First adopted in 1787; revised 1813. 2 R. L. chap. 60.

needless to enter into the question whether this restriction was applicable to the case of Trinity Church. The sanction to such conveyances is perfectly clear.

But the great mass of the property of the church is derived from the grant of 1705. That grant recited the Act of 1704, authorizing the corporation to take lands for the benefit of the said church, and other pious uses; and the habendum was, to "the Rector and Inhabitants of the City of New York in communion with the Church of England as by law established, and their successors forever."

So far as such property is concerned, there can be no doubt that transfers to incorporations of the Episcopal Church within the city, were legal. In my opinion transfers of such property, or its proceeds, to or for the use of churches, or any other pious purposes, out of the city, are unwarranted.

The fourth section of the act relates to the separation and incorporation of St. George's Chapel, then a church. It recites, that doubts had been entertained as to the legality of the act; confirms it, and sanctions the conveyance of the property.

I look upon this provision as utterly useless, and by suggesting the doubt, actually mischievous. There cannot be a point of ecclesiastical law more capable of demonstration, than the legality of the proceedings as to St. George's Church, under the charter. If the transfer of the land required any thing further, the third section of this act was enough.

The fifth section empowered the vestry of Trinity Church to set apart, as a separate church, any of the churches or chapels which formed part of the corporation, with the assent of a majority of the persons entitled to vote, belonging to the chapel to be set apart. They shall then cease to be members of Trinity Church; may become separately incorporated; and may receive from Trinity Church any grant of real or personal estate for its separate use.

This memorable statute so coveted, so assailed, and so resolutely defended, appears to me to be an act enfeebling the legal position of Trinity Church, rather than fortifying it. With perhaps the exception of the name, and the power to transfer real estate, every thing enacted was secured by the charter, and its essential inferential power. That charter, secured by the Constitution of 1777, was a most sure guaranty. Had there been a legislative invasion of rights thus strengthened, the tribunals of justice would have redressed it.

But the statute, in the points to which it extends, forms now the guide of the action of Trinity Church. It has withstood a fierce and persevering assault, and remains unshaken. But if repealed, the church could fall back upon a charter all sufficient for her security, and capable of development in legal conservative restrictions. The whole city of New York would be again, without a question, as perhaps it is even now, her parish, except where, by her consent or acquiescence, she has sanctioned the organization of independent churches and cures. Every dweller of the city, not allied to such independent churches, whose good lot it was to profess the faith and godly order of the Episcopal Church, would be her parishioner—to be nurtured at the mother altar, or the altar of a daughter chapel; and her office and mission would be, to rear such altars in all the waste places of her domain. She received the most admirable and comprehensive of charters; almost contemporaneously she was endowed with a munificent grant of property. It seems as if she was thus appointed and designed, as the instrument to preserve and to spread, in this city, the faith of Saints, reclaimed and restored in the true Church of England, and transplanted to our shore.

APPENDIX A.

ACT OF MAY 9, 1868, CHAPTER 803.

An Act to amend the Acts to provide for the Incorporation of Religious Societies, so far as the same relate to Churches in connection with the Protestant Episcopal Church. Passed May 9, 1868.

THE People of the State of New York, represented in Senate and Assembly, do enact as follows : —

§ 1. The first section of the act entitled " An Act to provide for the incorporation of Religious Societies," passed April 5, 1813, is hereby amended so as to read as follows : —

1. It shall be lawful for not less than six male persons, of full age, belonging to any church or congregation in communion with the Protestant Episcopal Church in this State, not already incorporated, to meet at any time at the usual place of public worship of such church or congregation, for the purpose of incorporating themselves under this act.

2. A notice of such meeting, specifying its object, and the time and place thereof, shall .be publicly read in the time of morning service, on two Sundays next previous thereto, by the rector or officiating minister, or, if there be none, by any other person belonging to such church or congregation ; and shall also be posted in a conspicuous place on the outside door, near the main entrance to such place of worship.

3. The rector, or if there be none, or he be necessarily absent, then one of the church-wardens or vestrymen, or any other person, called to the chair, shall preside at such meeting, and shall receive the votes.

4. The persons entitled to vote at such meeting shall be the male persons of full age belonging to the church or congregation, qualified as follows, and none other : —

First. Those who have been baptized in the Protestant Episcopal Church, or who have been received therein, either by the right of confirmation, or by receiving the holy communion ; or,

Second. Those who have purchased, and for not less than twelve months next prior to such meeting have owned, a pew or seat in such church; or who, during the same period of time, have hired and paid for a pew or seat in such church; or who, during the whole period aforesaid, have been contributors in money to the support of such church.

5. The persons so qualified shall, at such meeting, by a majority of votes, determine —

First. The name or title by which such church or congregation shall be known in law.

Second. On what day in Easter-week an annual election for church-wardens and vestrymen shall thereafter take place.

Third. What number of vestrymen, not less than four or more than eight, shall annually be elected, and shall, together with the rector (if there be one), and the two church-wardens, constitute the vestry of the church.

Fourth. And shall, by a majority of votes, elect two church-wardens and the number of vestrymen that it shall have been determined are to be annually elected, which church-wardens and vestrymen thus elected shall serve until the next regular election.

6. The polls shall continue open for one hour, and longer, in the discretion of the presiding officer, or if required, by the vote of a majority of voters present.

7. The presiding officer, together with two other persons, shall make a certificate, under their hands and seals, of —

First. The church-wardens and vestrymen so elected.

Second. Of the day in Easter-week so fixed for the annual election of their successors.

Third. Of the number of vestrymen (not less than four nor more than eight) so determined upon to be annually elected to constitute part of the vestry.

Fourth. Of the name or title by which such church or congregation shall be known in law.

Which certificate being duly acknowledged, or the execution and acknowledgment thereof being duly proven before any officer authorized to take the acknowledgment or proof of deeds or conveyances of real estate, to be recorded in the county where such church or place of worship of such congregation shall be situated, shall be recorded by the clerk of such county, or by the officer whose duty it is, or may hereafter be made, to record such instruments in the county in which such church or place of worship may be situated, in a book to be by him kept for such purpose.

8. The church-wardens and vestrymen so elected, and their successors in office, of themselves (but if there be a rector, then together with the rector of such church or congregation), shall form a vestry, and shall be the trustees of such church or congregation; and they and their successors shall thereupon by virtue of this act, be a body corporate, by the name or title expressed in such certificate.

9. The male persons qualified as aforesaid, provided· they shall also have belonged to such church or congregation for twelve months immediately preceding, shall, in every year thereafter, on the day in Easter-week so fixed for that purpose, elect two church-wardens, and as many vestrymen (not less than four nor more than eight) as shall have been legally determined to constitute part of the vestry.

10. Notice shall be given of such election by the rector, if there be one, or if there be none, or he be absent, by the officiating minister, or by a church-warden, for two Sundays next previous to the day so fixed, in the time of divine service.

11. Whenever a vacancy in the board so constituted shall happen, by death or otherwise, the vestry shall order a special election to supply such vacancy; of which notice shall be given in the time of divine service, at least ten days previous thereto.

12. The notice of any election, stated or otherwise, shall specify the place, day, and hour of holding the same. The provisions contained in the preceding sixth clause shall apply to all elections.

13. An election to supply a vacancy, and also the stated annual election, shall be holden immediately after morning service; and at all such elections, the rector, or if there be none, or he be absent, one of the church-wardens selected for the purpose by a majority of the duly qualified voters present; or if no warden be present, a vestryman (selected in like manner) shall preside, and receive the votes of the electors, and be the returning officer; and shall enter the proceedings in the book of the minutes of the vestry, and sign his name thereto, and offer the same to as many electors present as he shall think fit, to be by them also signed and certified.

14. The church-wardens and vestrymen chosen at any of the said elections, shall hold their offices until the expiration of the year for which they shall be chosen, and until others are chosen in their stead; and shall have power to call and induct a rector to such church or congregation as often as there shall be a vacancy therein, and to fix his salary or compensation.

15. No board, or meeting of such vestry shall be held, unless at least three days' notice thereof shall be given in writing, under the hand of the rector or of one of the church-wardens; except that for the first meeting after an election, twenty-four hours' notice shall be sufficient; and no such board shall be competent to transact any business unless the rector, if there be one, and at least one of the church-wardens, and a majority of the vestrymen be present. But if the rector be absent from the State, and shall have been so absent for over four calendar months, or if the meeting has been called by the rector, and he be absent therefrom, the board shall be competent to transact all business if there be present one church-warden, and a majority of the vestrymen; except that in the absence of the rector, no measure shall be taken for effecting a sale or disposition of the real property, nor may any sale or disposition of the capital or principal of the personal estate of such corporation be made, nor any act done which shall impair the rights of such rector.

16. The rector, if there be one, and if not, then the church-warden present, or if both the church-wardens be present, then the church-warden who shall be called to the chair by a majority of votes, shall preside and have the casting vote.

17. Whenever any corporation, organized under the provisions of this act, shall deem it for the interest of such corporation to change the number of its vestrymen, it shall and may be lawful for such corporation to change the same, provided that the number of such vestrymen shall not thereby be less than four or more than eight. And in order to effect such change, the same shall be authorized and approved by the vestry at a regular meeting thereof; and shall then at the next stated annual election for wardens and vestrymen be submitted to, and ratified by, a majority of the votes of all the qualified voters voting at such election; notice of which proposed change, and that the same will be submitted for ratification at such election, shall be given at the same time, and in the same manner as is required for notice of the said election; if such change be thus ratified, a certificate shall be made setting forth the resolution of the vestry, and the proceedings to ratify the same, together with the fact of the notice being given as required, and shall be acknowledged or proved and recorded in the same manner as is required for the original certificate of organization; and thereupon the number of vestrymen to constitute a part of the vestry of such corporation, shall be such as shall be fixed by the proceed-

ings to effect such change. But such change shall not take effect or be operative until the certificate above mentioned shall have been duly recorded.

§ 2. The provisions of the ninth, tenth, eleventh, twelfth, thirteenth, fourteenth, fifteenth, sixteenth, and seventeenth clauses of section one of this act shall apply to any church or corporation in communion with the Protestant Episcopal Church in this State heretofore incorporated under the act hereby amended, or under any of the acts amending the same, or under the several acts to provide for the incorporation of religious societies, passed April 6, 1784; March 27, 1801; or the Act for the Relief of the Protestant Episcopal Church in the State of New York, passed March 17, 1795; or by any special charter made or granted before or after July 4, 1776, whereof the vestry, at a regular meeting, shall by vote determine to adopt the same; and such vote shall, at the next ensuing stated annual election for wardens and vestrymen, be submitted to, and ratified by, a majority of the votes of all the qualified voters voting at such election, notice of such vote of the vestry, and of the proposed submission of the same for ratification, having been given at the same time and in the same manner as is required by the tenth clause of the first section of this act for notice of election. But such adoption shall not take effect, or be operative, until a certificate embodying a true copy of the resolution of the vestry, as entered upon their minutes, and the proceedings to ratify the same, together with the fact of the notice being given, as required, shall have been acknowledged or proved, and shall be recorded, as is required by the foregoing seventh clause of section one, for the certificate of incorporation.

§ 3. The first section of the act passed March 5, 1819, entitled " An Act to amend the Act entitled, 'An Act to provide for the Incorporation of Religious Societies,'" is hereby repealed.

§ 4. The third section of the act passed February 15, 1826, entitled " An Act to amend an Act entitled, ' An Act to provide for the Incorporation of Religious Societies,' " passed April 5, 1813, shall not apply to any church or congregation in connection with the Protestant Episcopal Church in this State.

§ 5. All acts and parts of acts inconsistent with the provisions of this act are hereby repealed.

NOTES TO THE ACT OF MAY, 1868.

§ 1. *Clause* 1.   The alteration is in requiring six male persons belonging to a church or congregation in communion with the Protestant Episcopal Church, in order to incorporate.

§ 1. *Clause* 2.   An officiating minister may give the notice.   A copy is to be posted in a conspicuous place on the outside door, near the main entrance.   See the form, Appendix No. 2.

§ 1. *Clause* 4.   Six male persons of full age must be present at the election.   The qualifications of voters are defined.   First, those who have been baptized in the Protestant Episcopal Church, or been received therein by being confirmed, or receiving the holy communion.   Thus, in strictness, the ecclesiastical qualifications are purely those of membership of the Protestant Episcopal Church.

And as to this class, there is no period of previous belonging to the church prescribed.   It results, however, that they must have belonged over the time which will allow the notice for two successive Sundays to be given.

The next class of voters are clearly defined.   Ownership of a pew or seat, or hiring and paying for the same, or contribution in money is required.   But in each case this must have lasted for not less than twelve months next before the election.

§ 1. *Clause* 3.   Instead of eight vestrymen the number may be not less than four nor more than eight.

Instead of the clause, "shall hold their office until the expiration of the year and until others be chosen in their stead," the provision is, "shall serve until the next regular election."

§ 1. *Clause* 6 is new.   The polls must continue open one hour. The presiding officer may extend the time, or a majority of voters present may require it to be done.

§ 1. *Clause* 7.   The certificate, besides what was before required, must state the number of vestrymen determined upon.   See the form, Appendix No. 3.

§ 1. *Clause* 9.   The provision as to belonging to such church for twelve months previous to all elections after the first, is made very definite.   No possible difference can now exist as to this point, for churches hereafter organized.   It has been shown, I trust, that it is the law now for all existing incorporated churches.   Such length of time of belonging, that is, stated attendance, is requisite in every case.

§ 1. *Clause* 15. The alteration of the law contained in this clause is important. If the rector be absent from the State, and for over four calendar months ; or, if the meeting be called by him, and he be voluntarily absent, the vestry, composed of one warden and a majority of vestrymen, may transact business, except they may not do any thing to effect a sale or disposition of real property, or the principal or capital of personal estate, or any thing impairing the rights of the rector.

§ 1. *Clause* 17. This provision is new, and enables the vestry, but with the assent of the qualified voters, to change the number of vestrymen originally fixed upon.

§ 2. Under this section, existing incorporations may avail themselves of the provisions of the act, and be governed by them. Certainly many advantages would arise from a uniform law governing every church incorporated throughout the State, and the few new points arising under the new law would soon be settled. Some experience of its practical working will probably be required before it is adopted by corporations organized before its passage.

§ 3. This repealed the first section of the Act of 1819, which defined the qualifications of voters at the first election, now provided for in the fourth clause of section 1.

§ 4. The third section of the Act of February 15, 1826, is a section authorizing the qualified voters of a religious society to change the day of the annual election before appointed. This, it is declared, shall not be applicable to churches of the Protestant Episcopal communion.

§ 5. All acts and parts of acts inconsistent with these provisions, are repealed.

APPENDIX B.

CHAPTER 471.

An Act for the Relief of certain Religious Societies in the City and County of New York, and in the Counties of Kings and of Westchester. Passed April 29, 1868.

WHEREAS several religious societies, whose places of worship are in the city of New York, or in the counties of Kings, or of Westchester, seeking to incorporate themselves under the provisions of the act entitled " An Act to provide for the Incorporation of Religious Societies," passed April 5, 1813, or of the several acts amending the same, have through mistake, caused the certificates provided for by the said act, to be recorded in the office of the clerk of the city and county of New York, or of the clerk of said county of Kings, or of the said county of Westchester, instead of the office of register of the city and county of New York, or of the register of the said counties of Kings or of Westchester respectively; therefore, the people of the State of New York, represented in Senate and Assembly do enact as follows:

§ 1. The recording of every such certificate alluded to in the foregoing preamble in either of the said offices of the clerk of the city and county of New York, or of the clerk of the county of Kings, or of the clerk of the county of Westchester, prior to the passage of this act, shall be regarded and construed, and such recording is hereby declared to be of the same validity, force and effect as would have been the recording of such certificate in the office of the register of the city and county of New York, or of the register of the county of Kings, or of the register of the county of Westchester, respectively. And every act, deed, matter and thing done or performed by every such religious society, since the recording of its certificate in the office of either of the said clerks of the city and county of New York, or of the county of Kings, or of the county of Westchester, is hereby ratified, confirmed and declared to be as valid in all respects, as if the said certificate had been properly and appropriately recorded in the office of the register of the city and county of New York, or of the register of the county of Kings, or of the register of the county of Westchester; but this act shall not affect any suit or proceeding already commenced, arising out of such original mistake.

§ 2. This act shall take effect immediately.

By an Act of March 12, 1852 (Laws, chap. 83), a register was to be elected for the county of Kings, and by section 7, all that part of the duty of the clerk of the county, which, in the city of New York, was required to be done by the register of deeds in such city, shall be done and performed by the register of deeds in and for the county of Kings, and the county clerk was prohibited from performing any of the duties devolved upon such register.

And by an Act of April 16, 1858 (Laws, chap. 293), a register was to be elected for the county of Westchester, and section 5 is the same as section 7 of the Act of 1852, as to the register in Kings County.

APPENDIX C. — Page 197.

OPINION UPON RECORDING PAPERS UPON A CHANGE OF NAME
AND IN THE REGISTER'S OFFICE GENERALLY.

By the Act of June 4, 1853, chap. 323, a religious society may present a petition for a change of name on the grounds specified in the manner prescribed by the act entitled " An Act to authorize Persons to change their Names, passed December 14, 1847, and upon fully complying with the requirements of said act, shall be known by such new and assumed name and by no other."

By that Act of December 14, 1847, chap. 464, within ten days after an order is granted for a change of name, a copy must be published in one newspaper in the county, and within twenty days after the order, the petition and verifications thereof, the order, and an affidavit of the publication, must be filed and recorded in the office of the clerk of the county.

By an Act of March 17, 1860 (Laws, chap. 80), the application for a change of name of persons was directed to be made to the county courts, and in New York to the Court of Common Pleas instead of the county judge, or a justice of the Supreme Court ; and the clerks of the counties (except of the county of New York) and the clerk of the Court of Common Pleas were to make a return of the changes of names made under the act.

Until the year 1854, the clerk of the county of New York, was the clerk of the Court of Common Pleas. By an Act of 12th day of April, 1854, chap. 198, the offices were separated. The clerk's office of the Court of Common Pleas was established, and the county clerk of the city and county of New York was to deliver to such clerk, all books, property, records, and papers, appertaining to said Court of Common Pleas.

The amendment of 1860, making changes in some particulars in the Act of 1847, in respect to the changing of names of individuals, cannot affect the provisions of the Act of 1853, embodying and regulating the proceedings for changing the names of religious corporations, according to the Act of 1847. The provisions of that act must be the guide and the decisive guide.

It would appear to follow that upon the change of names of individuals, the papers and proceedings are to be filed in the office of the clerk of the Common Pleas ; but even if that is a just result, it is produced by the statute of 1854, and cannot create a new rule as to the proceedings for changing the names of religious bodies, prescribed by the Act of 1847, and never expressly repealed, nor, by any just reasoning, impliedly repealed. I understand the practice, as to changes of the names of individuals, continues to be to file and record still in the county clerk's office.

The legislation, therefore, thus far stated, imports and declares, that the proceedings and papers on an application to change the corporate name of a religious society, must be filed and recorded in the office of the clerk of the county where the place of worship is situated.

But it is urged, and with considerable force, that the provisions of law respecting the register's office, supersede these enactments, and require a recording in that office.

The Act of 1813, for incorporating religious societies, was passed April 5, 1813, and directed the certificate to be recorded by the clerk of the county where the place of worship was located. The act to reduce the laws relating to the city of New York into one act, was passed April 9, 1813. This contained the provisions, not merely directing deeds and writings to be recorded in the register's office, but prohibiting the county clerks from recording them. So upon general principles the latter act would supersede the former. But by an Act of February 13, 1813, chap. 202, the revised acts passed at that session were not to take effect until December 1, 1813, notwithstanding anything in them to the contrary.

Hence these various provisions must be taken as declarations of the legislative will at one and the same period; and we must reconcile them, if it be possible. That can be done by reading them thus: Deeds and writings shall be recorded by the clerk of the county where, etc.; except that in the city of New York, this shall be done by the register of the city. So far as certificates of incorporation of religious bodies are concerned, the Act of April 21, 1863, chap. 287, and the Act of April 29, 1868, chap. 471, are plain legislative declarations, that they were not legally recorded in the clerk's office, but should have been in the register's. Both acts legalized the corporations which had made the mistake in recording.

The 160th section above cited, restrains the clerk of the county from registering mortgages and recording deeds, conveyances, and other writings, which are by law, or hereafter may be, directed and required to be recorded or registered.

When the direction of a law is merely that a particular writing be filed in the county clerk's office, the case does not fall within the prohibition. Thus by an Act of 1846, chap. 2, § 5, the bond of an auctioneer is to be filed with the clerk of the city and county of New York. So under the Act as to assignments by debtors (Laws, April 13, 1860, chap. 348), the bond to be given by the assignee is to be filed in the office of the county clerk where the assignment is recorded, the inventory is to be filed in the same office. But further, there are several acts which require the registering of writings, and expressly directs this to be done in the county clerk's office.

Such is the case in the Act for registering the names of members of a continuing firm (April 17, 1854, chap. 400, § 23). So in the Act as to debtors, assignments of April 13, 1860, before cited. The assignment shall be recorded in the clerk's office of the county where such debtor resides.

So by the Act of April 27, 1847, for the incorporation of rural cemeteries (chap. 133), the certificate prescribed in section 2, is to be recorded in the clerk's office of the county where the meeting is held, upon which the association becomes incorporated. While in an Act of April 11, 1862, chap. 215, the consent made necessary for a mortgage of a burying-ground, is to be proved or acknowledged in the same manner as deeds, and shall thereupon be recorded in the office of the register of the city, or clerk of the county in which such burying-ground is situated.

By an Act of April 29, 1833, chap. 273, chattel mortgages were to be filed in the city of New York in the office of the register of such city.

It seems to me that in order to harmonize these various provisions of law, we must read the 159th and 160th sections of the Act of 1813 to reduce the laws in relation to the city of New York, etc., in this manner.

That whenever a writing is directed to be registered or recorded and the place is not designated; or designated as to be in the proper office for registering or recording; or to be registered or recorded in the county where the place of business, etc. is located; in all such and similar cases, the register's office in New York is the only proper place. Where the registering or recording is expressly directed by a subsequent statute to be made elsewhere, as in the office of county clerk, that specific direction must prevail.

And where there is no direction as to either registering or recording, but a direction for filing papers only, the conclusion is stronger.

Certainly the legislature may indicate its understanding of the law in particular cases, by acts declaratory in their nature. It has done this in relation to religious bodies incorporated under the Act of 1813, and its amendatory acts, in the statutes of 1863 and 1868 referred to. The statute, reducing the laws, as to the city of New York, etc., is treated as continuing in force as to all cases of this character.

But the case of free churches, for example, is not within this rule and principle. They are incorporated under a particular act, neither amendatory nor supplementary. When such act prescribes a filing in the office of clerk of the county in which the church is established, it must be that a record in the register's office is not enough. (Act of April 13, 1854, chap. 218.)

The consideration of the subject would not be complete without adverting to the provisions of the Revised Statutes. (1 R. S. 762, § 38 and § 63.)

The thirty-eighth section defines the term, conveyance, among other things, as "a writing by which the title to any real estate may be affected in law or equity." And the sixty-third section directs that all the provisions of the chapter, except the eighteenth section shall extend and apply to the register of the city and county of New York, in the same manner as if he was county clerk of said county.

Two observations occur upon these provisions. It can scarcely be supposed, that papers and an order for the change of name of a religious society fall, by the largest constructions of the terms, within the thirty-eighth section. There is nothing on the face of the documents, directly or impliedly, affecting the title to land in any manner.

But if this were the case, then the positive direction of a subsequent statute, prescribing a different office for filing and recording, must prevail.

In Appendix B, *ante*, I have stated the Acts of 1852 and of 1858, establishing register's offices in the county of Kings and of Westchester. The duties performed by the register in New York were to be performed by the registers in such counties respectively, and the performance of such by the clerk of the county was forbidden. Whatever then, we find is to be done by the register in New York in relation to writings connected with religious corporations is to be done by the registers of the counties named.

The result appears to be: —

(1.) That certificates of incorporation under the second and third sections of the Act of 1813, and the amendments thereto;

under the supplementary Act of April 12, 1822, as to the Reformed Presbyterian Church ; under the amendatory Act of April 21, 1825, as to the True Reformed Dutch Church, must be recorded in the register's office in New York, Kings, and Westchester counties ; and in the office of county clerk in all other counties.

(2.) Certificates of incorporation under the Act of 1868 as to Protestant Episcopal Churches, and certificates of the adoption of that act by existing corporations of such Church, are to be recorded in the same offices respectively.

(3.) That certificates of the incorporation of free churches must be filed in the office of the county clerk in every case.

(4.) Certificates as to Roman Catholic Churches under the Act of March 25, 1863, must also be filed in the same office.

There is no direction as to recording in either of these statutes.

(5.) All the papers upon the change of name of an incorporated church, must be filed and recorded in the office of the county clerk where the church is located.

(6.) Deeds of real estate executed by a religious corporation are to be recorded in the register's office of the counties of New York, Kings, and Westchester, and in the county clerk's office elsewhere. .

No. 1.— See Page 48.

NOTICE OF MEETING TO INCORPORATE A PROTESTANT EPISCOPAL CHURCH.

NOTICE is hereby given that a meeting of the male persons of full age belonging to this church will be held on the   day of   , at   o'clock in the   noon, in this place (*the usual place of worship*), for the purpose of incorporating themselves under the acts of the legislature in such case provided, and to determine the name or title by which such church shall be known in law ; on what day in Easter-week an annual election for church-wardens and vestrymen shall thereafter take place ; what number of vestrymen, not less than four nor more than eight, shall annually be elected to constitute, together with the rector (if there be one), and the two church-wardens, the vestry of the church ; and by a majority of votes to elect two church-wardens, and the number of vestrymen determined to be annually elected, to serve until the next annual election.

[To be publicly read in the time of morning service, on two Sundays next previous to the meeting, by the rector or officiating minister; or if there be none, by any person belonging to the church; and a copy must be posted in a conspicuous place, on the outside door, near the main entrance to the place of worship.]

No. 2. — Page 50.

CERTIFICATE.

To all to whom these presents may come :   We, whose names are hereto subscribed do certify, that on the   day of   , male persons of full age, exceeding six in number, belonging to the church or congregation worshiping in (*the building*), in the of   , county of   , and State of New York, and in communion of the Protestant Episcopal Church, not before incorporated, met at their said place of public worship, for the purpose of incorporating themselves, under the laws of the legislature of the State of New York in such case provided, and doing the other acts therein directed to be done.

That the subscriber, the Rev.   , rector of such church, (or   , a church-warden, or a vestryman of such church, there being no rector), (or there being no rector, A. B., one of such persons), was called to the chair, and presided, and received the votes.

That at such meeting, C. D. and E. F. were duly elected church-wardens, and   were duly elected vestrymen.

That   in Easter-week was fixed upon for the annual election of the successors of such church-wardens and vestrymen.

That it was determined that the number of vestrymen to be annually elected should be   , and that the name or title by which such church or congregation should be known in law should be The   .

In testimony whereof, I, the presiding officer at such meeting, and we,   , and   , persons present during the same, have hereunto set our hands and seals this   day of   .

Signed and sealed }
in the presence of }

[This is to be acknowledged or proved before any person authorized to take the acknowledgment or proof of deeds. This certificate is then to be recorded in the office of the clerk of the county where such place of public worship is situated, or by the officer whose duty it is, or may be thereafter made, to record such instruments.

This is the register in the counties of New York, Kings, and Westchester, and an Act was passed April 29, 1868, legalizing the incorporation of those bodies, whose certificates had been filed in the clerk's office in those counties, instead of the register's office. (Laws, 1868, chap. 71.)].

No. 3.

NOTICE OF SUBSEQUENT ELECTIONS.[1]

Notice is hereby given, that an election for two church-wardens and vestrymen of this church, will be held at this place on the   day of   , at   o'clock,[2] the poll to remain open one hour, or longer if required.

No. 4.

NOTICE FOR A VACANCY.

The difference will be in stating that the election is to fill a vacancy of a warden or vestryman. It must be given in the time of Divine service, and ten days before the day fixed for the special election.

No. 5.

ENTRY OF ELECTION ON BOOK OF MINUTES.

An election was held on the   day of   , immediately after morning service, for the purpose of choosing wardens and

[1] To be read for two Sundays next previous to the election day.

[2] The hour must be specified in the notice, and the election is to be immediately after morning service. It is best to fix the hour, so as to admit the service being completed, and as nearly after as practicable.

vestrymen for the ensuing year (or for filling a vacancy in the office of church-warden or vestryman). The   presided and received the votes, and signs his name to this minute of proceedings, and we electors present have signed and certified the same.

[Signed by the presiding officer and the electors called by him to sign.]

No. 6.

CERTIFICATE OF ADOPTION OF ACT OF 1868.

This is to certify that at a regular meeting of the vestry of   Church, a church incorporated under the first section of the Act of the legislature passed the 5th of April, 1813, and its amendments, a resolution of which the following is a copy, was adopted by the vestry, and entered upon the minutes.

Resolved, that this church doth hereby determine to adopt the provisions of the ninth, tenth, eleventh, twelfth, thirteenth, fourteenth, fiftcenth, sixteenth, and seventeenth sections of the Act of the legislature passed the 9th day of May, 1868, entitled " An Act to amend the Acts for the Incorporation of Religious Societies, so far as the same relate to churches in connection with the Protestant Episcopal Church."

[To be signed by the presiding officer and two of the wardens or vestrymen, and acknowledged (or proven by a witness) before a judge of the Supreme Court, or of the Court of Common Pleas of the county, and to be recorded in the clerk's office of the county where the church is situated, but in the register's office if situated in the city of New York, or in Kings or Westchester county. See Appendix C.]

No. 7.

CERTIFICATE OF INCORPORATION UNDER THE THIRD SECTION OF ACT OF 1813, ETC.

We, whose names are hereto subscribed, two of the elders (or members) of the church or congregation known as The   , in which divine worship is celebrated according to the rites and discipline of the *Presbyterian* Church, do certify that on the   day of   , the male persons of full age who have statedly worshiped in such church or congregation, and not already incorporated, met at   , the place where they statedly attend for divine worship, and did then and there elect by plurality of voices,[1]   as trustees to take the charge of the estate and property belonging to such church or congregation, and to transact all affairs relative to the temporalities thereof. And further, that the name or title by which the said trustees and their successors should be known was, The   .

Witness our hands and seals }
  this   day of   }

No. 8.

CERTIFICATE OF INCORPORATION OF DUTCH REFORMED CHURCH.

WE the undersigned, the minister, elders and deacons (or if no minister), elders and deacons of the Reformed Protestant Dutch Church, known as   , worshiping in the   of   , county of   , State of New York, and trustees of such church, do hereby certify that on the   day of   , we assembled at our place of worship in said (*town*), for the purpose of forming ourselves, and our successors, into a body corporate, under the act or acts of this State, in such case provided. And we did thereupon fix upon the name or title of the

by which we and our successors, trustees, shall be known and designated.

In witness whereof, etc.

[To be acknowledged or proven before an officer authorized to take acknowledgments, and to be recorded in the register's office of New York, or Kings, or Westchester county. And in the clerk's office if in any other county. See Appendix C.]

No. 9.

CERTIFICATE OF ROMAN CATHOLIC CHURCH.

WE the undersigned, to wit, A. B. the Roman Catholic Archbishop (or Bishop) of the diocese of   , C. D. Vicar-General

---

[1] Not less than three, nor more than nine.

of such diocese, and E. F. pastor of the church of
in such diocese; and   laymen, members of the said
church, duly selected and appointed, hereby certify, that the name
or title of the   , is that by which they and their
successors shall be known and distinguished as a body corporate, by
virtue of the act of the legislature entitled " An Act supplementary
to an Act entitled ' An Act to provide for the Incorporation of Religious Societies, passed April 5, 1813,' passed March 25, 1863."

    Witness our hands, this day of

      Witness :

[Acknowledged or proven in the same manner as deeds of real
estate and filed in the office of the county clerk, and a copy in the
office of the Secretary of State.　See Appendix C.]

No. 10.

CERTIFICATE OF INCORPORATION OF FREE CHURCHES.

WE whose names are hereto subscribed, male persons of full
age, citizens of the United States, and a majority of whom are residents of the State of New York, do hereby certify that we have
associated ourselves together for the purpose of founding and continuing a free church in the city of   , State of New York;
that the name or title by which such society shall be known in
law was determined to be the Free Church of the   , in
the   of   .　That the purpose of its organization is the
ministering of the Word and Sacraments according to the doctrine
and worship and discipline of the Protestant Episcopal Church in
the United States of America.　That the following are the names
of seven trustees who are to manage the affairs of the said church
and body corporate, *five* of whom are not ministers of the Gospel
or priests of any denomination, namely :

[Signed in duplicate by all, and to be acknowledged, not proved,
and to be approved by a judge of the Supreme Court of the district, or of the Superior Court in New York, and filed in the office
of the county clerk, and a duplicate in the office of the Secretary
of State.　No recording is directed.]

No. 11.

PETITION FOR ORDER TO CHANGE NAME.

Supreme Court. In the matter of the application of   for a change of name.

THE petition of the   Street Baptist Church, respectfully showeth : —

That your petitioners are trustees of the above named church, a religious body incorporated under the act of the legislature of this State, in such case provided, and became so incorporated by the name and title above stated.

That it became desirable to change the location of its place of public worship, and an order has been obtained for selling the same ; that by reason thereof, the said name has become incongruous.

Your petitioners therefore pray that an order may be made, allowing the above corporation to change such, its corporate name, and to assume the name of the   .

[Affidavit of the truth of the facts to be made by one of the trustees.]

ORDER.

(See form No. 12.)

(*Another form.*)

Supreme Court. In the matter of the application of the rector, church-wardens, and vestrymen of the Church of the Intercessor, for a change of name.

THE petition of the rector, church-wardens and vestrymen of the Church of the Intercessor, in the city of New York, respectfully showeth : —

That your petitioners have become incorporated under the laws of this State, as a church in communion with the Protestant Episcopal Church in the United States of America, and as such corporation located in the city of New York.

That by reason of the similarity of their corporate name to that of another corporation in the said city and county, to wit, the Church of the Intercession, the corporate name of your petitioners has become incongruous and inconvenient, and that the location of such corporation will be more correctly and effectually designated by a change of name.

Your petitioners pray that their said corporate name may be changed to " The Rector, Church-wardens, and Vestrymen of St. Alban's Church in the city of New York."

Signed by the rector and attested by the clerk.

[The petition was sworn to by the rector, and there was a certificate attached by the clerk of the vestry, of a resolution being adopted by such vestry, authorizing an application for such change.]

No. 12.

ORDER FOR CHANGE OF NAME.

Supreme Court. In the matter of the application of, etc.

AT a Special Term of the Supreme Court, etc., held 14th February, 1867, — Present, —— ——, etc. It appearing from the petition of " The Rector," etc., a corporation incorporated under the laws of this State, hereto annexed, that the name by which such church and corporation is now known and designated, has become and is incongruous and inconvenient, and that by a change of its name the character and location of the same will be more correctly and effectually designated : It is ordered that on compliance with the provisions of the Revised Statutes, and of chapter 323 of the laws of 1853, and of chapter 464 of the laws of 1847, the said corporation be authorized to assume the name of " The Rector, Church-wardens, and Vestrymen of St. Albans' Church in the city of New York," and from and after the 20th day of March, 1867, be known by such new and assumed name and no other.

[This order is to be published within ten days after it is granted, in one of the public newspapers printed in the county in which the church is located. And within twenty days the petition, affidavit or affidavits, order and affidavit of publication, must be filed and recorded in the clerk's office of the county in which the church is located. Act of December 14, 1847, §§ 4, 5. See Appendix C.]

" When the requirements of this act shall be complied with, the applicant shall from and after the day specified for that purpose in such order, be known by the name which, by such order, he shall be authorized to assume, and by no other." (Act of December 14, 1847, § 6.)

No. 13.

PETITION FOR THE SALE OF REAL ESTATE.[1]

In the matter of, etc.

To the Justices of the   Court :

THE petition of the undersigned respectfully showeth : —

That they are trustees of the   , a religious corporation incorporated under the laws of the State of New York. That they own two parcels of real estate, one the lot of ground on which their place of worship stands, and another, a lot, a parcel in the town of   , bounded and described as follows : All, etc. That the said incorporation have incurred a debt of   hundred dollars in necessary repairs made to their church. That they have no personal property to pay the same. That such lot of ground is worth about the sum of $. That at a meeting of said society, held at their said house of worship, on the   day of   , at which there were present and voting, a majority of the legal voters of the said religious corporation, a resolution was passed instructing the said trustees to make this application, and effect a sale of such parcel of land; and that at a meeting of your petitioners, as a board of trustees, a resolution was passed to make this application accordingly.

[The petition should be verified by the president of the board, or clerk.

The conveyance, under the corporate seal, should, I think, be recorded in the register's office in New York, Westchester, or Kings county; and in the county clerk's office elsewhere. See Appendix C.]

No. 14.

PETITION FOR LEAVE TO CONVEY TO TRUSTEES OF A FREE CHURCH.

To the Justices of the Supreme Court :

THE petition of the rector, church-wardens, and vestrymen of the Church of the   , in the city of New York, respectfully showeth : —

That on or about the 3d day of November, 1853, in pursuance

[1] From Mr. Tyler's book, with slight changes. A good form.

of an act of the legislature of the State of New York, entitled
"An Act to provide for the Incorporation of Religious Societies,
passed April 5, 1813," they became a body corporate in communion
with the Protestant Episcopal Church, in the United States of
America ; that on or about the   day of   , 1853, they purchased four lots of ground situate, etc. That subsequently, they
caused to be erected a church upon such lots, which has since been
occupied and used for public worship, according to the rites and
ceremonies of such Protestant Episcopal Church, and that the
seats in such church have always been free to all worshipers.
That the value of such church and property is about the sum of
twenty thousand dollars.

Your petitioners further show that on or about the 28th of
February, 1856, the said corporation was indebted in the sum
of twelve thousand dollars, of which the sum of ten thousand five
hundred dollars was secured by mortgages upon such property.
That measures were taken to raise money by voluntary contributions, to enable your petitioners to discharge such indebtedness,
with the engagement and understanding that, if a sufficient sum for
such purpose could be procured, your petitioners would convey such
property to trustees, to be incorporated under the act of the legislature entitled " An Act for the Incorporation of Societies to establish Free Churches, passed April 13, 1854."

That upon such stipulation and engagement, sufficient funds have
been contributed to enable your petitioners to pay off the whole
of such indebtedness.

That on or about the 8th day of March, 1855, the Rev. J. J. E.
and L. M. H. etc. (seven in all), were duly incorporated trustees,
under the provisions of the said act for the establishment of free
churches, under the title of " The Trustees of the Church of the
            , in the city of New York." And for the purpose of
taking the title to the said property of your petitioners, to be held
by them in trust, under such last mentioned act.

Your petitioners further show, that for the purpose of better securing and perpetuating their said church and property as a free
church, and for the purpose of carrying into effect the condition
and engagement before mentioned, they are desirous of conveying
the said church property to the last mentioned trustees, on the condition that the same shall be used and occupied for public worship
as a free church, in communion with the Protestant Episcopal
Church in the United States of America.

Your petitioners therefore pray that an order may be granted allowing them to make such conveyance for the purpose. aforesaid.

[This was signed by the rector, wardens, and vestrymen, and sworn to by the rector.]

ORDER UPON SAME.

In the matter of the application of the rector, etc., for leave to convey property to the trustees of the Church of, etc.

AT, etc., 20th June, 1857, — Present, J. J. R., one of the judges, etc. On reading and filing the petition of the rector, etc., duly verified, and on motion of, etc., ordered that the said rector, etc., be authorized and empowered to convey these four lots of land situate and lying in, etc. (description), together with the church erected thereon, to the Rev. E. J. G., etc. (the trustees), as trustees under an act of the legislature of the State of New York, entitled " An Act for the Incorporation of Societies to establish Free Churches," passed August 13, 1854, to be held by them and their successors in trust, as a free church in communion with the Protestant Episcopal Church, in the United States of America.

INDEX.

———•———

A.

B.

C.

22

D.

E.

[1] Attention is particularly called to the Act of 1868, in Appendix A.

W.

WILL,

THE END.